PRAISE FOR ELENA FERRANTE'S NEAPOLITAN NOVELS

FROM THE UNITED STATES

"The Neapolitan quartet . . . now seems to me, at least within all that I've read, to be the greatest achievement in fiction of the post-war era." —Charles Finch, *The Chicago Tribune*

"Like Anna Karenina, Lila and Elena are volatile, full of desire and rage. They too break domestic conventions, but it thrills me that instead of killing them off, Ferrante allows them, in all their chaos and pain, to thrive." —Darcey Steinke, *The Los Angeles Times*

"Ferrante [. . .] adumbrates the mysterious beauty and brutality of personal experience." —Rachel Cusk, *The New York Times Book Review*

"It is the exploration of the women's mental underworld that makes the book so singular an achievement in feminist literature; indeed, in all literature." —Joan Acocella, *The New Yorker*

"Ferrante has written . . . a knowing and complex tale that encompasses an entire metropolis." —John Domini, *The Washington Post*

"Ferrante has created a mythic portrait of a female friendship." —*Kirkus Reviews* (starred)

"Ferrante's sentences have an incantatory power, as well as profound psychological and cultural insights." —Pasha Malla, *The Slate Book Review*

"Ferrante's writing is so unencumbered, so natural, and yet so lovely, brazen, and flush. The constancy of detail and the pacing that zips and skips then slows to a real-time crawl have an almost psychic effect, bringing you deeply into synchronicity with the discomforts and urgency of the characters' emotions. Ferrante is unlike other writers—not because she's innovative, but rather because she's unselfconscious and brutally, diligently honest."

—Minna Proctor, *Bookforum*

"Everyone should read anything with Ferrante's name on it."

—*The Boston Globe*

"In these bold, gorgeous, relentless novels, Ferrante traces the deep connections between the political and the domestic. This is a new version of the way we live now—one we need, one told brilliantly, by a woman."

—Roxana Robinson, *The New York Times Book Review*

"An intoxicatingly furious portrait of enmeshed friends Lila and Elena, bright and passionate girls from a raucous neighborhood in world-class Naples. Ferrante writes with such aggression and unnerving psychological insight about the messy complexity of female friendship that the real world can drop away when you're reading her." —*Entertainment Weekly*

"Ferrante can do a woman's interior dialogue like no one else, with a ferocity that is shockingly honest, unnervingly blunt."

—*Booklist*

"Elena Ferrante's gutsy and compulsively readable new novel, the first of a quartet, is a terrific entry point for Americans unfamiliar with the famously reclusive writer, whose go-for-broke tales of women's shadow selves—those ambivalent mothers and seething divorcées too complex or unseemly for polite society (and most literary fiction, for that matter)—shimmer with Balzacian human detail and subtle psychological suspense . . . The Neapolitan novels offer one of the more nuanced portraits of feminine friendship in recent memory—from the make-up and break-up quarrels of young girls to the way in which we carefully define ourselves against each other as teens—Ferrante wisely balances her mem-

"The through-line in all of Ferrante's investigations, for me, is nothing less than one long, mind-and-heart-shredding howl for the history of women (not only Neapolitan women), and its implicit *j'accuse* . . . Ferrante's effect, critics agree, is inarguable. 'Intensely, violently personal' and 'brutal directness, familial torment' is how James Wood ventures to categorize her—descriptions that seem mild after you've encountered the work."

—Joan Frank, *The San Francisco Chronicle*

"Lila, mercurial, unsparing, and, at the end of this first episode in a planned trilogy from Ferrante, seemingly capable of starting a full-scale neighborhood war, is a memorable character."

—*Publishers Weekly*

"Ferrante's own writing has no limits, is willing to take every thought forward to its most radical conclusion and backward to its most radical birthing."

—James Wood,*The New Yorker*

FROM THE UNITED KINGDOM

"Ferrante's writing seems to say something that hasn't been said before in a way so compelling its readers forget where they are, abandon friends and disdain sleep."

—Jo Biggs, *London Review of Books*

"I say this with more confidence than I have felt during 15 years of book reviewing: the Neapolitan novels are extraordinary."

—Theo Tait, *The Sunday Times*

"*The Story of the Lost Child* . . . confirms Ferrante—once again—as one of contemporary fiction's most compelling voices."

—*The Daily Telegraph*

"This is a great novel of female friendship, one that reveals admiration and envy, competition and self-sabotage, emotions that many women experience but do not discuss."

—*The Economist*

oir-like emotional authenticity with a wry sociological understanding of a society on the verge of dramatic change."
—Megan O'Grady, *Vogue*

"Elena Ferrante will blow you away."   —Alice Sebold

"An engrossing, wildly original contemporary epic about the
demonic power of human (and particularly female) creativity
checked by the forces of history and society."
—*The Los Angeles Review of Books*

"*My Brilliant Friend* is a sweeping family-centered epic that encompasses issues of loyalty, love, and a transforming Europe. This gorgeous novel should bring a host of new readers to one of Italy's
most acclaimed authors."   —*The Barnes and Noble Review*

"[Ferrante's Neapolitan Novels] don't merely offer a teeming
vision of working-class Naples, with its cobblers and professors,
communists and mobbed-up businessmen, womanizing poets and
downtrodden wives; they present one of modern fiction's richest
portraits of a friendship."   —John Powers, "Fresh Air", NPR

"Ferrante draws an indelible picture of the city's mean streets and
the poverty, violence and sameness of lives lived in the same place
forever . . . She is a fierce writer."   —*Shelf Awareness*

"Elena Ferrante: the best angry woman writer ever!"
—John Waters

"Beautifully translated by Ann Goldstein . . . Ferrante writes with
a ferocious, intimate urgency that is a celebration of anger.
Ferrante is terribly good with anger, a very specific sort of wrath
harbored by women, who are so often not allowed to give voice to
it. We are angry, a lot of the time, at the position we're in—
whether it's as wife, daughter, mother, friend—and I can think of
no other woman writing who is so swift and gorgeous in this rage,
so bracingly fearless in mining fury."
—Susanna Sonnenberg, *The San Francisco Chronicle*

"To the uninitiated, the Italian novelist Elena Ferrante is best described as Balzac meets *The Sopranos* and rewrites feminist theory." —*The Times*

"Nothing quite like it has ever been published." —*The Guardian*

"*The Story of a New Name*, like its predecessor, is fiction of the very highest order." —*Independent on Sunday*

"*My Brilliant Friend*, translated by Ann Goldstein, is stunning: an intense, forensic exploration of the friendship between Lila and the story's narrator, Elena. Ferrante's evocation of the working-class district of Naples where Elena and Lila first meet as two wiry eight-year-olds is cinematic in the density of its detail." —*The Times Literary Supplement*

"This is a story about friendship as a mass of roiling currents— love, envy, pity, spite, dependency and Schadenfreude coiling around one another, tricky to untangle." —*Intelligent Life*

"Elena Ferrante may be the best contemporary novelist you have never heard of. The Italian author has written six lavishly praised novels. But she writes under a pseudonym and will not offer herself for public consumption. Her characters likewise defy convention . . . Her prose is crystal, and her storytelling both visceral and compelling." —*The Economist*

FROM ITALY

"*Those Who Leave and Those Who Stay* evokes the vital flux of a heartbeat, of blood flowing through our veins." —*La Repubblica*

"We don't know who she is, but it doesn't matter. Ferrante's books are enthralling self-contained monoliths that do not seek friendship but demand silent, fervid admiration from her passionate readers . . . The thing most real in these novels is the intense, almost osmotic relationship that unites Elena and Lila, the two girls from a neighborhood in Naples who are the peerless protagonists of the Neapolitan novels." —*Famiglia Cristiana*

"Today it is near impossible to find writers capable of bringing smells, tastes, feelings, and contradictory passions to their pages. Elena Ferrante, alone, seems able to do it. There is no writer better suited to composing the great Italian novel of her generation, her country, and her time." —*Il Manifesto*

"Regardless of who is behind the name Elena Ferrante, the mysterious pseudonym used by the author of the Neapolitan novels, two things are certain: she is a woman and she knows how to describe Naples like nobody else. She does so with a style that recalls an enchanted spider web with its expressive power and the wizardry with which it creates an entire world." —*Huffington Post* (Italy)

"A marvel that is without limits and beyond genre." —*Il Salvagente*

"Elena Ferrante is proving that literature can cure our present ills; it can cure the spirit by operating as an antidote to the nervous attempts we make to see ourselves reflected in the present-day of a country that is increasingly repellent." —*Il Mattino*

"*My Brilliant Friend* flows from the soul like an eruption from Mount Vesuvius." —*La Repubblica*

FROM AUSTRALIA

"No one has a voice quite like Ferrante's. Her gritty, ruthlessly frank novels roar off the page with a barbed fury, like an attack that is also a defense . . . Ferrante's fictions are fierce, unsentimental glimpses at the way a woman is constantly under threat, her identity submerged in marriage, eclipsed by motherhood, mythologised by desire. Imagine if Jane Austen got angry and you'll have some idea of how explosive these works are." —John Freeman, *The Australian*

"One of the most astounding—and mysterious—contemporary Italian novelists available in translation, Elena Ferrante unfolds the tumultuous inner lives of women in her thrillingly menacing stories of lost love, negligent mothers and unfulfilled desires."
—*The Age*

"Ferrante bewitches with her tiny, intricately drawn world . . . *My Brilliant Friend* journeys fearlessly into some of that murkier psychological territory where questions of individual identity are inextricable from circumstance and the ever-changing identities of others."
—*The Melbourne Review*

"The Neapolitan novels move far from contrivance, logic or respectability to ask uncomfortable questions about how we live, how we love, how we singe an existence in a deeply flawed world that expects pretty acquiescence from its women. In all their beauty, their ugliness, their devotion and deceit, these girls enchant and repulse, like life, like our very selves."
—*The Sydney Morning Herald*

FROM SPAIN

"Elena Ferrante's female characters are genuine works of art . . . It is clear that her novel is the child of Italian neorealism and an abiding fascination with scene."
—*El País*

ALSO BY

ELENA FERRANTE

The Days of Abandonment
Troubling Love
The Lost Daughter
My Brilliant Friend
The Story of a New Name
Those Who Leave and Those Who Stay

THE STORY
OF THE LOST CHILD

Elena Ferrante

THE STORY
OF THE LOST CHILD

Book Four, The Neapolitan Novels
Maturity, Old Age

*Translated from the Italian
by Ann Goldstein*

Europa
editions

Europa Editions
214 West 29th Street
New York, N.Y. 10001
www.europaeditions.com
info@europaeditions.com

Translation by Ann Goldstein
Original title: *Storia della bambina perduta*
Translation copyright © 2015 by Europa Editions

Library of Congress Cataloguing in Publication Data is available
ISBN 978-1-60945-286-5

Ferrante, Elena
The Story of the Lost Child

Book design by Emanuele Ragnisco
www.mekkanografici.com

Cover photo © Cultura/Hybrid Images/Getty

Prepress by Grafica Punto Print – Rome

Printed in the USA

THE STORY
OF THE LOST CHILD

INDEX OF CHARACTERS

The Cerullo family (the shoemaker's family):

Fernando Cerullo, shoemaker, Lila's father.

Nunzia Cerullo, Lila's mother.

Raffaella Cerullo, called Lina, or Lila. She was born in August, 1944, and is sixty-six when she disappears from Naples without a trace. At the age of sixteen, she marries Stefano Carracci, but during a vacation on Ischia she falls in love with Nino Sarratore, for whom she leaves her husband. After the disastrous end of her relationship with Nino, the birth of her son Gennaro (also called Rino), and the discovery that Stefano is expecting a child with Ada Cappuccio, Lila leaves him definitively. She moves with Enzo Scanno to San Giovanni a Teduccio, but several years later she returns to the neighborhood with Enzo and Gennaro.

Rino Cerullo, Lila's older brother. He is married to Stefano's sister, Pinuccia Carracci, with whom he has two sons.

Other children.

The Greco family (the porter's family):

Elena Greco, called Lenuccia or Lenù. Born in August, 1944, she is the author of the long story that we are reading. After elementary school, Elena continues to study, with increasing success, obtaining a degree from the Scuola Normale, in Pisa, where she meets Pietro Airota. She marries him, and they move to Florence. They have two children, Adele, called Dede, and Elsa, but Elena, disappointed by marriage, begins an affair with Nino Sarratore, with whom she has been in love since childhood, and eventually leaves Pietro and the children.

Peppe, Gianni, and *Elisa,* Elena's younger siblings. Despite Elena's disapproval, Elisa goes to live with Marcello Solara.

The father, a porter at the city hall.

The mother, a housewife.

The Carracci family (Don Achille's family):

Don Achille Carracci, dealer in the black market, loan shark. He was murdered.

Maria Carracci, wife of Don Achille, mother of Stefano, Pinuccia, and Alfonso. The daughter of Stefano and Ada Cappuccio bears her name.

Stefano Carracci, son of Don Achille, shopkeeper and Lila's first husband. Dissatisfied by his stormy marriage to Lila, he initiates a relationship with Ada Cappuccio, and they start living together. He is the father of Gennaro, with Lila, and of Maria, with Ada.

Pinuccia, daughter of Don Achille. She is married to Lila's brother, Rino, and has two sons with him.

Alfonso, son of Don Achille. He resigns himself to marrying Marisa Sarratore after a long engagement.

The Peluso family (the carpenter's family):

Alfredo Peluso, carpenter and Communist, dies in prison.

Giuseppina Peluso, devoted wife of Alfredo, commits suicide after his death.

Pasquale Peluso, older son of Alfredo and Giuseppina, construction worker, militant Communist.

Carmela Peluso, called *Carmen.* Pasquale's sister, she was the girlfriend of Enzo Scanno for a long time. She subsequently marries Roberto, the owner of the gas pump on the *stradone,* with whom she has two children.

Other children.

The Cappuccio family (the mad widow's family):
Melina, a widow, a relative of Nunzia Cerullo. She nearly lost her mind after her relationship with Donato Sarratore ended.
Melina's *husband*, who died in mysterious circumstances.
Ada Cappuccio, Melina's daughter. For a long time the girl-friend of Pasquale Peluso, she becomes the lover of Stefano Carracci, and goes to live with him. From their relationship a girl, Maria, is born.
Antonio Cappuccio, her brother, a mechanic. He was Elena's boyfriend.
Other children.

The Sarratore family (the railway-worker poet's family):
Donato Sarratore, a great womanizer, who was the lover of Melina Cappuccio. Elena, too, at a very young age, gives herself to him on the beach in Ischia, driven by the suffering that the relationship between Nino and Lila has caused her.
Lidia Sarratore, wife of Donato.
Nino Sarratore, the oldest of the five children of Donato and Lidia, has a long secret affair with Lila. Married to Eleonora, with whom he has Albertino and Lidia, he begins an affair with Elena, who is also married and has children.
Marisa Sarratore, sister of Nino. Married to Alfonso Carracci. She becomes the lover of Michele Solara, with whom she has two children.
Pino, *Clelia*, and *Ciro Sarratore*, younger children of Donato and Lidia.

The Scanno family (the fruit-and-vegetable seller's family):
Nicola Scanno, fruit-and-vegetable seller, dies of pneumonia.
Assunta Scanno, wife of Nicola, dies of cancer.
Enzo Scanno, son of Nicola and Assunta, also a fruit-and-vegetable seller. He was for a long time the boyfriend of Carmen

Peluso. He takes on responsibility for Lila and her son, Gennaro, when she leaves Stefano Carracci, and takes them to live in San Giovanni a Teduccio. *Other children.*

The Solara family (the family of the owner of the Solara bar-pastry shop):

Silvio Solara, owner of the bar-pastry shop.

Manuela Solara, wife of Silvio, moneylender. As an old woman, she is killed in the doorway of her house.

Marcello and Michele Solara, sons of Silvio and Manuela. Rejected by Lila, *Marcello*, after many years, goes to live with Elisa, Elena's younger sister. *Michele*, married to Gigliola, the daughter of the pastry maker, takes Marisa Sarratore as his lover, and has two more children with her. Yet he continues to be obsessed with Lila.

The Spagnuolo family (the baker's family):

Signor Spagnuolo, pastry maker at the Solaras' bar-pastry shop.

Rosa Spagnuolo, wife of the pastry maker.

Gigliola Spagnuolo, daughter of the pastry maker, wife of Michele Solara and mother of two of his children. *Other children.*

The Airota family:

Guido Airota, professor of Greek literature.

Adele Airota, his wife.

Mariarosa Airota, their daughter, professor of art history in Milan.

Pietro Airota, a very young university professor, Elena's husband and the father of Dede and Elsa.

The teachers:

Ferraro, teacher and librarian.

Maestra Oliviero, teacher.

Professor Gerace, high-school teacher.

Professor Galiani, high-school teacher.

Other characters:

Gino, son of the pharmacist; Elena's first boyfriend.

Nella Incardo, the cousin of Maestra Oliviero.

Armando, doctor, son of Professor Galiani. Married to Isabella, with whom he has a son named Marco.

Nadia, student, daughter of Professor Galiani, was Nino's girl-friend. During a period of militant political activity, she becomes attached to Pasquale Peluso.

Bruno Soccavo, friend of Nino Sarratore and the heir to a sausage factory. He is killed in his factory.

Franco Mari, Elena's boyfriend during her first years at the university, has devoted himself to political activism. He loses an eye in a Fascist attack.

Silvia, a university student and political activist. She has a son, Mirko, from a brief relationship with Nino Sarratore.

MATURITY
THE STORY OF THE LOST CHILD

1.

From October 1976 until 1979, when I returned to Naples to live, I avoided resuming a steady relationship with Lila. But it wasn't easy. She almost immediately tried to reenter my life by force, and I ignored her, tolerated her, endured her. Even if she acted as if there were nothing she wanted more than to be close to me at a difficult moment, I couldn't forget the contempt with which she had treated me.

Today I think that if it had been only the insult that wounded me—You're an idiot, she had shouted on the telephone when I told her about Nino, and she had never, *ever* spoken to me like that before—I would have soon calmed down. In reality, what mattered more than that offense was the mention of Dede and Elsa. Think of the harm you're doing to your daughters, she had warned me, and at the moment I had paid no attention. But over time those words acquired greater weight, and I returned to them often. Lila had never displayed the slightest interest in Dede and Elsa; almost certainly she didn't even remember their names. If, on the phone, I mentioned some intelligent remark they had made, she cut me off, changed the subject. And when she met them for the first time, at the house of Marcello Solara, she had confined herself to an absentminded glance and a few pat phrases—she hadn't paid the least attention to how nicely they were dressed, how neatly their hair was combed, how well both were able to express themselves, although they were still small. And yet *I* had given birth to them, *I* had brought them up, they were part of me, who had been her friend forever: she should have taken this into account—I won't say out of affection but at least out of politeness—for my maternal pride. Yet she hadn't even attempted a little good-natured sarcasm; she had displayed indifference and nothing more. Only now—out of jealousy, surely, because I had taken Nino—did she remember the girls, and wanted to emphasize that I was a terrible mother, that although I was happy, I was causing them unhappiness. The minute I thought about it I became anxious. Had Lila worried about Gennaro when she left Stefano, when she abandoned the child to the neighbor because of her work in the factory, when she sent him to me as if to get him out of the way? Ah, I had my faults, but I was certainly more a mother than she was.

2.

Such thoughts became a habit in those years. It was as if Lila, who, after all, had uttered only that one malicious remark about Dede and Elsa, had become the defense lawyer for their needs as daughters, and, every time I neglected them to devote myself to myself, I felt obliged to prove to her that she was wrong. But it was a voice invented by ill feeling; what she really thought of my behavior as a mother I don't know. Only she can say if, in fact, she has managed to insert herself into this extremely long chain of words to modify my text, to purposely supply the missing links, to unhook others without letting it show, to say of me more than I want, more than I'm able to say. I wish for this intrusion, I've hoped for it ever since I began to write our story, but I have to get to the end in order to check all the pages. If I tried now, I would certainly get stuck. I've been writing for too long, and I'm tired; it's more and more difficult to keep the thread of the story taut within the chaos of the years, of events large and small, of moods. So either I tend to pass over my own affairs to recapture Lila and all the complications she brings with her or, worse, I let myself be carried away by the events of my life, only because it's easier to write them. But I have to avoid this choice. I mustn't take the first path, on which, if I set myself aside, I would end up finding ever fewer traces of Lila—since the very nature of our relationship dictates that I can reach her only by passing through myself. But I shouldn't take the second, either. That, in fact, I speak of my experience in increasingly greater detail is just what she would certainly favor. Come on—she would say—tell us what turn your life took, who cares about mine, admit that it doesn't even interest you. And she would conclude: I'm a scribble on a scribble, completely unsuitable for one of your books; forget it, Lenù, one doesn't tell the story of an erasure.

What to do, then? Admit yet again that she's right? Accept that to be adult is to disappear, is to learn to hide to the point of vanishing? Admit that, as the years pass, the less I know of Lila?

This morning I keep weariness at bay and sit down again at the desk. Now that I'm close to the most painful part of our story, I want to seek on the page a balance between her and me that in life I couldn't find even between myself and me.

3.

Of the days in Montpellier I remember everything except the city; it's as if I'd never been there. Outside the hotel, outside the vast assembly hall where the academic conference that Nino was attending took place, today I see only a windy autumn and a blue sky resting on white clouds. And yet in my memory that place-name, Montpellier, has for many reasons remained a symbol of escape. I had been out of Italy once, in Paris, with Franco, and I had felt exhilarated by my own audacity. But then it seemed to me that my world was and would forever remain the neighborhood, Naples, while the rest was like a brief outing in whose special climate I could imagine myself as I would never in fact be. Montpellier, on the other hand, although it was far less exciting than Paris, gave me the impression that my boundaries had burst and I was expanding. The pure and simple fact of being in that place constituted in my eyes the proof that the neighborhood, Naples, Pisa, Florence, Milan, Italy itself were only tiny fragments of the world and that I would do well not to be satisfied with those fragments any longer. In Montpellier I felt the limitations of my outlook, of the language in which I expressed myself and in which I had written. In Montpellier it seemed to me evident how restrictive, at thirty-two, being a wife and mother might be. And in all those days charged with love I felt, for the first time, freed from the chains I had accumulated over the years—those of my origins, those I had acquired through academic success, those derived from the choices I had made in life, especially marriage. There I also understood the reasons for the pleasure I had felt, in the past, on seeing my first book translated into other languages and, at the same time, the reasons for my disappointment at finding few readers outside Italy. It was marvelous to cross borders, to let oneself go within other cultures, discover the provisional nature of what I had taken for absolute. The fact that Lila had never been out of Naples, that she was afraid even of San Giovanni a Teduccio—if in the past I had judged it an arguable choice that she was nevertheless able, as usual, to turn into an advantage—now seemed to me simply a sign of mental limitation. I reacted the way you do to someone who insults you by using the same formulations that offended you. *You were wrong about me? No, my dear, it's I, I who was wrong about you: you will spend the rest of your life looking out at the trucks passing on the* stradone.

The days flew by. The organizers of the conference had reserved for Nino a single room in the hotel, and since I had decided so late to go with him, there was no way to change it to a double. So we had separate rooms, but every night I took a shower, got ready for bed, and then, with trepidation, went to his room. We slept together, clinging to each other, as if we feared that a hostile force would separate us in sleep. In the morning we had breakfast in bed, a luxury that I had seen only in movies; we laughed, we were happy. During the day I went with him to the assembly hall and, although the speakers read their endless pages in a bored tone, being with him was exciting; I sat next to him but without disturbing him. Nino followed the talks attentively, took notes, and every so often whispered in my ear ironic comments and words of love. At lunch and dinner we mixed with academics from all over the world, foreign names, foreign languages. Of course, the participants with bigger reputations were at a table of their own; we sat in a large group of younger scholars. But I was struck by Nino's mobility, both during the events and at the restaurants. How different he was from the student of long ago, even from the youth who had defended me in the bookstore in Milan almost ten years earlier. He had abandoned polemical tones, he tactfully crossed academic barriers, established relations with a serious yet engaging demeanor. Now in English (excellent), now in French (good), he conversed brilliantly, displaying his old devotion to figures and efficiency. I was filled with pride at how well liked he was. In a few hours he had charmed everyone, and was invited here and there.

There was a single moment when he changed abruptly. The evening before he was to speak at the conference, he became aloof and rude; he seemed overwhelmed by anxiety. He began to disparage the text he had prepared, he kept repeating that writing for him wasn't as easy as it was for me, he became angry because he hadn't had time to work well. I felt guilty—

was it our complicated affair that had distracted him?—and tried to help, hugging him, kissing him, urging him to read me the pages. He did read them, with the air of a frightened schoolboy, which touched me. To me the speech seemed as dull as the ones I had heard in the assembly hall, but I praised it and he calmed down. The next morning he performed with practiced warmth and was applauded. That evening one of the big-name academics, an American, invited him to sit with him. I was left alone, but I wasn't sorry. When Nino was there, I didn't talk to anyone, while in his absence I was forced to manage with my halting French, and I became friendly with a couple from Paris. I liked them because I quickly discovered that they were in a situation not very different from ours. Both considered the institution of the family suffocating, both had painfully left spouses and children, both seemed happy. He, Augustin, was around fifty, with a ruddy face, lively blue eyes, a bushy pale-blond mustache. She, Colombe, was a little over thirty, like me; she had very short black hair, eyes and lips drawn sharply on a tiny face, a charming elegance. I talked mainly to Colombe, who had a child of seven.

"In a few months," I said, "my older daughter will turn seven, but she's going into second grade this year—she's very bright."

"My son is extremely clever and imaginative."

"How did he take the separation?"

"Fine."

"He didn't get even a little upset?"

"Children aren't rigid, the way we are: they're flexible."

She dwelled on the flexibility she ascribed to childhood; it seemed to reassure her. She added: in our world it's fairly common for parents to separate, and children know it's possible. But just as I was saying that I didn't know other separated women, apart from one friend, her tone changed abruptly and she began to complain about the child: he's smart but slow, she exclaimed, at school they say he's unruly. I was struck by the change; she expressed herself without tenderness, almost bitterly, as if her son were behaving like that to spite her, and this made me anxious. Her companion must have noticed, and he interrupted, boasting about *his* two boys, fourteen and eighteen, and joking about how attractive they were to women, both old and young. When Nino returned, the two men—especially Augustin—began to criticize the speakers. Colombe joined in almost immediately, with a slightly artificial gaiety. The maliciousness soon created a bond. Augustin talked and drank a lot all evening, his companion laughed whenever Nino managed to say a word. They invited us to drive to Paris with them, in their car.

The conversation about children, and that invitation that we didn't say yes or no to, brought me back to reality. Until that moment Dede and Elsa, and also Pietro, had been on my mind constantly, but as if suspended in a parallel universe, motionless around the kitchen table in Florence, or in front of the television, or in their beds. Suddenly my world and theirs were back in communication. I realized that the days in Montpellier were about to end, that inevitably Nino and I would return to our homes, that we would have to face our respective marital crises, I in Florence, he in Naples. And the children's bodies rejoined mine, I felt the contact violently. I had no news of them for five days, and as I became aware of that I felt an intense nausea, an unbearable longing for them. I was afraid not of the future in general, which now seemed inescapably occupied by Nino, but of the hours that were about to come, of tomorrow, of the day after. I couldn't resist and although it was almost midnight—what's the difference, I said to myself, Pietro is always awake—I tried to telephone.

It was fairly laborious, but finally the call went through. Hello, I said. Hello, I repeated. I knew that Pietro was at the other end of the line, I called him by name: Pietro, it's Elena, how are the girls. The connection was cut off. I waited a few minutes, then I asked the operator to call again. I was determined to continue all night, but this time Pietro answered.

"What do you want?"

"Tell me about the children."

"They're sleeping."

"I know, but how are they?"

"What is it to you."

"They're my children."

"You left them, they don't want to be your children anymore."

"They told you?"

"They told my mother."

"You had Adele come?"

"Yes."

"Tell them I'll be home in a few days."

"No, don't come back. Neither I, nor the children, nor my mother wants to see you again."

4.

I had a cry, then I calmed down and went to Nino. I wanted to tell him about that phone call, I wanted him to console me. But as I was about to knock on his door I heard him talking to someone. I hesitated. He was on the phone. I couldn't understand what he was saying, or even what language he was speaking, but right away I thought that he was talking to his wife. So did this happen every evening? When I went to my room to get ready for the night and he was alone, he telephoned Eleonora? Were they looking for a way to separate without fighting? Or were they reconciling and, once the interlude of Montpellier was over, she would take him back?

I decided to knock. Nino broke off, silence, then he began

talking again but lowered his voice. I became nervous, I knocked again, nothing happened. I had to knock a third time, hard, before he came to the door. I immediately confronted him, I accused him of hiding me from his wife, I cried that I had telephoned Pietro, that my husband didn't want to let me see my children, that I was calling into question my entire life, while he was cooing on the telephone with Eleonora. It was a terrible night of quarreling; we struggled to make up. Nino tried everything to soothe me: he laughed nervously, he got angry at Pietro for the way he had treated me, he kissed me, I pushed him away, he said I was crazy. But no matter how I pressed him he never admitted that he was talking to his wife, in fact he swore on his son that since the day he left Naples he hadn't talked to her.

"Then who were you calling?"

"A colleague here in the hotel."

"At midnight?"

"At midnight."

"Liar."

"It's the truth."

I refused for a long time to make love, I couldn't, I was afraid that he no longer loved me. Then I yielded, in order not to have to believe that it was all already over.

The next morning, for the first time in almost five days of living together, I woke in a bad mood. We had to leave, the conference was nearly over. But I didn't want Montpellier to be merely an interlude; I was afraid to go home, afraid that Nino would go home, afraid of losing my children forever. When Augustin and Colombe again suggested that we drive to Paris with them, and even offered to put us up, I turned to Nino, hoping that he, too, wanted nothing more than the chance to extend this time, put off the return. But he shook his head sadly, he said: Impossible, we have to go back to Italy, and he talked about flights, tickets, trains, money. I was fragile, I

felt disappointment and rancor. I was right, I thought, he lied
to me, the break with his wife isn't conclusive. He had talked
to her every night, he had pledged to return home after the
conference, he couldn't delay even a couple of days. And me?
I remembered the publisher in Nanterre and my short,
scholarly story about the male invention of woman. Until that
moment I hadn't talked about myself to anyone, even Nino. I
had been the smiling but nearly mute woman who slept with
the brilliant professor from Naples, the woman always pasted
to him, attentive to his needs, to his thoughts. But now I said
with false cheer: It's Nino who has to return, I have an engagement in Nanterre; a work of mine is about to come out—or
maybe it's already out—a half essay, half story; I just might
leave with you, and stop in at the publisher's. The two looked
at me as if only at that moment had I actually begun to exist,
and they went on to ask me about my work. I told them, and
it turned out that Colombe knew well the woman who was the
head of the small but—as I discovered at that moment—prestigious publishing house. I let myself go, I talked with too
much vivacity and maybe I exaggerated a little about my literary career. I did it not for the two French people but, rather,
for Nino. I wanted to remind him that I had a rewarding life of
my own, that if I had been capable of leaving my children and
Pietro, then I could also do without him, and not in a week,
not in ten days: immediately.

He listened, then he said seriously to Colombe and
Augustin: All right, if it's not a bother for you we'll take advantage of the ride. But when we were alone he made me a speech
anxious in tone and passionate in content, whose sense was
that I should trust him, that although our situation was complicated we would surely untangle it, that to do so, however,
we had to go home, we couldn't flee from Montpellier to Paris
and then to who knows what other city, we had to confront our
spouses and begin our life together. Suddenly I felt that he was

not only reasonable but sincere. I was confused, I embraced him, I murmured agreement. And yet we left for Paris; I wanted just a few more days.

5.

It was a long trip. There was a strong wind, and sometimes rain. The landscape had a rust-caked pallor, but at times the sky broke and everything became brilliant, starting with the rain. I clung to Nino and, now and then, fell asleep on his shoulder; I began again to feel, with pleasure, that I was far beyond my margins. I liked the foreign language that echoed in the car, I was pleased that I was heading in the direction of a book that I had written in Italian and that, thanks to Mariarosa, was being published first in another language. What an extraordinary fact—how many amazing things were happening to me. That little volume was like a rock that I had hurled along an unpredictable trajectory and at a speed that had no comparison with that of the rocks that as girls Lila and I had thrown at the gangs of boys.

But the journey wasn't always pleasant; sometimes I became sad. And I quickly formed the impression that Nino was talking to Colombe in a tone that he didn't use with Augustin, not to mention that too often he touched her shoulder with his fingertips. My bad mood gradually worsened, as I saw the two of them were getting very friendly. When we arrived in Paris they were the best of friends, chatting away; she laughed often, smoothing her hair with a careless gesture.

Augustin lived in a nice apartment on Canal Saint-Martin; Colombe had recently moved in. Even after they showed us our room, they wouldn't let us to go bed. It seemed to me that they were afraid to be alone, they wouldn't stop talking. I was tired and nervous; I was the one who had wanted to go to

Paris, and now it seemed absurd to be in that house, among strangers, far from my daughters, with Nino paying scant attention to me. Once in the room I asked him:

"Do you like Colombe?"

"She's nice."

"I asked if you like her."

"Do you want to quarrel?"

"No."

"Then think about it: how can I like Colombe if I love you?"

It scared me when his tone became even slightly harsh; I was afraid I would have to acknowledge that something between us wasn't working. He is simply nice to anyone who has been nice to us, I said to myself, and fell asleep. But I slept badly. At one point I had the impression that I was alone in the bed; I tried to wake up, but was drawn back into sleep. I emerged again sometime later. Nino now was standing in the dark, or so it seemed to me. Sleep, he said. I fell asleep again.

The next day our hosts took us to Nanterre. The whole way Nino continued to joke with Colombe, to talk to her in an allusive way. I tried not to pay attention. How could I think of living with him if I had to spend my time watching him? When we reached our destination and he became genial and charming with Mariarosa's friend, the owner of the publishing house, and her partner—one around forty, the other sixty—I drew a sigh of relief. It's innocent, I concluded, he's like that with all women. And finally I felt better.

The two women greeted me warmly, full of praise, and asked about Mariarosa. I knew that my volume had only just arrived in the bookstores, but already a couple of reviews had appeared. The older woman showed them to me; she seemed amazed herself at how positive they were, and, turning to Colombe, to Augustin, to Nino, she kept repeating it. I read the articles, two lines here, four there. They were written by women—I had never heard of them, but Colombe and the two women had—and they praised the book enthusiastically. I should have been pleased; the day before, I had been compelled to sing my own praises, and now I no longer needed to. Yet I found that I couldn't feel excited. It was as if, since I loved Nino and he loved me, that love made everything good that happened to me and would happen to me nothing but a pleasant secondary effect. I showed my satisfaction graciously and gave a feeble assent to my publishers' plans for promotion. You'll have to return soon, the older woman exclaimed, or at least we hope so. The younger added: Mariarosa told us about your marital crisis; we hope you'll come out of it without too much suffering.

In this way I discovered that the news of the break between me and Pietro had reached not only Adele but Milan and even France. Better that way, I thought; it will be easier to make the separation permanent. I said to myself: I'll take what's mine, and I mustn't live in fear of losing Nino, I mustn't worry about Dede and Elsa. I'm fortunate, he will always love me, my daughters are my daughters, everything will work out.

6.

We returned to Rome. We promised each other everything as we said goodbye, we did nothing but promise. Then Nino left for Naples and I for Florence.

I returned home almost on tiptoe, convinced that one of the most difficult trials of my life awaited me. Instead the children greeted me with apprehensive joy, and began tagging after me through the house—not only Elsa but Dede, too—as if they were afraid that if they lost sight of me I would disappear again. Adele was polite and didn't mention even once the situation that had brought her to my house; Pietro, very pale, confined himself to handing me a piece of paper with a list of phone calls for me (Lila's name appeared at least four times), muttered that he had to go to work, and two hours later had disappeared, without even saying goodbye to his mother or the children.

It took a few days for Adele to manifest her opinion plainly: she wanted me to return to myself and to my husband. But it took several weeks to convince her that I really didn't want either of those things. In that time she never raised her voice, never lost her temper, didn't even comment sarcastically about my frequent long phone calls to Nino. She was more interested in the phone calls from the two women in Nanterre, who were keeping me informed of the progress of the book and of a calendar of engagements that would lead to a tour in France. She wasn't surprised at the positive reviews in the French papers; she was sure that the book would soon get the same attention in Italy, she said that in our papers she would have been able to obtain better. Above all she insistently praised my intelligence, my education, my courage, and on no account did she defend her son, who, besides, was never around.

I assumed that Pietro did not really have work obligations outside of Florence. Rather, I was immediately convinced, with rage and even a hint of contempt, that he had entrusted the resolution of our crisis to his mother and was holed up somewhere to work on his interminable book. Once, I couldn't contain myself and I said to Adele:

"It was really difficult to live with your son."

"There's no man it's not difficult to live with."

"With him, believe me, it's been especially difficult."

"You think it will go better with Nino?"

"Yes."

"I've asked around, the talk about him in Milan is very nasty."

"I don't need the talk of Milan. I've loved him for twenty

years and you can spare me the gossip. I know more about him than anyone else."

"How you like saying you love him."

"Why shouldn't I like it?"

"You're right, why? I was wrong: it's pointless to open the eyes of someone in love."

From then on we stopped talking about Nino. And when I left the girls with her to rush to Naples she didn't bat an eye. She didn't bat an eye even when I told her that, when I returned from Naples, I would have to go to France and would be there for a week. She asked only, with a slightly ironic inflection: "Will you be here for Christmas? Will you be with the children?"

The question almost offended me, I answered: "Of course."

I filled my suitcase mainly with elegant underwear and stylish dresses. At the announcement of my new departure Dede and Elsa, who never asked about their father, even though they hadn't seen him for a long time, were extremely upset. Dede went so far as to yell words that were surely not hers: go, get out, you're mean and hateful. I glanced at Adele, hoping that she would try to get her to play, and distract her, but she did nothing. When they saw me go to the door they began to cry. Elsa started it, shrieking, I want to come with you. Dede resisted, she tried to show me all her indifference, maybe even her scorn, but finally she gave in and became even more desperate than her sister. I had to tear myself away from them, they held on to my dress, they wanted me to leave the suitcase. Their cries pursued me to the street.

The trip to Naples seemed very long. Nearing the city I looked out the window. As the train slowed down, sliding into the urban space, I was seized by an anxious exhaustion. I noticed the ugliness of the periphery, with the small gray apartment buildings beyond the tracks; the pylons, the lights of the signals, the stone parapets. When the train entered the station it seemed to me that the Naples I felt bound to, the Naples I was returning to, was now summed up only in Nino. I knew that he was in worse trouble than I was. Eleonora had thrown him out of the house; for him, too, everything had become provisional. For several weeks he had been staying at the house of a university colleague who lived near the Duomo. Where would he take me, what would we do? And, above all, what decisions would we make, since we hadn't the least idea of a concrete solution to our situation? The only thing clear to me was that I was burning with desire, I couldn't wait to see him. I got out of the train terrified that something had kept him from coming to meet me. But he was there: tall as he was, he stood out in the stream of travelers.

This reassured me, and I was even more reassured to find that he had taken a room in a small hotel in Mergellina, thus showing that he had no intention of hiding me in his friend's house. We were mad with love, the time flew. In the evening we walked along the sea clinging to each other; he put an arm around my shoulders, and every so often leaned over to kiss me. I tried in every way possible to persuade him to go to France with me. He was tempted, then retreated, taking refuge behind his work at the university. He never spoke of Eleonora or Albertino, as if the mere mention of them could ruin the joy of our being together. I instead told him about the girls' desperation, I said we had to find a solution as quickly as possible. I felt he was nervous; I was sensitive to the slightest tension, I was afraid that at any moment he might say: I can't do it, I'm going home. But I was wide of the mark. When we went to dinner he revealed what the problem was. He said, becoming suddenly serious, that there was some vexing news.

"Let's hear it," I whispered.

"This morning Lina called me."

"Ah."

"She wants to see us."

7.

The evening was spoiled. Nino said it was my mother-in-law who had told Lila that I was in Naples. He spoke with great embarrassment, choosing his words carefully, emphasizing points like: she didn't have my address; she asked my sister for the phone number of my colleague; she telephoned a little before I was about to leave for the station; I didn't tell you right away because I was afraid you would get angry and our day would be ruined. He concluded, desolate:

"You know what she's like, I've never been able to say no to her. We have an appointment with her tomorrow at eleven, she'll be at the entrance to the metro at Piazza Amedeo."

I couldn't control myself:

"How long have you been back in touch? Have you seen each other?"

"What are you talking about? Absolutely not."

"I don't believe you."

"Elena, I swear I haven't talked to or seen Lila since 1963."

"You know the child wasn't yours?"

"She told me this morning."

"So you talked for a long time, and about intimate things."

"She was the one who brought up the child."

"And you—in all this time you were never curious to know more about it?"

"It's my problem, I don't see the need to discuss it."

"Your problems are also mine now. We have a lot to talk about, time is short, and I didn't leave my children to waste it with Lina. How could it possibly have occurred to you to make this date?"

"I thought it would please you. But there's the telephone: call your friend and tell her that we have a lot to do, you can't see her."

There, suddenly he lost patience, I was silent. Yes, I knew what Lila was like. Ever since I returned to Florence she had been calling often, but I had other things to think about and not only did I always hang up, I had also asked Adele—if she happened to answer—to say that I wasn't home. Lila, however, hadn't given up. It was therefore likely that she had found out from Adele about my presence in Naples, likely that she had taken for granted that I would not go to the neighborhood, likely that, to see me, she had found a way of getting in touch with Nino. What was the harm? And above all what did I expect? I had always known that he had loved Lila and that Lila had loved him. So? It had happened long ago, and to be jealous was inappropriate. I slowly caressed his hand, I murmured: All right, tomorrow we'll go to Piazza Amedeo.

We ate, and he talked for a long time about our future. Nino made me promise that I would ask for a separation as soon as I returned from France. Meanwhile he assured me that he had already been in touch with a lawyer friend of his and that even if it was all complicated, and certainly Eleonora and her relatives would make things hard for him, he had decided to go ahead. You know, he said, here in Naples these things are more difficult: when it comes to a backward mentality and bad manners my wife's relatives are no different from mine and yours, even if they have money and are high-ranking professionals. And, as if to explain himself better, he began to speak well of my in-laws. Unfortunately, he exclaimed, I'm not dealing, as you are, with respectable people, like the Airotas, people he described as having grand cultural traditions, admirable civility.

I listened, but now Lila was there between us, at our table, and I couldn't push her away. While Nino talked, I remembered the trouble she had got herself in just to be with him, heedless of what Stefano could do to her, or her brother, or Michele Solara. And the mention of our parents for a fraction of a second brought me back to Ischia, to the evening on the beach of the Maronti—Lila with Nino in Forio, I on the damp sand with Donato—and I felt horror. This, I thought, is a secret that I will never be able to tell him. How many words remain unsayable even between a couple in love, and how the risk is increased that others might say them, destroying it. His father and I, he and Lila. I tore away revulsion, I mentioned Pietro, what he was suffering. Nino flared up, it was his turn to be jealous, I tried to reassure him. He demanded clean breaks and full stops, I demanded them, too: they seemed to us indispensable to the start of a new life. We discussed when, where. Work chained Nino inescapably to Naples, the children chained me to Florence.

"Come and live here," he said suddenly. "Move as soon as you can."

"Impossible, Pietro has to be able to see the children."

"Take turns: you'll take them to him, the next time he'll come here."

"He won't agree."

"He'll agree."

The evening went on like that. The more we examined the question, the more complicated it seemed; the more we imagined a life together—every day, every night—the more we desired it and the difficulties vanished. Meanwhile in the empty restaurant the waiters whispered to each other, yawned. Nino paid, and we went back along the sea walk, which was still lively. For a moment, as I looked at the dark water and smelled its odor, it seemed that the neighborhood was much farther away than when I had gone to Pisa, to Florence. Even Naples, suddenly, seemed very far from Naples. And Lila from Lila, I felt that beside me I had not her but my own anxieties.

Only Nino and I were close, very close. I whispered in his ear: Let's go to bed.

8.

The next day I got up early and shut myself in the bathroom. I took a long shower, I dried my hair carefully, worrying that the hotel hair dryer, which blew violently, would give it the wrong wave. A little before ten I woke Nino, who, still dazed by sleep, was full of compliments for my dress. He tried to pull me down beside him, I drew back. Although I made an effort to pretend there was nothing wrong, I had trouble forgiving him. He had transformed our new day of love into Lila's day, and now the time was completely indelibly marked by that looming encounter.

I dragged him to breakfast, he followed submissively. He didn't laugh, he didn't tease me, he said, touching my hair with his fingertips: You look very nice. Evidently he perceived that I was anxious. And I was, I was afraid that Lila would arrive looking her best. I was made as I was made; she was elegant by nature. And, besides, she had new money, if she wanted she could take care of herself as she had done as a girl with Stefano's money. I didn't want Nino to be dazzled by her again.

We left around ten-thirty, in a cold wind. We walked, unhurried, toward Piazza Amedeo. I was shivering, even though I was wearing a heavy coat and he had an arm around my shoulders. We never mentioned Lila. Nino talked in a somewhat artificial way about how Naples had improved now that there was a Communist mayor, and he began pressing me again to join him as soon as possible with the children. He held me close as we walked, and I hoped he would keep holding me until we reached the subway station. I wanted Lila to be at the metro entrance, to see us from a distance, to find us handsome, to be forced to think: a perfect couple. But, a few meters from the

THE STORY OF THE LOST CHILD · 43

meeting place, he released his arm, lighted a cigarette. I took his hand instinctively, squeezed it hard, and we entered the piazza like that.

I didn't see Lila right away and for a moment I hoped she hadn't come. Then I heard her call me—she called me in her usual imperative way, as though it could never even occur to her that I wouldn't hear her, wouldn't turn, wouldn't obey her voice. She was in the doorway of the café opposite the metro tunnel, her hands stuck in the pockets of an ugly brown coat, thinner than usual, slightly bent, her shining black hair traversed by trails of silver and tied in a ponytail. She seemed to me the usual Lila, the adult Lila, a Lila marked by the factory experience: she had done nothing to dress up. She hugged me tight, in an intense embrace that I returned without energy, then she kissed me on the cheeks with two sharp smacks, and a contented laugh. She held out her hand to Nino absently.

We sat inside the café; she did almost all the talking and addressed me as if we were alone. She immediately confronted my hostility, which evidently she read in my face, and said affectionately, smiling: All right, I was wrong, I offended you, but now, enough, how is it that you've become so touchy, you know that I like everything about you, let's make up.

I avoided her, with tepid half-smiles, I didn't say yes or no. She was sitting opposite Nino, but she never looked or spoke to him. She was there for me; once, she took my hand but I quietly withdrew it. She wanted us to be reconciled, she intended to reinstate herself in my life again, even if she didn't agree with the direction I was taking it. I realized this from the way she added question to question without paying attention to the answers. She was so eager to reoccupy every corner that she had scarcely touched on one subject when she immediately went on to another.

"With Pietro?"

"Badly."

"And your daughters?"

"They're well."

"You'll get divorced?"

"Yes."

"And you two will live together?"

"Yes."

"Where, what city?"

"I don't know."

"Come back here to live."

"It's complicated."

"I'll find you an apartment."

"If it's necessary I'll let you know."

"Are you writing?"

"I've published a book."

"Another?"

"Yes."

"No one's said anything about it."

"For now it's only come out in France."

"In French?"

"Yes."

"A novel?"

"A story, but it has a thesis."

"What's it about?"

I was vague, I cut her off. I preferred to ask about Enzo, about Gennaro, about the neighborhood, about her work. At the mention of her son she took on a look of amusement, and declared that I would see him soon; he was still at school now, but he was coming with Enzo and there would also be a nice surprise. About the neighborhood, on the other hand, she assumed an attitude of indifference. Alluding to the terrible death of Manuela Solara and the turmoil it had unleashed, she said: It's nothing, people are murdered here the way they are everywhere in Italy. Then, surprisingly, she mentioned my mother, praising her energy and her resourcefulness, even though she was well aware of our turbulent relationship. And, just as surprisingly, she seemed affectionate toward her own parents; she said that she was putting money aside to buy the apartment where they had always lived, to give them some peace of mind. It's a pleasure for me—she explained, as if she had to apologize for that generosity—I was born there, I'm attached to it, and if Enzo and I work hard we can afford it. She worked as much as twelve hours a day now, not only for Michele Solara but also for other clients. I'm studying—she said—a new machine, the System 32, much better than the one I showed you when you came to Acerra: it's a white case that incorporates a tiny six-inch monitor, a keyboard, and a printer. She talked on and on about more advanced systems that were coming. She was very well informed, as usual she got excited about the new things, even though she'd be sick of them in a few days. The new machine had a beauty of its own, according to her. Too bad, she said, that apart from the machine, every-thing was shit.

At that point Nino broke in, and did exactly the opposite of what until that moment I had done: he began to give her detailed information. He spoke with excitement about my book, he said that it was coming out soon in Italy, too; he cited the success of the French reviews, he pointed out that I had a lot of problems with my husband and my daughters, he talked about his break with his wife, he repeated that the only solu-tion was to live in Naples, he even encouraged her to find us a house, he asked some knowledgeable questions about her and Enzo's work.

I listened somewhat apprehensively. His manner as he spoke was distant, to show me, first, that he really hadn't seen Lila before; and, second, that she no longer had any influence over him. And not for an instant did he use the seductive tones that he had used with Colombe and which habitually came to him with women. He didn't invent sentimental locutions, he never looked her straight in the eye, he didn't touch her: his voice became a little warmer only when he praised me.

This didn't prevent me from remembering the beach at Citara, and how he and Lila had made use of the most varied subjects to reach an understanding and cut me out. But it seemed to me that now the opposite was happening. Even when they asked each other questions and answered them, they ignored each other and addressed me, as if I were their only interlocutor.

They went on talking for a good half hour without agreeing about anything. I was surprised especially by the way they insisted on their differences about Naples. My political knowledge was by now feeble: the care of the children, the study in preparation for my little book, the writing of it, and, above all, the upheaval of my personal life had kept me even from reading the newspaper. The two of them, on the other hand, knew everything about everything. Nino listed names of Neapolitan Communists and socialists he knew well, and trusted. He praised an administration that, finally, was honest, led by a mayor whom he called respectable, likable, a stranger to the usual old corruption. He concluded: now at last there are good reasons to live and work here, this is a great opportunity, we have to be part of it. But Lila made sarcastic comments about everything he said. Naples, she said, is disgusting, exactly as it was before, and if you're not teaching the monarchists, fascists, and Christian Democrats a good lesson for all the filthy things they've done, if you just forget about it, as the left is doing, soon the shopkeepers—she laughed a little harshly after saying the word—will take back the city, along with the city bureaucracy, the lawyers, the accountants, the banks, and the Camorrists. I was quickly forced to realize that even at the center of that discussion they had put me. They both wanted me to return to Naples, but each was openly intent on detaching me from the influence of the other and was urging me to move to the city that each was imagining: Nino's was at peace and heading toward good government; Lila's was taking revenge on all the predators, it didn't give a damn about Communists and socialists, it was starting over from zero.

I studied them the whole time. It struck me that, the more complex the themes that emerged in the conversation, the more Lila tended to unfold her secret Italian, which I knew she was capable of but which on that occasion astonished me, because every sentence demonstrated that she was more cultured than she wished to appear. As for Nino, who was usually brilliant, self-confident, he chose his words warily, and at times seemed intimidated. They're both uneasy, I thought. In the past they exposed themselves to each other openly and now they're ashamed of having done so. What is happening at this moment? Are they deceiving me? Are they really fighting over me or are they only trying to keep their old attraction under control? I purposely gave signs of impatience. Lila noticed, she got up and disappeared as if to go to the bathroom. I didn't say a word, I was afraid of seeming aggressive toward Nino, and he, too, was silent. When Lila returned, she exclaimed cheerfully:

"Come on, it's time, let's go see Gennaro."

"We can't," I said, "we have an engagement."

"My son is really fond of you, he'll be disappointed."

"Say hello from me, tell him I love him, too."

"I have an appointment in Piazza dei Martiri: it's just ten minutes, we'll say hello to Alfonso and then you'll go."

I stared at her, she suddenly narrowed her eyes as if to hide them. Was that her plan, then? She wanted to take Nino to the Solaras' old shoe store, take him back to the place where, for almost a year, they had been secret lovers?

I answered with a half smile: No, I'm sorry, we really have to run. And I glanced at Nino, who immediately gestured to the waiter, to pay. Lila said: I've already done it, and while he protested she turned to me again, insisting in a cajoling tone:

"Gennaro isn't coming by himself, Enzo's bringing him. And someone else is coming with them, someone who's dying to see you, it would really be terrible if you left without seeing him."

The person was Antonio Cappuccio, my teenage boyfriend, whom the Solaras, after the murder of their mother, had swiftly recalled from Germany.

9.

Lila told me that Antonio had come by himself for Manuela's funeral, so thin that he was almost unrecognizable. Within a few days he had rented a place near Melina, who lived with Stefano and Ada, and had sent for his German wife and three children. It was true, then, that he was married, it was true that he had children. Separate segments of life came together in my head. Antonio was an important part of the world I came from, Lila's words about him diminished the weight of the morning: I felt lighter. I whispered to Nino: Just a few minutes, all right? He shrugged his shoulders and we set off toward Piazza dei Martiri.

All the way, as we went along Via dei Mille and Via Filangieri, Lila monopolized me, and while Nino followed us, hands in pockets, head lowered, certainly in a bad mood, she talked to me with her usual assurance. She said that at the first opportunity I should meet Antonio's family. She vividly described his wife and children. She was beautiful, fairer than I was, and the three children were also fair, not one had taken after their father, who was as dark as a Saracen: when the five of them walked along the *stradone*, the wife and children, so pale, with those shining heads, seemed like prisoners of war he was leading around the neighborhood. She laughed, then she listed those who, besides Antonio, were waiting to greet me: Carmen—who, however, had to work, she would stay a few minutes and rush off with Enzo—Alfonso, of course, who still managed the Solaras' shop, Marisa with the children. Give them just a few minutes, she said, and you'll make them happy: they love you.

While she talked, I thought that all those people I was about to see again would spread through the neighborhood the news of the end of my marriage, that my parents, too, would find out, that my mother would learn I had become the lover of the son of Sarratore. But I noticed that it didn't bother me, in fact it pleased me that my friends would see me with Nino, that they would say behind my back: She's a person who does as she likes, she's left her husband and children, she's gone with someone else. I realized, to my surprise, that I *wanted* to be officially associated with Nino, I wanted to be seen with him, I wanted to erase the Elena-Pietro couple and replace it with the Nino-Elena couple. And I felt suddenly calm, almost well disposed toward the net in which Lila wished to trap me.

The words followed one another without pause; at one point, assuming an old habit, she took me by the arm. That gesture left me indifferent. She wants to prove that we're still the same, I said to myself, but it's time to acknowledge that we've used each other up, that arm of hers is like a wooden limb or the phantom remains of the thrilling contact of long ago. I remembered, by contrast, the moment when, years before, I had wished that she would get sick and die. Then—I thought—in spite of everything our relationship was alive, intense, therefore painful. Now there was a new fact. All the passion I was capable of—even what had harbored that terrible wish—was concentrated on the man I had always loved. Lila thought that she still had her old power, that she could drag me with her where she wanted. But in the end what had she orchestrated: the revisiting of bitter loves and adolescent passions? What a few moments earlier had seemed to me malicious suddenly appeared as harmless as a museum. Something else was important for me, whether she liked it or not. Nino and I were important, Nino and I, and even to cause scandal in the small world of the neighborhood seemed a pleasing recognition of us as a couple. I no longer felt Lila, there was no life in her arm, it was only fabric against fabric.

We arrived in Piazza dei Martiri. I turned to Nino to warn him that his sister and her children were also at the shop. He muttered in irritation. The sign appeared—SOLARA—we entered, and even though all eyes were on Nino, I was greeted as if I were alone. Only Marisa spoke to her brother, and neither seemed pleased by the encounter. She immediately reproached him because she never heard from him or saw him, exclaiming: Mamma is ill, Papa is unbearable, and you don't give a damn. He didn't answer, he kissed his nephews absentmindedly, and only because Marisa continued to attack him he said: I've got my own troubles, Marì, leave me alone. While I was pulled affectionately this way and that, I continued to keep my eye on him, not jealously now—I was worried only about his uneasiness. I didn't know if he remembered Antonio, if he recognized him, I alone knew about the beating my former boyfriend had given him. I saw that they exchanged a very reserved greeting—a movement of the head, a slight smile—no different from what right afterward occurred between Enzo and him, Alfonso and him, Carmen and him. For Nino they were all strangers, Lila's and my world, he had had almost nothing to do with it. Afterward, he wandered through the shop smoking, and no one, not even his sister, said a word to him. He was there, he was present, it was he I had left my husband for. Even Lila—especially Lila—had finally to acknowledge the fact. Now that everyone had studied him carefully, I wanted to drag him out of there as quickly as possible and take him away with me.

10.

For the half hour that I was in that place there was a chaotic collision of past and present: the shoes Lila designed, her wedding photograph, the evening of the inauguration and the miscarriage, she who for her own purposes had transformed the shop into a salon and a love nest; and the present-day plot, all of us over thirty, with our very different stories, the open rumors, the secret ones.

I affected composure, I assumed a happy tone. I exchanged kisses, hugs, and a few words with Gennaro, who was now an overweight boy of twelve with a dark strip of fuzz on his upper lip, so similar in features to the adolescent Stefano that Lila, in conceiving him, seemed to have taken away herself entirely. I felt obliged to be equally affectionate with Marisa's children and with Marisa herself, who, pleased with my attention, began to make allusive remarks, the remarks of someone who knew the turn my life was taking. She said: Now that you'll be in Naples more often, please, come see us; we know you two are busy, you're scholarly people and we aren't, but you'll find a little time.

She sat next to her husband and restrained her children, who were eager to run outside. In vain I sought in her face traces of a blood tie with Nino, but she had nothing of her brother or even of her mother. Now that she was heavier she resembled, rather, Donato; she had also inherited his artificial patter, with which she was trying to give me the impression that she had a lovely family and a good life. And Alfonso, to support her, nodded yes, and smiled at me silently, displaying gleaming white teeth. How disorienting his looks were. He was stylishly dressed, and his long black hair, tied in a ponytail, showed off the grace of his features, but there was something in his gestures, in his face, that I couldn't understand, something unexpected that made me uneasy. He was the only one there, except for Nino and me, who had had an education, and—it seemed to me—rather than fading over time it had more profoundly penetrated his slender body, the fine contours of his face. How handsome he was, how polite. Marisa had wanted him at all costs, even though he fled, and now look at them, she who as she aged was taking on masculine features, he who fought virility by becoming more feminine, and those two children of theirs, who were said to be the children of Michele Solara. Yes, Alfonso whispered, joining his wife's invitation, if you would come to dinner sometime at our house you would make us very happy. And Marisa: When will you write a new book, Lenù? We're waiting; but you have to keep up. You seemed dirty, but you weren't dirty enough—have you seen the pornographic stuff they write today?

Although no one there showed any liking for Nino, there was no hint of criticism for my change of feeling, not even a glance, or a half smile. On the contrary, as I did my rounds, hugging and talking, they tried to impress on me their affection and their respect. Enzo put into his embrace the force of his seriousness, and although he merely smiled, without a word, it seemed to me that he was saying: I love you whatever you decide to do. Carmen, instead, drew me almost immediately into a corner—she was very nervous, and kept looking at the clock—and spoke in a rush about her brother, as one speaks to a good authority who knows everything and can do everything, and no false step can dim that aura. She made no mention of her children, her husband, her personal life or mine. I realized that she had taken upon herself the weight of Pasquale's reputation as a terrorist, but only in order to recast it. In our few minutes of conversation she did not confine herself to saying that her brother was unjustly persecuted: she wanted to restore courage and goodness to him. Her eyes were burning with the determination to be always and no matter what on his side. She said that she had to know where to find me, she wanted my telephone number and my address. You are an important person, Lenù—she whispered—you know people who, if Pasquale isn't murdered, can help him. Then she indicated Antonio, who was standing apart, a few steps from Enzo. Come here—she said softly—you tell her, too. And Antonio came over, head down, and spoke timid phrases whose meaning was: I know Pasquale trusts you, he came to your house before making the choice he made, so if you see him again, warn him. He has to disappear, he'd better not be seen in Italy; because, as I told Carmen, too, the problem isn't the carabinieri, the problem is the Solaras. They're convinced that he murdered Signora Manuela, and if they find him—now, tomorrow, years from now—I can't help him. While he was making that speech, in a grave tone, Carmen kept interrupting to ask me: Do you understand, Lenù? She watched me with an anxious gaze. Finally she hugged me, kissed me, whispered: You and Lina are my sisters, and she went off with Enzo, they had things to do.

So I remained alone with Antonio. I seemed to have before me two people present in the same body and yet very distinct. He was the boy who long ago had held me tight at the ponds, who had idolized me, and whose intense odor had remained in my memory like a desire that is never truly satisfied. And he was the man of now, without an ounce of fat, all big bones and taut skin that went from his hard blank face to his feet, in enormous shoes. I said, embarrassed, that I didn't know anyone who could help Pasquale, that Carmen overestimated me. But I realized right away that if Pasquale's sister had an exaggerated idea of my prestige, his was even more exaggerated. Antonio said that I was modest as usual, that he had read my book, in German no less, that I was known all over the world. Although he had lived for a long time abroad, and had certainly seen and done terrible things for the Solaras, he had remained someone from the neighborhood and continued to imagine—or maybe he was pretending, who knows, to please me—that I had power, the power of respectable people, because I had a degree, because I spoke in Italian, I wrote books. I said, laughing: you're the only person in Germany who bought that book. And I asked about his wife, his children. He answered in monosyllables, but meanwhile he drew me outside, into the square. There he said kindly:

"Now you have to admit that I was right."

"In what."

"You wanted him, and you lied to me."

"I was a girl."

"No, you were grown up. And you were more intelligent than me. You don't know the harm you did letting me believe I was crazy."

"Stop it."

He was silent, I retreated toward the shop. He followed me, and held me back on the threshold. For a few seconds he stared at Nino, who had sat down in a corner. He murmured:

"If he hurts you, too, tell me."

I laughed: "Of course."

"Don't laugh, I talked to Lina. She knows him well, she says you shouldn't trust him. We respect you, he doesn't."

Lila. Here she was using Antonio, making him her messenger of possible misfortunes. Where had she gone? I saw that she was off in a corner, playing with Marisa's children, but in fact she was observing each one of us, with her eyes narrowed. And in her usual way she was ruling over everyone: Carmen, Alfonso, Marisa, Enzo, Antonio, her son and the children of others, perhaps even the owners of the shop. I told myself again that she would no longer exercise any authority over me, that that long phase was over. I said goodbye, she hugged me tight, as if she wanted to pull me into herself. As I said goodbye to them all, one by one, I was again struck by Alfonso, but this time I understood what had disturbed me. The little that had marked him as the son of Don Achille and Maria, as the brother of Stefano and Pinuccia, had disappeared from his face. Now, mysteriously, with that long hair in a ponytail, he resembled Lila.

11.

I returned to Florence, I talked to Pietro about our separation. We quarreled violently while Adele tried to protect the children and perhaps herself, shutting herself up with them in her room. At a certain point we realized not that we were overdoing it but that the presence of our daughters did not allow us to overdo it as we felt the need to do. So we went out, continuing to fight in the street. When Pietro walked off, I don't know where—I was furious, I didn't want to see or hear him anymore—I went home. The children were sleeping. I found Adele sitting in the kitchen reading.

I said: "You see how he treats me?"

"And you?"

"I?"

"Yes, you: do you see how you treat him, how you've treated him?"

I turned away and shut myself in the bedroom, slamming the door. The contempt she had put into those words surprised me, wounded me. It was the first time she had turned against me so explicitly.

I left the next day for France, full of guilt because of the children's crying and the books I had to study on the trip. But as I concentrated on the reading, the pages became more and more mixed up with Nino, Pietro, my daughters, the defense of Pasquale made by his sister, Antonio's words, Alfonso's mutation. I arrived in Paris after an exhausting train trip, more confused than ever. Yet at the station, when I recognized the younger of the two women publishers on the platform, I became cheerful, I found again the pleasure of extending myself that I had had with Nino in Montpellier. This time there were no hotels and monumental lecture halls; everything was more modest. The two women took me around to big cities and small towns, every day a journey, every evening a debate in a bookstore or even in a private apartment. As for meals and sleep, there was home cooking, a cot, or, occasionally, a couch. I was very tired, and paid less and less attention to my appearance; I lost weight. And yet my editors and the audiences I encountered night after night liked me. Moving here and there, discussing with this and that person in a language that wasn't mine but that I rapidly learned to manage, I gradually rediscovered an aptitude that I had displayed years before, with my previous book: I had a natural ability to transform small private events into public reflection. Every night I improvised successfully, starting from my own experience. I talked about the world I came from, about the poverty and squalor, male and also female rages, about Carmen and her bond with her brother, her justifications for violent actions that she would surely never commit. I talked about how, since I was a girl, I had observed in my mother and other women the most humiliating aspects of family life, of motherhood, of subjection to males. I talked about how, for love of a man, one could be driven to be guilty of every possible infamy toward other women, toward children. I talked about my difficult relationship with the feminist groups in Florence and Milan, and, as I did, an experience that I had underestimated suddenly became important: I discovered in public what I had learned by watching that painful effort of excavation. I talked about how, to assert myself, I had always sought to be male in intelligence—I started off every evening saying I felt that I had been invented by men, colonized by their imagination—and I told how I had recently seen a male childhood friend of mine make every effort possible to subvert himself, extracting from himself a female.

I drew often on that half hour spent in the Solaras' shop, but I only realized it later, maybe because Lila never came to my mind. I don't know why I didn't at any point allude to our friendship. Probably it seemed to me that, although she had dragged me into the swelling sea of her desires and those of our childhood friends, she didn't have the capacity to decipher what she had put before my eyes. Did she see, for example, what in a flash I had seen in Alfonso? Did she reflect on it? I ruled that out. She was mired in the *lota*, the filth, of the neighborhood, she was satisfied with it. I, on the other hand, in those French days, felt that I was at the center of chaos and yet had tools with which to distinguish its laws. That conviction, reinforced by the small success of my book, helped me to be somewhat less anxious about the future, as if, truly, everything that I was capable of adding up with words written and spoken were destined to add up in reality as well. Look, I said to myself, the couple collapses, the family collapses, every cultural cage collapses, every possible social-democratic accommodation collapses, and meanwhile everything tries violently to assume another form that up to now would have been unthinkable: Nino and me, the sum of my children and his, the hegemony of the working class, socialism and Communism, and above all the unforeseen subject, the woman, I. Night after night, I went around recognizing myself in an idea that suggested general disintegration and, at the same time, new composition.

Meanwhile, always somewhat breathlessly, I telephoned Adele and talked to the children, who answered in monosyllables, or asked, over and over, like a refrain: When are you coming home? Around Christmas, I tried to take leave of my publishers, but by now they had taken my fate to heart, and didn't want to let me go. They had read my first book, they wanted to republish it, and to this purpose they dragged me to the offices of the French publishing house that had printed it years earlier, unsuccessfully. I timidly got involved in discussions and negotiations, sustained by the two women, who, unlike me, were very combative, and knew how to cajole and threaten. Finally, in part thanks to the mediation of the Milan publisher, they came to an agreement: my text would be reissued the following year under the imprint of my new publishers.

I told Nino on the phone, and he seemed very excited. But then, sentence by sentence, his displeasure emerged.

"Maybe you don't need me anymore," he said.

"What are you talking about? I can't wait to hold you."

"You're so involved in your own affairs that there's not even a tiny spot left for me."

"You're wrong. It's thanks to you that I wrote this book, that I seem to have everything clear in my mind."

"Then let's see each other in Naples, or even in Rome, now, before Christmas."

But by this point a meeting was impossible, the editorial matters had taken up my time, I had to get back to the children. Yet I couldn't resist, and we decided to meet in Rome at least for a few hours. I traveled in a sleeping car, and arrived in the capital exhausted on the morning of December 23rd. I spent pointless hours in the station: Nino wasn't there. I was worried, I was desolate. I was about to take a train for Florence when he appeared, sweating despite the cold. He had had endless difficulties, and had come by car, by train he would never have made it. We ate something quickly, we found a hotel in Via Nazionale, close to the station, and shut ourselves in the room. I wanted to go in the afternoon, but I didn't have the strength to leave him, and I delayed my departure until the next day. We woke up happy to have slept together: ah, it was wonderful to stretch out a foot and discover, after the unconsciousness of sleep, that he was there in the bed, beside me. It was Christmas Eve, and we went

out to get each other presents. My departure was postponed
hour by hour and so was his. Not until the late afternoon did I
drag myself with my suitcase to his car, I couldn't leave him.
Finally he started the engine, drove off, disappeared in the traffic. Laboriously I trudged from Piazza della Repubblica to the
station, but I had delayed too long, and I missed the train by a
few minutes. I was desperate: I would arrive in Florence in the
middle of the night. And yet it had happened that way. I
resigned myself to telephoning home. Pietro answered.

"Where are you?"

"In Rome, the train is stuck here in the station and I don't
know when it's leaving."

"Ah, these trains. Shall I tell the girls that you won't be here
for Christmas Eve dinner?"

"Yes, I probably won't arrive in time."

He burst into laughter, he hung up.

I traveled in a totally empty, frigid train. Not even the con-
ductor came by. I felt as if I had lost everything and was heading toward nothingness, prisoner of a bleakness that accentuated my guilt. I arrived in Florence in the middle of the night,
and couldn't find a taxi. I carried my suitcase through the cold,
on the deserted streets; even the Christmas bells had long since
vanished into the night. I used my keys to enter. The apartment
was dark and there was an anguished silence. I went through
the rooms, no trace of the children, or of Adele. Tired, terrified, but also exasperated, I looked for at least a note that
would tell me where they had gone. Nothing.

The house was in perfect order.

12.

I had ugly thoughts. Maybe Dede or Elsa or both had got
sick and Pietro and his mother had taken them to the hospital.

Or my husband had ended up in the hospital, because he had done some mad thing, and Adele and the children were with him.

I wandered through the house consumed by anxiety, I didn't know what to do. At some point I thought that, whatever had happened, it was likely that my mother-in-law had told Mariarosa, and although it was three in the morning I decided to call her. My sister-in-law answered eventually; I had a hard time waking her. But finally I found out from her that Adele had decided to take the children to Genoa—they had left two days earlier—to allow me and Pietro to confront our situation freely, and Dede and Elsa to enjoy Christmas vacation in peace.

On the one hand, the news calmed me, on the other it made me furious. Pietro had lied to me: when I telephoned he already knew there would be no Christmas Eve dinner, that the children weren't expecting me, that they had left with their grandmother. And Adele? How dare she take away my daughters! I vented on the telephone while Mariarosa listened to me in silence. I asked: Am I wrong about everything, do I deserve what is happening to me? She took a serious tone, but she was encouraging. She said that I had the right to have my life and the duty to continue to study and write. Then she offered to let me stay with her, along with the children, any time I found myself in trouble.

Her words soothed me, yet I couldn't sleep. I turned things over and over in my breast: anguish, rage, desire for Nino, unhappiness because he would spend the holiday with his family, with Albertino, and I was reduced to a woman alone, without affection, in an empty house. At nine in the morning I heard the door open, it was Pietro. I confronted him immediately, I yelled at him: Why did you hand over the children to your mother without my permission? He was disheveled, unshaven, he stank of wine, but he didn't seem drunk. He let me scream without reacting, he merely repeated over and over, in a depressed tone: I have work to do, I can't take care of them, and you have your lover, you don't have time for them.

I forced him to sit down, in the kitchen. I tried to calm myself, I said:

"We have to come to an agreement."

"Explain yourself, what type of agreement."

"The children will live with me, and you'll see them on the weekend."

"On the weekend where?"

"At my house."

"And where is your house?"

"I don't know, I'll decide later: here, in Milan, in Naples."

That word was enough: Naples. As soon as he heard it he jumped to his feet, opened his eyes wide, opened his mouth as if to bite me, raised his fist with such a ferocious expression that I was terrified. It was an endless moment. The faucet was dripping, the refrigerator humming, someone laughed in the courtyard. Pietro was large, he had big white knuckles. He had already hit me once, I knew that he would hit me now so violently that he would kill me, and I raised my arms abruptly to protect myself. But suddenly he changed his mind, turned, and once, twice, three times punched the metal closet where I kept the brooms. He would have continued if I hadn't clung to his arm crying: Stop it, enough, you'll hurt yourself.

The result of that rage was that what I had feared on my return really happened: we ended up in the hospital. His arm was put in a cast, and on the way home he seemed almost cheerful. I remembered that it was Christmas and I made something to eat. We sat down at the table, and he said, point-blank:

"Yesterday I called your mother."

I jumped.

"How did that occur to you?"

"Well, someone had to tell her. I told her what you did to me."

"It was my job to talk to her."

"Why? To lie to her the way you lied to me?"

I became agitated again, but I tried to contain myself; I was afraid that he would start breaking his bones again to avoid breaking mine. Instead I saw that he smiled calmly, looking at his arm in the cast.

"So I can't drive," he muttered.

"Where do you have to go?"

"To the station."

I discovered that my mother had set out by train on Christmas Day—the day she normally assumed domestic centrality, the highest of her responsibilities—and was about to arrive.

13.

I was tempted to flee. I thought of going to Naples—escaping to my mother's city just as she was arriving in mine—and seeking some tranquility with Nino. But I didn't move. Although I felt that I was changed, I had remained the disciplined person who had never avoided anything. And besides, I said to myself, what can she do to me? I'm a woman, not a child. At most she'll bring something good to eat, like that Christmas ten years ago, when I was sick and she came to see me in the dormitory at the Normale.

I went with Pietro to get my mother at the station; I drove. She got off the train proudly, she had new clothes, a new purse, new shoes, even a little powder on her cheeks. You look well, I said, you're very stylish. She hissed: No thanks to you, and didn't say another word to me. To make up for it she was very affectionate toward Pietro. She asked about his cast, and since he was vague—he said he had bumped into a door—she began to mumble in hesitant Italian: Bumped, I know who made you bump it. I imagine, bumped.

Once we got home she ended her feigned composure. She made me a long speech, limping back and forth in the living room. She praised my husband in an exaggerated fashion, she ordered me to ask his forgiveness immediately. When I didn't, she began to beg him herself to forgive me and swore on Peppe, Gianni, and Elisa that she would not go home if the two of us did not make peace. At first, with all her hyperbole, she seemed to be making fun of both me and my husband. The list she made of Pietro's virtues appeared infinite, and—I have to admit—she didn't stint on mine, either. She emphasized endlessly that, when it came to intelligence and scholarship, we were made for each other. She urged us to think of Dede's good—Dede was her favorite granddaughter, she forgot to mention Elsa—the child understood everything and it wasn't right to make her suffer.

My husband, while she spoke, appeared to agree, even though he wore the incredulous expression he assumed in the face of any spectacle of excess. She hugged him, kissed him, thanked him for his generosity, before which—she shouted at me—I should go down on my knees. She kept pushing us with rude claps toward each other, so that we would hug and kiss each other. I drew back, I was aloof. The whole time I thought: I can't bear her, I can't bear that at a moment like this, in front of Pietro, I *also* have to account for the fact that I am the daughter of this woman. And meanwhile I tried to calm myself by saying: It's her usual scene, soon she'll get tired and go to bed. But when she grabbed me for the hundredth time, insisting I admit that I had made a serious mistake, I couldn't take it anymore, her hands offended me and I pulled away. I said something like: Enough, Ma, it's pointless, I can't stay with Pietro anymore, I love someone else.

It was a mistake. I knew her, she was just waiting for a small provocation. Her litany broke off, things changed in a flash. She slapped me violently, shouting nonstop: Shut up, you whore, shut up, shut up. And she tried to grab me by the hair, she cried that she couldn't stand it any longer, that it wasn't possible that I, *I*, should want to ruin my life, running after Sarratore's son, who was worse, much worse, than that man of shit who was his father. Once, she cried, I thought it was your friend Lina leading you on this evil course, but I was wrong, you, *you*, are the shameless one; without you, she's become a fine person. Damn me that I didn't break your legs when you were a child. You have a husband of gold who makes you a lady in this beautiful city, who loves you, who has given you two daughters, and you repay him like this, bitch? Come here, I gave birth to you and I'll kill you.

She was on me, I felt as if she really wanted to kill me. In those moments I felt all the truth of the disappointment that I was causing her, all the truth of the maternal love that despaired of subjecting me to what she considered my good—that is, what she had never had and what I instead had and what until the day before had made her the most fortunate mother in the neighborhood—and was ready to turn into hatred and destroy me to punish me for my waste of God's gifts. So I pushed her away, I pushed her shouting louder than she was. I pushed her involuntarily, instinctively, with such force that I made her lose her balance and she fell to the floor.

Pietro was frightened. I saw it in his face, in his eyes: my world colliding with his. Certainly in all his life he had never witnessed a scene like that, words so aggressive, reactions so frenzied. My mother had overturned a chair, she had fallen heavily. Now she had trouble getting up, because of her bad leg, she was waving one arm in an effort to grab the edge of the table and pull herself up. But she didn't stop, she went on screaming threats and insults at me. She didn't stop even when Pietro, shocked, helped her up with his good arm. Her voice choked, angry and at the same time truly grieved, eyes staring, she gasped: You're not my child anymore, he's my child, him,

not even your father wants you anymore, not even your siblings; Sarratore's son is bound to stick you with the clap and
syphilis, what did I do wrong to come to a day like this, oh
God, oh God, God, I want to die this minute, I want to die
now. She was so overwhelmed by her suffering that—incredibly—she burst into tears.

I ran away and locked myself in the bedroom. I didn't know
what to do; never would I have expected that a separation
would involve such torture. I was frightened, I was devastated.
From what obscure depth, what presumption, had come the
determination to push back my mother with her own physical
violence? I became calmer only when, after a while, Pietro
knocked and said softly, with an unexpected gentleness: Don't
open the door, I'm not asking you to let me in; I just want to say
that I didn't want this, it's too much, not even you deserve it.

14.

I hoped that my mother would soften, that in the morning,
with one of her abrupt swerves, she would find a way of affirm-
ing that she loved me and in spite of everything was proud of
me. But she didn't. I heard her talking to Pietro all night. She
flattered him, she repeated bitterly that I had always been her
cross, she said, sighing, that one had to have patience with me.
The next day, to avoid quarreling again, I wandered through
the house or tried to read, without ever joining their councils.
I was very unhappy. I was ashamed of the shove I had given
her, I was ashamed of her and of myself, I wanted to apologize,
embrace her, but I was afraid that she would misunderstand and be convinced that I had given in. If she had gone so
far as to assert that I was the black soul of Lila, and not Lila
mine, I must have been a truly intolerable disappointment to
her. I said to myself, to excuse her: her unit of measure is the

neighborhood; there everything, in her eyes, is arranged for the best; she feels related to the Solaras thanks to Elisa; her sons finally work for Marcello, whom she proudly calls her son-in-law; in those new clothes she wears the sign of the prosperity that has rained down on her; it's natural therefore that Lila, working for Michele Solara, in a stable home with Enzo, so rich she wants to bequeath her parents the small apartment they live in, appears to her much more successful than me. But arguments like that served only to further mark the distance between her and me; we no longer had any point of contact.

She departed without our having spoken a word to each other. Pietro and I took her to the station in the car, but she acted as if I were not driving. She confined herself to wishing Pietro all the best and urging him, until a moment before the train left, to keep her informed about his broken arm and about the children.

As soon as she left I realized with some surprise that her irruption had had an unhoped-for effect. My husband, as we were returning home, went beyond the few phrases of solidarity whispered outside my door the night before. That intemperate encounter with my mother must have revealed to him about me, about how I had grown up, more than what I had told him and he had imagined. He felt sorry for me, I think. He returned abruptly to himself, our relations became polite, a few days later we went to a lawyer, who talked for a moment about this and that, then asked:

"You're sure you don't want to live together anymore?"

"How can one live with a person who no longer loves you?" Pietro answered.

"You, Signora, you no longer want your husband?"

"It's my business," I said. "All you have to do is settle the practical details of the separation."

When we were back on the street Pietro laughed: "You're just like your mother."

"It's not true."

"You're right, it's not true: you're like your mother if she had had an education and had started writing novels."

"What do you mean?"

"I mean you're worse."

I was angry but not very. I was glad that within the limits of the possible he had come to his senses. I drew a sigh of relief and began to focus on what to do. In the course of long phone calls to Nino, I told him everything that had happened since the moment we parted, and we discussed my moving to Naples; out of prudence I didn't tell him that Pietro and I had begun to sleep under the same roof, even if in separate rooms, naturally. Most important, I talked to my daughters often and I told Adele, with explicit hostility, that I would come to get them.

"Don't worry," my mother-in-law tried to reassure me, "you can leave them as long as you need to."

"Dede has school."

"We can send her here, nearby, I would take care of everything."

"No, I need them with me."

"Think about it. A woman separated, with two children and your ambitions, has to take account of reality and decide what she can give up and what she can't."

Everything, in that last sentence, bothered me.

15.

I wanted to leave immediately for Genoa, but I got a phone call from France. The older of my two publishers asked me to put into writing, for an important journal, the arguments she had heard me make in public. So right away I found myself in a situation in which I had to choose between going to get my daughters and starting work. I put off my departure, I worked day and night with the anxiety of doing well. I was still trying to give my text an acceptable form when Nino announced to me that, before returning to the university, he had some free days and was eager to see me. I couldn't resist; we drove to Argentario. I was dazed by love. We spent marvelous days devoted to the winter sea and, as had never happened with either Franco or, even less, Pietro, to the pleasure of eating and drinking, conversation, sex. Every morning at dawn I dragged myself out of bed and began writing.

One evening, in bed, Nino gave me some pages he had written, saying that he would value my opinion. It was a complicated essay, on Italsider in Bagnoli. I read it lying close beside him, while now and then he murmured, self-critical: I write badly, correct it if you want, you're better, you were better in high school. I praised his work highly, and suggested some corrections. But he wasn't satisfied, he urged me to intervene further. Then, finally, as if to convince me of the need for my corrections, he said that he had a terrible thing to reveal to me. Half embarrassed, half ironic, he described this secret: "the most shameful thing I've done in my life." And he said that it had to do with the article I had written in high school about my fight with the religion teacher, the one that he had commissioned for a student magazine.

"What did you do?" I asked, laughing.

"I'll tell you, but remember I was just a boy."

I felt that he was seriously ashamed and I became slightly worried. He said that when he read my article he couldn't believe that someone could write in such a pleasing and intelligent way. I was content with that compliment, I kissed him, I remembered how I had labored over those pages with Lila, and meanwhile I described to him in a self-ironic way the disappointment, the pain I had felt when the magazine hadn't had space to publish it.

"I told you that?" Nino asked, uneasily.

"Maybe, I don't remember now."

He had an expression of dismay.

"The truth is that there was plenty of space."

"Then why didn't they publish it?"

"Out of envy."

I burst out laughing.

"The editors were envious of me?"

"No, it was *I* who felt envy. I read your pages and threw them in the wastebasket. I couldn't bear that you were so good."

For a few moments I said nothing. How important that article had been to me, how much I had suffered. I couldn't believe it: was it possible that Professor Galiani's favorite had been so envious of the lines of a middle-school student that he threw them away? I felt that Nino was waiting for my reaction, but I didn't know how to place such a petty act within the radiant aura I had given him as a girl. The seconds passed and I tried, disoriented, to keep it close to me, so that it could not reinforce the bad reputation that, according to Adele, Nino had in Milan, or the invitation not to trust him that had come to me from Lila and Antonio. Then I shook myself, the positive side of that confession leaped to my eyes, and I embraced him. There was, in essence, no need for him to tell me that episode, it was a bad deed that was very distant in time. And yet he had just told me, and that need of his to be sincere, greater than any personal gain, even at the risk of putting himself in a terrible light, moved me. Suddenly, starting from that moment, I felt that I could always believe him.

We loved each other that night with more passion than usual. Upon waking I realized that, in confessing his sin, Nino had confessed that in his eyes I had always been a girl out of the ordinary, even when he was Nadia Galiani's boyfriend, even when he had become Lila's lover. Ah, how exciting it was to feel that I was not only loved but esteemed. He entrusted his text to me, I helped him give it a more brilliant form. In those days in Argentario I had the impression that I had now definitively expanded my capacity to feel, to understand, to express myself, something that—I thought with pride—was confirmed by the modest welcome that the book I had written goaded by him, to please him, had received outside Italy. I had everything, at that moment. Only Dede and Elsa were left in the margins.

16.

I said nothing to my mother-in-law about Nino. I told her instead about the French journal and portrayed myself as being fully absorbed by what I was writing. Meanwhile, if reluctantly, I thanked her for taking care of her grandchildren.

Although I didn't trust her, I understood at that point that Adele had raised a real problem. What could I do to keep my life and my children together? Certainly I intended to go and live with Nino soon, somewhere, and in that case we would help each other. But meanwhile? It wouldn't be easy to balance the need to see each other, Dede, Elsa, the writing, the public engagements, the pressures that Pietro, although he had become more reasonable, would nevertheless subject me to. Not to mention the problem of money. Very little remained of my own, and I still didn't know how much the new book would earn. It was out of the question that at the moment I could pay rent, telephone, daily life for my daughters and me. And then where would our daily life take shape? Any moment now, I would go and get the children, but to take them where? To Florence, to the apartment where they were born and in which, finding a gentle father, a courteous mother, they would be convinced that everything had miraculously gone back to normal? Did I want to delude them, knowing that as soon as Nino burst in I would disappoint them even more? Should I

tell Pietro to leave, even though I was the one who had broken
with him? Or was it up to me to leave the apartment?

I went to Genoa with a thousand questions and no decision.
My in-laws received me with polite coldness, Elsa with
uncertain enthusiasm, Dede with hostility. I didn't know the
house in Genoa well, only an impression of light remained in my
mind. In reality there were entire rooms full of books, old furniture, crystal chandeliers, floors covered with precious carpets,
heavy curtains. Only the living room was bright: it had a big window that framed a section of light and sea, displaying it like a
prized object. My daughters—I realized—moved through the
entire apartment with more freedom than in their own house:
they touched everything, they took what they wanted with never
a reproach, and they spoke to the maid in the courteous but
commanding tones they had learned from their grandmother. In
the first hours after I arrived they showed me their room, they
wanted me to get excited about the many expensive toys that
they would never have received from me and their father, they
told me about the many wonderful things they had done and
seen. I slowly realized that Dede had become very attached to
her grandfather, while Elsa, although she had hugged and kissed
me as much as she could, turned to Adele for anything she
needed or, when she was tired, climbed up on her lap and
looked at me from there with a melancholy gaze, her thumb in
her mouth. Had the children learned to do without me in so
short a time? Or, rather, were they exhausted by what they had
seen and heard in the past months and now, apprehensive of the
swarm of disasters I conjured up, were afraid to take me back?
I don't know. Certainly I didn't dare to say immediately: Pack
your things and let's go. I stayed a few days, I began to care for
them again. And my in-laws never interfered; rather, at the first
recourse to their authority against mine, especially by Dede, they
withdrew, avoiding any conflict.

Guido in particular was very careful to speak about other

things; at first he didn't even allude to the break between me
and his son. After dinner, when Dede and Elsa went to bed and
he, politely, stayed with me for a while before shutting himself
in his study to work late into the night (evidently Pietro did little more than apply his father's model), he was embarrassed.
He usually took refuge in political talk: the deepening crisis of
capitalism, the cure-all of austerity, the broadening area of mar-
ginalization, the earthquake in Friuli as the symbol of a precar-
ious Italy, the great difficulties of the left, old parties and fac-
tions. But he did it without displaying any interest in my
opinions, and I, in turn, made no effort to have any. If he actually decided to encourage me to say something, he fell back on
my book, whose Italian edition I saw for the first time in that
house: it was a slender volume, not very conspicuous, which
arrived along with the many books and magazines that piled up
continuously on the tables, waiting to be perused. One evening
he asked some questions, and I—knowing that he hadn't read
it and wouldn't—summarized for him the arguments, read him
a few lines. In general he listened seriously, attentive. In one
case only did he offer some learned criticisms on a passage of
Sophocles that I had cited inappropriately, and he assumed
professorial tones that shamed me. He was a man who
emanated authority, even though authority is a patina and at
times it doesn't take much to crack it, if only for a few minutes,
and glimpse a less edifying person. At a mention of feminism
Guido's composure suddenly shattered, an unexpected malice
appeared in his eyes, and he began to hum sarcastically, red in
the face—he who in general had an anemic complexion—a
couple of slogans he had heard: *Sex, sex behind the wall, who
has orgasms of us all? No one*; and also: *We're not machines for
reproduction but women fighting for liberation.* He sang in a low
voice and laughed, all excited. When he realized that he had
unpleasantly surprised me, he grabbed his glasses, cleaned
them carefully, withdrew to his study.

On those few evenings Adele was almost always silent, but I soon realized that both she and her husband were looking for a way to draw me out into the open. Since I wouldn't bite, my father-in-law finally confronted the problem in his own way. When Dede and Elsa said good night, he asked his grand-daughters in a sort of good-humored ritual:

"What is the name of these two lovely young ladies?"

"Dede."

"Elsa."

"And then? Grandfather wants to hear the whole name."

"Dede Airota."

"Elsa Airota."

"Airota like who?"

"Like Papa."

"And also?"

"Like Grandpa."

"And what's Mamma's name?"

"Elena Greco."

"And is your name Greco or Airota?"

"Airota."

"Bravo. Good night, dear ones, sweet dreams."

Then, as soon as the children left the room, accompanied by Adele, he said as if following a thread that started from the answers of the two children: I've learned that the break with Pietro is due to Nino Sarratore. I jumped, I nodded yes. He smiled, he began to praise Nino, but not with the absolute support of years earlier. He said that he was very intelligent, someone who knew what was what, but—he said, emphasizing the adversative conjunction—he is *fickle*, and he repeated the word as if to make sure that he had chosen the right one. Then he emphasized: I didn't like Sarratore's most recent writings. And in a suddenly contemptuous tone he relegated him to the heap of those who considered it more urgent to make the gears of neocapitalism function rather than to continue to demand transformations in social relations and in production. He used that language, but giving every word the substance of an insult. I couldn't bear it. I struggled to convince him that he was wrong. Adele returned just as I was citing the essays of Nino's that seemed to me most radical, and Guido listened to me, emitting the dull sound he usually resorted to when he was suspended between agreement and disagreement. I suddenly stopped, rather agitated. For a few minutes my father-in-law seemed to soften his judgment (*After all, it's difficult for all of us to orient ourselves in the chaos of the Italian crisis, and I can understand that young men like him find themselves in trouble, especially when they have a desire to act*), then he rose to go to his study. But before he disappeared he had a second thought. He paused in the doorway and uttered harshly: *But there is doing and doing, Sarratore is intelligence without traditions, he would rather be liked by those in charge than fight for an idea, he'll become a very useful technocrat.* And he broke off, but still he hesitated, as if he had something much crueler on the tip of his tongue. He confined himself instead to muttering good night and went into his study.

I felt Adele's gaze on me. I ought to retreat, I thought, I have to make up an excuse, say I'm tired. But I hoped that Adele would find a conciliating phrase that might soothe me, and so I asked:

"What does it mean that Nino is intelligence without traditions?"

She looked at me ironically.

"That he's no one. And for a person who is no one to become someone is more important than anything else. The result is that this Signor Sarratore is an unreliable person."

"I, too, am an intelligence without traditions."

She smiled.

"Yes, you are, too, and in fact you are unreliable."

Silence. Adele had spoken serenely, as if the words had no

emotional charge but were limited to recording the facts. Still, I felt offended.

"What do you mean?"

"That I trusted a son to you and you didn't treat him honestly. If you wanted someone else, why did you marry him?"

"I didn't know I wanted someone else."

"You're lying."

I hesitated, I admitted: "I'm lying, yes, but why do you force me to give you a linear explanation; linear explanations are almost always lies. You also spoke badly of Pietro, in fact you supported me against him. Were you lying?"

"No. I was really on your side, but within a pact that you should have respected."

"What pact?"

"Remaining with your husband and children. You were an Airota, your daughters were Airotas. I didn't want you to feel unsatisfied and unhappy, I tried to help you be a good mother and a good wife. But if the pact is broken everything changes. From me and from my husband you'll have nothing anymore, in fact I'll take away everything I've given you."

I took a deep breath, I tried to keep my voice calm, just as she continued to do.

"Adele," I said, "I am Elena Greco and my daughters are my daughters. I don't give a damn about you Airotas."

She nodded, pale, and her expression was now severe.

"It's obvious that you are Elena Greco, it's now far too obvious. But the children are my son's daughters and we will not allow you to ruin them."

17.

That was the first clash with my in-laws. Others followed, though they never reached such explicit contempt. Later my in-laws confined themselves to demonstrating in every possible way that, if I insisted on being concerned with myself above all, I had to entrust Dede and Elsa to them.

I resisted, naturally: there was not a day that I didn't get angry and decide to take my children away with me immediately, to Florence, to Milan, to Naples—anywhere, just so as not to leave them in that house a moment longer. But soon I would give in, put off my departure; something always happened that bore witness against me. Nino, for example, telephoned and, unable to refuse, I rushed to meet him wherever he wanted. And then in Italy, too, the new book had begun to make a small wave, and, although it was ignored by the reviewers of the big papers, it was nevertheless finding an audience. So often I added encounters with readers to the meetings with my lover, which extended the time that I was away from the children.

I separated from them unwillingly. I felt their accusing gaze on me, and I suffered. And yet already in the train, as I studied, as I prepared for some public discussion, as I imagined my meeting with Nino, an impudent joy began to bubble up inside me. I soon discovered that I was getting used to being happy and unhappy at the same time, as if that were the new, inevitable law of my life. When I returned to Genoa I felt guilty—Dede and Elsa were now comfortable, they had school, friends, everything they wanted, independently of me—but as soon as I left the guilt became a tedious obstacle; it weakened. I realized this, naturally, and the alternation made me wretched. It was humiliating to have to admit that a little fame, and love for Nino, could obscure Dede and Elsa. And yet it was so. The echo of Lila's phrase, *Think of the harm you're doing to your daughters,* became in that period a sort of permanent epigraph that introduced unhappiness. I traveled, I was often in a new bed, often I couldn't sleep. My mother's curses returned to mind, and were mixed up with Lila's words.

She and my friend, although they had always been, for me, the opposite of one another, in those nights often came together. Both were hostile, estranged from my new life: on the one hand this seemed the proof that I had finally become an autonomous person; on the other it made me feel alone, at the mercy of my troubles.

I tried to repair relations with my sister-in-law. As usual she showed herself to be very willing, and organized an event in honor of my book at a bookstore in Milan. Most of those who came were women, and I was now much criticized, now much praised by opposing groups. At first I was frightened, but Mariarosa interceded with authority and I discovered in myself an unsuspected capacity to summarize disagreement and agreement, choosing in the meantime a role as mediator. I was good at saying in a convincing way: *That isn't exactly what I meant.* In the end I was celebrated by everyone, especially by her.

Afterward I had dinner and stayed at her house. I found Franco there, I found Silvia with her son Mirko. The whole time, all I did was observe the child—I calculated that he must be eight—and register the physical resemblances to Nino, and even resemblances in personality. I had never told him that I knew about that child and had decided that I never would, but all evening I talked to him, cuddled him, played with him, held him on my lap. In what disorder we lived, how many fragments of ourselves were scattered, as if to live were to explode into splinters. In Milan, there was this child, in Genoa my daughters, in Naples Albertino. I couldn't restrain myself, I began talking about that dispersion with Silvia, with Mariarosa, with Franco, assuming the attitude of a disillusioned thinker. In reality I expected that my former boyfriend would, as usual, take over the conversation and arrange everything according to a skillful dialectic that settled the present and anticipated the future, reassuring us. But he was the true surprise of the evening. He spoke of the imminent end of a period that had been *objectively*—he used the adverb sarcastically—revolutionary but that now, he said, was declining, was sweeping away all the categories that had served as a compass.

"I don't think so," I objected, but only to provoke him. "In Italy things are very lively and combative."

"You don't think so because you're pleased with yourself."

"Not at all, I'm depressed."

"The depressed don't write books. People who are happy write, people who travel, are in love, and talk and talk with the conviction that, one way or another, their words always go to the right place."

"Isn't that how it is?"

"No, words rarely go to the right place, and if they do, it's only for a very brief time. Otherwise they're useful for speaking nonsense, as now. Or for pretending that everything is under control."

"Pretending? You who have always kept everything under control, you were pretending?"

"Why not? It's unavoidable to pretend a little. We who wanted to enact the revolution were the ones who, even in the midst of chaos, were always inventing an order and pretending to know exactly how things were going."

"You're accusing yourself?"

"Yes. Good grammar, good syntax. An explanation ready for everything. And such great skill in logic: this derives from that and leads necessarily to that. The game is over."

"It doesn't work anymore?"

"Oh, it works very well. It's so comfortable never to be confused by anything. No infected bedsores, no wound without its stitches, no dark room that frightens you. Only that at a certain point the trick no longer functions."

"Meaning what?"

"Blah blah blah, Lena, blah blah blah. The meaning is leaving the words."

And he didn't stop there. He mocked what he had just said, making fun of himself and of me. Then he said: What a lot of nonsense I'm talking, and he spent the rest of the evening listening to the three of us.

It struck me that if in Silvia the terrible marks of violence had completely disappeared, in him the beating suffered several years earlier had gradually exposed another body and another spirit. He got up often to go to the bathroom; he limped, though not conspicuously; the purple socket, in which the false eye was clumsily set, seemed more combative than the other eye, which, although it was alive, seemed opaque with depression. Above all, both the pleasantly energetic Franco of long ago and the shadowy Franco of convalescence had disappeared. He seemed gently melancholy, capable of an affectionate cynicism. While Silvia said that I should take my daughters back, and Mariarosa said that, as long as I hadn't found a stable arrangement, Dede and Elsa were fine with their grandparents, Franco exaggerated his praise of my capacities, ironically defined as male, and insisted that I should continue to refine them without getting lost in female obligations.

When I went to my room I had trouble falling asleep. What was bad for my children, what was their good? And bad for me, and my good, what did those consist of, and did they correspond to or diverge from what was bad and good for the children? That night Nino faded into the background, Lila reemerged. Lila alone, without the support of my mother. I felt the need to argue with her, shout at her: Don't just criticize me, take responsibility, tell me what to do. Finally I slept. The next day I returned to Genoa and said point-blank to Dede and Elsa, in the presence of my in-laws:

"Girls, I have a lot of work at the moment. In a few days I have to leave again and then again and again. Do you want to come with me or stay with your grandparents?"

Even today as I write that question I'm ashamed.

First Dede and then, right afterward, Elsa answered: "With Grandma and Grandpa. But come back whenever you can and bring us presents."

18.

It took me more than two years, filled with joys, torments, nasty surprises, and agonizing mediations, to put some order into my life. Meanwhile, although I was privately suffering, publicly I continued to be successful. The scant hundred pages I had written to make a good impression on Nino were translated into German and English. My book of ten years earlier reappeared in both France and Italy, and I began writing again for newspapers and journals. My name and my physical person gradually reacquired their modest fame, the days became crowded, as they had been in the past, I gained the interest, and at times the respect, of people who at the time were well known on the public stage. But what helped my self-confidence was some gossip from the director of the Milan publishing house, who had liked me from the start. One evening when I was having dinner with him to talk about my publishing future, but also—I have to say—to propose a collection of Nino's essays, he revealed that, the preceding Christmas, Adele had pressured him to block the publication of my book.

He said, jokingly, "The Airotas are used to plotting the rise of an undersecretary at breakfast and deposing a minister at dinner, but with your book they didn't succeed. The volume was ready and we sent it to the printer."

According to him, my mother-in-law was also behind the meager number of reviews in the Italian press. As a result, if the book had nevertheless made a name for itself, certainly the credit should go not to kind second thoughts from Dottoressa Airota but to the force of my writing. Thus I learned that this time I owed nothing to Adele, although she continued to tell me I did whenever I went to Genoa. That gave me confidence, made me proud, I was finally convinced that the period of my dependence was over.

Lila didn't notice at all. She, from the depths of the neighborhood, from that area that now seemed to me infinitesimal, continued to consider me an appendage of hers. From Pietro she got the telephone number in Genoa, and she began to use it without worrying about annoying my in-laws. When she managed to reach me she pretended not to notice my terseness and talked for both of us, without pause. She talked about Enzo, about work, about her son, who was doing well in school, about Carmen, about Antonio. When I wasn't there, she persisted in telephoning, with neurotic perseverance, enabling Adele—who wrote in a notebook the calls that came for me, putting down, I don't know, such and such month, such and such day, Sarratore (three calls), Cerullo (nine calls)—to complain about the nuisance I caused. I tried to convince Lila that if they said I wasn't there it was pointless to insist, that the house in Genoa wasn't my house, and that she was embarrassing me. Useless. She went so far as to call Nino. It's hard to say how things really went: he was embarrassed, he made light of it, he was afraid of saying something that would irritate me. Early on he told me that Lila had telephoned Eleonora's house repeatedly, angering her, then I gathered that she had tried to get him on the phone at Via Duomo directly, finally that he himself had hastened to track her down to prevent her from constantly telephoning his wife. Whatever had happened, the fact was that Lila had forced him to meet her. Not alone, however: Nino was immediately eager to explain that she had come with Carmen, since it was Carmen—mainly Carmen—who urgently needed to get in touch with me.

I listened to the account of the meeting without emotion. First, Lila had wanted to know in detail how I behaved in public when I talked about my books: what dress I wore, how I did my hair and my makeup, if I was shy, if I was entertaining, if I read, if I improvised. Otherwise she was silent, she had left the field to Carmen. So it turned out that all that eagerness to talk to me had to do with Pasquale. Through her own channels, Carmen had found out that Nadia Galiani had fled to safety abroad, and so she wanted to ask a favor again, that I get in touch with my high-school teacher to ask her if Pasquale, too, was safe. Carmen had exclaimed a couple of times: I don't want the children of the rich people to get out and not the ones like my brother. Then she had urged him to let me know—as if she herself considered her worry about Pasquale to be an indictable crime that could involve me, too—that if I wanted to help her I shouldn't use the telephone either to get in touch with the professor or to get in touch with her. Nino concluded: Both Carmen and Lina are imprudent, better to let it go, they can get you in trouble.

I thought that, a few months earlier, an encounter between Nino and Lila, even in the presence of Carmen, would have alarmed me. Now I was discovering instead that it left me indifferent. Evidently I was now so sure of Nino's love that, although I couldn't rule out that she wanted to take him away from me, it seemed impossible that she could succeed. I caressed his cheek, I said, amused, Don't *you* get into trouble, please: How is it that you never have a free moment and now you found the time for this?

19.

I noted for the first time, during that period, the rigidity of the perimeter that Lila had established for herself. She was less and less interested in what happened outside the neighborhood. If she became excited by something whose dimensions were not merely local, it was because it concerned people she had known since childhood. Even her work, as far as I knew, interested her only within a very narrow radius. Enzo occasionally had to spend time in Milan, or Turin. Not Lila, she had never moved, and I only began to notice that closing off of herself seriously when my own taste for travel intensified.

I took every possible opportunity to travel outside of Italy, at the time, especially if it was possible to do so with Nino. For example, when the small German publisher who had brought out my little book organized a promotional tour in West Germany and Austria, Nino canceled all his engagements and acted as my cheerful and obedient driver. We travelled all over for some two weeks, gliding from one landscape to the next as if beside paintings with dazzling colors. Every mountain or lake or city or monument entered our life as a couple only to become part of the pleasure of being there, at that moment, and it always seemed like a refined contribution to our happiness. Even when rude reality intervened and frightened us because it corresponded to the darkest words that I uttered night after night in front of radical audiences, we recounted the fear to each other afterward as if it had been a pleasant adventure.

One night when we were driving back to the hotel, the police stopped us. The German language, in the dark, in the mouths of men in uniform, guns in hand, sounded, both to my ear and to Nino's, sinister. The police pulled us out of the car, and separated us; I ended up, yelling, in one car, Nino in another. We were reunited in a small room, left to ourselves, then brutally questioned: documents, reason for our stay, job. On one wall there was a long row of photos: grim faces, mostly bearded, some women with short hair. I surprised myself by looking anxiously for the faces of Pasquale and Nadia; I didn't find them. We were released at dawn, returned to the place where we had been forced to leave our car. No one apologized:

we had an Italian license plate, we were Italians, the check was obligatory.

I was surprised by my instinct to seek in Germany, among the mug shots of criminals all over the world, that of the very person who was then close to Lila's heart. Pasquale Peluso, that night, seemed to me a sort of rocket launched from the narrow space in which Lila had enclosed herself to remind me, in my much broader space, of her presence in the whirlwind of planetary events. For a few seconds Carmen's brother became the point of contact between her diminishing world and my expanding world.

On the evenings when I talked about my book in foreign cities I knew nothing about, there was a host of questions on the harshness of the political climate, and I got by with generic phrases that in essence rotated around the word "repress." As a fiction writer, I felt obliged to be imaginative. No space is spared, I said. A steamroller is moving from land to land, from West to East, to put the whole planet in order: the workers to work, the unemployed to waste away, the starving to perish, the intellectuals to speak nonsense, blacks to be black, women to be women. But at times I felt the need to say something truer, genuine, my own, and I told the story of Pasquale in all its tragic stages, from childhood to the choice of a clandestine life. I didn't know how to make more concrete speeches, the vocabulary was what I had appropriated ten years earlier, and I felt that the words had meaning only when I connected them to certain facts of the neighborhood, for it was only old, worn-out material, of certain effect. What's more, if at the time of my first book I had sooner or later ended by appealing to revolution, as that seemed to be the general feeling, now I avoided the word: Nino had begun to find it naïve; from him I was learning the complexity of politics and I was more cautious. I resorted, rather, to the formula *to rebel is just*, and immediately afterward added that it was necessary to broaden the consensus, that the state would last longer than we had imagined, that it was urgent to learn to govern. I wasn't always satisfied with myself on those evenings. In some cases it seemed to me that I lowered my tone only to make Nino happy, as he sat listening to me in smoky rooms, among beautiful foreigners who were my age or younger. Often I couldn't resist and I overdid it, indulging the old obscure impulse that in the past had pushed me to argue with Pietro. It happened mainly when I had an audience of women who had read my book and expected cutting remarks. We must be careful not to become policemen of ourselves, I said then, the struggle is to the last drop of blood and will end only when we win. Nino teased me afterward, he said that I always had to exaggerate, and we laughed together.

Some nights I curled up next to him and tried to explain myself to myself. I confessed that I liked subversive words, words that denounced the compromises of the parties and the violence of the state. Politics—I said—politics the way you think about it, *as it certainly is*, bores me, I leave it to you, I'm not made for that sort of engagement. But then I had second thoughts and added that I didn't feel cut out, either, for the other sort of engagement that I had forced myself into in the past, dragging the children along with me. The threatening shouts of the demonstrators frightened me, as did the aggressive fringes, the armed gangs, the dead on the streets, the revolutionary hatred of everything. I have to speak in public, I confessed, and I don't know what I am, I don't know to what point I seriously believe what I say.

Now, with Nino, I seemed able to put into words the most secret feelings, even things I didn't say to myself, even the incongruities, the acts of cowardice. He was so sure of himself, solid, he had detailed opinions about everything. I felt as if I had pasted onto the chaotic rebellion of childhood neat cards bearing phrases suited to making a good impression. At a conference in Bologna—we were part of a determined exodus headed to the city of freedom—we ran into constant police checks, and were stopped at least five times. Weapons leveled against us, out of the car, documents, there against the wall. I was frightened, at the time, even more than in Germany: it was my land, it was my language, I became anxious, I wanted to be silent, to obey, and instead I began to shout, I slipped into dialect without realizing it, I unloaded insults at the police for pushing me rudely. Fear and rage were mixed up, and often I couldn't control either one. Nino instead remained calm, he joked with the policemen, humored them, calmed me. For him only the two of us counted. Remember that we're here, now, together, he said, the rest is background and will change.

20.

We were always moving, in those years. We wanted to be present, observe, study, understand, argue, bear witness, and most of all love each other. The wailing police sirens, the checkpoints, the crack of helicopter blades, the murdered—all were paving stones on which we marked the time of our relationship, the weeks, the months, the first year, and then a year and a half, starting from the night when, in the house in Florence, I had gone to Nino in his room. It was then that—we said to each other—our true life had begun. And what we called *true life* was that impression of miraculous splendor that never abandoned us even when everyday horrors took the stage.

We were in Rome in the days following the kidnapping of Aldo Moro. I had joined Nino, who was to discuss a book by a Neapolitan colleague on southern politics and geography. Very little was said about the volume, while there was a lot of argument about Moro, the head of the Christian Democrats. Part of the audience rose up, scaring me, when Nino said it was

Moro himself who threw mud at the state, who embodied its worst aspects, who created the conditions for the birth of the Red Brigades, and thus obscured uncomfortable truths about his corrupt party, and indeed identified it with the state to avoid every accusation and every punishment. Even when he concluded that defending the institutions meant not hiding their misdeeds but making them transparent, without omissions, efficient, capable of justice in every nerve center, the people didn't calm down, and insults flew. I saw Nino turn pale, and I dragged him away as soon as possible. We took refuge in us as if in shining armor.

The times had that rhythm. Things went badly for me, too, one evening, in Ferrara. Moro's body had been found a little more than a month earlier and I let slip a description of his kidnappers as murderers. It was always difficult with words, my audience required that I calibrate them according to the current usage of the radical left, and I was very careful. But often I would get excited and then I made pronouncements with no filter. "Murderers" did not sit well with that audience—*the fascists are the murderers*—and I was attacked, criticized, jeered. I was silent. How I suffered in situations where approval suddenly vanished: I lost confidence, I felt dragged down to my origins, I felt politically incapable, I felt I was a woman who would have been better off not opening her mouth, and for a while I avoided every occasion of public confrontation. *If one murders someone, is one not a murderer?* The evening ended unpleasantly, Nino nearly came to blows with someone at the back of the room. But even in that situation only the return to the two of us counted. That's how it was: if we were together, there was no critic who could truly touch us; in fact we became arrogant, nothing else made sense except our opinions. We hurried to dinner, to good food, wine, sex. We wanted only to hold each other, cling to each other.

21.

The first cold shower arrived at the end of 1978, from Lila, naturally. It was the end of a series of unpleasant events that began in mid-October, when Pietro, returning from the university, was openly attacked by a couple of kids—reds, blackshirts, who knew anymore—armed with clubs. I hurried to the hospital, convinced that I would find him more depressed than ever. Instead, in spite of his bandaged head and a black eye, he was cheerful. He greeted me with a conciliatory tone, then he forgot about me and talked the whole time with some of his students, among whom a very pretty girl was conspicuous. When most of them left, she sat next to him, on the edge of the bed, and took one of his hands. She wore a white turtleneck sweater and a blue miniskirt, and her brown hair hung down her back. I was polite, I asked her about her studies. She said she had two more exams before getting her degree, but she was already working on her thesis, on Catullus. She's very good, Pietro praised her. Her name was Doriana and the whole time we were in the ward she only let go of his hand to rearrange the pillows.

That night, in the house in Florence, my mother-in-law appeared with Dede and Elsa. I talked to her about the girl, she smiled with satisfaction, she knew about her son's relationship. She said: You left him, what did you expect. The next day we all went together to the hospital. Dede and Elsa were immediately charmed by Doriana, by her necklaces and bracelets. They paid little attention to either their father or me, they went out to the courtyard to play with her and their grandmother. A new phase has begun, I said to myself, and I cautiously tested the ground with Pietro. Even before the beating his visits to his daughters had decreased, and now I understood why. I asked him about the girl. He talked about her as he knew how to do, with devotion. I asked: Will she come to live with you? He said that it was too soon, he didn't know, but yes, maybe so. We have to discuss the children, I said. He agreed.

As soon as possible, I took up this new situation with Adele. She must have thought that I wanted to complain but I explained that I wasn't unhappy about it, my problem was the children.

"What do you mean?" she asked, alarmed.

"Until now I've left them with you out of necessity and because I thought that Pietro needed to resettle himself, but now that he has a life of his own things have changed. I, too, have the right to some stability."

"And so?"

"I'll take a house in Naples and move there with my daughters."

We had a violent quarrel. She was very attached to the girls and didn't trust leaving them to me. She accused me of being too self-absorbed to take care of them properly. She insinuated that setting up house with a stranger—she meant Nino—when you have two female children was a very serious imprudence. Finally she swore that she would never allow her grandchildren to grow up in a disorderly city like Naples.

We shouted insults. She brought up my mother—her son must have told her about the terrible scene in Florence.

"When you have to go away who will you leave them with, her?"

"I'll leave them with whoever I like."

"I don't want Dede and Elsa to have any contact with people who are out of control."

I answered:

"In all these years I believed that you were the mother figure I'd always felt the need for. I was wrong, my mother is better than you."

22.

I subsequently brought up the subject again with Pietro, and it became evident that, despite his protests, he would agree to whatever arrangement allowed him to be with Doriana as much as possible. At that point I went to Naples to talk to Nino; I didn't want to reduce such a delicate moment to a phone call. I stayed in the apartment on Via Duomo, as I had often done now. I knew that he was still living there, it was his home, and although I always had a sense of temporariness and the dirty sheets annoyed me, I was glad to see him and I went there willingly. When I told him that I was ready to move, with my daughters, he had a real explosion of joy. We celebrated, he promised to find us an apartment as soon as possible, he wanted to take on all the inevitable annoyances.

I was relieved. After so much running around and traveling and pain and pleasure, it was time to settle down. Now I had some money, I would get some from Pietro for the children's maintenance, and I was about to sign a favorable contract for a new book. I felt that I was finally an adult, with a growing reputation, in a state in which returning to Naples could be an exciting risk and fruitful for my work. But mainly I wished to live with Nino. How lovely it was to walk with him, meet his friends, talk, come home late. I wanted to find a light-filled house, with a view of the sea. My daughters mustn't feel the lack of the comforts of Genoa.

I avoided calling Lila and telling her my decision. I assumed that she would inevitably get mixed up in my affairs and I didn't want her to. Instead I called Carmen, with whom in the past year I had established a good relationship. To please her I had met Nadia's brother, Armando, who—I had discovered—was now, besides a doctor, a prominent member of the Proletarian Democracy party. He had treated me with great respect. He had praised my last book, insisting that I come and talk about it somewhere in the city, had brought me to a popular radio station he had founded; there, in the most wretched disorder, he had interviewed me. But as for what he ironically called my recurrent curiosity about his sister, he had been evasive. He said that Nadia was well, that she had gone on a long trip with their mother, and nothing else. About Pasquale he knew nothing nor was he interested in knowing: people like him—he had said emphatically—had been the ruin of an extraordinary political period.

To Carmen, obviously, I had given a toned-down report of that meeting, but she was unhappy just the same. A decorous unhappiness, which in the end had led me to see her occasionally when I went to Naples. I felt in her an anguish that I understood. Pasquale was *our* Pasquale. We both loved him, whatever he had done or was doing. Of him I now had a drifting, fragmentary memory: the time we had been together at the neighborhood library, the time of the fight in Piazza dei Martiri, the time he had come in the car to take me to Lila, the time he had showed up at my house in Florence with Nadia. Carmen on the other hand I felt as more consistent. Her suffering as a child—I had a clear memory of her father's arrest—was welded to her suffering for her brother, to the tenacity with which she tried to watch over his fate. If she had once been only the childhood friend who had ended up behind the counter in the Carraccis' new grocery store thanks to Lila, now she was a person I saw willingly and was fond of.

We met in a coffee shop on Via Duomo. The place was dark, and we sat near the street door. I told her in detail about my plans, I knew she would talk to Lila and I thought: That's as it should be. Carmen, wearing dark colors, with her dark complexion, listened attentively and without interrupting. I felt frivolous in my elegant outfit, talking about Nino and my desire to live in a nice house. At a certain point she looked at the clock, announced:

"Lina's coming."

That made me nervous; I had a date with her, not with Lila. I looked in turn at the clock, and said, "I have to go."

"Wait, five minutes and she'll be here."

She began to speak of her with affection and gratitude. Lila took care of her friends. Lila took care of everyone: her parents, her brother, even Stefano. Lila had helped Antonio find an apartment and had become very friendly with the German woman he had married. Lila intended to set up her own computer business. Lila was sincere, she was rich, she was generous, if you were in trouble she reached into her purse. Lila was ready to help Pasquale in any way. Ah, she said, Lenù, how lucky you two are to have always been so close, how I envied you. And I seemed to hear in her voice, to recognize in a movement of her hand, the tones, the gestures of our friend. I thought again of Alfonso, I remembered my impression that he, a male, resembled Lila even in his features. Was the neighborhood settling in her, finding its direction?

"I'm going," I said.

"Wait a minute, Lila has something important to tell you."

"You tell me."

"No, it's up to her."

I waited, with growing reluctance. Finally Lila arrived. This time she had paid much more attention to her looks than when I'd seen her in Piazza Amedeo, and I had to acknowledge that, if she wanted, she could still be very beautiful. She exclaimed:

"So you've decided to return to Naples."

"Yes."

"And you tell Carmen but not me?"

"I would have told you."

"Do your parents know?"

"No."

"And Elisa?"

"Not her, either."

"Your mother's not well."

"What's wrong?"

"She has a cough, but she won't go to the doctor."

I became restless, I turned to look at the clock.

"Carmen says you have something important to tell me."

"It's not a nice thing."

"Go ahead."

"I asked Antonio to follow Nino."

I jumped.

"Follow in what sense?"

"See what he does."

"Why?"

"I did it for your own good."

"I'll worry about my own good."

Lila glanced at Carmen as if to get her support, then she turned back to me.

"If you act like that I'll shut up: I don't want you to feel offended again."

"I'm not offended, go on."

She looked me straight in the eye and revealed, in curt phrases, in Italian, that Nino had never left his wife, that he continued to live with her and his son, that as a reward he had been named, just recently, the director of an important research institute financed by the bank that his father-in-law headed. She concluded gravely:

"Did you know?"

I shook my head.

"No."

"If you don't believe me let's go see him and I'll repeat everything to his face, word for word, just as I told you now."

I waved a hand to let her know there was no need.

"I believe you," I whispered, but to avoid her eyes I looked out the door, at the street.

Meanwhile from very far away came Carmen's voice saying:

If you're going to Nino I want to come, too; the three of us will settle things properly. I felt her lightly touching my arm to get my attention. As small girls we had read photo-romances in the garden next to the church and had felt the same urge to help the heroine when she was in trouble. Now, surely, she had the same feeling of solidarity of those days, but with the gravity of today, and it was a genuine feeling, brought on by a wrong that was not fictional but real. Lila on the other hand had always scorned such reading and there was no doubt that at that moment she was sitting across from me with other motives. I imagined that she felt satisfied, as Antonio, too, must have been when he discovered Nino's falseness. I saw that she and Carmen exchanged a look, a sort of mute consultation, as if to make a decision. It was a long moment. No, I read on Carmen's lips, and that breath was accompanied by an imperceptible shaking of her head.

No to what?

Lila stared at me again, her mouth half open. As usual she was taking on the job of sticking a pin in my heart not to stop it but to make it beat harder. Her eyes were narrowed, her broad forehead wrinkled. She waited for my reaction. She wanted me to scream, weep, hand myself over to her. I said softly:

"I really have to go now."

23.

I cut Lila out of everything that followed.

I was hurt, not because she had revealed that for more than two years Nino had been telling me lies about the state of his marriage but because she had succeeded in proving to me what in fact she had said from the start: that my choice was mistaken, that I was stupid.

A few hours later I met Nino, but I acted as if nothing were wrong, I limited myself only to avoiding his embraces. I was swallowed up by bitterness. I spent the whole night with my eyes wide open, the desire to cling to that long male body was ruined. The next day he wanted to take me to see an apartment on Via Tasso, and I agreed when he said: If you like it, don't worry about the rent, I'll take care of it, I'm about to get a position that will resolve all our financial problems. But that night I couldn't take it anymore and I exploded. We were in the apartment on Via Duomo, and his friend as usual wasn't there. I said to him:

"Tomorrow I'd like to see Eleonora."

He looked at me in bewilderment.

"Why?"

"I have to talk to her. I want to know what she knows about us, when you left home, when you stopped sleeping together. I want to know if you asked for a legal separation. I want her to tell me if her father and mother know that your marriage is over."

He remained calm.

"Ask me: if something isn't clear I'll explain it to you."

"No, I trust only her, you're a liar."

At that point I started yelling, I switched to dialect. He gave in immediately, he admitted everything, I had no doubt that Lila had told me the truth. I hit him in the chest with my fists and as I did I felt as if there were a me unglued from me who wished to hurt him even more, who wanted to beat him, spit in his face as I had seen people do as a child in the neighborhood quarrels, call him a shit, scratch him, tear out his eyes. I was surprised, frightened. *Am I always this furious other I? I, here in Naples, in this filthy house, I, who if I could would kill this man, plunge a knife into his heart with all my strength? Should I restrain this shadow—my mother, all our female ancestors—or should I let her go?* I shouted, I hit him. And at first he warded off the blows, pretending to be amused, then suddenly he darkened, sat down heavily, stopped defending himself.

I slowed down, my heart was about to burst. He murmured:

"Sit down."

"No."

"At least give me a chance to explain."

I collapsed onto a chair, as far away as possible, and let him speak. You know—he began in a choked voice—that before Montpellier I had told Eleonora everything and that the break was irreparable. But when he returned, he said, things had become complicated. His wife had gone crazy, even Albertino's life seemed in danger. Thus, to be able to continue he had had to tell her that we were no longer seeing each other. For a while the lie had held up. But since the explanations he gave Eleonora for all his absences were increasingly implausible, the scenes had begun again. Once his wife had grabbed a knife and tried to stab herself in the stomach. Another time she had gone out on the balcony and wanted to jump. Yet another time she had left home, taking the child; she had disappeared for an entire day and he was dying with fear. But when he finally tracked her down at the house of a beloved aunt, he realized that Eleonora had changed. She was no longer angry, there was just a hint of contempt. One morning—Nino said, breathlessly—she asked if I had left you. I said yes. And she said: All right, I believe you. She said it just like that and from then on she began to pretend to believe me, *pretend*. Now we live in this fiction and things are working well. In fact, as you see, I'm here with you, I sleep with you, if I want I'll go away with you. And she knows everything, but she behaves as if she knew nothing.

Here he took a breath, cleared his throat, tried to understand if I was listening or harboring only rage. I continued to say nothing, I looked in another direction. He must have thought that I was yielding and he continued to explain with greater determination. He talked and talked, he was good at it, he put everything into it. He was winning, self-mocking, suffering, desperate. But when he tried to approach, I pushed him away, shouting. Then he couldn't bear it and burst into tears. He gesticulated, he leaned toward me, he murmured between tears: I don't want you to pardon me, I want only to be understood. I interrupted him, angrier than ever, I cried: You lied to her and you lied to me, and you didn't do it for love of either of us, you did it for yourself, because you don't have the courage of your choices, because you're a coward. Then I moved on to repugnant words in dialect, and he let himself be insulted, he muttered just some phrases of regret. I felt as if I were suffocating, I gasped, I was silent, and that allowed him to return to the charge. He tried again to demonstrate that lying to me had been the only way to avoid a tragedy. When it seemed to him that he had succeeded, when he whispered to me that now, thanks to Eleonora's acquiescence, we could try to live together without trouble, I said calmly that it was over between us. I left, I returned to Genoa.

24.

The atmosphere in my in-laws' house became increasingly tense. Nino telephoned constantly, I either hung up on him or quarreled too loudly. A couple of times Lila called, she wanted to know how it was going. I said to her: Well, very well, just the way you wanted it to go, and hung up. I became intractable, I yelled at Dede and Elsa for no reason. But mainly I began to fight with Adele. One morning I threw in her face what she had done to hinder the publication of my book. She didn't deny it, in fact she said: It's a pamphlet, it doesn't have the dignity of a book. I replied: If I write pamphlets, you in your

whole life haven't been capable of writing even that, and it's
not clear where all this authority of yours comes from. She was
offended, she hissed: You don't know anything about me. Oh
no, I knew things that she couldn't imagine. That time I managed to keep my mouth shut, but a few days later I had a violent quarrel with Nino; I yelled on the phone in dialect, and
when my mother-in-law reproached me in a contemptuous
tone I reacted by saying:

"Leave me alone, worry about yourself."

"What do you mean?"

"You know."

"I don't know anything."

"Pietro told me that you've had lovers."

"I?"

"Yes, you, don't be so taken aback. I assumed my responsibilities in front of everyone, even Dede and Elsa, and I'm paying for the consequences of my actions. You, who give yourself
so many airs, you're just a hypocritical little bourgeois who
hides her dirt under the carpet."

Adele turned pale, she was speechless. Rigid, her face tense,
she got up and closed the door of the living room. Then she
said to me in a low voice, almost a whisper, that I was an evil
woman, that I couldn't understand what it meant to truly love
and to give up one's beloved, that behind a pleasing and docile
façade I concealed an extremely vulgar craving to grab everything, which neither studying nor books could ever tame. Then
she concluded: Tomorrow get out, you and your children; I'm
sorry only that if the girls had grown up here they might have
tried not to be like you.

I didn't answer, I knew I had gone too far. I was tempted to
apologize but I didn't. The next morning Adele ordered the
maid to help me pack. I'll do it myself, I exclaimed, and without even saying goodbye to Guido, who was in his study pretending nothing was happening, I found myself at the station

loaded with suitcases, the two children watching me, trying to understand what my intentions were.

I remember the exhaustion, the echo of the station hall, the waiting room. Dede reproached me for shoving: Don't push me, don't always shout, I'm not deaf. Elsa asked: Are we going to Papa? They were cheerful because there was no school, but I felt that they didn't trust me and they asked cautiously, ready to be silent if I got angry: What are we doing, when are we going back to Grandma and Grandpa's, where are we going to eat, where will we sleep tonight.

At first, desperate as I was, I thought of going to Naples and showing up with the children, without warning, at Nino and Eleonora's house. I said to myself: Yes, that's what I should do, my daughters and I are in this situation because of him, and he has to pay. I wanted my disorder to crash into him and overwhelm him, as it was overwhelming me. He had deceived me. He had held on to his family and, like a toy, me, too. I had chosen definitively, he hadn't. I had left Pietro, he had kept Eleonora. I was in the right, then. I had the right to invade his life and say to him: Well, my dear, we are here; if you're worried about your wife because she does crazy things, now I'm doing crazy things, let's see how you manage it.

But while I was preparing for a long, excruciating journey to Naples I changed my mind in a flash—an announcement on the loudspeaker was enough—and left for Milan. In this new situation I needed money more than ever. I said to myself that first of all I should go to a publisher and beg for work. Only on the train did I realize the reason for that abrupt change of plan. In spite of everything, love writhed fiercely inside me and the mere idea of doing harm to Nino was repugnant to me. Although I now wrote about women's autonomy and discussed it everywhere, I didn't know how to live without his body, his voice, his intelligence. It was terrible to confess it, but I still wanted him, I loved him more than my own daughters. At the idea of hurting him and of no longer seeing him I withered painfully, the free and educated woman lost her petals, separated from the woman-mother, and the woman-mother was disconnected from the woman-lover, and the woman-lover from the furious whore, and we all seemed on the point of flying off in different directions. As I traveled toward Milan, I discovered that, with Lila set aside, I didn't know how to give myself substance except by modeling myself on Nino. *I was incapable of being a model for myself.* Without him I no longer had a nucleus from which to expand outside the neighborhood and through the world, I was a pile of debris.

I arrived worn out and frightened at Mariarosa's house.

25.

How long did I stay there? Several months, and at times it was a difficult cohabitation. My sister-in-law already knew about the fight with Adele and she said with her usual frankness: You know I love you, but you were wrong to treat my mother like that.

"She behaved very badly."

"Now. But she helped you before."

"She did it only so that her son wouldn't look bad."

"You're unfair."

"No, I'm direct."

She looked at me with an irritation that was unusual in her. Then, as if she were stating a rule whose violation she could not tolerate, she said:

"I want to be direct, too. My mother is my mother. Say what you like about my father and my brother, but leave her alone."

Otherwise she was polite. She welcomed us to her house in her casual way, assigned us a big room with three cots, gave us towels, and then left us to ourselves, as she did with all the guests who appeared and disappeared in the apartment. I was struck, as usual, by her vivacious gaze; her entire organism seemed to hang from her eyes like a worn dressing gown. I scarcely noticed that she had an unusual pallor and had lost weight. I was absorbed in myself, in my suffering, and soon I paid her no attention at all.

I tried to put some order into the room, which was dusty, dirty, crowded with things. I made my bed and the girls' beds. I made a list of everything they and I needed. But that organizational effort didn't last long. My head was in the clouds, I didn't know what decisions to make, and for the first days I was constantly on the telephone. I missed Nino so much that I immediately called him. He got Mariarosa's number and from then on he called me continuously, even if every conversation ended in a fight. At first I was overjoyed to hear his voice, and at times I was close to giving in. I said to myself: I hid from him the fact that Pietro returned home and we were sleeping under the same roof. Then I grew angry with myself, I realized that it wasn't the same thing: I had never slept with Pietro, he slept with Eleonora; I had started the process of separation, he had consolidated his marriage bond. So we started quarreling again, I told him, shouting, never to call again. But the telephone rang regularly morning and evening. He said that he couldn't do without me, he begged me to come to Naples. One day he announced that he had rented the apartment on Via Tasso and that everything was ready to welcome me and my daughters. He said, he declared, he promised, he appeared ready for everything, but he could never make up his mind to say the most important words: *It's really over now with Eleonora.* So there was always a moment when, paying no attention to the children or to the people coming and going around the house, I screamed at him to stop tormenting me and hung up angrier than ever.

26.

I lived those days despising myself, I couldn't tear Nino out of my mind. I finished my work lethargically, I departed out of duty, I returned out of duty, I despaired, I was collapsing. And I felt that the facts were proving Lila right: I was forgetting my daughters, I was leaving them with no care, with no school.

Dede and Elsa were enchanted by the new arrangement. They scarcely knew their aunt, but they adored the sense of absolute freedom that she radiated. The house in Sant'Ambrogio continued to be a port in a storm; Mariarosa welcomed everyone with the tone of a sister or perhaps a nun without prejudices, and she didn't care about dirt, mental problems, crime, drugs. The girls had no duties; they wandered through the rooms until late at night, curious. They listened to speeches and jargons of every type, they were entertained when people made music, when they sang and danced. Their aunt went out in the morning to the university and returned in the late afternoon. She was never anxious, she made them laugh, she chased them around the apartment, played hide-and-seek or blind-man's buff. If she stayed home, she undertook great cleaning efforts, involving me, them, stray guests. But more than our bodies she looked after our minds. She had organized evening courses, and invited her colleagues from the university. Sometimes she herself gave lectures that were witty and packed with information, and she kept her nieces beside her, addressing them, involving them. The apartment at those times was crowded with her friends, men and women, who came just to listen to her.

One evening, during one of those lessons, there was a knock on the door and Dede ran to open it; she liked to greet people. Returning to the living room, she said excitedly: It's the police. In the small assembly there was an angry, almost threatening murmur. Mariarosa rose calmly and went to speak to the police. There were two, they said that the neighbors had complained, or something like that. She was cordial, insisted that they come in, almost forced them to sit with us in the living room, and returned to her lecture. Dede had never seen a policeman up close, and started talking to the younger one, resting her elbow on his knee. I remember her opening remark, by which she intended to explain that Mariarosa was a good person:

"In fact," she said, "my aunt is a professor."

"In fact," the cop said faintly, with an uncertain smile.

"Yes."

"How well you speak."

"Thank you. In fact, her name is Mariarosa Airota and she teaches art history."

The boy whispered something to his older companion. They remained prisoners for ten minutes or so and then they left. Dede led them to the door.

Later I, too, was assigned one of these educational projects, and for my evening more people showed up than usual. My daughters sat on cushions in the first row, in the big living room, and they listened obediently. Starting then, I think, Dede began to observe me with curiosity. She had great respect for her father, her grandfather, and now Mariarosa. She knew nothing about me and didn't want to know anything. I was her mother, I forbade everything, she couldn't stand me. She must have been amazed that I was listened to with an attention that she on principle would never have given me. And maybe she also liked the composure with which I responded to criticisms; that evening they came surprisingly from Mariarosa. My sister-in-law was the only one among the women present who did not agree with even a word of what I was saying—she who, long ago, had encouraged me to study, to write, to publish. Without asking my permission, she told the story of the fight I had had with my mother in Florence, demonstrating that she knew about it in detail. "Resorting to many learned citations," she theorized that a woman without love for her origins is lost.

27.

When I had to travel I left the children to my sister-in-law, but I soon realized that it was really Franco who took care of them. Generally he stayed in his room, he didn't join in the lectures, he paid no attention to the constant coming and going. But he was fond of my daughters. When necessary he cooked for them, he invented games, in his way he instructed them. Dede learned from him to challenge the silly fable—so she described it, telling me about it—of Menenius Agrippa, which she had been taught in the new school I had decided to enroll her in. She laughed and said: *The patrician Menenius Agrippa, Mamma, bewildered the common people with his talk, but he couldn't prove that one man's limbs are nourished when another man's stomach is filled. Ha ha ha.* From him she also learned, on a big map of the world, the geography of inordinate prosperity and intolerable poverty. She couldn't stop repeating: It's the greatest injustice.

One evening when Mariarosa wasn't there, my boyfriend from the days of Pisa said, in a serious tone of regret, alluding to the children, who followed him around the house with drawn-out cries: Imagine, they could have been ours. I corrected him: They'd be a few years older by now. He nodded yes. I observed him for a few seconds while he stared at his shoes. I compared him in my mind to the rich, educated student of fifteen years earlier: it was him and yet it was not him. He no longer read, he didn't write, within the past year he had reduced to the minimum his participation in assemblies, debates, demonstrations. He talked about politics—his only true interest—without his former conviction and passion; rather, he accentuated the tendency to mock his own grim prophecies of disaster. In hyperbolic tones he listed the catastrophes that in his view were approaching: one, the decline of the revolutionary subject par excellence, the working class; two, the definitive dispersion of the political patrimony of socialists and Communists, who were already perverted by their daily quarrel over which was playing the role of capital's crutch; three, the end of every hypothesis of change, what was there was there and we would have to adapt to it. I asked skeptically: You really think it's going to end like that? Of course— he laughed—but you know that I'm a skilled debater, and if you want I'll prove to you, by means of thesis, antithesis, and synthesis, the exact opposite: Communism is inevitable, the dictatorship of the proletariat is the highest form of democracy, the Soviet Union and China and North Korea and Thailand are much better than the United States, shedding blood in rivulets or rivers in certain cases is a crime and in certain others is just. Would you prefer that I do that?

Only twice did I see him as he had been as a youth. One morning Pietro appeared, without Doriana, assuming the attitude of someone who was making an inspection to check on what conditions his daughters were living in, what school I had put them in, if they were happy. It was a moment of great tension. The children perhaps told him too much, and with a childish taste for fantastic exaggeration, about the way they were living. So he began to quarrel ponderously first with his sister and then with me, he said to us both that we were irresponsible. I lost my temper, and shouted at him: You're right, take them away, you take care of them, you and Doriana. And at that point Franco came out of his room, intervened, rolled out his old skill with words, which in the past had enabled him to control raucous meetings. He and Pietro ended up having a learned discussion on the couple, the family, the care of children, and even Plato, forgetting about Mariarosa and me. My husband left, his face flushed, his eyes clear, nervous and yet pleased to have found someone with whom he could have an intelligent and civilized conversation.

Stormier—and terrible for me—was the day when Nino appeared without warning. He was tired from the long drive, unkempt in appearance, very tense. At first I thought he had come to decide, on his own authority, the fate of me and the children. Enough, I hoped he would say, I've cleared up my situation and we're going to live in Naples. I felt disposed to give in without any more nonsense, I was exhausted by the provisional nature of things. But it didn't turn out like that. We closed ourselves in a room, and he, amid endless hesitations, twisting his hands, his hair, his face, repeated, against all my expectations, that it was impossible for him to separate from his wife. He was agitated, he tried to embrace me, he struggled to explain that only by staying with Eleonora would it be possible for him not to give up me and our life together. At another moment I would have pitied him; it was evident that his suffering was sincere. But, at the time, I didn't care in the least how much he was suffering, I looked at him in astonishment.

"What are you saying to me?"

"That I can't leave Eleonora, but I can't live without you."

"So if I understand you: you are proposing, as if it were a reasonable solution, that I abandon the role of lover and accept that of parallel wife."

"What do you mean, it's not like that."

I attacked him, *Of course it's like that*, and I pointed to the door: I was tired of his tricks, his inspired ideas, his every wretched word. Then, in a voice that strained to come out of his throat, and yet with the air of someone who is uttering definitively the irrefutable reasons for his own behavior, he confessed to me a thing that—he cried—*he didn't want others to tell me*, and so he had come to tell me in person: Eleonora was seven months pregnant.

28.

Now that much of my life is behind me I know that my reaction to that news was overblown, and as I write I realize that I'm smiling to myself. I know many men and many women who can recount experiences that aren't very different: love and sex are unreasonable and brutal. But at the time I couldn't bear it. That fact—*Eleonora is seven months pregnant*—seemed to me the most intolerable wrong that Nino could do to me. I remembered Lila, the moment of uncertainty when she and Carmen had looked at each other, as if they had had something else to tell me. Had Antonio discovered the pregnancy, too? Did they know? And why had Lila relinquished her chance to tell me? Had she claimed the right to measure out my suffering in doses? Something broke in my chest and in my stomach. While Nino was suffocating with anxiety and struggling to justify himself, saying that the pregnancy, if on the one hand it had served to calm his wife, on the other had made it even more difficult to leave her, I was doubled over with suffering, arms locked, my whole body was ill, I couldn't speak, or cry out. Only Franco was in the apartment. No crazy women, desolate women, singers, sick people. Mariarosa had taken the children out to give Nino and me time to confront each other. I opened the door of the room and called my old boyfriend from Pisa in a weak voice. He came right away and I pointed to Nino. I said in a sort of rattle: throw him out.

He didn't throw him out, but he signaled him to be silent. He avoided asking what had happened, he grabbed my wrists, he held me steady, he let me retake possession of myself. Then he led me to the kitchen, made me sit down. Nino followed us.

I was gasping for breath, making choking sounds of despair. Throw him out, I repeated, when Nino tried to come near me. Franco kept him away, said calmly: Leave her alone, leave the room. Nino obeyed and I told Franco everything in the most confused way. He listened without interrupting, until he realized that I had no more energy. Only at that point did he say, in his refined way, that it was a good rule not to expect the ideal but to enjoy what is possible. I got mad at him, too: The usual male talk, I shouted, who gives a damn about the possible, you're talking nonsense. He wasn't offended, he wanted me to examine the situation for what it was. All right, he said, this man has lied to you for two and a half years, he told you he had left his wife, he said he didn't have relations with her, and now you discover that seven months ago he made her pregnant. You're right, it's horrible, Nino is an abject being. But once it was known—he pointed out—he could have disappeared, forgotten about you. Why, then, did he drive from Naples to Milan, why did he travel all night, why did he humiliate himself, accusing himself, why did he beg you not to leave him? All that should signify something. It signifies, I cried, that he is a liar, that he is a superficial person, that he is incapable of making a choice. And he kept nodding yes, he agreed. But then he asked: What if he loved you, seriously, and yet knew that he could love you only in this way?

I didn't have time to say that that was exactly Nino's argument. The house door opened and Mariarosa appeared. The girls recognized Nino with charming bashfulness and at the idea of getting his attention immediately forgot that that name had for days, for months, sounded in their father's mouth like a curse. He devoted himself to them, Mariarosa and Franco took care of me. How difficult everything was. Dede and Elsa were now talking in loud voices, laughing, and my two hosts turned to me with serious arguments. They wanted to help me reason, but with underlying feelings that not even they could keep under control. Franco revealed a surprising tendency to give space to affectionate mediation instead of to clean breaks, as he used to do. My sister-in-law at first was full of understanding for me, then she also tried to understand Nino's motives and, especially, Eleonora's plight, in the end wounding me, maybe without wishing to, maybe intentionally. Don't get angry, she said, try to reflect: what does a woman of your understanding feel at the idea that her happiness becomes the ruin of someone else?

It went on like that. Franco urged me to take what I could within the limits imposed by the situation, Mariarosa portrayed Eleonora abandoned with a small child and another on the way, and advised me: establish a relationship with her, look at one another. The nonsense of someone who doesn't know, I thought, with no energy now, of someone who can't understand. Lila would come out of it as she always does, Lila would advise me: You've already made a big enough mistake, spit in their faces and get out, it was the ending she'd always wished for. But I was frightened, I felt even more confused by what Franco and Mariarosa were saying, I was no longer listening to them. I observed Nino instead. How handsome he was as he regained my daughters' trust. Here, he was coming back into the room with them, pretending nothing had happened, praising them as he addressed Mariarosa—See, aunt, what exceptional young ladies?—and the charm came naturally to him, the light touch of his fingers on her bare knee. I dragged him out of the house, insisted on a long walk through Sant'Ambrogio.

It was hot, I remember. We drifted alongside a red brick stain, the air was full of fuzz flying off the plane trees. I told him that I had to get used to doing without him, but that for now I couldn't, I needed time. He answered that he, instead, would never be able to live without me. I replied that he had never been able to separate himself from anything or anyone. He repeated that it wasn't true, that circumstances were to blame, that to have me he was compelled to hold on to everything. I understood that to force him to go beyond that position was in vain, he could see before him only an abyss and he was frightened by it. I walked him to his car, I sent him away. A moment before he left he asked: What do you think you'll do. I didn't answer, even I didn't know.

29.

What happened a few weeks later made my decision for me. Mariarosa had gone, she had an engagement in Bordeaux. Before she left she took me aside and delivered a confused speech about Franco, on the need for me to stay close to him during her absence. She described him as very depressed, and I suddenly understood what until that moment I had only intuited in fits and starts and then missed through distraction: with Franco she was playing the good Samaritan as she did with everyone; she loved him seriously, she had become for him mother-sister-lover, and her expression of suffering, her withered body were due to permanent anxiety about him, the certainty that he had become too fragile and might break at any moment.

She was away for eight days. With some effort—I had other things on my mind—I was cordial to Franco. I stayed up late talking with him every evening, and I was glad that instead of talking about politics he preferred to recall, to himself more than to me, how well we had got on together: our walks through Pisa in the spring, the terrible smell of the street along the Arno, the times he had confided to me things he'd never said to anyone about his childhood, his parents, his grandparents. Above all I was pleased that he let me talk about my anxieties, about the new contract I had signed with the publishing house, about the need therefore to write a new book, about a possible return to Naples, about Nino. He never attempted generalizations or superfluous words. He was, rather, sharp, almost vulgar. If he is more important to you than yourself— he said one evening, seeming almost dazed—you should take him as he is: wife, children, that permanent tendency to sleep with other women, the vulgar things he is and will be capable of. Lena, Lenuccia, he murmured, affectionately, shaking his head. And then he laughed, got up from the chair, said obscurely that in his view love ended only when it was possible to return to oneself without fear or disgust, and left the room with shuffling steps, as if he wanted to reassure himself of the materiality of the floor. I don't know why Pasquale came to mind, that night, a person very far from him in social background, culture, political choices. And yet, for an instant, I imagined that if my friend from the neighborhood had managed to reemerge alive from the darkness that had swallowed him he would have the same way of walking.

For an entire day Franco didn't come out of his room. That night I had an engagement for work, I knocked, I asked him if he could give Dede and Elsa dinner. He promised to do it. I got home late, and, contrary to his usual habit, he had left the kitchen in great disorder. I cleared the table, I washed the dishes. I didn't sleep much, at six I was already awake. On the way to the bathroom I passed his room and was attracted by a sheet of notebook paper attached to the door with a thumbtack. On it was written: *Lena, don't let the children in.* I thought that Dede and Elsa had been bothering him, or that the evening before they had made him angry, and I went to make breakfast with the intention of scolding them. Then I thought again. Franco had a good relationship with my daughters, I ruled out that he was angry with them for some reason. Around eight I knocked discreetly. No answer. I knocked harder, I opened the door cautiously, the room was dark. I called him, silence, I turned on the light.

There was blood on the pillow and on the sheet, a large blackish stain that extended to his feet. Death is so repellent. Here I will say only that when I saw that body deprived of life, that body which I knew intimately, which had been happy and active, which had read so many books and had been exposed to so many experiences, I felt both repulsion and pity. Franco had been a living material saturated with political culture, with generous purposes and hopes, with good manners. Now he offered a horrible spectacle of himself. He had rid himself so fiercely of memory, language, the capacity to find meaning that it seemed obvious the hatred he had for himself, for his own skin, for his moods, for his thoughts and words, for the brutal corner of the world that had enveloped him.

In the days that followed I thought of Pasquale and Carmen's mother, Giuseppina. She, too, had stopped being able to tolerate herself and the segment of life that remained to her. But Giuseppina came from the time that preceded me, Franco instead was of my time, and that violent removal from it didn't just make an impression, it was devastating. I thought for a long time about his note, the only one he left. It was addressed to me and in substance was saying: Don't let the children in, I don't want them to see me; but you can enter, you *must* see me. I still think about that double imperative, one explicit, one implicit. After the funeral, which was attended by a crowd of militants with weakly clenched fists (Franco was still at the time well known and highly respected), I tried to re-establish a bond with Mariarosa. I wanted to be close to her, I wanted to talk about him, but she wouldn't let me. Her untidy appearance got worse, her features took on a morbid distrust that diminished even the vivacity of her eyes. The house slowly emptied. Any sisterly feeling toward me vanished, and she became increasingly hostile. Either she stayed at the university all the time or, if she was at home, she shut herself in her room and didn't want to be disturbed. She got angry if the girls made noise playing, she got even angrier if I scolded them for their noisy games. I packed the bags, I left for Naples with Dede and Elsa.

30.

Nino had been sincere, he had actually rented the apartment on Via Tasso. I went to live there right away, even though it was infested with ants and the furniture came down to a double bed without a headboard, cots for the children, a table, some chairs. I didn't talk about love, I didn't mention the future.

I told him that my decision had to do mostly with Franco, and I limited myself to bringing him good news and bad. The good was that my publisher had agreed to bring out his collection of essays, provided he made a new draft that was a little less dry; the bad was that I didn't want him to touch me. He greeted the first piece of news joyfully, he was desperate about the second. But then, as it turned out, we spent every evening sitting together, rewriting his essays, and with that closeness I couldn't keep my rage alive. Eleonora was still pregnant when we began to love each other again. And when she gave birth to a girl, who was named Lidia, Nino and I had returned to being lovers, a couple with our habits, a nice house, two children, an intense life, both private and public.

"Don't think," I said from the start, "that I'm at your command: I'm not capable of leaving you now, but sooner or later it will happen."

"It won't happen, you won't have any reason to."

"I have plenty of reasons."

"Everything will change soon."

"We'll see."

But it was a stage set, I passed off as very reasonable what was in fact unreasonable and humiliating. I'm taking—I said, adapting Franco's words—what is indispensable to me now, and as soon as I've consumed his face, his words, every desire, I'll send him away. When I waited for him in vain for days I told myself it was better that way, I was busy, he was with me too much. And when I felt the sting of jealousy I tried to calm myself by whispering: *I am the woman he loves.* And if I thought of his children I said to myself: He spends more time with Dede and Elsa than with Albertino and Lidia. Naturally it was all true and all false. Yes, the force of Nino's attraction would wear out. Yes, I had a lot of things to do. Yes, Nino loved me, he loved Dede and Elsa. But there were also others, yes, whom I pretended to ignore. Yes, I was more attracted to him than ever. Yes, I was ready to neglect everything and everyone if he needed me. Yes, his ties to Eleonora, Albertino, and the newborn Lidia were at least as strong as his ties to me and my daughters. I lowered dark curtains over those yeses, and if in fact here or there a tear in the fabric made evident the true state of things I quickly resorted to big words about the world to come: everything is changing, we are inventing new forms of living together, and other nonsense of the sort that I myself uttered in public or wrote every time it happened.

But the difficulties hammered at me every day, cracks were continually opening up. The city hadn't improved at all, its malaise wore me out immediately. Via Tasso turned out to be inconvenient. Nino got me a used car, a white Renault 4 that I immediately became attached to, but then I was always stuck in traffic, and I soon gave it up. I struggled to meet the endless demands of daily life much more than I ever had in Florence, Genoa, Milan. From the first day of school Dede hated her teacher and her classmates. Elsa, now in first grade, always came home depressed, her eyes red, and refused to tell me what had happened to her. I began to scold them both. I said they didn't know how to deal with adversity, they didn't know how to assert themselves, they didn't know how to adapt, and they had to learn. As a result the two sisters joined forces against me: they began to speak of their grandmother Adele and aunt Mariarosa as if they were divinities who had organized a happy world made just for them, they mourned them in an increasingly explicit way. When, in an attempt to win them back, I drew them to me, cuddled them, they hugged me unwillingly, and sometimes pushed me away. And my work? It became more and more evident that, especially in that successful period, I would have done better to stay in Milan and find a job at a publisher's. Or even settle in Rome, since I had met people on my promotional tours who had offered to help me. What were my daughters and I doing in Naples? Were we there just to make Nino happy? Was I lying to myself when I portrayed myself as free and autonomous? And was I lying to my audience when I played the part of someone who, with her two small books, had sought to help every woman confess what she couldn't say to herself? Were they mere formulas that it was convenient for me to believe in while in fact I was no different from my more traditional contemporaries? In spite of all the talk was I letting myself be *invented* by a man to the point where his needs were imposed on mine and those of my daughters?

I learned to avoid myself. It was enough for Nino to knock on the door and the bitterness vanished. I said to myself: Life *now* is this and can't be other. Meanwhile I tried to give myself some discipline, I didn't resign myself, I tried to be assertive, sometimes I even managed to feel happy. The house shone with light. From my balcony I saw Naples stretching to the edges of the yellow-blue reflection of the sea. I had taken my daughters away from the temporariness of Genoa and Milan, and the air, the colors, the sounds of the dialect in the streets, the cultured people Nino brought to see me even late into the night gave me confidence, made me cheerful. I took the girls to see Pietro in Florence and was pleased when he came to see them in Naples. Over Nino's protests I let him stay in my house. I made him a bed in the girls' room; their affection for him was a performance, as if they wanted to keep him with them through a display of how much they loved him. We tried to have a casual relationship, I inquired about Doriana, I asked about his book, which was always about to be published when further details emerged that had to be examined. When the children held tight to their father, ignoring me, I took a little break. I went down through the Arco Mirelli and walked along Via Caracciolo, beside the sea. Or I went up to Via Aniello Falcone and came to the Floridiana. I chose a bench, I read.

31.

From Via Tasso the old neighborhood was a dim, distant rockpile, indistinguishable urban debris at the foot of Vesuvius. I wanted it to stay that way: I was another person now, I would make sure that it did not recapture me. But in that case, too, the purpose I tended to attribute to myself was fragile. A mere three or four days after the first harried arrangement of the apartment I gave in. I dressed the children carefully, dressed up myself, and said: Now let's go see Grandmother Immacolata and Grandfather Vittorio and the uncles.

We left early in the morning and at Piazza Amedeo took the metro; the children were excited by the violent wind produced by the train's arrival, which ruffled their hair, pasted their dresses to their bodies, took away their breath. I hadn't seen or talked to my mother since the scene in Florence. I was afraid she would refuse to see me and maybe for that reason I didn't telephone to announce my visit. But I have to be honest, there was another, more obscure reason. I was reluctant to say to myself: I am here for this or that other reason, I want to go here or I want to go there. The neighborhood for me, even more than my family, was Lila: to plan that visit would also mean asking myself how I wanted to arrange things with her. And I still didn't have definite answers, and so leaving it to chance was better. In any case, since it was possible that I would run into her, I had devoted the greatest attention to the children's appearance and to my own. If it happened, I wanted her to realize that I was a lady of refinement and that my daughters weren't suffering, weren't falling apart, were doing very well.

It turned out to be an emotionally charged day. I went through the tunnel, I avoided the gas pump where Carmen worked with her husband, Roberto, and crossed the courtyard. My heart pounding, I climbed the crumbling stairs of the old building where I was born. Dede and Elsa were very excited, as if they were heading into some unknown adventure; I arrayed them in front of me and rang the bell. I heard the limping gait of my mother, she opened the door, she widened her eyes as if we were ghosts. I, too, in spite of myself, showed astonishment. The person I expected to see had come unglued from the one who was in fact before me. My mother was very changed. For a fraction of a second she seemed to be a cousin of hers whom I had seen a few times as a child, and who resembled her, although she was six or seven years older. She was much thinner, the bones of her face, her nose, her ears seemed enormous.

I tried to hug her, she drew back. My father wasn't there, nor were Peppe and Gianni. To find out anything about them was impossible, for a good hour she barely spoke a word to me. With the children she was affectionate. She praised them mightily and then, enveloping them in large aprons, she began making sugar candies with them. For me it was very awkward; the whole time she acted as if I weren't there. When I tried to say to the children that they were eating too many candies, Dede quickly turned to her grandmother:

"Can we have some more?"

"Eat as many as you want," my mother said, without looking at me.

The same scene was repeated when she told her grandchildren that they could go play in the courtyard. In Florence, in Genoa, in Milan I had never let them go out alone. I said: "No, girls, you can't, stay here."

"Grandma, can we go?" my daughters asked, almost in unison.

"I told you yes."

We remained alone. I said to her anxiously, as if I were still a child: "I moved. I've taken an apartment on Via Tasso."

"Good."

"Three days ago."

"Good."

"I've written another book."

"What do I care?"

I was silent. With an expression of disgust, she cut a lemon in two and squeezed the juice into a glass.

"Why are you having a lemonade?" I asked.

"Because seeing you turns my stomach."

She added water to the lemon, put in some bicarbonate of soda, drank the foamy effervescence in one gulp.

"Are you not well?"

"I'm very well."

"It's not true. Have you been to the doctor?"

"Imagine if I'll throw away money on doctors and medicine."

"Elisa knows you don't feel well?"

"Elisa is pregnant."

"Why didn't you or she tell me anything?"

She didn't answer. She placed the glass on the sink with a long, tired sigh, wiped her lips with the back of her hand. I said:

"I'll take you to the doctor. What else do you feel?"

"Everything that you brought on. Because of you a vein in my stomach ruptured."

"What do you mean?"

"Yes, you've killed this body."

"I love you very much, Mamma."

"Not me. You've come to stay in Naples with the children?"

"Yes."

"And your husband's not coming?"

"No."

"Then don't ever show up in this house again."

"Ma, today it's not like it used to be. You can be a respectable person even if you leave your husband, even if you go with someone else. Why do you get so angry with me when you don't say anything about Elisa, who's pregnant and not married?"

"Because you're not Elisa. Did Elisa study the way you did? From Elisa did I expect what I expected from you?"

"I'm doing things you should be happy about. Greco is becoming an important name. I even have a little reputation abroad."

"Don't boast to me, you're nobody. What you think you are means nothing to normal people. I'm respected here not because I had you but because I had Elisa. She didn't study, she didn't even graduate from middle school, but she's a lady. And you who have a university degree—where did you end up? I'm just sorry for the two children, so pretty and they speak so well. Didn't you think of them? With that father they were growing up like children on television, and you, what do you do, you bring them to Naples?"

"I'm the one who brought them up, Ma, not their father. And wherever I take them they'll still grow up like that."

"You are presumptuous. *Madonna*, how many mistakes I made with you. I thought Lina was the presumptuous one, but

it's you. Your friend bought a house for her parents, did you
do that? Your friend orders everyone around, even Michele
Solara, and who do you order around, that piece of shit son of
Sarratore?"

At that point she began to sing Lila's praises: Ah, how pretty
Lina is, how generous, now she's got her own business, no less,
she and Enzo—they've known how to get ahead. I understood
that the greatest sin she charged to me was forcing her to
admit, with no way out, that I was worth less than Lila. When
she said she wanted to cook something for Dede and Elsa,
deliberately excluding me, I realized that it would pain her to
invite me to lunch and, taking the children, I went away bitterly.

32.

Once on the *stradone* I hesitated: wait at the gate for my
father's return, wander the streets in search of my brothers, see
if my sister was home? I found a telephone booth, I called Elisa,
I dragged the girls to her big apartment, from which you could
see Vesuvius. My sister showed no signs yet of pregnancy, and
yet I found her very changed. The simple fact of being pregnant
must have made her expand suddenly, but distorting her. She
was as if coarsened in her body, in her words, in her voice. She
had an ashy complexion and was so poisoned by animosity that
she welcomed us reluctantly. Not for a moment did I find any
trace of the affection nor the slightly childish admiration she
had always had for me. And when I mentioned our mother's
health she took an aggressive tone that I wouldn't have thought
her capable of, at least with me. She exclaimed:

"Lenù, the doctor said she's fine, it's her soul that suffers.
Mamma is very healthy, she has her health, there's nothing to
treat except sorrow. If you hadn't disappointed her the way
you have she wouldn't be in this state."

"What sort of nonsense is that?"

She became even more rancorous.

"Nonsense? I'll just tell you this: my health is worse than Mamma's. And anyway, now that you're in Naples and you know more about doctors, you take care of her, don't leave it all on my shoulders. Enough for you to give her a bit of attention and she'll be healthy again."

I tried to control myself, I didn't want to quarrel. Why was she talking to me like that? Had I, too, changed for the worse, like her? Were our good times as sisters over? Or was Elisa, the youngest of the family, the outward sign that the life of the neighborhood was even more ruinous than in the past? I told the children, who sat obediently, in silence, but disappointed that their aunt paid them not the slightest attention, that they could finish the candies from their grandmother. Then I asked my sister:

"How are things with Marcello?"

"Very good, how should they be? If it weren't for all the worries he's had since his mother died, we'd really be happy."

"What worries?"

"Worries, Lenù, worries. Go think about your books, life is something else."

"Peppe and Gianni?"

"They work."

"I never see them."

"Your fault that you never come around."

"I'll come more often now."

"Good for you. Then try to talk to your friend Lina, too."

"What's happening?"

"Nothing. But among Marcello's many worries she's one."

"What do you mean?"

"Ask Lina, and if she answers, tell her that she'd better stay where she belongs."

I recognized the threatening reticence of the Solaras and I

realized that we would never regain our old intimacy. I told her that Lila and I had grown apart, but I had just heard from our mother that she had stopped working for Michele and had set up on her own. Elisa muttered:

"Set up on her own with our money."

"Explain."

"What is there to explain, Lenù? She twists Michele around her finger. But not my Marcello."

33.

Elisa didn't invite us to lunch, either. Only when she led us to the door did she seem to become aware that she had been rude, and she said to Elsa: Come with your aunt. They disappeared for a few minutes, making Dede suffer; she clutched my hand in order not to feel neglected. When they reappeared Elsa had a serious expression but a cheerful gaze. My sister, who seemed worn out by being on her feet, closed the door as soon as we started down the stairs.

Once we were in the street the child showed us her aunt's secret gift: twenty thousand lire. Elisa had given her money the way, when we were small, certain relatives did who were scarcely better off than we were. But at that time the money was only in appearance a gift for us children: we were bound to hand it over to my mother, who spent it on necessities. Elisa, too, evidently, had wanted to give the money to me rather than to Elsa, but for another purpose. With that twenty thousand lire—the equivalent of three books in quality bindings—she meant to prove to me that Marcello loved her and she led a life of luxury.

I calmed the children, who were squabbling. Elsa had to be subjected to persistent questioning in order to admit that, according to their aunt's wishes, the money should be divided, ten thousand to her and ten thousand to Dede. They were still wrangling and tugging at each other when I heard someone calling me. It was Carmen, bundled up in a blue gas-station attendant's smock. Distracted, I hadn't taken a detour around the gas pump. Now she was making signs of greeting, her hair curly and black, her face broad.

It was hard to resist. Carmen closed the pump, wanted to take us to her house for lunch. Her husband, whom I had never met, arrived. He had gone to get the children at school: two boys, one the same age as Elsa, the other a year younger. He turned out to be a gentle, very cordial man. He set the table, getting the children to help him, he cleared, he washed the dishes. Until that moment I had never seen a couple of my generation get along so well, so obviously content to live together. Finally I felt welcomed, and I saw that my daughters, too, were at ease: they ate heartily, with maternal tones they devoted themselves to the two boys. In other words I felt reassured, I had a couple of hours of tranquility. Then Roberto hurried out to reopen the pump, and Carmen and I were alone.

She was discreet, she didn't ask about Nino, if I had moved to Naples to live with him, even though she seemed to know everything. Instead she talked about her husband, a hard worker, and attached to the family. Lenù, she said, amid so much suffering he and the children are the only consolation. She recalled the past: the terrible story of her father, the sacrifices of her mother and her mother's death, the period when she worked in Stefano Carracci's grocery store, and then when Ada replaced Lila and had tortured her. We even laughed a little about the time when she was Enzo's girlfriend: What nonsense, she said. She didn't mention Pasquale even once; I had to ask. But she stared at the floor, shook her head, jumped up as if to push away something she wouldn't or couldn't tell me.

"I'm going to call Lina," she said. "If she knows we saw each other and I didn't tell her she'll never speak to me again."

"Forget it, she'll be working."

"Come on, she's the boss now and she does as she likes."

I tried to keep her talking, and asked her cautiously about the relations between Lila and the Solaras. But she was embarrassed, she answered that she didn't know much about it and went to call. I heard her announcing excitedly that my daughters and I were in her house. When she returned she said: "She's very pleased, she'll be right over."

From that moment I began to get nervous. And yet I felt well disposed, it was comfortable in that modest, respectable house, the four children playing in the other room. The bell rang, Carmen went to the door, there was Lila's voice.

34.

I didn't notice Gennaro at first, nor did I see Enzo. They became visible only after a long series of seconds in which I heard only Lila and felt an unexpected sense of guilt. Maybe it seemed wrong that it was she, yet again, who was eager to see me, while I insisted on keeping her outside of my life. Or maybe it seemed to me rude that she continued to be interested in me, while I, by my silence, by my absence, intended to signal to her that she no longer interested me. I don't know. Certainly as she hugged me I thought: if she doesn't attack me with spiteful talk about Nino, if she pretends not to know about his new child, if she is nice to my daughters, I'll be polite, then we'll see.

So we sat down. We hadn't seen each other since the meeting in the bar on Via Duomo. It was Lila who spoke first. She pushed Gennaro forward—a large adolescent, his face marked by acne—and immediately began to complain about his scholastic performance. She said, but in an affectionate tone: he did well in elementary school, he did well in middle school, but this year they're failing him, he can't manage Latin and

Greek. I gave the boy a pat, I consoled him: you just have to practice, Gennà, come to me, I'll tutor you. And impulsively I decided to take the initiative, confronting what for me was the burning issue, I said: I moved to Naples a few days ago, things with Nino are resolved within the limits of the possible, everything's fine. Then, calmly, I called my daughters, and when they looked in I exclaimed, Here are the children, how do you find them, see how they've grown. There was confusion. Dede recognized Gennaro and happily pulled him after her with a seductive look, she nine and he nearly fifteen; Elsa in turn tugged at him, in order not to be outdone by her sister. I looked at them with motherly pride and was glad that Lila meanwhile said: You've done well to return to Naples, one should do what one feels like doing, the girls look really well, how pretty they are.

At that point I felt relieved. Enzo, making conversation, asked me about work. I boasted a little about the success of the last book, but I immediately understood that though people in the neighborhood had heard of my first book at the time and some had even read it, not even Enzo and Carmen, or Lila, knew about the second. So I circled around it in a self-mocking tone and then I asked about their activities, I said, laughing: I know you've gone from being workers to bosses. Lila made a face as if to disparage this, and turned to Enzo, who tried to explain in simple terms. He said that computers in recent years had evolved, he said that IBM had put machines on the market that were completely different from the earlier ones. As usual he got lost in technical details that bored me. He cited products, the System 34, the 5120, and explained that there were no longer either perforated cards or punch-card machines and checkers but a different programming language, BASIC, while the machines kept getting smaller, with less power for calculation and storage but much less costly. In the end I understood only that that new technology had been crucial for them; they had begun to study up and had decided that they could go out on their own. So they had started their own business, Basic Sight—*in English, because otherwise they don't take you seriously*—and of that business, with headquarters in the rooms of their house (*hardly bosses*), he, Enzo, was the majority partner and administrator, but the soul, the true soul—Enzo pointed to her with a gesture of pride—was Lila. Look at the logo, he said, she designed it.

I examined the logo, a swirl around a vertical line. I stared at it with sudden emotion, as a further manifestation of her ungovernable mind—I wondered how many I had missed. I felt a sudden longing for the good moments of our past. Lila learned, set aside, learned. She couldn't stop, she never retreated: the 34, the 5120, BASIC, Basic Sight, the logo. Lovely, I said, and I felt then the way I hadn't felt with my mother and my sister. They all seemed happy to have me among them again, and drew me generously into their lives. Enzo, as if to demonstrate that his ideas hadn't changed in spite of prosperity, began to relate in his dry manner what he saw when he went around to the factories: people were working in terrible conditions for practically nothing, and sometimes he was ashamed at having to transform the filth of exploitation into the tidiness of programming. Lila, for her part, said that to obtain that tidiness the bosses had been forced to show her all their dirt close up, and she spoke sarcastically about the duplicity, the tricks, the scams that were behind the façade of orderly accounts. Carmen was not to be outdone, she talked about gas, she exclaimed: Here, too, there's shit everywhere. And only at that point she mentioned her brother, citing all the right reasons that had led him to do wrong things. She recalled the neighborhood of our childhood and adolescence. She told the story—she had never told it before—of when she and Pasquale were children and their father listed point by point what the fascists, led by Don Achille, had done to him: the time he had been beaten up right at the entrance to the tunnel; the time they'd made him kiss the photograph of Mussolini but he had spit on it, and if they hadn't murdered him, if he hadn't disappeared like so many comrades—*there is no history of those whom the fascists killed and then "disappeared"*—it was only because he had the carpentry shop and was well known in the neighborhood, and if they had removed him from the face of the earth everyone would have noticed.

So the time passed. At a certain point there was such a strong feeling of friendship that they decided to give me real proof of it. Carmen consulted Enzo and Lila with a look, then she said warily: We can trust Lenuccia. When she saw that they agreed she said that they had recently seen Pasquale. He had appeared one night at Carmen's house, and she had called Lila, and Lila had hurried over with Enzo. Pasquale was well. He was clean, not a hair out of place, very well dressed, he looked like a surgeon. But they had found him sad. His ideas had remained the same, but he was incredibly sad. He had said that he would never surrender, that they would have to kill him. Before leaving he had looked in at his nephews as they slept: he didn't even know their names. Carmen here began to cry, but silently, so that her children wouldn't come in. We said, she first of all, she more than me, more than Lila (Lila was laconic, Enzo confined himself to nodding), that we didn't like Pasquale's choices, that we felt horror at the bloody disorder of Italy and the world, but that he knew the same essential things that we knew, and even if he had committed whatever terrible acts—among those you read about in the papers—and even if we were comfortable with our lives in information technology, Latin and Greek, books, gas, we would never reject him. None of those who loved him would do so.

The day ended there. There was only one last question, which I asked Lila and Enzo, because I was feeling at ease and had in mind what Elisa had said to me a little earlier. I asked:

And the Solaras? Enzo immediately stared at the floor. Lila shrugged, she said: The usual pieces of shit. Then she said sarcastically that Michele had gone mad: after his mother's death he had left Gigliola, he had thrown his wife and children out of the house on Posillipo and if they showed up there he beat them. The Solaras—she said, with a hint of gratification—are finished: imagine, Marcello goes around saying it's my fault that his brother is behaving like that. And here she narrowed her eyes, with an expression of satisfaction, as if what Marcello said were a compliment. Then she concluded: A lot of things have changed, Lenù, since you left; you should stay with us now; give me your phone number, we ought see each other as much as we can; and then I want to send you Gennaro, you have to see if you can help him.

She took a pen and got ready to write. I dictated the first two numbers right away, then I got confused, I had learned the number only a few days earlier and I couldn't remember it. When, however, it did come to mind precisely, I hesitated again, I was afraid she would come back and settle in my life; I dictated two more numbers, and got the other numbers wrong on purpose.

It was a good thing. Just as I was about to leave with the girls Lila asked me in front of everyone, including Dede and Elsa: "Will you have a child with Nino?"

35.

Of course not, I responded, and laughed in embarrassment. But on the street I had to explain, to Elsa especially—Dede was grimly silent—that I would not have other children, they were my children and that was that. And for two days I had a headache, I couldn't sleep. A few deliberately placed words and Lila had disrupted an encounter that had seemed to me pleasant. I said to myself: There's nothing to be done, she's incurable, she always knows how to complicate my existence. And I wasn't alluding only to the anxieties she had unleashed in Dede and Elsa. Lila had struck with precision a point in myself that I kept carefully hidden and which had to do with the urge for motherhood I'd noticed for the first time a dozen years ago, when I had held little Mirko, in Mariarosa's house. It had been a completely irrational impulse, a sort of command of love, which at the time had overwhelmed me. I had intuited even then that it was not a simple wish to have a child, I wanted a particular child, a child like Mirko, a child of Nino's. And in fact that yearning had not been alleviated by Pietro and the conception of Dede and Elsa. Rather, it had reemerged recently, when I saw Silvia's child and, especially, when Nino had told me that Eleonora was pregnant. Now, with increasing frequency, it rummaged around in me, and Lila, with her usual acute gaze, *had seen* it. It's her favorite game—I said to myself—she does it with Enzo, with Carmen, with Antonio, with Alfonso. She must have behaved the same way with Michele Solara, with Gigliola. She pretends to be a kind and affectionate person, but then she gives you a slight nudge, she moves you a tiny bit, and she ruins you. She wants to go back to acting like that with me, and with Nino, too. She had managed to bring out into the open a secret tremor that in general I tried to ignore, as one ignores the twitching of an eyelid.

For days, in the house on Via Tasso, alone and in company, I was constantly agitated by the question: *Will you have a child with Nino?* But now it wasn't Lila's question, I asked it of myself.

36.

After that, I returned often to the neighborhood, especially when Pietro came to stay with the girls. I walked to Piazza

Amedeo, I took the metro. Sometimes I stopped on the railroad bridge and looked down on the *stradone*, sometimes I just went through the tunnel and walked to the church. But more often I went to fight with my mother, insisting that she go to a doctor, and I involved my father, Peppe, Gianni in that battle. She was a stubborn woman, she got angry at her husband and sons as soon as they alluded to her health problems. With me, it was always the same, she cried: Shut up, you're the one who's killing me, and she threw me out, or locked herself in the bathroom.

Lila instead had what it takes, and everyone knew it; Michele, for example, had realized it long ago. So Elisa's aversion toward her was due not only to some disagreement with Marcello but to the fact that Lila had yet again broken off from the Solaras and, after using them, had done well. Basic Sight was earning her a growing reputation for innovation and for profit. It was no longer a matter of the brilliant person who since she was a child had had the capacity to take the disorder from your head and heart to give it back to you well organized or, if she couldn't stand you, to confuse your ideas and leave you depressed. Now she also embodied the possibility of learning a new job, a job that no one knew anything about but was lucrative. The business was going so well—people said—that Enzo was looking for a space for a proper office and not the makeshift one that he had installed between the kitchen and the bedroom. But who was Enzo, clever though he might be? Only a subordinate of Lila. It was she who moved things, who made and unmade. So, to exaggerate just slightly, the situation in the neighborhood seemed in a short time to have become the following: you learned either to be like Marcello and Michele or to be like Lila.

Of course, it might be that it was my obsession, but in that phase, at least, I seemed increasingly to see her in all the people who had been or were close to her. Once, for example, I ran into Stefano Carracci, much heavier, his complexion yellowish, shabbily dressed. There was absolutely nothing left of the young shopkeeper Lila had married, least of all his money. And yet from the little conversation we had it seemed to me that he used many of his wife's phrases. And Ada, too, who at that point had great respect for Lila and said nice things about her, because of the money she gave Stefano, seemed to imitate her gestures, maybe even her way of laughing.

Relatives and friends crowded around her in search of a job, making an effort to appear suitable. Ada herself was hired out of the blue at Basic Sight, she was to begin by answering the telephone, then maybe she would learn other things. Rino, too—who one bad day had quarreled with Marcello and left the supermarket—inserted himself into his sister's activity without even asking permission, boasting that he could learn in no time all there was to learn. But the most unexpected news for me—Nino told me one night, he had heard it from Marisa—was that even Alfonso had ended up at Basic Sight. Michele Solara, who continued to act in a crazy way, had closed the shop in Piazza dei Martiri for no reason and Alfonso was left without a job. As a result now he, too—and success-fully—was being retrained, thanks to Lila.

I could have found out more, and maybe I would have liked to, all I had to do was call her, stop by. But I never did. Once only I met her on the street and stopped reluctantly. She must have been offended that I had told her the wrong phone number, that I had offered to give lessons to her son and instead had disappeared, that she had done everything to reconcile with me and I had withdrawn. She said she was in a hurry, she asked in dialect:

"Are you still living on Via Tasso?"

"Yes."

"It's out of the way."

"It has a view of the sea."

"What's the sea, from up there? A bit of color. Better if

you're closer, that way you notice that there's filth, mud, piss, polluted water. But you who read and write books like to tell lies, not the truth."

I cut her short, I said:

"For now I'm there."

She cut me even shorter:

"One can always change. How many times do we say one thing and then do another? Take a place here."

I shook my head, I said goodbye. Was that what she wanted? To bring me back to the neighborhood?

37.

Then in my already complicated life two completely unexpected things happened at the same time. Nino's research institute was invited to New York for some important job and a tiny publishing house in Boston published my book. Those two events turned into a possible trip to the United States.

After endless hesitations, endless discussions, some quarrels, we decided to take that vacation. But I would have to leave Dede and Elsa for two weeks. Even under normal conditions I had a hard time making arrangements: I wrote for some journals, I did translations, I took part in debates in places large and small, I compiled notes for a new book, and to arrange for the children with all that hectic activity was always extremely difficult. In general I turned to Mirella, a student of Nino's, who was very reliable and didn't ask much, but if she wasn't available I left them with Antonella, a neighbor of around fifty, the competent mother of grown children. This time I tried to get Pietro to take them, but he said it was impossible just then to have them for so long. I examined the situation (I had no relationship with Adele, Mariarosa had left and no one knew where she was, my mother was weakened by her elusive illness, Elisa was increasingly hostile), and there didn't seem to be an acceptable solution. It was Pietro who finally said to me: Ask Lina, she left her son with you for months, she's in your debt. I had a hard time making up my mind. The more superficial part of me imagined that, although she had showed that in spite of her work obligations she was available, she would treat my daughters like fussy, demanding little dolls, she would torment them, or leave them to Gennaro; while a more hidden part, which perhaps upset me more than the first, considered her the only person I knew who would devote herself entirely to making them comfortable. It was the urgency of finding a solution that drove me to call her. To my tentative and evasive request she responded without hesitation, as usual surprising me:

"Your daughters are more than my daughters, bring them to me whenever you like and go do your things as long as you want."

Even though I had told her that I was going with Nino, she never mentioned him, not even when, with all kinds of cautions, I brought her the children. And so in May of 1980, consumed by misgivings and yet excited, I left for the United States. It was an extraordinary experience. I felt again that I had no limits, I was capable of flying over oceans, expanding over the entire world: an exhilarating delirium. Naturally the two weeks were very exhausting and very expensive. The women who had published my book had no money and even though they were generous I still spent a lot. As for Nino, he had trouble getting reimbursed even for his airplane ticket. Yet we were happy. I, at least, have never been so happy as in those days.

When we got back I was sure I was pregnant. Already before leaving for America I had had some suspicions, but I hadn't said anything to Nino and for the entire vacation I had savored the possibility in secret, with a heedless pleasure. But when I went to get my daughters I had no more doubts and, feeling so literally full of life, I was tempted to confide in Lila. As usual, however, I gave up on the idea, I thought: She'll say something unpleasant, she'll remind me that I claimed I didn't want another child. I was radiant and Lila, as if my happiness had infected her, greeted me with an air that was no less content, she exclaimed: How beautiful you look. I gave her the gifts I had brought for her, for Enzo, and for Gennaro. I told her in detail about the cities I had seen, the encounters I'd had. From the plane, I said, I saw a piece of the Atlantic Ocean through a hole in the clouds. The people are very friendly, they're not reserved the way they are in Germany, or arrogant, as in France. Even if you speak English badly they listen to you with attention and make an effort to understand. In the restaurants everybody shouts, more than in Naples. If you compare the skyscraper on Corso Novara with the ones in Boston or New York, you realize it's not a skyscraper. The streets are numbered, they don't have the names of people everyone's forgotten by now. I never mentioned Nino, I didn't say anything about him and his work, I acted as if I had gone by myself. She listened attentively, she asked questions I wasn't able to answer, and then she praised my daughters sincerely, she said she had got on very well with them. I was pleased, and again I was on the point of telling her that I was expecting a child. But Lila didn't give me time, she whispered seriously: Lucky you're back, Lenù, I've just had some good news and it makes me happy to tell you first of all. She, too, was pregnant.

38.

Lila had dedicated herself to the children body and soul. And it could not have been easy to wake them in time in the morning, get them washed and dressed, give them a solid but quick breakfast, take them to school in the Via Tasso neighborhood amid the morning chaos of the city, pick them up punctually in that same turmoil, bring them back to the neighborhood, feed them, supervise their homework, and keep up with her job, her domestic tasks. But, when I questioned Dede and Elsa closely, it became clear that she had managed very well. And now for them I was a more inadequate mother than ever. I didn't know how to make pasta with tomato sauce the way Aunt Lina did, I didn't know how to dry their hair and comb it with the skill and gentleness she had, I didn't know how to perform any task that Aunt Lina didn't approach with a superior sensitivity, except maybe singing certain songs that they loved and that she had admitted she didn't know. To this it should be added that, especially in Dede's eyes, that marvelous woman whom I didn't visit often enough (*Mamma, why don't we go see Aunt Lina, why don't you let us sleep at her house more, don't you have to go away anymore?*) had a specific quality that made her unequalled: she was the mother of Gennaro, whom my older daughter usually called Rino, and who seemed to her the most wonderful person of the male sex in the world.

At the moment I was hurt. My relations with the children were not wonderful and their idealization of Lila made things worse. Once, at yet another criticism of me, I lost my patience, I yelled: O.K., go to the market of mothers and buy another one. That market was a game of ours that generally served to alleviate conflicts and reconcile us. I would say: Sell me at the market of mothers if I'm no good for you; and they would answer, no, Mamma, we don't want to sell you, we like you the way you are. On that occasion, however, maybe because of my harsh tone, Dede answered: Yes, let's go right now, we can sell you and buy Aunt Lina.

That was the atmosphere for a while. And certainly it wasn't the best one for telling the children that I had lied to them. My emotional state was complicated: shameless, shy, happy, anxious, innocent, guilty. And I didn't know where to begin, the conversation was difficult: children, I thought I didn't want another child, but I did, and in fact I'm pregnant, you'll have a little brother or maybe another sister, but the father isn't your father, the father is Nino, who already has a wife and two children, and I don't know how he'll take it. I thought about it, thought about it again, and put it off.

Then out of the blue came a conversation that surprised me. Dede, in front of Elsa, who listened in some alarm, said in the tone she took when she wanted to explain a problem full of perils:

"You know that Aunt Lina sleeps with Enzo, but they're not married?"

"Who told you?"

"Rino. Enzo isn't his father."

"Rino told you that, too?"

"Yes. So I asked Aunt Lina and she explained to me."

"What did she explain?"

She was tense. She observed me to see if she was making me angry.

"Shall I tell you?"

"Yes."

"Aunt Lina has a husband just as you do, and that husband is Rino's father, his name is Stefano Carracci. Then she has Enzo, Enzo Scanno, who sleeps with her. And the exact same thing happens with you: you have Papa, whose name is Airota, but you sleep with Nino, whose name is Sarratore."

I smiled to reassure her.

"How did you ever learn all those surnames?"

"Aunt Lina talked to us about it, she said that they're stupid. Rino came out of her stomach, he lives with her, but he's called Carracci like his father. We came out of your stomach, we live much more with you than with Papa, but we're called Airota."

"So?"

"Mamma, if someone talks about Aunt Lina's stomach he doesn't say this is Stefano Carracci's stomach, he says this is Lina Cerullo's stomach. The same goes for you: your stomach is Elena Greco's stomach, not Pietro Airota's."

"And what does that mean?"

"That it would be more correct for Rino to be called Rino Cerullo and us Dede and Elsa Greco."

"Is that your idea?"

"No, Aunt Lina's."

"What do you think?"

"I think the same thing."

"Yes?"

"Yes, absolutely."

But Elsa, since the atmosphere seemed favorable, tugged at me and intervened:

"It's not true, Mamma. She said that when she gets married she'll be called Dede Carracci."

Dede exclaimed furiously: "Shut up, you're a liar."

I turned to Elsa:

"Why Dede Carracci?"

"Because she wants to marry Rino."

I asked Dede:

"You like Rino?"

"Yes," she said in an argumentative tone, "and even if we don't get married I'll sleep with him just the same."

"With Rino?"

"Yes. Like Aunt Lina with Enzo. And also like you with Nino."

"Can she do that, Mamma?" Elsa asked, dubiously.

I didn't answer, I was evasive. But that exchange improved my mood and initiated a new phase. It didn't take much, in fact, to recognize that with this and other conversations about real and pretend fathers, about old and new last names, Lila

had managed to make the living situation into which I had cast
Dede and Elsa not only acceptable in their eyes but even inter-
esting. In fact almost miraculously my daughters stopped talking about how they missed Adele and Mariarosa; they stopped
saying, when they returned from Florence, that they wanted to
go and stay forever with their father and Doriana; they stopped
making trouble for Mirella, the babysitter, as if she were their
worst enemy; they stopped rejecting Naples, the school, the
teachers, their classmates, and, above all, the fact that Nino
slept in my bed. In short, they seemed more serene. And I
noted those changes with relief. However vexing it might be
that Lila had entered the lives of my daughters, binding them
to her, the last thing I could accuse her of was not having given
them the utmost affection, the utmost care, assistance in reduc-
ing their anxieties. That was the Lila I loved. She could emerge
unexpectedly from within her very meanness, surprising me.
Suddenly every offense faded—*she's malicious, she always has
been, but she's also much more, you have to put up with her*—
and I acknowledged that she was helping me do less harm to
my daughters.

One morning I woke up and thought of her without hostility for the first time in a long while. I remembered when she
got married, her first pregnancy: she was sixteen, only seven or
eight years older than Dede. My daughter would soon be the
age of the ghosts of our girlhood. I found it inconceivable that
in a relatively small amount of time, my daughter could wear a
wedding dress, as Lila had, end up brutalized in a man's bed,
lock herself into the role of Signora Carracci; I found it equally
inconceivable that, as had happened to me, she could lie under
the heavy body of a grown man, at night, on the Maronti,
smeared with dark sand, damp air, and bodily fluids, just for
revenge. I remembered the thousands of odious things we had
gone through and I let the solidarity regain force. What a waste
it would be, I said to myself, to ruin our story by leaving too

much space for ill feelings: ill feelings are inevitable, but the essential thing is to keep them in check. I grew close to Lila again with the excuse that the children liked seeing her. Our pregnancies did the rest.

39.

But we were two very different pregnant women. My body reacted with eager acceptance, hers with reluctance. And yet from the beginning Lila emphasized that she had *wanted* that pregnancy, she said, laughing: I planned it. Yet there was something in her body that, as usual, put up resistance. Thus while I immediately felt as if a sort of rose-colored light flickered inside me, she became greenish, the whites of her eyes turned yellow, she detested certain smells, she threw up continuously. What should I do, she said, I'm happy, but that thing in my belly isn't, it's mad at me. Enzo denied it, he said: Come on, he's happier than anyone. And according to Lila, who made fun of him, he meant: I put it in there, trust me, I saw that it's good and you mustn't worry.

When I ran into Enzo I felt more liking for him than usual, more admiration. It was as if to his old pride a new one had been added, which was manifested in a vastly increased desire to work and, at the same time, in a vigilance at home, in the office, on the street, all aimed at defending his companion from physical and metaphysical dangers and anticipating her every desire. He took on the task of giving Stefano the news; he didn't blink, he half grimaced and withdrew, maybe because by now the old grocery made almost nothing and the subsidies he got from his ex-wife were essential, maybe because every connection between him and Lila must have seemed to him a very old story, what did it matter to him if she was pregnant, he had other problems, other desires.

But, mainly, Enzo took on the job of telling Gennaro. Lila in fact had reasons to feel embarrassment with her son that were no different from mine—but certainly more justified—for feeling embarrassed with Dede and Elsa. Gennaro wasn't a child and childish tones and words couldn't be used with him. He was a boy in the full crisis of puberty who couldn't find an equilibrium. Failed twice in a row in high school, he had become hypersensitive, unable to hold back tears, or emerge from his humiliation. He spent days wandering the streets or in his father's grocery, sitting in a corner, picking at the pimples on his broad face and studying Stefano in every gesture and expression, without saying a word.

He'll take it really badly, Lila worried, but meanwhile she was afraid that someone else would tell him, Stefano for example. So one evening Enzo took him aside and told him about the pregnancy. Gennaro was impassive, Enzo urged him: Go hug your mother, let her know that you love her. The boy obeyed. But a few days later Elsa asked me in secret:

"Mamma, what's a tramp?"

"A beggar."

"You're sure?"

"Yes."

"Rino told Dede that Aunt Lina is a tramp."

Problems, in other words. I didn't talk to Lila about it, that seemed pointless. And then I had my own difficulties: I couldn't bring myself to tell Pietro, I couldn't tell the children, mainly I couldn't tell Nino. I was sure that when Pietro found out I was pregnant he would be resentful, even though he now had Doriana, and would turn to his parents, would induce his mother to make trouble for me in every way possible. I was sure that Dede and Elsa would become hostile again. But my real worry was Nino. I hoped that the birth of the child would bind him definitively to me. I hoped that Eleonora, once she found out about that new fatherhood, would leave him. But it was a feeble hope, usually fear predominated. Nino had told me clearly: he preferred that double life—even though it caused all sorts of problems, anxieties, tensions—to the trauma of an absolute break with his wife. I was afraid he would ask me to have an abortion. So every day I was on the point of telling him and every day I said to myself: No, better tomorrow.

Instead everything began to sort itself out. One night I telephoned Pietro and told him: I'm pregnant. There was a long silence, he cleared his throat, he said softly that he expected it. He asked:

"Have you told the children?"

"No."

"Do you want me to tell them?"

"No."

"Be careful."

"All right."

That was it. He began to call more often. His tone was affectionate, he was worried about how the girls would react, he offered every time to talk to them about it. But in the end it was neither of us. It was Lila, who, although she had refused to tell her own son, convinced Dede and Elsa that it would be a wonderful thing to occupy themselves, when the time came, with the funny live doll that I had made with Nino and not with their father. They took it well. Since Aunt Lina had called it a doll, they began to use the same word. They were interested in my stomach, and every morning when they woke up they asked, Mamma, how's the doll?

Between telling Pietro and telling the girls, I finally confronted Nino. It went like this. One afternoon when I felt especially anxious I went to see Lila to complain, and asked her:

"What if he wants me to have an abortion?"

"Well," she said, "then everything becomes perfectly clear."

"What's clear?"

"That his wife and children come first, then you."

Direct, brutal. Lila hid many things from me, but not her aversion to my union. I wasn't sorry, in fact I knew that it did me good to speak explicitly. In the end she had said what I didn't dare say to myself, that Nino's reaction would provide proof of the solidity of our bond. I muttered something like: It's possible, we'll see. When, soon afterward, Carmen arrived with her children, and Lila drew her, too, into the conversation, the afternoon became like afternoons of our adolescence. We confided in each other, we plotted, we planned. Carmen got mad, she said that if Nino was opposed she was ready to go and speak to him in person. And she added: I don't understand how it's possible, Lenù, that a person at your level can let someone walk all over you. I tried to justify myself and to justify my companion. I said that his in-laws had helped and were helping him, that everything Nino and I could afford was possible only because, thanks to his wife's family, he had a good income. I admitted that, with what I got from my books and from Pietro, the girls and I would have a hard time scraping by in a respectable way. And I added: Don't get the wrong idea, though, Nino is very affectionate, he sleeps at my house at least four times a week, he has always avoided humiliating me in any way, when he can he takes care of Dede and Elsa as if they were his. But as soon as I stopped speaking Lila almost ordered me: "Then tell him tonight."

I obeyed. I went home and when he arrived we had dinner, I put the children to bed, and finally I told him that I was pregnant. There was a very long moment, then he hugged me, kissed me, he was very happy. I whispered with relief: I've known for a while, but I was afraid you would be angry. He reproached me, and said something that amazed me: We have to go with Dede and Elsa to my parents and give them this good news, too—my mother will be pleased. He wanted in that way to sanction our union, he wanted to make his new paternity official. I gave a halfhearted sign of agreement, then I said:

"But you'll tell Eleonora?"

"It's none of her business."

"You're still her husband."

"It's pure form."

"You'll have to give your name to our child."

"I'll do it."

I became agitated.

"No, Nino, you won't do it, you'll pretend it's nothing, as you've done up to now."

"Aren't you happy with me?"

"I'm very happy."

"Do I neglect you?"

"No. But *I* left my husband, *I* came to live in Naples, *I* changed my life from top to bottom. *You* instead still have yours, and it's intact."

"My life is you, your children, this child who's about to arrive. The rest is a necessary background."

"Necessary to whom? To you? Certainly not to me."

He hugged me tight, he whispered:

"Have faith."

The next day I called Lila and said to her: Everything's fine, Nino was really happy.

40.

Complicated weeks followed; I often thought that if my body hadn't reacted with such delighted naturalness to pregnancy, if I had been in Lila's state of continuous physical suffering, I wouldn't have held up. My publisher, after much resistance, finally brought out Nino's collection of essays, and I—continuing to imitate Adele, in spite of our terrible relationship—took on the job of persuading both the few prominent people I knew to cover it in the newspapers, and the many, very many, he knew, but out of pride refused to telephone. Around at the same time, Pietro's book also was published, and he brought a copy to me himself when he came to Naples to see his daughters. He waited anxiously while I read the dedication (embarrassing: *to Elena, who taught me to love with suffering*), we were both excited, he invited me to a celebration in his honor in Florence. I had to go, if only to bring the children. But then I was forced to face not only the open hostility of my in-laws but also, before and after, Nino's agitation: he was jealous of every contact with Pietro, angry about the dedication, surly because I had said that my ex-husband's book was really good and was talked about with great respect within the academic world and outside it, unhappy because his volume was going completely unnoticed.

How exhausting our relationship was, and how many hazards were concealed in every gesture, in every sentence that I uttered, that he uttered. He didn't even want to hear Pietro's name, he darkened if I recalled Franco, he became jealous if I laughed too much with some friend of his, yet he found it completely normal to divide himself between me and his wife. A couple of times I ran into him on Via Filangieri with Eleonora and the two children: the first time they pretended not to see me, and kept going; the second I stopped in front of them with a warm smile, I said a few words referring to my pregnancy, even though it wasn't visible, I went off in a rage, with my heart pounding in my throat. When, later, he reproached me for what he called a needlessly provocative attitude, we quarreled (I *didn't tell her that you're the father: all I said was I'm pregnant*), I threw him out of the house, I welcomed him back.

At those moments I saw myself suddenly for what I was: a slave, willing to always do what he wanted, careful not to exaggerate in order not to get him in trouble, not to displease him.

I wasted my time cooking for him, washing the dirty clothes he left in the house, listening to all his troubles at the university and in the many responsibilities that he was accumulating, thanks to the aura of good feeling that surrounded him and the small powers of his father-in-law; I always welcomed him joyfully, I wanted him to be happier with me than in the other house, I wanted him to relax, to confide, I felt sorry that he was continuously overwhelmed by obligations; I even wondered if Eleonora might love him more than I did, since she accepted every insult just to feel that he was still hers. But sometimes I couldn't stand it anymore and I yelled at him, despite the risk that the girls might hear: Who am I for you, tell me why I'm in this city, why I wait for you every night, why I tolerate this situation.

He became frightened and begged me to calm down. It was probably to show me that I—I alone—was his wife, and Eleonora had no importance in his life, that he really wanted to take me to lunch one Sunday at his parents', in their house on Via Nazionale. I didn't know how to say no. The day passed slowly and the mood was one of affection. Lidia, Nino's mother, was an old woman, worn down by weariness; her eyes seemed terrified not by the external world but by a threat she felt from within. As for Pino, Clelia, and Ciro, whom I had known as children, they were adults, who studied, who worked, Clelia had recently gotten married. Soon Marisa and Alfonso arrived with their children, and the lunch began. There were innumerable courses, and it lasted from two in the afternoon until six at night, in an atmosphere of forced gaiety, but also of sincere feeling. Lidia, especially, treated me as if I were her real daughter-in-law, she wanted to keep me beside her, she complimented my daughters, and congratulated me for the child I carried in my womb.

Naturally the only source of tension was Donato. Seeing him after twenty years made an impression on me. He wore a dark blue smoking jacket, and on his feet brown slippers. He was as if shrunken and broadened, he kept waving his stubby hands, with their dark age spots and a blackish arc of dirt under the nails. His face seemed to have spread over the bones, his gaze was opaque. He covered his bald crown with his sparse hair, dyed a vaguely reddish color, and when he smiled the spaces where the teeth were missing showed. At first he tried to assume his former attitude of a man of the world, and he kept staring at my bosom, and made allusive remarks. Then he began to complain: Nothing is in its place, the Ten Commandments have been abolished, women, who can restrain them, it's all a whorehouse. But his children shut him up, ignored him, and he was silent. After lunch he drew Alfonso into a corner—so refined, so delicate, as good-looking in my eyes as Lila and more—to indulge his craving to be the center of attention. Every so often I looked, incredulous, at that old man, I thought: it's not possible that I, I as a girl, at the Maronti was with that foul man, it can't really have happened. Oh, my God, look at him: bald, slovenly, his obscene glances, next to my so deliberately feminine classmate, a young woman in male clothes. And I in the same room with him, so very different from the me of Ischia. What time is *now*, what time was *then*.

At a certain point Donato called me over, he said politely, Lenù. And Alfonso, too, insisted with a gesture, a look, that I join them. I went to their corner uneasily. Donato began to praise me loudly, as if he were speaking to a vast audience: This woman is a great scholar, a writer who has no equal anywhere in the world; I'm proud to have known her as a girl; at Ischia, when she came to vacation at our house she was a child, she discovered literature through her interest in my poor verses, she read my book before going to sleep:—isn't it true, Lenù?

He looked at me uncertainly, suddenly a supplicant. His eyes pleaded with me to confirm the role of his words in my literary vocation. And I said yes, it's true, as a girl I couldn't believe that I knew personally someone who had written a book of poetry and whose thoughts were printed in the newspaper. I thanked him for the review that a dozen years earlier he had given my first book, I said it had been very useful. And Donato turned red with joy, he took off, he began to celebrate himself and at the same time to complain that the envy of mediocrities had kept him from becoming known as he deserved. Nino had to intervene, and roughly. He brought me over to his mother again.

On the street he reproached me, saying: You know what my father's like, there's no need to encourage him. I nodded, and meanwhile I looked at him out of the corner of my eye. Would Nino lose his hair? Would he get fat? Would he utter rancorous words against those who had been more fortunate? He was so good-looking now, I didn't even want to think about it. He was saying of his father: he can't resign himself, the older he gets the worse he is.

41.

During that same period my sister, after endless anxieties and protests, gave birth. She had a boy whom she named Silvio, after Marcello's father. Since our mother was still not well I tried to help Elisa. She was white with exhaustion and terrified by the newborn. Seeing her son all smeared with blood and liquids had given her the impression of a small body in its death throes and she was disgusted. But Silvio was all too alive, he wailed desperately with clenched fists. And she didn't know how to hold him, how to bathe him, how to take care of the wound from the umbilical cord, how to cut his nails. Even the fact that he was a male repulsed her. I tried to instruct her, but it didn't last long. Marcello, always rather clumsy, treated me immediately with an apprehension beneath which I perceived annoyance, as if my presence in the house complicated his day. And Elisa, too, instead of being grateful, appeared annoyed by everything I said, by my very generosity. Every day I said to myself: that's it, I have so many things to do, tomorrow I won't go. But I kept going, until events decided for me. Terrible events. One morning when I was at my sister's house—it was very hot and the neighborhood was dozing in the burning-hot dust; several days earlier the station in Bologna had been blown up—a phone call came from Peppe: our mother had fainted in the bath. I hurried to her, she was in a cold sweat, trembling, she had an unbearable pain in her stomach. Finally I managed to make her see a doctor. Tests of various sorts followed and in a short time a serious illness was diagnosed, an evasive term that I learned to use immediately. The neighborhood resorted to it whenever the problem was cancer and the doctors did the same. They translated their diagnosis into a similar formula, maybe just a little more refined: the illness, rather than serious, was *inexorable*.

My father at that news immediately fell apart, he couldn't tolerate the situation, and became depressed. My brothers, their expressions vaguely dazed, their complexions pasty, hovered for a while with an air of wanting to help, and then, absorbed day and night by their mysterious jobs, disappeared, leaving money, which was needed for doctors and medicines. As for my sister, she stayed in her house, frightened, untidy, in her nightgown, ready to stick a nipple in Silvio's mouth if he merely hinted at a wail. Thus, in the fourth month of my pregnancy, the full weight of my mother's illness fell on me.

I wasn't sorry, I wanted my mother to understand, even if she had always tormented me, that I loved her. I became very active: I involved both Nino and Pietro, asking them to direct me to the best doctors; I took her to the various luminaries; I stayed with her in the hospital when she had an urgent operation, when she was discharged. I took care of everything once I brought her home.

The heat was unbearable, and I was constantly worried. While my stomach began to swell happily and in it grew a heart different from the one in my breast, I daily observed, with sorrow, my mother's decline. I was moved by her clinging to me in order not to get lost, the way I, a small child, had clung to her hand. The frailer and more frightened she became, the prouder I was of keeping her alive.

At first she was as ill-tempered as usual. Whatever I said, she always objected with rude refusals, there was nothing she didn't claim to be able to do without me. The doctor? She wanted to see him alone. The hospital? She wanted to go alone. The treatments? She wanted to take care of them alone. I don't need anything, she grumbled, get out, you only bother me. Yet she got angry if I was just a minute late (*Since you had other things to do it was pointless to tell me you were coming*); she insulted me if I wasn't ready to bring her immediately what she asked for and she would set off with her limping gait to show me that I was worse than Sleeping Beauty, that she was much more energetic than I (*There, there, who are you thinking about, your head's not there, Lenù, if I wait for you I'll get cold*); she criticized me fiercely for being polite to doctors and nurses, hissing, *If you don't spit in their faces, those pieces of shit don't give a damn about you, they only help if they're scared of you.* But meanwhile inside her something was changing. Often she was frightened by her own agitation. She moved as if she feared that the floor might open beneath her feet. Once when I surprised her in front of the mirror—she looked at herself often, with a curiosity she had never had—she asked me, in embarrassment, do you remember when I was young? Then, as if there were a connection, she insisted—returning to her old violence—that I swear I wouldn't take her to the hospital again, that I wouldn't let her die alone in a ward. Her eyes filled with tears.

What worried me most was that she became emotional

easily: she had never been that way. She was moved if I mentioned Dede, if she suspected that my father had no clean socks, if she spoke of Elisa struggling with her baby, if she looked at my growing stomach, if she remembered the countryside that had once extended all around the houses of the neighborhood. With the illness there came, in other words, a weakness she hadn't had before, and that weakness lessened her anxiety, transformed it into a capricious suffering that frequently brought tears to her eyes. One afternoon she burst out crying because she had thought of Maestra Oliviero, although she had always detested her. You remember, she said, how she insisted that you take the test for admission to middle school? And the tears poured down without restraint. Ma, I said, calm down, what's there to cry about? It shocked me seeing her so desperate for nothing, I wasn't used to it. She, too, shook her head, incredulous, she laughed and cried, she laughed to let me know that she didn't know what there was to cry about.

42.

It was this frailty that slowly opened the way to an intimacy we had never shared. At first she was ashamed of being ill. If my father or my brothers or Elisa and Silvio were present at a moment of weakness she hid in the bathroom, and when they urged her tactfully (*Ma, how do you feel, open the door*) she wouldn't open it, she answered inevitably: I'm fine, what do you want, why don't you leave me in peace in the bathroom, at least. With me, on the other hand, out of the blue, she let go, she decided to show me her sufferings unashamedly.

It began one morning, at her house, when she told me why she was lame. She did it spontaneously, with no preamble. The angel of death, she said proudly, touched me when I was a child, with the exact same illness as now, but I screwed him, even though I was just a girl. And you'll see, I'll screw him again, because I know how to suffer—I learned at the age of ten, I haven't stopped since—and if you know how to suffer the angel respects you, after a while he goes away. As she spoke she pulled up her dress and showed me the injured leg like the relic of an old battle. She smacked it, observing me with a fixed half-smile on her lips and terrified eyes.

From then on her periods of bitter silence diminished and those of uninhibited confidences increased. Sometimes she said embarrassing things. She revealed that she had never been with any man but my father. She revealed with coarse obscenities that my father was perfunctory, she couldn't remember if sleeping with him had ever truly given her pleasure. She revealed that she had always loved him and that she still did, but as a brother. She revealed that the only good thing in her life was the moment I came out of her belly, I, her first child. She revealed that the worst sin she had committed—a sin for which she would go to Hell—was that she had never felt attached to her other children, she had considered them a punishment, and still did so. She revealed finally, without circumlocutions, that her only true child was me. When she said this—I remember that we were at the hospital for an examination—her distress was such that she wept even more than usual. She whispered: I worried only about you, always, the others for me were stepchildren; so I deserve the disappointment you've given me, what a blow, Lenù, what a blow, you shouldn't have left Pietro, you shouldn't have gone with Sarratore's son, he's worse than the father, an honest man who is married, who has two children, doesn't take someone else's wife.

I defended Nino. I tried to reassure her, I told her that there was divorce now, that we would both get divorced and then would marry. She listened without interrupting me. She had almost completely used up the energy with which she once rebelled, and insisted on being right, and now she confined herself to shaking her head. She was skin and bones, pale, if she contradicted me she did it with the slow voice of despair.

"When? Where? Must I watch you become worse than me?"

"No, Ma, don't worry, I'll move forward."

"I don't believe it anymore, Lenù, you've come to a halt."

"You'll see, I'll make you happy, we'll all make you happy, my siblings and I."

"I abandoned your brothers and sister and I'm ashamed."

"It's not true. Elisa has everything she wants, and Peppe and Gianni work, have money, what more do you want?"

"I want to fix things. I gave all three of them to Marcello and I was wrong."

Like that, in a low voice. She was inconsolable, she sketched a picture that surprised me. Marcello is more criminal than Michele, she said, he pulled my children into the mud, he seems the better of the two but it's not true. He had changed Elisa, who now felt more Solara than Greco and was on his side in everything. She talked for hours, whispering, as if we were waiting our turn not in the ugly, crowded waiting room of one of the best hospitals in the city but in some place where Marcello lurked nearby. I tried to make light of it, to calm her, illness and old age were making her exaggerate. You worry too much, I said. She answered: I worry because I know and you don't, ask Lina if you don't believe me.

It was here, on the wave of those melancholy words describing how the neighborhood had changed for the worse (*We were better off when Don Achille Carracci was in charge*), that she began to talk about Lila with an even more marked approval than before. Lila was the only one capable of putting things in order in the neighborhood. Lila was capable of harnessing the good and, even more, the bad. Lila knew everything, even the most terrible acts, but she never condemned you, she understood that anyone can make a mistake, herself first of all, and so she helped you. Lila appeared to her as a kind of holy warrior who spread avenging light over the *stradone*, the gardens, amid the old buildings and the new.

As I listened it seemed to me that now I counted, in her eyes, only because of my relationship with the neighborhood's new authority. She described the friendship between me and Lila as a useful friendship, which I ought to cultivate forever, and I immediately understood why.

"Do me a favor," she said, "talk to her and to Enzo, see if they can take your brothers off the street, see if they can hire them."

I smiled at her, I smoothed a lock of gray hair. She claimed she had never taken care of her other children, meanwhile, bent over, hands trembling, nails white as she clutched my arm, she worried about them most of all. She wanted to take them away from the Solaras and give them to Lila. It was her way of remedying a tactical mistake in the war between the desire to do harm and the desire to do good in which she had been engaged forever. Lila, I observed, seemed to her the incarnation of the desire to do good.

"Mamma," I said, "I'll do everything you want, but Peppe and Gianni, even if Lina would take them—and I don't think she would, they'd need to study there—would never go to work for her, they earn more with the Solaras."

She nodded bleakly, but insisted:

"Try anyhow. You've been away and you're not well informed, but here everyone knows how Lina put down Michele. And now that she's pregnant, you'll see, she'll become stronger. The day she makes up her mind to, she'll crush both of the Solaras."

43.

The months of pregnancy passed quickly for me, in spite of my worries, and very slowly for Lila. We couldn't avoid noting that the feelings of expecting were very different for each of us. I said things like I'm *already* at the fourth month, she said things like I'm *only* at the fourth month. Of course, Lila's complexion soon improved, her features softened. But our bodies, although undergoing the same process of reproducing life, continued to experience the phases in different ways, mine with active collaboration, hers with dull resignation. And even the people we dealt with were surprised at how time hurried along for me and dragged for her.

I remember that one Sunday we were walking along Toledo with the children and we ran into Gigliola. That encounter was important; it was disturbing to me and proved that Lila really had had something to do with Michele Solara's crazy behavior. Gigliola was wearing heavy makeup but she was shabbily dressed, her hair was uncombed, she flaunted her uncontainable breasts and hips, her broad buttocks. She seemed happy to see us, she wouldn't let us go. She made a fuss over Dede and Elsa, she dragged us to Gambrinus, she ordered all sorts of things, both salty and sweet, and ate greedily. She soon forgot about my children, and they her: when she began to tell us in detail, in a very loud voice, about all the wrongs Michele had done to her, they got bored and, curious, went off to explore the restaurant.

Gigliola couldn't accept the way she had been treated. He's a beast, she said. He went so far as to shout at her: Don't just threaten to do it, kill yourself for real, jump off the balcony, die. Or he thought he could fix everything with no concern for her feelings, sticking in her bosom and in her pocket hundreds of thousands of lire. She was furious, she was desperate. She recounted—turning to me, because I had been away for a long time and wasn't up to date—that her husband had thrown her out of the house on Posillipo, kicking and hitting her, that he had sent her to live, with the children in the old neighborhood, in two dark rooms. But the moment she began to wish on Michele all the most atrocious diseases she could think of and a terrible death, she switched listeners, and addressed herself exclusively to Lila. I was amazed, she spoke to her as if she could help her make the curses effective, she considered her an ally. You did well, she said excitedly, to make him pay dearly for your work and then quit. In fact, even better if you screwed him out of some money. Lucky you, you know how to treat him, you have to keep making him bleed. She screamed: What he can't bear is that you don't care, he can't accept that the less you see him the better off you are, well done, well done, make him go nuts for good, make him die cursed.

At that point she drew a sigh of false relief. She remembered our two pregnant bellies, she wanted to touch them. She placed her broad hand almost on my pubic bone, she asked what month I was in. As soon as I said the fourth she exclaimed: No way you're already in the fourth. Of Lila, on the other hand, she said, suddenly unfriendly: There are women who never give birth, they want to keep the child inside forever, you're one of those. It was pointless to remind her that we were in the same month, that we would both give birth in January of the following year. She shook her head, she said to Lila: Just think, I was sure you'd already had it. And she added, with an incoherent note of pain: The more Michele sees you with that belly, the more he suffers; so make it last a long time, you can manage, stick it in front of him, let him drop dead. Then she announced that she had very urgent things to do, but meanwhile she repeated two or three times that we ought to see each other more often (*Let's reestablish the group from when we were girls, ah, how nice it was, we should have said fuck off to all those shits and thought only of ourselves*). She

didn't even wave goodbye to the children, who were now playing outside, and she went off after making some obscene
remarks to the waiter, laughing.

"She's an idiot," Lila said, sulkily. "What's wrong with my
stomach?"

"Nothing."

"And me?"

"Nothing, don't worry."

44.

It was true, nothing was wrong with Lila: nothing new. She
remained the same restless creature with an irresistible force of
attraction, and that force made her special. Every one of her
affairs, for better or for worse (how she was reacting to the
pregnancy, what she had done to Michele and how she had
subdued him, how she was asserting herself in the neighborhood), continued to seem to us more intense than ours, and it
was for that reason that time for her seemed to move slowly. I
saw her frequently, above all because my mother's illness
brought me to the neighborhood. But with a new sense of balance. Maybe because of my public persona, maybe because of
all my private troubles, I felt more mature than Lila by now,
and I was increasingly convinced that I could welcome her
back into my life, acknowledging her fascination without suffering from it.

In those months I rushed frantically here and there, but the
days flew by; paradoxically I felt light even when I crossed the
city to take my mother to a doctor's appointment in the hospital. If I didn't know what to do with the children I turned to
Carmen, or sometimes even Alfonso, who had telephoned me
often to tell me I could count on him. But naturally the person
in whom I had the most confidence, the one whom Dede and

Elsa went to most willingly, was Lila, although she was always burdened by work and exhausted by pregnancy. The differences between my belly and hers were increasing. I had a large, wide stomach, which seemed to expand sideways rather than forward; she had a small stomach, squeezed between narrow hips, sticking out like a ball that was about to tumble out of her lap.

As soon as I told Nino about my condition, he took me to a gynecologist who was the wife of a colleague, and since I liked the doctor—very skilled, very available, very different in manner and perhaps also in competence from the gruff doctors in Florence—I had told Lila about her enthusiastically and urged her to come with me at least once, to try. Now we went together for our examinations, and had arranged to see her at the same time: when it was my turn, she stood quietly in a corner, and when it was her turn, I held her hand, because doctors still made her nervous. But the best part was in the waiting room. In those moments I forgot about my mother's suffering and we became girls again. We liked sitting next to each other, I fair, she dark, I calm, she anxious, I likable, she malicious, the two of us opposite and united, and separate from the other pregnant women, whom we observed ironically.

It was a rare hour of joy. Once, thinking of the tiny creatures who were defining themselves in our bodies, I remembered when—sitting next to each other in the courtyard, as we were now in the waiting room—we played at being mothers with our dolls. Mine was called Tina, hers Nu. She had thrown Tina into the shadows of the cellar and I, out of spite, had done the same with Nu. Do you remember, I asked. She seemed bewildered, she had the faint smile of someone struggling to recapture a memory. Then, when I whispered to her, with a laugh, how fearful we were, how bold, climbing up to the door of the terrible Don Achille Carracci, the father of her future husband, and accusing him of the theft of our dolls, she began to find it funny, we laughed like idiots, disturbing the inhabited stomachs of the other patients, who were more sedate.

We stopped only when the nurse called us, Cerullo and Greco: we had both given the surnames we had had as girls. She was a large good-humored woman, who never failed to say to Lila, touching her stomach, There's a boy in here; and to me, Here's a girl. Then she showed us in and I whispered to Lila: I already have two girls, if you really have a boy will you give it to me: and she replied, Yes, let's do an exchange, no problem.

The doctor always found us in good health, the tests were excellent, everything was going smoothly. Or rather—since she focused her attention on our weight, and Lila remained as usual very thin while I tended to get fat—at every examination she judged that Lila was healthier than me. And although we both had many worries, on those occasions we were almost always happy to have found again, at the age of thirty-six, a pathway to affection: though distant in every way we were still close.

But when I went back up to Via Tasso and she hurried to the neighborhood, the gap that we put between us made other gaps conspicuous. This new solidarity was undoubtedly real. We liked being together, it lightened our lives. But there was one unequivocal fact: I told her almost everything about myself, she said almost nothing about herself. While I couldn't not tell her about my mother, or an article that I was writing, or problems with Dede and Elsa, or even about my situation as a lover-wife (it was enough not to specify the lover-wife of whom, not to utter the name of Nino too often; otherwise I could confide freely), when she talked about herself, her parents, her siblings, Rino, the anxieties Gennaro caused her, our friends and acquaintances, Enzo, Michele and Marcello Solara, the entire neighborhood, she was vague, she didn't seem to trust me completely. Evidently I remained the one who had gone away, and who, even though I had returned, now had another view, lived in upper-class Naples, could not be fully welcomed back.

45.

That I had a sort of double identity was true. Up on Via Tasso Nino brought me his educated friends, who treated me with respect, loved my second book in particular, wanted me to look at what they were working on. We talked late into the night with an attitude of worldliness. We wondered if there was still a proletariat or not, we alluded to the socialist left and, with bitterness, to the Communists (*They're more cops than the cops and the priests*), we argued about the governability of an increasingly depleted country, some boldly used drugs, we were sarcastic about a new illness that everyone thought was an exaggeration of Pope John Paul II's to block the free expression of sexuality in all its possible versions.

But I wasn't confined to Via Tasso; I moved around, I didn't want to be a prisoner of Naples. I often went to Florence with the children. Pietro, who had long since broken politically with his father, was now—unlike Nino, who was growing closer to the socialists—openly Communist. I stayed a few hours, listening to him in silence. He sang the praises of the competent honesty of his party, he cited the problems of the university, he informed me of the success his book was having among academics, especially the English and Americans. Then I set off again. I left the girls with him and Doriana and went to Milan, to the publisher, in particular to oppose the campaign of denigration in which Adele was persisting. My mother-in-law—the director himself had reported, one evening when he took me to dinner—did not miss any opportunity to say bad things about me and was labeling me with the reputation of a fickle and unreliable person. As a result I tried to be engaging with everyone I happened to meet at the publisher's. I made sophisticated conversation, I was agreeable to every request from the publicity department, I claimed to the editor that my new book was at a good point, even though I hadn't even started it. Then I set off again, stopped to get the children, and slipped into Naples, readjusting to the chaotic traffic, to the endless transactions to obtain each thing that was mine by right, to exhausting and quarrelsome lines, to the struggle to assert myself, to the permanent anxiety of going with my mother to doctors, hospitals, labs for tests. The result was that on Via Tasso and throughout Italy I felt like a woman with a small reputation, whereas in Naples, especially in the neighborhood, I lost my refinement, no one knew anything about my second book, if injustices enraged me I moved into dialect and the coarsest insults.

The only bond between high and low seemed to me blood. There was more and more killing, in the Veneto, in Lombardy, in Emilia, in Lazio, in Campania. I glanced at the newspaper in the morning and sometimes the neighborhood seemed more tranquil than the rest of Italy. It wasn't true, of course, the violence was the same. Men fought with each other, women were beaten, people were murdered for obscure reasons. Sometimes, even among the people I loved, the tension rose and tones became threatening. But I was treated with respect. Toward me there was the benevolence that is shown to a guest who is welcomed but mustn't stick her nose into matters she's not familiar with. And in fact I felt like an external observer, with inadequate information. I constantly had the impression that Carmen or Enzo or others knew much more than I did, that Lila told them secrets that she didn't reveal to me.

One afternoon I was with the children in the office of Basic Sight—three little rooms from whose windows you could see the entrance to our elementary school—and, knowing I was there, Carmen also stopped by. I alluded to Pasquale out of sympathy, out of affection, even though I imagined him now as a fighter on the run, ever more deeply involved in infamous crimes. I wanted to know if there was news, but it seemed to me that both Carmen and Lila stiffened, as if I had said something reckless. They didn't avoid it, on the contrary, we talked for a long time about him, or rather we let Carmen go on about her anxieties. But I had the impression that for some reason they had decided that they couldn't say more to me.

Two or three times I also ran into Antonio. Once he was with Lila, another, I think, with Lila, Carmen, and Enzo. It struck me how the friendship among them had solidified again, and it seemed surprising that he, a henchman of the Solaras, behaved as if he had changed masters, he seemed to be working for Lila and Enzo. Of course, we had all known each other since we were children, but I felt it wasn't a question of old habits. The four of them, on seeing me, behaved as if they had met by chance, and it wasn't true, I perceived a sort of secret pact that they didn't intend to extend to me. Did it have to do with Pasquale? With the operations of the business? With the Solaras? I don't know. Antonio said only, on one of those occasions, but absentmindedly: you're very pretty with that belly. Or at least that's the only remark of his that I remember.

Was it distrust? I don't think so. At times I thought that, because of my *respectable* identity, I had lost, especially in Lila's eyes, the capacity to understand and so she wanted to protect me from moves that I might in my ignorance misunderstand.

46.

Yet something wasn't right. It was a sensation of indeterminacy, which I felt even when everything appeared explicit and it seemed only one of Lila's old childish diversions: to orchestrate situations in which she let you perceive that under the facts there was something else.

One morning—again at Basic Sight—I exchanged a few words with Rino, whom I hadn't seen for many years. He seemed unrecognizable. He was thin, his eyes were dull, he greeted me with exaggerated affection, he even touched me as if I were made of rubber. He talked a lot of nonsense about computers, about the great business affairs he managed. Then suddenly he changed, he was seized by a kind of asthma attack, and for no evident reason he began, in a low voice, to rail against his sister. I said: Calm down, and wanted to get him a glass of water, but he stopped me in front of Lila's closed door and disappeared as if he were afraid that she would reprimand him.

I knocked and went in. I asked her warily if her brother was sick. She had an expression of irritation, she said: You know what he's like. I nodded yes, I thought of Elisa, I said that with siblings things aren't always straightforward. Meanwhile I thought of Peppe and Gianni, I said my mother was worried about them, she wanted to get them away from Marcello Solara and had asked me to see if she had any way of giving them a job. But those phrases—*get them away from Marcello Solara, give them a job*—made her narrow her eyes, she looked at me as if she wanted to know how far my knowledge when it came to meaning of the words I had uttered. Since she must have decided that I didn't know their real meaning, she said bitterly: I can't take them here, Lenù; Rino's already enough, not to mention the risks that Gennaro runs. At first I didn't know how to answer. *Gennaro, my brothers, hers, Marcello Solara.* I returned to the subject, but she retreated, she talked about other things.

That evasiveness happened later in the case of Alfonso, too. He now worked for Lila and Enzo, but not like Rino, who hung around there without a job. Alfonso had become very good, they sent him to the companies they consulted for to collect data. The bond between him and Lila, however, immediately seemed to me much stronger than anything to do with work. It wasn't the attraction-repulsion that Alfonso had confessed to me in the past but something more. There was on his part a need—I don't know how to put it—not to lose sight of her. It was a singular relationship, based on a secret flow that, moving from her, remodeled him. I was soon convinced that the closing of the shop in Piazza dei Martiri and the firing of Alfonso had to do with that flow. But if I tried to ask questions—what happened with Michele, how did you manage to get rid of him, why did he fire Alfonso—Lila gave a little laugh, she said: what can I say, Michele doesn't know what he wants, he closes, he opens, he creates, he destroys, and then he gets mad at everyone.

The laugh wasn't of mockery, of contentment, or of satisfaction. The laugh served to prevent me from insisting. One afternoon we went shopping on Via dei Mille and since that area had for years been Alfonso's domain, he offered to go with us, he had a friend with a shop that would suit us. People knew by now of his homosexuality. He continued formally to live with Marisa, but Carmen had confirmed to me that his children were Michele's, and she had whispered: Marisa is now Stefano's lover—yes, Stefano, Alfonso's brother, Lila's ex-husband, that was the new gossip. But—she added with explicit understanding—Alfonso doesn't give a damn, he and his wife lead separate lives and they get on. So I wasn't surprised that the shopkeeper friend—as Alfonso himself introduced him, smiling—was a homosexual. What surprised me instead was the game that Lila led him into.

We were trying on maternity clothes. We came out of the dressing rooms, looked at ourselves in the mirror, and Alfonso and his friend admired, recommended, recommended against, in a generally pleasant atmosphere. Then for no reason Lila began to get restless, scowling. She didn't like anything, she touched her pointy stomach, she was tired, she made remarks to Alfonso like: What are you saying, don't give me bad advice, would you wear a color like this?

I perceived in what was happening around me the usual

oscillation between the visible and the hidden. At a certain point Lila grabbed a beautiful dark dress and, as if the mirror in the shop were broken, said to her former brother-in-law: show me how it looks on *me*. She said those incongruous words as if they expressed a normal request, so that Alfonso didn't wait to be asked again, he grabbed the dress and shut himself up in the dressing room for a long time.

I continued to try on clothes. Lila looked at me absent-mindedly, the owner of the shop complimented every item I put on, and I waited in bewilderment for Alfonso to reappear. When he did I was speechless. My old desk mate, with his hair down, in the elegant dress, was a copy of Lila. His tendency to resemble her, which I had long noted, came abruptly into focus, and maybe at that moment he was even handsomer, more beautiful than she, a male-female of the type I had talked about in my book, ready, male and female, to set off on the road leading to the black Madonna of Montevergine.

He asked Lila with some anxiety: Do you like it, this way? And the shop owner applauded enthusiastically, he said conspiratorially: I know exactly who'd like you, you're beautiful. Allusions. Facts that I didn't know and they did. Lila had a malicious smile, she muttered: I want to give it to you. Nothing more. Alfonso accepted it happily but nothing else was said, as if Lila had commanded him and his friend, silently, that it was enough, I had seen and heard enough.

47.

That deliberate oscillation of hers between the obvious and the opaque struck me in a particularly painful way once—the only time—when things went badly at one of our appointments with the gynecologist. It was November and yet the city gave off heat as if summer had never ended. Lila felt sick on the way, and we sat in a café for a few minutes, then went, slightly alarmed, to the doctor. Lila explained to her in self-mocking tones that the now large thing she had inside was kicking her, pushing her, stifling her, disturbing her, weakening her. The gynecologist listened, amused, calmed her, said: You'll have a son like you, very lively, very imaginative. All good, then, very good. But before leaving I insisted with the doctor:

"You're sure everything's all right?"

"Very sure."

"What's the matter with me?" Lila protested.

"Nothing that has to do with your pregnancy."

"What does it have to do with?"

"With your head."

"What do you know about my head?"

"Your friend Nino was full of praise for it."

Nino? Friend? Silence.

When we left I had to struggle to persuade Lila not to change doctors. Before going off she said, in her fiercest tones: your lover is certainly not my friend, but in my view he's not your friend, either.

Here I was, then, driven forcefully into the heart of my problems: the unreliability of Nino. In the past Lila had showed me that she knew things about him I didn't know. Was she now suggesting that there were still other facts known to her and not to me? It was pointless to ask her to explain; she left, cutting short any conversation.

48.

Afterward I quarreled with Nino for his lack of tact, for the confidences that, although he denied it indignantly, he must surely have made to the wife of his colleague, for everything I kept inside me and that this time, too, in the end I stifled.

I didn't say to him: Lila considers you a traitorous liar. It was pointless, he would have started laughing. But the suspicion remained that that mention of his unreliability alluded to something concrete. It was a slow, reluctant suspicion, I myself had no intention of transforming it into some intolerable certainty. And yet it persisted. So one Sunday in November, I went first to my mother, then, around six, to Lila's house. My daughters were in Florence with their father, Nino was celebrating his father-in-law's birthday with his family (that was how I put it now: *your* family). I knew that Lila was alone; Enzo had had to go and see some relatives of his in Avellino and had taken Gennaro.

The creature in my womb was nervous, I blamed the heavy air. Lila, too, complained that the baby was moving too much, she said it was forever creating a choppy sea in her belly. To calm him she wanted to take a walk, but I had brought pastries; I made the coffee myself, I wanted to have a private conversation, in the intimacy of that bare house with windows onto the *stradone*.

I pretended I was in the mood for idle talk. I mentioned matters that interested me less—*Why does Marcello say you're the ruin of his brother, what did you do to Michele*—and in a tone partly of fun, as if they were just something to laugh about. I counted on slowly getting to the question that I really cared about: What do you know about Nino that I don't know.

Lila answered unwillingly. She sat down, she got up, she said her stomach felt as if she had swallowed liters of carbonated drinks, she complained about the smell of the cannoli, which she usually liked but which now seemed to her bad. Marcello—you know what he's like, she said, he's never forgotten what I did to him as a girl, and since he's a coward he doesn't say things to your face, he acts like a good person, harmless, but he spreads gossip. Then she took the tone she always had in that phase, affectionate and at the same time slightly teasing: But you're a lady, forget my troubles, tell me how your mother is. As usual she wanted me to talk about myself, but I didn't yield. Moving from my mother, from her worries about Elisa and my brothers, I led her back to the Solaras. She grumbled, she said sarcastically that men place such an enormous importance on fucking, she laughed: not Marcello—although even he doesn't joke—but Michele, who went crazy, he's been obsessed with me for a long time, and even runs after the shadow of my shadow. She repeated that expression allusively—*shadow of my shadow*—she said that was why Marcello was angry and threatened her, he couldn't bear the fact that she had put a leash on his brother and led him in directions that in his view were humiliating. She laughed again, she muttered: Marcello thinks he can scare me, but look, the only person who really knew how to scare people was his mother and you know how she ended up.

As she talked she kept touching her forehead, she complained of the heat, of the slight headache she'd had since the morning. I understood that she wanted to reassure me but also, in a contradictory manner, show me a little of what was there where she lived and worked every day, behind the façade of the houses, on the streets of the new neighborhood and the old one. Thus on the one hand she repeatedly denied the danger, on the other drew me a picture of spreading crime, extortion, assault, theft, usury, revenge followed by revenge. The secret red book that Manuela maintained and that after her death had passed to Michele was now controlled by Marcello, who was also taking away from his brother—out of distrust—the management of the legal and illegal trafficking, the political friendships. She said suddenly: Marcello has been bringing drugs to the neighborhood for several years, and I want to see where it's going to end up. A remark like that. She was very pale, fanning herself with the edge of her skirt.

Of all her allusions, only the one to drugs struck me, particularly because of her tone of disgust and disapproval. Drugs for me at that time meant Mariarosa's house, or, on certain evenings, the apartment on Via Tasso. I had never used drugs, apart from smoking once or twice, out of curiosity, but I wasn't outraged if others did, in the circles I had frequented and did frequent no one was outraged. So, to keep the conversation going, I stated an opinion, drawing on the days in Milan, and on Mariarosa, for whom taking drugs was one of many channels for individual well-being, a way of freeing oneself from taboos, a cultivated form of release. But Lila shook her head in opposition: What release, Lenù, the son of Signora Palmieri died two weeks ago, they found him in the gardens. And I perceived the irritation she felt at that word, *release*, at my way of saying it, assigning it a positive value. I stiffened, I ventured: He must have had some heart trouble. She answered, He had heroin trouble, and she quickly added: That's enough, I'm fed up, I don't want to spend Sunday talking about the revolting activities of the Solaras.

Yet she had done so, and more than usual. A long moment slipped by. Out of restlessness, out of weariness, out of choice—I don't know—Lila had slightly widened the net of her conversation, and I realized that even if she hadn't said much she had filled my head with new images. I had long known that Michele wanted her—wanted her in that abstractly obsessive way that was harmful to him—and it was clear that she had taken advantage of it by bringing him to his knees. But now she had evoked the *shadow of her shadow*, and with that expression had thrust before my eyes Alfonso, the Alfonso who posed as a reflection of her in a maternity dress in the store on Via dei Mille, and I had seen Michele, a dazzled Michele, lifting his dress, holding him tight. As for Marcello, in a flash drugs stopped being what they had seemed to me, a liberating game for wealthy people, and moved into the sticky theater of the

gardens beside the church, they had become a viper, a poison
that spread through the blood of my brothers, of Rino, perhaps
of Gennaro, and murdered, and brought money into the red
book once kept by Manuela Solara and now—having passed
from Michele to Marcello—by my sister, in her house. I felt all
the fascination of the way Lila governed the imagination of
others or set it free, at will, with just a few words: that speaking,
stopping, letting images and emotions go without adding anything else. I'm wrong, I said to myself in confusion, to write as
I've done until now, recording everything I know. I should
write the way she speaks, leave abysses, construct bridges and
not finish them, force the reader to establish the flow:
Marcello Solara who takes off quickly with my sister Elisa,
with Silvio, with Peppe, with Gianni, with Rino, with Gennaro,
with Michele enthralled by the shadow of the shadow of Lila;
suggest that they all slip inside the veins of Signora Palmieri's
son, a boy I don't even know and who now causes me pain,
veins far away from those of the people Nino brings to Via
Tasso, from Mariarosa's, from those of a friend of hers—I now
remembered—who was sick, and had to detox, and my sister-
in-law, too, wherever she is, I haven't heard from her for a long
time, some people are always saved and some perish.

I tried to expel images of voluptuous penetrations between
men, of needles in veins, of desire and death. I tried to resume
the conversation but something wasn't right, I felt the heat of
that late afternoon in my throat, I remember that my legs felt
heavy and my neck was sweaty. I looked at the clock on the
kitchen wall, it was just after seven-thirty. I discovered I no
longer felt like talking about Nino, like asking Lila, sitting
opposite me in a low yellowish light, what do you know about
him that I don't know. She knew a lot, too much, she could
make me imagine whatever she wanted and I would never be
able to erase the images from my mind. They had slept
together, they had studied together, she had helped him write

his articles, as I had done with the essays. For a moment jealousy and envy returned. They hurt me and I repressed them. Or probably what actually repressed them was a kind of thunder under the building, under the *stradone*, as if one of the trucks that were constantly passing had swerved in our direction, was descending rapidly underground with the engine at top speed, and running into our foundations, crashing and shattering everything.

49.

My breath was cut short, and for a fraction of a second I couldn't understand what was happening. The coffee cup trembled on the saucer, the leg of the table bumped my knee. I jumped up, and realized that Lila, too, was alarmed, she was trying to get up. The chair was tilting backward, she tried to grasp it, but slowly, bent over, one hand reaching in front of her, in my direction, the other extended toward the chair back, her eyes narrowing, the way they did when she concentrated before reacting. Meanwhile thunder rumbled beneath the building, a stormy underground wind lifted waves of a secret sea against the floor. I looked at the ceiling; the light was swaying, along with the pink glass cover.

Earthquake, I cried. The earth was moving, an invisible tempest exploding under my feet, shaking the room with the howl of a forest subdued by gusts of wind. The walls creaked, they appeared distended, they came unstuck and were pasted together again at the corners. A cloud of dust rained down from the ceiling, adding to the cloud that came out of the walls. I rushed toward the door, shouting again: earthquake. But the movement was mere intention, I couldn't take a step. My feet were like lead, everything was heavy, my head, my chest, above all my stomach. And yet the ground on which I wanted to step was receding: for a fraction of a second it was there and then immediately it subsided. I remembered Lila, I sought her with my gaze. The chair had finally fallen over, the ceiling light was swaying, the furniture—especially an old sideboard with its knickknacks, glasses, silverware, chinoiserie—vibrated along with the windowpanes, like weeds growing in the eaves, stirred by the breeze. Lila was standing in the middle of the room, leaning forward, head down, eyes narrowed, brow furrowed, her hands holding her stomach as if she were afraid that it would slip away from her and get lost in the cloud of plaster dust. The seconds slid by, but nothing appeared to want to return to order; I called to her. She didn't respond, she seemed solid, the only one of all the shapes impervious to jolts, tremors. She seemed to have erased every feeling: her ears didn't hear, her throat didn't inhale air, her mouth was locked, her eyelids canceled her gaze. She was a motionless organism, rigid, alive only in the hands that, fingers spread, gripped her stomach.

Lila, I called. I moved to grab her, drag her away, it was the most urgent thing to do. The lower part of me, the part I thought was exhausted but, instead, here it was reviving, suggested to me: maybe you should be like her, stand still, bend over to protect your infant, don't run away, think calmly. I struggled to make up my mind, to reach her was difficult, and yet it was just a step. Finally I seized her by the arm, I shook her, and she opened her eyes, which seemed white. The noise was unbearable, the whole city was making noise, Vesuvius, the streets, the sea, the old houses of the Tribunali and the Quartieri, the new ones of Posillipo. She wriggled free, she cried: Don't touch me. It was an angry shout, and shocked me even more than the long seconds of the earthquake. I realized that I was mistaken: Lila, always in control of everything, at that moment wasn't in control of anything. She was immobilized by horror, fearful that if I merely touched her she would break.

50.

I dragged her outside, tugging her violently, pushing, entreating. I was afraid the tremor that had paralyzed us would be followed immediately by another, more terrible, final, and that everything would collapse on top of us. I admonished her, I begged her, I reminded her that we had to rescue the creatures we carried in our wombs. So we flung ourselves into the wake of terrified cries, a growing clamor joined to frenzied movements—it seemed that the heart of the neighborhood, of the city, was about to burst. As soon as we reached the courtyard, Lila threw up; I fought the nausea that gripped my stomach.

The earthquake—the earthquake of November 23, 1980, with its infinite destruction—entered into our bones. It expelled the habit of stability and solidity, the confidence that every second would be identical to the next, the familiarity of sounds and gestures, the certainty of recognizing them. A sort of suspicion of every form of reassurance took over, a tendency to believe in every prediction of bad luck, an obsessive attention to signs of the brittleness of the world, and it was hard to take control again. Minutes and minutes and minutes that wouldn't end.

Outside was worse than inside, everything was moving and shouting, we were assaulted by rumors that multiplied the terror. Red flashes could be seen in the direction of the railroad. Vesuvius had reawakened. The sea was beating against Mergellina, the city hall, Chiatamone. The cemetery of the Pianto had sunk, along with the dead, Poggioreale had collapsed entirely. The prisoners were either under the ruins or had escaped and now were murdering people just for the hell of it. The tunnel that led to the Marina had collapsed, burying half the fleeing neighborhood. Fantasies fed on one another, and Lila, I saw, believed everything, she trembled as she clung to my arm. The city is dangerous, she whispered, we have to go, the houses are cracking, everything is falling on us, the sewers are spurting into the air, look how the rats are escaping. Since people were running to their cars and the streets were becoming congested, she began to pull me, she whispered, they're all going to the countryside, it's safer there. She wanted to run to her car, she wanted to get to an open space where only the sky, which seemed weightless, could fall on our heads. I couldn't calm her.

We reached the car, but Lila didn't have the keys. We had fled without taking anything, we had pulled the door shut behind us and, even if we had found the courage, we couldn't go back to the house. I seized one of the door handles with all my strength and pulled it, shook it, but Lila shrieked, she put her hands over her ears as if my action produced intolerable sounds and vibrations. Looking around, I saw a big rock that had fallen out of a wall, and used it to break a window. I'll get it fixed later, I said, now let's stay here, it will pass. We settled ourselves in the car, but nothing passed, we felt a continuous trembling of the earth. Beyond the dusty windshield, we watched the people of the neighborhood, who had gathered in small groups to talk. But when at last things seemed quiet someone ran by shouting, which caused a general stampede, and people slammed into our car with heart-stopping violence.

51.

I was afraid, yes, I was terrified. But to my great amazement I wasn't as frightened as Lila. In those seconds of the earthquake she had suddenly stripped off the woman she had been until a moment before—the one who was able to precisely calibrate thoughts, words, gestures, tactics, strategies—as if in that situation she considered her a useless suit of armor. Now she was someone else. She was the person I had glimpsed the time

Melina walked along the *stradone* eating soap; or the one of the night of New Year's Eve in 1958, when the fireworks war broke out between the Carraccis and the Solaras; or the one who had sent for me in San Giovanni a Teduccio, when she worked in Bruno Soccavo's factory and, thinking something was wrong with her heart, wanted to leave me Gennaro because she was sure she would die. But now that other person seemed to have emerged directly from the churning guts of the earth; she bore almost no resemblance to the friend who a few minutes before I had envied for her ability to choose words deliberately; there was no resemblance even in the features, disfigured by anguish.

I could never have undergone such an abrupt metamorphosis, my self-discipline was stable, the world existed around me, in a natural way, even in the most terrible moments. I knew that Dede and Elsa were with their father in Florence, and Florence was an elsewhere out of danger, which in itself calmed me. I hoped that the worst had passed, that no house in the neighborhood had collapsed, that Nino, my mother, my father, Elisa, my brothers were surely, like us, frightened, but surely, like us, alive. She, on the other hand, no, she couldn't think in that way. She writhed, she trembled, she caressed her stomach, she no longer seemed to believe in solid connections. For her Gennaro and Enzo had lost every connection with each other and with us, they were destroyed. She emitted a sort of death rattle, eyes wide, she clutched herself, held tight. And she repeated obsessively adjectives and nouns that were completely incongruous with the situation we were in, she uttered sentences without sense and yet she uttered them with conviction, tugging on me.

For a long time it was useless for me to point out people we knew, to open the window, wave my arms, call out to anchor her to names, to voices that would have their own stories of that terrible experience and so draw her into an orderly conversation. I pointed out Carmen with her husband and children, and others, hurrying, on foot, toward the station. I

pointed out Antonio with his wife and children, I was astonished at how handsome they all were, like characters in a film,
as they calmly got into a green van, which then left. I pointed
out to her the Carracci family and their relations, husbands,
wives, fathers, mothers, people living together, lovers—that is
to say Stefano, Ada, Melina, Maria, Pinuccia, Rino, Alfonso,
Marisa, and all their children—who appeared and disappeared
in the throng, shouting continuously for fear of losing each
other. I pointed out Marcello Solara's fancy car that was trying,
with a roar, to get free of the jam of vehicles; he had my sister
Elisa with her child next to him, and in the back seat the pale
shadows of my mother and father. I shouted names with the
window open, I tried to involve Lila, too. But she wouldn't
move. In fact, I realized that the people—especially those we
knew well—frightened her even more, especially if they were
agitated, if they were shouting, if they were running. She
squeezed my hand hard and closed her eyes when, against all
the rules, Marcello's car went up on the sidewalk honking and
made its way amid the people who were standing there talking,
or were hauling things along. She exclaimed: Oh Madonna, an
expression I had never heard her use. What's wrong, I asked.
Gasping for breath, she cried out that the car's boundaries
were dissolving, the boundaries of Marcello, too, at the wheel
were dissolving, the thing and the person were gushing out of
themselves, mixing liquid metal and flesh.

She used that term: *dissolving boundaries*. It was on that
occasion that she resorted to it for the first time; she struggled
to elucidate the meaning, she wanted me to understand what
the dissolution of boundaries meant and how much it frightened her. She was still holding my hand tight, breathing hard.
She said that the outlines of things and people were delicate,
that they broke like cotton thread. She whispered that for her
it had always been that way, an object lost its edges and poured
into another, into a solution of heterogeneous materials, a

merging and mixing. She exclaimed that she had always had to struggle to believe that life had firm boundaries, for she had known since she was a child that it was not like that—*it was absolutely not like that*—and so she couldn't trust in their resistance to being banged and bumped. Contrary to what she had been doing, she began to utter a profusion of overexcited sentences, sometimes kneading in the vocabulary of the dialect, sometimes drawing on the vast reading she had done as a girl. She muttered that she mustn't ever be distracted: if she became distracted real things, which, with their violent, painful contortions, terrified her, would gain the upper hand over the unreal ones, which, with their physical and moral solidity, pacified her; she would be plunged into a sticky, jumbled reality and would never again be able to give sensations clear outlines. A tactile emotion would melt into a visual one, a visual one would melt into an olfactory one, ah, what is the real world, Lenù, nothing, nothing, nothing about which one can say conclusively: it's like that. And so if she didn't stay alert, if she didn't pay attention to the boundaries, the waters would break through, a flood would rise, carrying everything off in clots of menstrual blood, in cancerous polyps, in bits of yellowish fiber.

52.

She spoke for a long time. It was the first and last time she tried to explain to me the feeling of the world she moved in. Up to now, she said—and here I summarize in my own words, of the present—I thought it was a matter of bad moments that came and then passed, like a childhood illness. Do you remember New Year's Eve of 1958, when the Solaras shot at us? The shots were the least frightening part. First, even before they started shooting, I was afraid that the colors of the fireworks were sharp—the green and the purple especially were razorlike—that they could butcher us, that the trails of the rockets were scraping my brother Rino like files, like rasps, and broke his flesh, caused another, disgusting brother to drip out of him, whom I had to put back inside right away—inside his usual form—or he would turn against me and hurt me. All my life I've done nothing, Lenù, but hold back moments like those. Marcello scared me and I protected myself with Stefano. Stefano scared me and I protected myself with Michele. Michele scared me and I protected myself with Nino. Nino scared me and I protected myself with Enzo. But what does that mean, protect, it's only a word. I could make you, now, a detailed list of all the coverings, large and small, that I constructed to keep myself hidden, and yet they were of no use to me. Do you remember how the night sky of Ischia horrified me? You all said how beautiful it is, but I couldn't. I smelled an odor of rotten eggs, eggs with a greenish-yellow yolk inside the white and inside the shell, a hard-boiled egg cracked open. I had in my mouth poisoned egg stars, their light had a white, gummy consistency, it stuck to your teeth, along with the gelatinous black of the sky, I crushed it with disgust, I tasted a crackling of grit. Am I clear? Am I making myself clear? And yet on Ischia I was happy, full of love. But it was no use, my head always finds a chink to peer through, beyond—above, beneath, on the side—where the fear is. In Bruno's factory, for example, the bones of the animals cracked in your fingers if you merely touched them, and a rancid marrow spilled out. I was so afraid that I thought I was sick. But was I sick? Did I really have a murmur in my heart? No. The only problem has always been the disquiet of my mind. I can't stop it, I always have to do, redo, cover, uncover, reinforce, and then suddenly undo, break. Take Alfonso, he's always made me nervous, ever since he was a boy, I've felt that the cotton thread that held him together was about to break. And Michele? Michele thought he was who knows what, and yet all I had to do was find his boundary line and pull, oh, oh, oh, I broke it, I broke his cotton thread and tangled it with Alfonso's, male material inside male material, the fabric that I weave by day is unraveled by night, the head finds a way. But it's not much use, the terror remains, it's always in the crack between one normal thing and the other. It's there waiting, I've always suspected it, and since yesterday evening I've known for certain: nothing lasts, Lenù, even here in my belly, you think the creature will endure but it won't. You remember when I married Stefano and I wanted the neighborhood to start again from the beginning, to be only beautiful things, the ugliness of before was not supposed to be there anymore. How long did it last? Good feelings are fragile, with me love doesn't last. Love for a man doesn't last, not even love for a child, it soon gets a hole in it. You look in the hole and you see the nebula of good intentions mixed up with the nebula of bad. Gennaro makes me feel guilty, this thing here in my belly is a responsibility that cuts me, scratches me. Loving courses together with hating, and I can't, I can't manage to solidify myself around any goodwill. Maestra Oliviero was right, I'm bad. I don't even know how to keep friendship alive. You're kind, Lenù, you've always had a lot of patience. But tonight I finally understood it: there is always a solvent that acts slowly, with a gentle heat, and undoes everything, even when there's no earthquake. So please, if I insult you, if I say ugly things to you, stop up your ears, I don't want to do it and yet I do. Please, please, don't leave me, or I'll fall in.

53.

Yes—I kept saying—all right, but now rest. I held her tight beside me, and finally she fell asleep. I stayed awake watching her, as she had once begged me to do. Every so often I felt new small aftershocks, someone in a car shouted with terror. Now the *stradone* was empty. The infant moved in my belly like rolling waters, I touched Lila's stomach, hers was moving, too. Everything was moving: the sea of fire under the crust of the earth, and the furnaces of the stars, and the planets, and the universes, and the light within the darkness and the silence in the cold. But, even now as I pondered the wave of Lila's distraught words, I felt that in me fear could not put down roots, and even the lava, the fiery stream of melting matter that I imagined inside the earthly globe, and the fear it provoked in me, settled in my mind in orderly sentences, in harmonious images, became a pavement of black stones like the streets of Naples, a pavement where I was always and no matter what the center. I gave myself weight, in other words, I knew how to do that, whatever happened. Everything that struck me—my studies, books, Franco, Pietro, the children, Nino, the earthquake— would pass, and I, whatever *I* among those I was accumulating, *I* would remain firm, I was the needle of the compass that stays fixed while the lead traces circles around it. Lila on the other hand—it seemed clear to me now, and it made me proud, it calmed me, touched me—struggled to feel stable. She couldn't, she didn't believe it. However much she had always dominated all of us and had imposed and was still imposing a way of being, on pain of her resentment and her fury, she perceived herself as a liquid and all her efforts were, in the end, directed only at containing herself. When, in spite of her defensive manipulation of persons and things, the liquid prevailed, Lila lost Lila, chaos seemed the only truth, and she—so active, so courageous—erased herself and, terrified, became nothing.

54.

The neighborhood emptied, the *stradone* became quiet, the air turned cold. In the buildings, transformed into dark rocks, there was not a single lamp lighted, no colorful glow of a television. I, too, fell asleep. I awoke with a start, it was still dark. Lila had left the car, the window on her side was half open. I opened mine, I looked around. The stopped cars were all inhabited, people coughed, groaned in their sleep. I didn't see Lila, I grew concerned, I went toward the tunnel. I found her not far from Carmen's gas pump. She was moving amid fragments of cornices and other debris, she looked up toward the windows of her house. Seeing me she had an expression of embarrassment. I wasn't well, she said, I'm sorry, I filled your head with nonsense, luckily we were together. There was the hint of an uneasy smile on her face, she said one of the many almost incomprehensible phrases of that night—*"Luckily" is a breath of perfume that comes out when you press the pump*—and she shivered. She still wasn't well, I persuaded her to return to the car. In a few minutes she fell asleep again.

As soon as it was day I woke her. She was calm, she wanted to apologize. She said softly, making light of it: You know I'm like that, every so often there's something that grabs me here in my chest. I said: It's nothing, there are periods of exhaustion, you're looking after too many things, and anyway it's been terrible for everyone, it wouldn't end. She shook her head: I know how I'm made.

We organized ourselves, we found a way of returning to her house. We made a great number of phone calls, but either they didn't go through or the phone rang in vain. Lila's parents didn't answer, the relatives in Avellino, who could have given us news of Enzo and Gennaro, didn't answer, no one answered at Nino's number, his friends didn't answer. I talked to Pietro, he had just found out about the earthquake. I asked him to keep the girls for a few days, long enough to be sure the danger had passed. But as the hours slid by, the dimensions of the disaster grew. We hadn't been frightened for nothing. Lila murmured as if to justify herself: You see, the earth was about to split in two.

We were dazed by emotions and by weariness, but still we walked through the neighborhood and through a sorrowing city, now silent, now streaked by the nagging sounds of sirens. We kept talking to alleviate anxiety: where was Nino, where was Enzo, where was Gennaro, how was my mother, where had Marcello Solara taken her, where were Lila's parents. I realized that she needed to return to the moments of the earthquake, and not so much to recount again its traumatic effects as to feel them as a new heart around which to restructure sensibility. I encouraged her every time, and it seemed to me that the more she regained control of herself the more evident became the destruction and death of entire towns of the South. Soon she began to speak of the terror without being ashamed and I was reassured. But something indefinable nevertheless remained: her more cautious steps, a hint of apprehension in her voice. The memory of the earthquake endured, Naples contained it. Only the heat was departing, like a foggy breath that rose from the body of the city and its slow, strident life.

We reached the house of Nino and Eleonora. I knocked for a long time, I called, no answer. Lila stood a hundred meters away, staring at me, her belly stretched, pointed, a sulky expression on her face. I talked to a man who came out of the entrance with two suitcases, he said that the whole building was deserted. I stayed another moment, unable to make up my mind to leave. I observed Lila's figure. I remembered what she had said and implied shortly before the earthquake, I had the impression that a legion of demons was pursuing her. She used Enzo, she used Pasquale, she used Antonio. She remodeled Alfonso. She subdued Michele Solara, leading him into a mad love for her, for him. And Michele was thrashing about to free himself, he fired Alfonso, he closed the shop in Piazza dei Martiri, but in vain. Lila humiliated him, continued to humiliate him, subjugating him. How much did she know now of the two brothers' business. She had set eyes on their affairs when she collected data for the computer, she even knew about the drug money. That's why Marcello hated her, that's why my sister Elisa hated her. Lila knew everything. She knew everything out of pure, simple fear of all that was living or dead. Who knows how many ugly facts she knew about Nino. She seemed to say to me from a distance: Forget him, we both know that he's safely with his family and doesn't give a damn about you.

55.

It turned out to be essentially true. Enzo and Gennaro returned to the neighborhood in the evening, worn-out, overwhelmed, looking like survivors of an atrocious war, with a single preoccupation: How was Lila. Nino, on the other hand, reappeared many days later, as if he'd come back from a vacation. I couldn't understand anything, he said, I took my children and fled.

His children. What a responsible father. And the one I carried in my belly?

He said in his confident voice that he had taken refuge with the children, Eleonora, his in-laws in a family villa in Minturno. I sulked. I kept him away for days, I didn't want to see him, I was worried about my parents. I heard from Marcello himself, who had returned alone to the neighborhood, that he had brought them to a safe place, with Elisa and Silvio, to a property he had in Gaeta. Another savior of *his* family.

Meanwhile I returned to Via Tasso, alone. It was very cold now, the apartment was freezing. I checked the walls one by one, there didn't seem to be any cracks. But at night I was afraid to fall asleep, I feared that the earthquake would return, and I was glad that Pietro and Doriana had agreed to keep the children for a while.

Then Christmas came; I couldn't help it, I made peace with

Nino. I went to Florence to get Dede and Elsa. Life began again but like a convalescence whose end I couldn't see. Now, every time I saw Lila, I felt on her part a mood of uncertainty, especially when she took an aggressive tone. She looked at me as if to say: You know what is behind my every word.

But did I really know? I crossed barricaded streets and passed by countless uninhabitable buildings, shored up by strong wooden beams. I often ended up in the havoc caused by the basest complicit inefficiency. And I thought of Lila, of how she immediately returned to work, to manipulate, motivate, deride, attack. I thought of the terror that in a few seconds had annihilated her, I saw the trace of that terror in her now habitual gesture of holding her hands around her stomach with the fingers spread. And I wondered apprehensively: who is she now, what can she become, how can she react? I said to her once, to underline that a bad moment had passed:

"The world has returned to its place."

She replied teasingly:

"What place?"

56.

In the last month of pregnancy everything became a struggle. Nino was hardly ever around: he had to work, and that exasperated me. When he did appear, he was rude. I thought: I'm ugly, he doesn't want me anymore. And it was true, by now I couldn't look at myself in the mirror without disgust. I had puffy cheeks and an enormous nose. My bosom and stomach seemed to have consumed the rest of my body, I saw myself without a neck, with short legs and fat ankles. I had become like my mother, but not the one of now, who was a thin, frightened old woman; rather, I resembled the venomous figure I had always feared, who now existed only in my memory.

That persecuting mother was unleashed. She began to act through me, venting because of the difficulties, the anxieties, the pain the dying mother was causing me with her frailties, the gaze of a person who is about to drown. I became intractable, every complication seemed like a plot, I often started shouting. I had the impression, in my moments of greatest unhappiness, that the chaos of Naples had settled even in my body, that I was losing the capacity to be nice, to be likable. Pietro called to talk to the children and I was brusque. The publisher called me, or some daily paper, and I protested, I said: I'm in my ninth month, I'm stressed, leave me alone.

With my daughters, too, I got worse. Not so much with Dede, since she resembled her father, and I was by now accustomed to her mixture of intelligence, affection, and harassing logic. It was Elsa who began to upset me. The meek little girl was becoming a being with blurry features, whose teacher did nothing but complain about her, calling her sly and violent, while I myself, in the house or on the street, constantly scolded her for picking fights, taking others' things and breaking them when she had to give them back. A fine trio of women we are, I said to myself, it's obvious that Nino is avoiding us, that he prefers Eleonora, Albertino, and Lidia. When I couldn't sleep at night because of the creature stirring in my womb, as if it were made of mobile air bubbles, I hoped against every prediction that the new baby would be a male, that he would resemble Nino, that he would please him, and that Nino would love him more than his other children.

But although I forced myself to return to the image I preferred of myself—I had always wanted to be an even-tempered person who wisely curbed petty or even violent feelings—in those final days I was unable to find an equilibrium. I blamed the earthquake, which at the time didn't seem to have disturbed me a great deal but perhaps remained deep inside, right in my belly. If I drove through the tunnel of Capodimonte I was gripped by panic, I was afraid that a new shock would make it collapse. If I took the Corso Malta viaduct, which vibrated anyway, I accelerated to escape the shock that might shatter it at any moment. In that phase I even stopped battling the ants, which often and willingly appeared in the bathroom: I preferred to let them live and every so often observe them; Alfonso claimed that they could anticipate disaster.

But it wasn't only the aftermath of the earthquake that upset me; Lila's fantastical hints also entered into it. I now looked on the streets for syringes like the ones I had absent-mindedly noticed in the days of Milan. And if I saw some in the gardens in the neighborhood a querulous mist rose around me, I wanted to go and confront Marcello and my brothers, even if it wasn't clear to me what arguments I would use. Thus I ended up doing and saying hateful things. To my mother, who harassed me, asking if I had talked to Lila about Peppe and Gianni, I responded rudely one day: Ma, Lina can't take them, she already has a brother who's a drug addict, and she's afraid for Gennaro, you can't all burden her with the problems you can't fix. She looked at me in horror, she had never alluded to drugs, I had said a word that shouldn't be said. But if in earlier times she would have started shouting in defense of my brothers and against my lack of sensitivity, now she shut herself in a dark corner of the kitchen and didn't breathe a word, so that I had to say, repentant: Don't worry, come on, we'll find a solution.

What solution? I made things even more complicated. I tracked down Peppe in the gardens—who knows where Gianni was—and made an angry speech about how terrible it was to earn money from the vices of others. I said: Go find any job but not this, you'll ruin yourself and make our mother die of worry. The whole time he was cleaning the nails of his right hand with the nail of his left thumb, and he listened to me uneasily, eyes lowered. He was three years younger than me and felt like the little brother in front of the big sister who was an important person. But that didn't keep him from saying to me, at the end, with a sneer: Without my money Mamma would already be dead. He went away with a faint wave of farewell. That answer got me even more upset. I let a day or two go by and went to see Elisa, hoping to find Marcello, too. It was very cold, the streets of the new neighborhood were as damaged and dirty as those of the old. Marcello wasn't there; the house was untidy; and I found my sister's slovenliness annoying: she hadn't washed or dressed, all she did was take care of her son. I almost scolded her: Tell your husband—and I stressed that word *husband* even though they weren't married—that he's ruining our brothers; if he has to sell drugs, let him do it himself. I expressed myself like that, in Italian, and she turned pale, she said: Lenù, leave my house immediately, who do you think you're talking to, all those fancy people you know? Get out, you're presumptuous, you always were. As soon as I tried to reply she shouted: Don't ever come here again acting like the professor about my Marcello: he's a good person, we owe everything to him; if I want to I can buy you, that whore Lina, and all the shits you admire so much.

57.

I got more and more involved in the neighborhood that, because of Lila, I had glimpsed, and realized only later that I was getting mixed up in activities that were difficult to sort out, and was violating among other things a rule I had made when I returned to Naples: not to be sucked back into the place where I was born. One afternoon when I had left the children with Mirella, I went to see my mother, and then, I don't know whether to soothe my agitation or to give vent to it, I went to Lila's office. Ada opened the door, cheerfully. Lila was closed in her room and arguing with a client, Enzo had gone with Rino to visit some business or other, and she felt it her duty to keep me company. She entertained me with talk about her daughter, Maria, on how big she was, how good she was in school. But then the telephone rang, she hurried to answer, calling to Alfonso: Lenuccia's here, come. With a certain embarrassment, my former schoolmate, more feminine than ever in his ways, in his hair, in the colors of his clothes, led me into a small bare space. There to my surprise I found Michele Solara.

I hadn't seen him for a long time, and an unease took possession of all three of us. Michele seemed very changed. He had gone gray, and his face was lined, although his body was still young and athletic. But the oddest thing was that he appeared to be embarrassed by my presence, and behaved in a completely uncharacteristic way. First of all he stood up when I entered. Then he was polite but said very little, his usual teasing patter had disappeared. He kept looking at Alfonso as if he were seeking help, then immediately looked away, as if merely looking at him could be compromising. And Alfonso was just as uncomfortable. He kept smoothing his long hair, he smacked his lips in search of something to say, and the conversation soon languished. The moments seemed fragile to me. I became nervous, but I didn't know why. Maybe it annoyed me that they were hiding—*from me*, no less, as if I couldn't understand; *from me,* who had frequented and did frequent circles more progressive than that little neighborhood room, who had written a book praised even abroad on how brittle sexual identities were. On the tip of my tongue was the wish to exclaim: If I've understood correctly, you are lovers. I didn't do it only out of fear of having mistaken Lila's hints. But certainly I couldn't bear the silence and I talked a lot, pushing the conversation in that direction.

I said to Michele:

"Gigliola told me you're separated."

"Yes."

"I'm also separated."

"I know, and I also know you you're with."

"You never liked Nino."

"No, but people have to do what they feel like, otherwise they get sick."

"Are you still in Posillipo?"

Alfonso interrupted enthusiastically:

"Yes, and the view is fabulous."

Michele looked at him with irritation, he said:

"I'm happy there."

I answered:

"People are never happy alone."

"Better alone than in bad company," he answered.

Alfonso must have perceived that I was looking for a chance to say something unpleasant to Michele and he tried to focus my attention on himself.

He exclaimed:

"And I am about to separate from Marisa." And he related in great detail certain quarrels with his wife on money matters. He never mentioned love, sex, or even her infidelities. Instead he continued to insist on the money, he spoke obscurely of Stefano and alluded only to the fact that Marisa had pushed out Ada (*Women take men away from other women without any scruples, in fact with great satisfaction*). His wife, in his words, seemed no more than an acquaintance whose doings could be talked about with irony. Think what a waltz, he said, laughing—Ada took Stefano from Lila and now Marisa is taking him away from her, hahaha.

I sat listening and slowly rediscovered—but as if I were dragging it up from a deep well—the old solidarity of the time when we sat at the same desk. Yet only then did I understand that even if I had never been aware that he was different, I was fond of him precisely because he wasn't like the other boys, precisely because of that peculiar alienation from the male

behaviors of the neighborhood. And now, as he spoke, I discovered that that bond endured. Michele, on the other hand,
annoyed me more than ever. He muttered some vulgarities
about Marisa, he was impatient with Alfonso's conversation, at
a certain point he interrupted in the middle of a sentence almost
angrily (Will you let me have a word with Lenuccia?) and asked
about my mother, he knew she was ill. Alfonso became suddenly
silent, blushing. I started talking about my mother, purposely
emphasizing how worried she was about my brothers. I said:
  "She's not happy that Peppe and Gianni work for your
brother."
  "What's the problem with Marcello?"
  "I don't know, you tell me. I heard that you don't get along
anymore."
  He looked at me almost in embarrassment.
  "You heard wrong. And anyway, if your mother doesn't like
Marcello's money, she can send them to work under someone
else."
  I was on the point of reproaching him for that *under*: my
brothers *under* Marcello, *under* him, *under* someone else: *my*
brothers, whom I hadn't helped with school and now, because
of me, they were *under*. Under? No human being should be
under, much less under the Solaras. I felt even more dissatis-
fied and had a desire to quarrel. But Lila came out.
  "Ah, what a crowd," she said, and turned to Michele: "You
need to talk to me?"
  "Yes."
  "Will it take long?"
  "Yes."
  "Then first I'll talk to Lenuccia."
  He nodded timidly. I got up, and, looking at Michele but touch-
ing Alfonso on the arm as if to push him toward Michele, said:
  "One of these nights you two must invite me to Posillipo,
I'm always alone. I can do the cooking."

Michele opened his mouth but no sound came out, Alfonso intervened anxiously:

"There's no need, I'm a good cook. If Michele invites us, I'll do everything."

Lila led me away.

She stayed in her room with me for a long time, we talked about this and that. She, too, was near the end of her term, but the pregnancy no longer seemed to weigh on her. She said, smiling, as she placed her hand in a cup shape under her stomach: Finally I've gotten used to it, I feel good, I'd almost keep the child inside forever. With a vanity that she had rarely displayed, she turned sideways to be admired. She was tall, and her slender figure had beautiful curves: the small bosom, the stomach, the back and the ankles. Enzo, she said, laughing, with a trace of vulgarity, likes me pregnant even more, how annoying that it'll end. I thought: the earthquake seemed so terrible to her that each moment now is uncertain, and she would like everything to stand still, even her pregnancy. Every so often I looked at the clock, but she wasn't worried that Michele was waiting; rather, she seemed to be wasting time with me on purpose.

"He's not here for work," she said when I reminded her that he was waiting, "he's pretending, he's looking for excuses."

"For what?"

"Excuses. But you stay out of it: either mind your own business, or these are matters you have to take seriously. Even that remark about dinner at Posillipo, maybe it would have been better if you hadn't said it."

I was embarrassed. I murmured that it was a time of constant tensions, I told her about the fight with Elisa and Peppe, I told her I intended to confront Marcello. She shook her head, she repeated:

"Those, too, are things you can't interfere in and then go back up to Via Tasso."

"I don't want my mother to die worrying about her sons."

"Comfort her."

"How."

She smiled.

"With lies. Lies are better than tranquilizers."

58.

But in those low-spirited days I couldn't lie even for a good cause. Only because Elisa reported to our mother that I had insulted her and as a result she wanted nothing more to do with me; only because Peppe and Gianni shouted at her that she must never dare send me to make speeches like a cop, I finally decided to tell her a lie. I told her that I had talked to Lila and Lila had promised to take care of Peppe and Gianni. But she perceived that I wasn't really convinced and she said grimly: Yes, well done, go home, go, you have children. I was angry at myself, and on the following days she was even more agitated, she grumbled that she wanted to die soon. But once when I took her to the hospital she seemed more confident.

"She telephoned me," she said in her hoarse, sorrowful voice.

"Who?"

"Lina."

I was speechless with surprise.

"What did she tell you?"

"That I can stop worrying, she'll take care of Peppe and Gianni."

"In what sense?"

"I don't know, but if she promised it means she'll find a solution."

"That's certainly true."

"I trust her, she knows what's right."

"Yes."

"Have you seen how pretty she looks?"

"Yes."

"She told me if she has a girl she'll call her Nunzia, like her mother."

"She'll have a boy."

"But if it's a girl she'll call her Nunzia," she repeated, and as she spoke she looked not at me but at the other suffering faces in the waiting room. I said:

"I am certainly going to have a girl, just look at this belly."

"So?"

I forced myself to promise her:

"Then I'll give her your name, don't worry."

"Sarratore's son will want to name her for his mother."

59.

I denied that Nino had a say in it, at that stage the mere mention of him made me angry. He had vanished, he always had something to do. But on the day I made that promise to my mother, in the evening, as I was having dinner with the children, he unexpectedly appeared. He was cheerful, he pretended not to notice that I was bitter. He ate with us, he put Dede and Elsa to bed with jokes and stories, he waited for them to fall asleep. His casual superficiality made my mood worse. He had dropped in now, but he would leave again and who could say for how long. What was he afraid of, that my labor would start while he was in the house, while he was sleeping with me? That he would have to take me to the clinic? That he would then have to say to Eleonora: I have to stay with Elena because she is bringing my child into the world?

The girls were asleep, he came back to the living room. He caressed me, he knelt in front of me, he kissed my stomach. It was a flash, Mirko came to mind: how old would he be now, maybe twelve.

"What do you hear about your son?" I asked without preamble.

He didn't understand, naturally, he thought I was talking about the child I had in my belly, and he smiled, disoriented. Then I explained, with pleasure breaking the promise I had long ago made to myself:

"I mean Silvia's child, Mirko. I've seen him, he's identical to you. But you? Did you acknowledge him? Have you ever had anything to do with him?"

He frowned, he got up.

"Sometimes I don't know what to do with you," he murmured.

"Do what? Explain."

"You're an intelligent woman, but every so often you become another person."

"What do you mean? Unreasonable? Stupid?"

He gave a small laugh and made a gesture as if to brush off an annoying insect.

"You pay too much attention to Lina."

"What does Lina have to do with it?"

"She ruins your head, your feelings, everything."

Those words made me lose my temper completely. I said to him:

"Tonight I want to sleep alone."

He didn't resist. With the expression of someone who in order to live peacefully gives in to a serious injustice he softly closed the door behind him.

Two hours later, as I was wandering around the house, with no desire to sleep, I felt small contractions, as if I had menstrual cramps. I called Pietro, I knew that he still spent the nights studying. I said: I'm about to give birth, come and get Dede and Elsa tomorrow. I had barely hung up when I felt a warm liquid drip down my legs. I grabbed a bag that I had long since packed with what I needed, then I kept my finger on the neighbors' doorbell until they answered. I had already made an arrangement with Antonella, and though she was half asleep she wasn't surprised. I said:

"The time has come, I'm leaving you the girls."

Suddenly my rage and all my anxieties disappeared.

60.

It was January 22, 1981, the day my third child was delivered. Of the first two experiences I didn't have a particularly painful memory, but this one was absolutely the easiest, so much so that I considered it a happy liberation. The gynecologist praised my self-control, she was happy that I hadn't caused her any problems. If only they were all like you, she said: You're made for bringing children into the world. She whispered: Nino is waiting outside, I've let him know.

The news pleased me, but I was even happier to discover that my resentments were gone. Delivering the child relieved me of the bitterness of the past month and I was glad, I felt capable again of a good nature that could take things less seriously. I welcomed the new arrival lovingly, she was a girl of seven pounds, purple, bald. I said to Nino, when I let him come in, after neatening myself to hide the evidence of the exertion: now we're four females, I'll understand if you leave me. I made no allusion to the quarrel we had had. He embraced me, kissed me, swore he couldn't do without me. He gave me a gold necklace with a pendant. I thought it was beautiful.

As soon as I felt better I called the neighbor. I learned that Pietro, diligent as usual, had arrived. I talked to him, he wanted to come to the clinic with the children. I had him put them on the phone, but they were distracted by the pleasure of being with their father, and answered in monosyllables. I told my ex-husband I would prefer that he take them to Florence for a few days. He was very affectionate, I would have liked to thank him for his care, tell him that I loved him. But I felt Nino's inquiring gaze and I gave up on the idea. Right afterward I called my parents. My father was cold, maybe out of timidity, maybe because my life seemed to him a disaster, maybe because he shared my brothers' resentment at my recent tendency to stick my nose in their business, when I had never let them meddle in mine. My mother wanted to see the child immediately, and I struggled to calm her down. Afterward I called Lila, she commented, amused: Things always go smoothly for you, for me nothing's moving yet. Maybe because she was busy with work she was brusque, she didn't mention a visit to the clinic. Everything normal, I thought, good-humoredly, and fell asleep.

When I woke I took it for granted that Nino had disappeared, but he was there. He talked for a long time with his friend the gynecologist, he asked about acknowledgment of paternity, he showed no anxiety about Eleonora's possible reaction. When I said I wanted to give the baby my mother's name he was pleased. And as soon as I recovered we went to a city clerk to officially register the child I had just delivered as Immacolata Sarratore.

Nino didn't appear uncomfortable on that occasion, either. I was the confused one, I said that I was married to Giovanni Sarratore, I corrected myself, I said *separated* from Pietro Airota, I came out with a disorderly pile of names, surnames, imprecise information. But the moment seemed lovely to me and I went back to believing that, to put my life in order, I needed only a little patience.

In those early days Nino neglected his endless duties and demonstrated in every possible way how important I was to him. He darkened only when he discovered that I didn't want to baptize the child.

"Children are baptized," he said.

"Are Albertino and Lidia baptized?"

"Of course."

Thus I learned that, in spite of the anti-religiousness that he often flaunted, baptism seemed necessary to him. There were moments of embarrassment. I had thought, ever since we were in high school, that he wasn't a believer, and he, on the other hand, said to me that, precisely because of the argument with the religion teacher in middle school, he was sure that I was a believer.

"Anyway," he said, bewildered, "believer or not, children are baptized."

"What sort of reasoning is that."

"It's not reasoning, it's feeling."

I assumed a playful tone.

"Let me be consistent," I said. "I didn't baptize Dede and Elsa, I won't baptize Immacolata. They'll decide themselves when they grow up."

He thought about it for a moment and burst out laughing: "Well, yes, who cares, it was an excuse for a celebration."

"Let's do it anyway."

I promised that I would organize something for all his friends. In those first hours of our daughter's life I observed him in every gesture, in the expressions of disappointment and those of approval. I felt happy and yet disoriented. Was it him? Was he the man I had always loved? Or a stranger I was forcing to assume a clear and definite character?

61.

None of my relatives, none of my friends from the neighborhood came to the clinic. Maybe—I thought, once I got home—I should have a little party for them, too. I had kept my origins so far from myself that, although I spent quite a bit of time in the neighborhood, I had never invited a single person who had to do with my childhood and adolescence to the apartment on Via Tasso. I regretted it, I felt that sharp separation as a residue of more fragile periods of my life, almost a sign of immaturity. I still had that thought in mind when the telephone rang. It was Lila.

"We're about to arrive."

"Who."

"Your mother and I."

It was a cold afternoon, Vesuvius had a dusting of snow on top, that visit seemed ill-timed.

"In this cold? Going out will make her ill."

"I told her but she won't listen."

"In a few days I'll have a party, I'll invite everyone, tell her she'll see the baby then."

"You tell her."

I gave up the discussion, but every idea of celebration left me, I felt that visit as an intrusion. I had only been home for a short time. With feeding, bathing, some sutures that bothered me, I was tired. And at that moment Nino was in the house. I didn't want my mother to be unhappy, and it made me uneasy that he and Lila should meet at a moment when I wasn't yet in shape. I tried to get rid of Nino, but he didn't seem to understand, in fact he seemed happy that my mother was coming, and stayed.

I went into the bathroom to fix myself up. When they knocked I rushed to open the door. I hadn't seen my mother for ten days. The contrast was violent between Lila, still carrying two lives, beautiful and energetic, and my mother, gripping her arm like a life preserver in a storm, more bent over than ever, at the end of her strength, close to sinking. I had her lean on me, I led her to a chair at the window. She murmured: how beautiful the bay is. And she stared past the balcony, maybe so as not to look at Nino. But he came over to her and in his winning way began to point out to her the foggy outlines between sea and sky: That's Ischia, there is Capri, come, you can see better here, lean on me. He never spoke to Lila, he didn't even greet her. I talked to her.

"You've recovered quickly," she said.

"I'm a little tired but I'm well."

"You insist on staying up here, it's hard to get here."

"But it's beautiful."

"Well."

"Come, let's go get the baby."

I took her into Immacolata's room.

"You already have your looks back," she praised me. "Your hair is so nice. And that necklace?"

"Nino gave it to me."

I picked the baby up from the cradle. Lila sniffed her, put her nose in her neck, said she smelled her scent as soon as she came into the house.

"What scent?"

"Of talcum powder, milk, disinfectant, newness."

"You like it?"

"Yes."

"I expected her to weigh more. Evidently only I was fat."

"Who knows what mine is like."

She spoke of him always in the masculine now.

"He'll be wonderful."

She nodded yes, but as if she hadn't heard, she was looking at the baby carefully. She ran a finger over her forehead, one ear. She repeated the pact we had jokingly made:

"If necessary we'll make an exchange."

I laughed, I brought the baby to my mother, who was leaning on Nino's arm, near the window. She was staring up at him with pleasure, she was smiling, it was as if she had forgotten herself and imagined that she was young.

"Here's Immacolata," I said.

She looked at Nino. He exclaimed quickly:
"It's a beautiful name."
My mother murmured:
"It's not true. But you can call her Imma, which is more modern."
She left Nino's arm, she gestured to me to give her her granddaughter. I did, but fearful that she didn't have the strength to hold her.
"*Madonna*, how beautiful you are," she whispered, and turned to Lila: "Do you like her?"
Lila was distracted, she was staring at my mother's feet.
"Yes," she said without taking her eyes off them. "But sit down."
I also looked where she was looking. Blood was dripping from under my mother's black dress.

62.

I snatched the infant with an instinctive jerk. My mother realized what was happening and I saw in her face disgust and shame. Nino grabbed her a moment before she fainted. Mamma, mamma, I called while he struck her lightly on one cheek with his fingertips. I was alarmed, she didn't regain consciousness, and meanwhile the baby began to wail. She'll die, I thought, terrified, she held out until the moment she saw Immacolata and then she let go. I kept repeating *Mamma* in a louder and louder voice.
"Call an ambulance," Lila said.
I went to the telephone, I stopped, confused, I wanted to give the baby to Nino. But he avoided me, he turned to Lila instead, he said that it would be quicker to take her to the hospital in the car. I felt my heart in my throat, the baby was crying, my mother regained consciousness and began to moan.

She whispered, weeping, that she didn't want to set foot in the hospital, she reminded me, pulling on my skirt, that she had been admitted once and didn't want to die in that abandonment. Trembling, she said: I want to see the baby grow up. Nino at that point assumed the firm tone he had had even as a student when he had to confront difficult situations. Let's go, he said and picked up my mother in his arms. Since she protested weakly he reassured her, he told her that he would take care of arranging everything. Lila looked at me perplexed, I thought: the professor who attends to my mother at the hospital is a friend of Eleonora's family, Nino at this moment is indispensable, lucky he's here. Lila said, leave me the baby, you go. I agreed, I was about to hand her Immacolata but with a hesitant gesture, I was connected to her as if she were still inside me. And, anyway, I couldn't separate myself now, I had to feed her, bathe her. But to my mother, too, I felt bound as never before, I was shaking, what was that blood, what did it mean.

"Come on," Nino said impatiently to Lila, "hurry up."

"Yes," I said, "go and let me know."

Only when the door closed did I feel the wound of that situation: Lila and Nino together were taking my mother away, they were taking care of her when it should have been me.

I felt weak and confused. I sat on the couch, giving my breast to Immacolata to soothe her. I couldn't take my eyes off the blood on the floor as I imagined the car speeding over the frozen streets of the city, the handkerchief outside the window signaling an emergency, the finger on the horn, my mother dying in the back seat. The car was Lila's, was she driving or had he gotten behind the wheel? I have to stay calm, I said to myself.

I placed the baby in the cradle, and decided to call Elisa. I minimized what had happened, I was silent about Nino, I mentioned Lila. My sister immediately lost her temper, burst out crying, insulted me. She shouted that I had sent our mother who knows where with a stranger, that I should have called an ambulance, that I thought only of my own affairs and convenience, that if our mother died I was responsible. Then I heard her calling Marcello repeatedly in a commanding tone unfamiliar to me, petulant yet anguished cries. I said to her: What does "who knows where" mean, Lina took her to the hospital, why must you speak like that. She slammed down the telephone.

But Elisa was right. I had lost my head. I really should have called an ambulance. Or torn the baby away and given her to Lila. I was subject to Nino's authority, to that craving of men to make a good impression by appearing determined, saviors. I waited by the telephone for them to call me.

An hour passed, an hour and a half, finally the phone rang. Lila said calmly:

"They admitted her. Nino knows the doctors, they told him it's all under control. Be calm."

"Is she alone?"

"Yes, they won't let anyone in."

"She doesn't want to die alone."

"She won't die."

"She's frightened, Lila, do something, she's not what she used to be."

"That's how the hospital works."

"Did she ask about me?"

"She said you should bring her the baby."

"What are you doing now?"

"Nino is still with the doctors, I'm going."

"Go, yes, thank you, don't get tired."

"He'll phone as soon as he can."

"O.K."

"And stay calm, otherwise your milk won't come."

That allusion to the milk helped me. I sat next to Immacolata's cradle as if her nearness could preserve my swollen breasts. What was the body of a woman: I had nourished my daughter in the womb, now that she was out she was nourished by my breast. I thought, there was a moment when I, too, had been in my mother's womb, had sucked at her breast. A breast as big as mine, or maybe even bigger. Until shortly before my mother got sick my father had often alluded obscenely to that bosom. I had never seen her without a bra, in any stage of her life. She had always concealed herself, she didn't trust her body because of the leg. Yet at the first glass of wine she would counter my father's obscenities with words just as coarse in which she boasted of her attractions, an exhibition of shamelessness that was pure show. The telephone rang again and I hurried to answer. It was Lila again, now she had a curt tone.

"There's trouble here, Lenù."

"Is she worse?"

"No, the doctors are confident. But Marcello showed up and he's acting crazy."

"Marcello? What does Marcello have to do with it?"

"I don't know."

"Let me talk to him."

"Wait, he's arguing with Nino."

I recognized in the background Marcello's thick voice, loaded with dialect, and Nino's, in good Italian, but strident, which happened when he lost his temper.

"Tell Nino to forget it, in fact send him away."

Lila didn't answer, I heard her join a discussion that I was ignorant of and then suddenly shout in dialect: What the fuck are you saying, Marcè, go fuck yourself, get out. Then she shouted at me: Talk to this shit, please, you two come to an agreement, I don't want to get involved. Distant voices. After a few seconds Marcello came to the phone. He said, trying to assume a polite tone, that Elisa had insisted that we not leave our mother in the hospital and that he had come to get her and

take her to a nice clinic in Capodimonte. He asked as if he seri-
ously sought my permission:
"Am I right? Tell me if I'm right."
"Calm down."
"I'm calm, Lenù. But you gave birth in a clinic, Elisa gave
birth in a clinic: why should your mother die here?"
I said uneasily:
"The doctors who are taking care of her work there."
He became aggressive as he had never been toward me:
"The doctors are where the money is. Who's in charge here,
you, Lina, or that shit?"
"It's not a question of being in charge."
"Yes, it is. Either tell your friends that I can take her to
Capodimonte or I'll break someone's face and take her all the
same."
"Give me Lina," I said.
I had trouble standing up, my temples were pounding. I
said: Ask Nino if my mother can be moved, make him talk to
the doctors, then call me back. I hung up wringing my hands,
I didn't know what to do.
A few minutes went by and the phone rang again. It was
Nino.
"Lenù, control that beast, otherwise I'll call the police."
"Did you ask the doctors if my mother can be moved?"
"No, she can't be moved."
"Nino, did you ask or not? She doesn't want to stay in the
hospital."
"Private clinics are even more disgusting."
"I know, but calm down."
"I'm perfectly calm."
"All right, but come home now."
"And here?"
"Lina will take care of it."
"I can't leave Lina with that guy."

I raised my voice:

"Lina can take care of herself. I can't stand up, the baby's crying, I have to bathe her. I told you, come home right now."

I hung up.

63.

Those were difficult hours. Nino arrived distraught, he was speaking in dialect, he was extremely nervous, he repeated: Now let's see who wins. I realized that my mother's admission to the hospital had become for him a question of principle. He was afraid that Solara really would take her to some unsuitable place, one of those which operate just to make money. In the hospital, he exclaimed, returning to Italian, your mother has high-level specialists available, professors who, in spite of the advanced stage of the illness, have so far kept her alive in a dignified way.

I shared his fears, and he took the matter to heart. Although it was dinnertime he telephoned important people, names well known in Naples at the time, I don't know if to complain or to gain support in a possible battle against Marcello's aggression. But I could hear that as soon as he uttered the name Solara the conversation became complicated, and he was silent, listening. He calmed down only around ten. I was in despair, but I tried not to let him see it, so that he wouldn't decide to go back to the hospital. My agitation spread to Immacolata. She wailed, I nursed her, she was quiet, she wailed again.

I didn't close my eyes. The telephone rang again at six in the morning, I rushed to answer hoping that neither the baby nor Nino would wake up. It was Lila, she had spent the night in the hospital. She gave me the report in a tired voice. Marcello had apparently given in, and had left without even saying goodbye to her. She had sneaked through stairways and corridors, had found the ward where they had brought my mother. It was a room of agony, there were five other suffering women, they groaned and cried, all abandoned to their suffering. She had found my mother, who, motionless, eyes staring, was whispering at the ceiling, *Madonna*, let me die soon, her whole body shaking with the effort of enduring the pain. Lila had squatted beside her, had calmed her. Now she had had to get out because it was day and the nurses were beginning to show up. She was pleased at how she had violated all the rules; she always enjoyed disobedience. But in that circumstance it seemed to me that she was pretending, in order not to make me feel the weight of the effort she had undertaken for me. She was close to giving birth, I imagined her exhausted, tortured by her own needs. I was worried about her at least as much as about my mother.

"How do you feel?"

"Fine."

"Sure?"

"Very sure."

"Go and sleep."

"Not until Marcello arrives with your sister."

"You're sure they'll be back?"

"As if they would give up making a scene."

While I was on the phone Nino appeared, sleepy. He listened for a while, then said:

"Let me speak to her."

I didn't hand him the phone, I muttered: She already hung up. He complained, he said he had mobilized a series of people to ensure that my mother would have the best care possible and he wanted to know if there had been any result of his interest. For now, no, I answered. We made a plan for him to take me to the hospital with the baby, even though there was a strong, cold wind. He would stay in the car with Immacolata and I would go to my mother between feedings. He said all right, and his helpfulness softened me toward him, then annoyed me, because he had taken care of everything except the practicality of noting the visiting hours. I called to find out, we carefully bundled up the baby, and went. Lila hadn't been heard from; I was sure we would find her in the hospital. But when we arrived we found that not only was she not there but neither was my mother. She had been discharged.

64.

I learned later from my sister what had happened. She told me as if she were saying: You give yourself a lot of airs, but without us you are no one. At exactly nine Marcello had arrived at the hospital with some head physician—he had taken the trouble himself to pick him up at home in the car. Our mother had been immediately transferred by ambulance to the Capodimonte clinic. There, Elisa said, she's like a queen, we relatives can stay as much as we want, there's a bed for Papa, who will keep her company at night. And she specified, contemptuously: Don't worry, we'll pay for it. What followed was explicitly threatening. Maybe your friend the professor, she said, doesn't understand who he's dealing with, you'd better explain it to him. And tell that shit Lina that she may be very intelligent, but Marcello has changed, Marcello isn't her little boyfriend from long ago, and he's not like Michele, whom she twists around her little finger: Marcello said that if she raises her voice again with me, if she insults me the way she did in front of everyone in the hospital, he'll kill her.

I didn't report anything to Lila and I didn't even want to know in what terms she had quarreled with my sister. But in the days that followed I became more affectionate, I telephoned often to let her know that I was grateful, that I loved her and couldn't wait until she, too, gave birth.

"Everything all right?" I asked.

"Yes."

"Nothing moving?"

"Of course not. Do you want help today?"

"No, tomorrow if you can."

The days were intense, with a complicated adding up of old restraints and new. My whole body was still in symbiosis with Imma's tiny organism, I couldn't separate from her. But I also missed Dede and Elsa, so I telephoned Pietro and he finally brought them back. Elsa immediately pretended to love her new little sister dearly, but she didn't hold out for long, in a few hours she began to make faces of disgust at her, she said: You made her really ugly. Dede, on the other hand, wanted to prove that she could be a much more capable mamma than I was and was in constant danger of dropping her or drowning her in the bath.

I needed a lot of help, at least in those early days, and I have to say that Pietro offered it. He, who as a husband had barely exerted himself to make things easier, now that we were officially separated didn't want to leave me alone with three children, one of whom was a newborn, and offered to stay for a few days. But I had to send him away, and not because I didn't want his help but because during the few hours he was in Via Tasso Nino harassed me, he kept calling to find out if Pietro had gone and if he could come *to his house* without being forced to meet him. Naturally when my ex-husband left Nino was overwhelmed by his job and his political engagements, so I was on my own: in order to shop, take the children to school, pick them up, read a book or write a few lines, I had to leave Imma with the neighbor.

But that was the least of it. Much more complicated was arranging to go and see my mother in the clinic. I didn't trust Mirella, two children and a newborn seemed too much for her. So I decided to take Imma with me. I bundled her up, called a taxi, and was driven to Capodimonte, taking advantage of the time when Dede and Elsa were in school.

My mother had recovered. Of course, she was frail, and if she didn't see us children every day she feared catastrophe and began to cry. Also, she was permanently in bed, while before, even if laboriously, she had moved, gone out. But it seemed indisputable that the luxuries of the clinic were beneficial to her. To be treated like a great lady became a game that distracted her from the illness and that, with the help of some drug, diminished the pain, making her at times euphoric. She liked the large luminous room, she found the mattress comfortable, she was proud of having her own bathroom, and in the room, no less. A real bathroom—she pointed out—not a toilet, and she wanted to get up and show it to me. Not to mention that there was the new granddaughter. When I went with Imma to see her she held the baby next to her, talked to her in baby talk, grew excited, claiming—which was very unlikely—that Imma had smiled at her.

But in general her interest in the infant didn't last long. She began to speak of her own childhood, of adolescence. She went back to when she was five, then she slid to twelve, then fourteen, and she related to me from within those ages things that had happened to her and her companions of that time. One morning she said to me in dialect: As a child I knew about death, I've always known about it, but I never thought it would happen to me, and even now I can't believe it. Another time, following her own thoughts, she began to laugh, and whispered: You're right not to baptize the baby, it's nonsense; now that I'm dying I know that I'll turn into little bits and pieces. But mostly it was in those slow hours that I truly felt I was her favorite child. When she embraced me before I left, it was as if she meant to slip inside me and stay there, as once I had been inside her. That contact with her body, which had irritated me when she was healthy, I now liked.

65.

It was odd how the clinic soon became a place of meeting for the old and the young of the neighborhood.

My father slept there with my mother, and when I saw him in the morning his beard was unshaven, his eyes were frightened. We barely greeted each other, but that didn't seem unusual. I had never had much contact with him: at times affectionate, often distracted, occasionally in support of me against my mother. But it had almost always been superficial. My mother had given him a role and taken it away according to convenience, and especially when it came to me—making and unmaking my life was to be only for her—she had pushed him into the background. Now that the energy of his wife had almost completely vanished, he didn't know how to talk to me nor I to him. I said hi, he said hi, then he added: while you keep her company, I'll go smoke a cigarette. Sometimes I wondered how he had managed to survive, a man so ordinary, in the fierce world he had moved in, in Naples, in his job, in the neighborhood, even at home.

When Elisa arrived with her baby I saw that there was a greater intimacy between her and our father. Elisa treated him with affectionate authority. Often she stayed all day and sometimes all night, sending him home to sleep in his own bed. As soon as she arrived, my sister had to criticize everything, the dust, the windows, the food. She did it to make herself respected, she wanted it to be clear that she was in charge. And Peppe and Gianni matched her. When they felt my mother was suffering and my father desperate, both would get upset, press the bell, call the nurse. If the nurse delayed, my brothers reprimanded her harshly and then, contradicting themselves, gave her lavish tips. Gianni especially, before leaving, would stick some money in her pocket, saying: Stay right outside the door and hop up as soon as Mamma calls you, have your coffee

when you're off duty, is that clear? Then, to let it be understood that our mother was a person of consequence, he would
mention three or four times the name of the Solaras. Signora
Greco—he would say—is the Solaras' business.

The Solaras' business. Those words enraged me, I was
ashamed. But meanwhile I thought, either this or the hospital,
and I said to myself: but *afterward* (what I meant by *afterward*
I didn't admit even to myself) I'll have to clear up a lot of
things with my siblings and with Marcello. For now it gave me
pleasure to arrive in the room and find my mother with her
friends from the neighborhood, all her contemporaries, to
whom she boasted weakly, saying things like, My children
wanted it like this, or, pointing to me: Elena is a famous writer,
she has a house on Via Tasso from which the sea is visible, look
what a beautiful baby, she's called Immacolata, like me. When
her friends left, murmuring, Sleep, I went in to check on her,
then returned with Imma to the corridor, where the air seemed
fresher. I left the door of the room open so I could monitor my
mother's heavy breathing; after the fatigue of those visits, she
often fell asleep and groaned in her sleep.

Occasionally the days were simpler. Carmen, for example,
sometimes came to get me in her car. And Alfonso did the
same. Naturally it was a sign of affection for me. They spoke
respectfully to my mother, at most they gave her some satisfaction by praising her granddaughter and the comfort of the
room. The rest of the time they spent either talking in the corridor with me or waiting outside, in the car, to be in time to
take me to pick up the girls at school. The mornings with them
were always intense and created a curious effect: they brought
together the neighborhood of my mother, now near its end,
and the one being constructed under Lila's influence.

I told Carmen what our friend had done for my mother. She
said with satisfaction: You know no one can stop Lina, and she
spoke of her as if she attributed to her magical powers. But I

learned more from a quarter of an hour spent with Alfonso in the spotless corridor of the clinic, while the doctor was with my mother. He, too, usually, was inflamed with gratitude toward Lila, but what struck me was that for the first time he talked explicitly about himself. He said: Lina taught me a job with a great future. He exclaimed: Without her what would I have been, nothing, a piece of living flesh, without fulfillment. He compared Lila with his wife's behavior: I left Marisa free to betray me as much as she wanted, I gave my name to her children, but just the same she's angry at me, she tormented me and torments me, she has spit in my face countless times, she says I cheated her. He defended himself: How did I cheat, Lenù, you're an intellectual and you can understand me, the one who was cheated was me, cheated by myself, and if Lina hadn't helped me I would have died cheated. His eyes were shining. The most beautiful thing she did for me was to impose clarity on me, teach me to say: If I touch the bare foot of this woman I feel nothing, while I die of desire if I touch the foot of that man, there, and caress his hands, cut his nails with scissors, squeeze his blackheads, be with him on a dance floor and say to him, If you know how to waltz lead me, let me feel how well you lead. He recalled faraway events: Do you remember when you and Lina came to my house to ask my father to give you back the dolls and he called me, he asked, teasing, Alfò, did you take them—because I was the shame of the family, I played with my sister's dolls and I tried on Mamma's necklaces? He explained to me, but as if I already knew everything and was useful only in enabling him to express his true nature. Even as a child, he said, I knew I wasn't what the others thought but not what I thought, either. I said to myself: I'm another thing, a thing that is hidden in the veins, it has no name and waits. But I didn't know what that thing was and especially I didn't know how it could be me, until Lila forced me—I don't know how to say it—to take a little of her. You know what she's like, she said: start here and see what happens; so we were mixed up—it was a lot of fun—and now I'm not what I was and I'm not Lila, either, but another person who is slowly defining himself.

He was happy to share these confidences and I was happy, too, that he made them. A new intimacy arose between us, different from when we used to walk home from school. And with Carmen, too, I had the impression that our relationship was becoming more trusting. Then I realized that both, if in different ways, were asking something more of me. It happened twice, both times connected to Marcello's presence in the clinic.

My sister Elisa and her baby were usually driven to the clinic by an old man named Domenico. Domenico left them there and drove our father back to the neighborhood. But sometimes it was Marcello himself who brought Elisa and Silvio. One morning when he appeared in person Carmen was there with me. I was sure there would be tensions between them, but they exchanged a greeting that wasn't warm but not confrontational, either, and she hovered around him like an animal ready to approach at the first hint of favor. Once we were alone she confided to me nervously, in a low voice, that even if the Solaras hated her she was trying to be friendly and she did it for love of Pasquale. But—she exclaimed—I can't do it, Lenù, I hate them, I want to strangle them, it's only out of necessity. Then she asked: How would you act in my place?

Something similar happened with Alfonso. One morning when he took me to see my mother, Marcello appeared and Alfonso panicked just at the sight of him. And yet Solara behaved just as he usually did: he greeted me with awkward politeness, and gave Alfonso a nod, pretending not to see the hand that he had mechanically extended. To avoid friction I pushed my friend into the hall with the excuse that I had to nurse Imma. Once outside the room Alfonso muttered: If they murder me, remember it was Marcello. I said: Don't exaggerate.

But he was tense, he began sarcastically to make a list of the people in the neighborhood who would gladly kill him, people I didn't know and people I knew. On the list he put his brother Stefano (he laughed; *he fucks my wife only to demonstrate that we're not all fags in the family*) and also Rino (he laughed; *ever since he realized I'm able to look like his sister, he would do to me what he can't do to her*). But at the top he always left Marcello, according to him it was Marcello who hated him most. He said it with satisfaction and yet anguish: he thinks Michele went mad because of me. And he added, sneering: Lila encouraged me to be like her, she likes the effort I make, she likes to see how I distort her, she's pleased with the effect that this distortion has on Michele, and I'm pleased, too. Then he stopped, he asked me: What do you think?

I listened, nursing the baby. He and Carmen were not satisfied that I lived in Naples, that every so often we met: they wanted me to be fully reintegrated into the neighborhood, they asked me to stand beside Lila as a guardian deity, they urged that we act as divinities at times in agreement, at times in competition, but in any case attentive to their problems. That request for greater involvement in their affairs, which in her way Lila, too, often made and which in general seemed an inappropriate pressure, in that situation moved me, I felt that it reinforced the tired voice of my mother when she proudly pointed me out to her friends of the neighborhood as an important part of herself. I hugged Imma to my breast and adjusted the blanket to protect her from the drafts.

66.

Only Nino and Lila never came to the clinic. Nino was explicit: I have no desire to meet that Camorrist, I'm sorry for your mother, give her my best, but I can't go with you. Sometimes

I convinced myself that it was a way of justifying his disappearances, but more often he seemed truly hurt, because he had gone to a lot of trouble for my mother and then I and my whole family had ended up going along with the Solaras. I explained to him that it was a difficult system. I said: It doesn't have to do with Marcello, we only agreed to what made our mother happy. But he grumbled: that's why Naples will never change.

As for Lila, she said nothing about the move to the clinic. She continued to help me out even though she was about to give birth herself at any moment. I felt guilty. I said: Don't worry about me, you should look after yourself. But no—she answered pointing to her stomach with an expression between sarcasm and alarm—he's late, I don't want to and he doesn't want to. And as soon as I needed something she hurried over. Naturally, she never offered to drive me to Capodimonte, as Carmen and Alfonso did. But if the children had a fever and I couldn't send them to school—as happened several times in Immacolata's first three weeks of life, which were cold and rainy—she was available, she left the job to Enzo and Alfonso, she came up to Via Tasso to take all three of them.

I was glad; the time Dede and Elsa spent with Lila was always valuable. She was able to bring the two sisters closer to the third, making Dede take responsibility, keeping Elsa under control, soothing Imma without sticking the pacifier in her mouth, as Mirella did. The only problem was Nino. I was afraid I would discover that—though he was always busy when I was alone—he had miraculously managed to find time to help Lila when she was with the girls. And so in a hidden corner of myself I was never really serene. Lila arrived, I gave her endless advice, I wrote down the number of the clinic, I alerted my neighbor just in case, I hurried to Capodimonte. I stayed with my mother no longer than an hour and then I slipped away to get home in time for nursing, for cooking. But sometimes, on the way home, I'd have a flash of entering the house and finding Nino and Lila together, talking about everything under the sun, as they used to do in Ischia. I also tended, naturally, to more intolerable fantasies, but I repressed them, horrified. The most persistent fear was a different one, and, while I drove, it appeared to me the most well founded. I imagined that her labor would begin while Nino was there, so that he would have to take her to the emergency room, leaving Dede to play, terrified, the part of the sensible woman, Elsa to rummage in Lila's bag and steal something, Imma to wail in her cradle, tormented by hunger and diaper rash.

Something like that did happen, but Nino had no part in it. I returned home one morning, punctual, within the half hour, and discovered that Lila wasn't there; her labor had begun. An intolerable anguish seized me. More than anything she feared the shaking and bending of matter, she hated illness in any form, she detested the hollowness of words when they were emptied of any possible meaning. So I prayed that she would hold up.

67.

I know about the birth from two sources, her and the gynecologist. Here I'll put down the stories in succession and summarize the situation in my own words. It was raining. I had given birth three weeks earlier. My mother had been in the clinic for a couple of weeks and, if I didn't appear, she wept like an anxious child. Dede had a slight fever, Elsa refused to go to school, insisting that she wanted to take care of her sister. Carmen wasn't available, nor was Alfonso. I called Lila, I set out the usual conditions: If you don't feel well, if you have to work, forget it, I'll find another solution. She replied in her teasing way that she felt very well and that when you're the boss you give the orders and take all the time off you want. She loved the two girls, but she especially liked taking care of Imma with them; it was a game that made all four of them happy. I'm leaving right away, she said. I figured that she would arrive in an hour at most, but she was late. I waited a while, but since I knew that she would keep her promise, I said to the neighbor: It's a matter of minutes, and left the children with her to go to my mother.

But Lila was late because of a sort of presentiment in her body. Although she wasn't having contractions she didn't feel well and, finally, as a precaution, had Enzo take her to my house. Even before she went in she felt the first pains. She immediately called Carmen, ordering her to come and give the neighbor a hand, then Enzo took her to the clinic where our gynecologist worked. The contractions suddenly became violent but not decisive: the labor lasted sixteen hours.

Lila's account was almost funny. It's not true, she said, that you suffer only with the first child and afterward it's easier—you always suffer. And she brought out arguments as fierce as they were humorous. It seemed to her pointless to safeguard the child in your womb and at the same time long to get rid of it. It's ridiculous, she said, that this exquisite nine months of hospitality is accompanied by the desire to throw out the guest as violently as possible. She shook her head indignantly at the inconsistency of the mechanism. It's crazy, she exclaimed, resorting to Italian, it's your own body that's angry with you, and in fact rebels against you until it becomes its own worst enemy, until it achieves the most terrible pain possible. For hours she had felt in her belly sharp cold flames, an unbearable flow of pain that hit her brutally in the pit of her stomach and then returned, penetrating her kidneys. Come on, she said sarcastically, you're a liar, where is the great experience. And she swore—this time seriously—that she would never get pregnant again.

But according to the gynecologist, whom Nino invited to dinner one night with her husband, the delivery had been normal, any other woman would have given birth without all that talk. What complicated it was only Lila's teeming head. The doctor had been very irritated. You're doing the opposite of what you should, she had reprimanded her, you hold on when instead you should push: go on, go, push. According to her— she now felt an open aversion toward her patient, and there in my house, at dinner, she didn't hide it but, rather, displayed it in a conspiratorial way, especially to Nino—Lila had done her best not to bring her infant into the world. She held onto it with all her strength and meanwhile gasped: Cut my stomach open, you get it out, I can't do it. When the gynecologist continued to encourage her, Lila shouted vulgar insults at her. She was soaked in sweat, the gynecologist told us, her eyes were bloodshot below her broad forehead, and she was screaming: You talk, you give orders, you come here and do it, you piece of shit, you push the baby out if you can, it's killing me.

I was annoyed and I said to the doctor: You shouldn't tell us these things. She became even more irritated, she exclaimed: I'm telling you because we're among friends. But then, stung, she assumed the tone of the doctor and said with an affected seriousness that if we loved Lila we should (she meant Nino and me, obviously) help her concentrate on something that truly gave her satisfaction, otherwise, with her dancing brain (she used precisely that expression), she would get herself and those around her in trouble. Finally, she repeated that in the delivery room she had seen a struggle against nature, a terrible clash between a mother and her child. It was, she said, a truly unpleasant experience.

The infant was a girl, a girl and not a boy as everyone had predicted. When I was able to go to the clinic, Lila, although she was exhausted, showed me her daughter proudly. She asked:

"How much did Imma weigh?"

"Seven pounds."

"Nunzia weighs almost nine pounds: my belly was small but she is large."

She really had named her for her mother. And in order not to upset Fernando, her father, who was even more irascible in old age than he'd been as a young man, and Enzo's relatives, she had her baptized in the neighborhood church and held a big party in the Basic Sight offices.

68.

The babies immediately became an excuse to spend more time together. Lila and I talked on the phone, met to take them for a walk, spoke endlessly, no longer about ourselves but about them. Or at least so it seemed to us. In reality a new richness and complexity in our relationship began to manifest itself through a mutual attention to our daughters. We compared them in every detail as if to assure ourselves that the health or illness of the one was the precise mirror of the health or illness of the other and as a result we could readily intervene to reinforce the first and cut off the second. We told each other everything that seemed good and useful for healthy development, engaging in a sort of virtuous competition of who could find the best food, the softest diaper, the most effective cream for a rash. There was no pretty garment acquired for Nunzia—but now she was called Tina, the diminutive of Nunziatina—that Lila did not also get for Imma, and I, within the limits of my finances, did the same. This onesie was cute on Tina, so I got one for Imma, too—she'd say—or these shoes were cute on Tina and I got some for Imma, too.

"You know," I said one day, smiling, "that you've given her the name of my doll?"

"What doll?"

"Tina, you don't remember?"

She touched her forehead as if she had a headache, and said:

"It's true, but I didn't do it on purpose."

"She was a beautiful doll—I was attached to her."

"My daughter is more beautiful."

Meanwhile the weeks passed; already the scents of spring were flaring. One morning my mother got worse, and there was a moment of panic. Since the doctors at the clinic didn't seem qualified even to my siblings, the idea of taking her back to the hospital was mentioned. I asked Nino to find out if, through the doctors who were connected to his in-laws and had taken care of my mother before, it would be possible to avoid the wards and get a private room. But Nino said that he was opposed to using connections or appeals, that in a public institution treatment should be the same for everyone, and he muttered ill-humoredly: in this country we have to stop thinking that even for a bed in the hospital you have to be a member of a lodge or rely on the Camorra. He was angry with Marcello, naturally, not with me, but I felt humiliated anyway. On the other hand I'm sure that in the end he would have helped if my mother, although suffering atrociously, hadn't made it clear in every way possible that she preferred to die amid comforts rather than return, even for a few hours, to a hospital ward. So one morning Marcello, surprising us yet again, brought to the clinic one of the specialists who had treated our mother. The specialist, who had been curt when he was working in the hospital, was extremely cordial and returned often, greeted deferentially by the doctors in the private clinic. Things improved.

But soon the clinical picture worsened again. At that point my mother gathered all her strength and did two contradictory but in her eyes equally important things. Lila just then had found a way of getting jobs for Peppe and Gianni with a client of hers in Baiano, but they had disregarded the offer, so she— heaping blessings on my friend for her generosity—summoned her two sons and became, at least for a moment, what she had been in the past. Her eyes were furious, she threatened to pursue them from the kingdom of the dead if they didn't accept the offer: she made them weep, she reduced them to lambs, she didn't let go until she was sure she had subdued them. Then she took up an initiative that ran in the opposite direction. She summoned Marcello, from whom she had just wrested Peppe and Gianni, and made him swear solemnly that he would marry her younger daughter before she closed her eyes forever. Marcello reassured her, he told her that he and Elisa had put off getting married only because they were waiting for her to recover, and now that her recovery was imminent he would immediately take care of the paperwork. Now my mother brightened. She made no distinction between the power she attributed to Lila and that which she attributed to Marcello. She had pressured both and was happy to have gained benefits for her children from the most important people in the neighborhood; that is, in her view, in the world.

For a few days she lingered in a state of peaceful joy. I brought Dede, whom she loved dearly, and I let her hold Imma. She was even affectionate toward Elsa, whom she had never liked much. I observed her: she was a gray, wrinkled old woman, even though she wasn't a hundred but sixty. I then first felt the impact of time, the force that was pushing me toward forty, the velocity with which life was consumed, the concreteness of the exposure to death: *If it's happening to her*, I thought, *there's no escape, it will happen to me as well.*

One morning, when Imma was just over two months old, my mother said weakly: Lenù, I'm truly content now, it's only you I'm worried about, but you are you and you've always been able to arrange things as you liked, so I have confidence. Then she went to sleep and fell into a coma. She held out for a few more days; she didn't want to die. I remember that I was in her room with Imma; by now the death rattle was continuous, it had become one of the ordinary sounds of the clinic. My father, who couldn't bear to hear it anymore, had stayed home that night, weeping. Elisa had taken Silvio out to the courtyard to get some air, my brothers were smoking in a room nearby. I stared for a long time at that insubstantial bulge under the sheet. My mother was diminished almost to nothing, and yet she had been truly burdensome, weighing on me, making me feel like a worm under a rock, protected and crushed. I wished that wheeze would stop, right away, now, and, to my surprise, it did. Suddenly the room was silent. I waited, I couldn't find the strength to get up and go to her. Then Imma clicked her tongue and the silence was broken. I left the chair, went over to the bed. The two of us—I and the infant, greedily seeking my nipple in her sleep, to feel that she was still part of me— were, in that place of illness, the only living and healthy part of my mother that remained.

That day, I don't know why, I had put on the bracelet she had given me more than twenty years before. I hadn't worn it for a long time; I usually wore the finer jewelry that Adele had recommended. From then on I wore it often.

69.

I struggled to accept my mother's death. Even though I didn't shed a tear, the pain lasted for a long time and perhaps has never really gone away. I had considered her an insensitive and vulgar woman, I had feared her and fled. Right after her funeral I felt the way you feel when it suddenly starts raining hard, and you look around and find no place to take shelter. For weeks I saw and heard her everywhere, night and day. She was a vapor that in my imagination continued to burn without a wick. I missed the different way of being together we had dis- covered during her illness, I prolonged it by retrieving positive memories of when I was a child and she was young. My sense of guilt wanted to compel her to endure. In a drawer I put a hairpin of hers, a handkerchief, a pair of scissors, but they all seemed inadequate objects, even the bracelet was worthless. My pregnancy had brought back the pain in my hip and Imma's birth hadn't relieved it, but maybe that was why I decided not to go to the doctor. I nurtured that pain like a bequest preserved in my body.

The words she had said to me at the end (*You're you, I have confidence*) also stayed with me for a long time. She died convinced that because of how I was made, because of the resources I had accumulated, I would not be overwhelmed by anything. That idea worked inside me and in the end helped me. I decided to prove to her that she had been right. I began again in a disciplined way to take care of myself. I returned to using every bit of empty time for reading and writing. I lost what little interest I'd had in petty politics—I couldn't get excited at the intrigues of the five governing parties and their quarrels with the Communists, as Nino now was actively doing—but I continued to follow closely the corrupt and violent drift of the country. I collected feminist readings and, still fortified by the small success of my last book, proposed articles to the new journals directed at women. But, I have to admit, a great part of my energy was focused on convincing my publisher that I was moving along with the new novel.

A few years earlier half of a substantial advance had been paid, but in the meantime I had done very little, I was stumbling along, still looking for a story. The editor in chief, who was responsible for that generous sum, had never pressured me, he inquired discreetly, and if I was elusive, because to admit the truth seemed to me shameful, he let me be elusive. Then a small unpleasant event occurred. A semi-sarcastic article appeared in the *Corriere della Sera* that, after praising a first novel that had had a modest success, alluded to the failed promise of the new

Italian literature, and included my name. A few days later the editor passed through Naples—he was to take part in a prestigious conference—and asked if we could meet.

His serious tone immediately worried me. In almost fifteen years he had never insisted on his authority, he had sided with me against Adele, he had always treated me kindly. With forced warmth I invited him to dinner on Via Tasso, which cost me anxiety and hard work, but I did it partly because Nino wanted to propose a new collection of essays.

The editor was polite but not affectionate. He expressed his condolences for my mother, he praised Imma, he gave Dede and Elsa some colorful books, he waited patiently for me to maneuver between dinner and daughters, leaving Nino to talk to him about his possible book. When we got to dessert he brought up the true reason for the meeting: he wanted to know if he could plan to bring out my novel the following fall. I turned red.

"Fall of 1982?"

"Fall of 1982."

"Maybe, but I'll know better in a little while."

"You have to know now."

"I'm still nowhere near the end."

"You could let me read something."

"I don't feel ready."

Silence. He took a sip of wine, then said in a serious tone:

"Up to now you've been very lucky, Elena. The last book went particularly well, you're respected, you've gained a good number of readers. But readers have to be cultivated. If you lose them, you lose the chance to publish other books."

I was displeased. I understood that Adele, by force of repetition, had gotten through even to that very civilized and polite man. I imagined the words of Pietro's mother, her choice of terms—*She's an untrustworthy southerner who behind a charming appearance weaves crafty tissues of lies*—and I hated myself because I was proving to that man that those words

were true. At dessert, the editor, in a few curt phrases, liqui-
dated Nino's proposal, saying that it was a difficult moment for
essays. The awkwardness increased, no one knew what to say,
I talked about Imma until finally the guest looked at his watch
and said that he had to go. At that point I couldn't take it and
I said:

"All right, I'll deliver the book in time for it to come out in
the fall."

70.

My promise soothed the editor. He stayed another hour, he
chatted about this and that, he made an effort to be more well
disposed to Nino. He embraced me as he left, whispering, I'm
sure you're writing a wonderful story.

As soon as I closed the door I exclaimed: Adele is still plotting against me, I'm in trouble. But Nino didn't agree. Even
the slim possibility that his book would be published had
cheered him. Besides, he had been in Palermo recently for the
Socialist Party Congress, where he had seen both Guido and
Adele, and the professor had indicated that he admired some
of his recent work. So he said, conciliatory:

"Don't exaggerate the intrigues of the Airotas. All you had
to do was promise you'd get to work and you saw how things
changed?"

We quarreled. I had just promised a book, yes, but how,
when would I be able to write it with the necessary concentration and continuity? Did he realize what my life had been, and
still was? I listed randomly the illness and death of my mother,
the care of Dede and Elsa, the household tasks, the pregnancy,
the birth of Imma, his lack of interest in her, the rushing from
this conference to that congress, more and more often without
me, and the disgust, yes, the disgust at having to share him with

Eleonora. *I*, I shouted at him, *I* am now nearly divorced from Pietro, and you wouldn't even separate. Could I work among so many tensions, by myself, without any help from him? The fight was pointless, Nino reacted as he always did. He looked depressed, he whispered: You don't understand, you can't understand, you're unfair, and he swore fiercely that he loved me and couldn't do without Imma, the children, me. Finally he offered to pay for a housekeeper.

He had encouraged me on other occasions to find someone who could take care of the house, the shopping, the cooking, the children, but, in order not to seem excessively demanding, I had always responded that I didn't want to be a bigger economic burden than necessary. Generally I tended to give more importance not to what would be helpful to me but to what he would appreciate. And then I didn't want to admit that the same problems I had already experienced with Pietro were surfacing in our relationship. But this time, surprising him, I said immediately: Yes, all right, find this woman as soon as possible. And it seemed to me that I was speaking in the voice of my mother, not in the feeble voice of recent times but in strident tones. Who gave a damn about the shopping, I had to take care of my future. And my future was to write a novel in the next few months. And that novel had to be very good. And nothing, not even Nino, would prevent me from doing my work well.

71.

I examined the situation. The two previous books, which for years had produced a little money, partly thanks to translations, had stopped selling. The advance I had received for my new book and hadn't yet earned was nearly gone. The articles I wrote, working late into the night, either brought in little or were not paid at all. I lived, in other words, on the money that Pietro contributed punctually every month and that Nino supplemented by taking on the rent for the house, the bills, and, I have to admit, often giving me money for clothes for myself and the children. But as long as I had had to confront all the upheavals and inconveniences and sufferings that followed my return to Naples, it had seemed fair. Now instead—after that evening—I decided that it was urgent to become as autonomous as possible. I had to write and publish regularly, I had to reinforce my profile as an author, I had to earn money. And the reason was not any literary vocation, the reason had to do with the future: Did I really think that Nino would take care of me and my daughters forever?

It was then that a part of me—only a part—began to emerge that consciously, without particular suffering, admitted that it couldn't really count on him. It wasn't just the old fear that he would leave me; rather it seemed to me an abrupt contraction of perspective. I stopped looking into the distance, I began to think that in the immediate future I couldn't expect from Nino more than what he was giving me, and that I had to decide if it was enough.

I continued to love him, of course. I liked his long slender body, his methodical intelligence. And I had a great admiration for his work. His old ability to assemble facts and interpret them was a skill that was much in demand. Recently he had published a highly regarded work—maybe that was the one Guido had liked so much—on the economic crisis and on the karstic movement of capital that was being shifted from sources to be investigated toward construction, finance, private television. Yet something about him had begun to bother me. For example, I was wounded by his delight in finding favor with my former father-in-law. Nor did I like the way he had begun again to differentiate Pietro—*a petty professor with no imagination, highly praised only because of his surname and*

his obtuse activity in the Communist Party—from his father, the
real Professor Airota, whom he praised unrestrainedly as the
author of fundamental volumes on Hellenism and as an out-
standing and combative figure of the socialist left. His renewed
liking for Adele further wounded me; he was constantly calling
her a great lady, extraordinary at public relations. He seemed
to me, in other words, sensitive to the approval of those who
had authority and ready to catch out, or even, at times, humiliate, out of envy, those who did not yet have enough of it and
those who did not have it at all but could have it. Something
that marred the image that I had always had of him and that he
generally had of himself.

It wasn't only that. The political and cultural climate was
changing, other readings were emerging. We had all stopped
making extreme speeches, and I was surprised to find myself
agreeing with positions that years earlier I had opposed in
Pietro, out of a wish to contradict him, out of the need to quarrel. But Nino went too far, he now found ridiculous not only
every subversive statement but also every ethical declaration,
every display of purity. He said, making fun of me:

"There are too many sensitive souls around."

"Meaning?"

"People who are outraged, as if they didn't know that either
the parties do their job or you get armed gangs and Masonic
lodges."

"What do you mean?"

"I mean that a party can't be anything other than a distrib-
utor of favors in exchange for support, ideals are part of the
furniture."

"Well, then I'm a sensitive soul."

"I know that."

I began to find his craving to be politically surprising
unpleasant. When he organized dinners at my house he embarrassed his own guests by defending from the left positions of

the right. The fascists—he maintained—aren't always wrong and we should learn to talk to each other. Or: You can't simply condemn, you have to get your hands dirty if you want to change things. Or even: Justice should as soon as possible be subordinated to the rights of those who have the task of governing, otherwise the judges become loose cannons, dangerous for the preservation of the democratic system. Or again: Wages have to be frozen, the mechanism of the wage index scale is ruinous for Italy. If someone disagreed with him he became contemptuous, he sneered, he let it be understood that it wasn't worth the trouble to argue with people wearing blinders, whose heads were full of old slogans.

I retreated into an uneasy silence, in order not to take sides against him. He loved the shifting sands of the present, the future for him was decided there. He knew about everything that happened in the parties and in parliament, about the internal movements of capital and of the organization of labor. I, on the other hand, persisted in reading only what had to do with the dark conspiracies, the kidnappings and bloody last-ditch efforts of the armed red gangs, the debate on the decline of the centrality of workers, the identification of new opposition subjects. As a result I felt more comfortable with the language of the other diners than with his. One evening he quarreled with a friend who taught in the school of architecture. He became inflamed by passion, disheveled, handsome.

"You can't distinguish between a step forward, a step back, and standing still."

"What's a step forward?" the friend asked.

"A prime minister who isn't the same old Christian Democrat."

"And standing still?"

"A demonstration by steelworkers."

"And a step back?"

"Asking who's cleaner, the socialists or the Communists."

"You're turning cynical."

"You, on the other hand, have always been a shit."

No, Nino no longer persuaded me the way he used to. He expressed himself, I don't know how to say it, in a provocative and yet opaque way, as if precisely he, who extolled the long view, were able to follow only the daily moves and counter-moves of a system that to me, to his own friends, seemed rotten to the core. Enough, he would insist, let's end the childish aversion to power: one has to be on the inside in the places where things are born and die: the parties, the banks, television. And I listened, but when he turned to me I lowered my gaze. I no longer concealed from myself that his conversation partly bored me, and partly seemed to point to a brittleness that dragged him down.

One time he was lecturing Dede, who had to do some sort of crazy research for her teacher, and to soften his pragmatism I said:

"The people, Dede, always have the possibility of turning everything upside down."

Good-humoredly he replied, "Mamma likes to make up stories, which is a great job. But she doesn't know much about how the world we live in functions, and so whenever there's something she doesn't like she resorts to a magic word: let's turn everything upside down. You tell your teacher that we have to make the world that exists function."

"How?" I asked.

"With laws."

"But if you say that the judges should be controlled."

Displeased with me, he shook his head, just as Pietro used to do.

"Go and write your book," he said, "otherwise you'll complain it's our fault that you can't work."

He started a lesson with Dede on the division of powers, which I listened to in silence and agreed with from A to Z.

72.

When Nino was home he staged a comic ritual with Dede and Elsa. They dragged me into the little room where I had my desk, ordered me peremptorily to get to work, and shut the door behind them, scolding me in chorus if I dared to open it. In general, if he had time, he was very available to the children: to Dede, whom he judged very intelligent but too rigid, and to Elsa, whose feigned acquiescence, behind which lurked malice and cunning, amused him. But what I hoped would happen never did: he didn't become attached to little Imma. He played with her, of course, and sometimes he really seemed to enjoy himself. For example, with Dede and Elsa he would bark at her, to get her to say the word "dog." I heard them howling through the house as I sought in vain to make some notes, and if Imma by pure chance emitted from the depths of her throat an indistinct sound that resembled *d*, Nino shrieked in unison with the children: she said it, hooray, *d*. But nothing more. In fact he used the infant as a doll to entertain Dede and Elsa. The increasingly rare times when he spent a Sunday with us and the weather was fine, he went with them and Imma to the Floridiana, encouraging them to push their sister's stroller along the paths of the park. When they returned they were all pleased. But a few words were enough for me to guess that Nino had abandoned Dede and Elsa to play mamma to Imma, while he went off to converse with the real mothers of the Vomero who were taking their children out for air and sun.

Over time I had become used to his penchant for seductive behavior, I considered it a sort of tic. I was used above all to the way women immediately liked him. But at a certain point something was spoiled there, too. I began to notice that he had an impressive number of women friends, and that they all seemed to brighten in his vicinity. I knew that light well, I wasn't surprised. Being close to him gave you the impression of being visible, especially to yourself, and you were content. It was natural, therefore, that all those girls, and older women, too, were fond of him, and if I didn't exclude sexual desire I also didn't consider it essential. I stood confused on the edge of the remark made long ago by Lila, *In my opinion he's not your friend, either*, and tried as infrequently as possible to transmute it into the question: *Are these women his lovers?* So it wasn't the hypothesis that he was betraying me that disturbed me but something else. I was convinced that Nino encouraged in those people a sort of maternal impulse to do, within the limits of the possible, what could be useful to him.

Shortly after Imma's birth, things began to go better for him. When he appeared he told me proudly of his successes, and I was quickly forced to register that, just as in the past his career had had a boost thanks to his wife's family, so, too, behind every new responsibility he got was the mediation of a woman. One had obtained for him a biweekly column in *Il Mattino*. One had recommended him for the keynote speech at an important conference in Ferrara. One had put him on the managing editorial board of a Turinese journal. Another—originally from Philadelphia and married to a NATO officer stationed in Naples—had recently added his name as a consultant for an American foundation. The list of favors was continuously lengthening. Besides, hadn't I myself helped him publish a book with an important publishing house? And, if I thought about it, hadn't Professor Galiani been the source of his reputation as a high-school student?

I began to study him while he was engaged in that work of seduction. He often invited young and not so young women to dinner at my house, alone or with their husbands or companions. I observed with some anxiety that he knew how to give them space: he ignored the male guests almost completely, making the women the center of his attention, and at times focusing on one in particular. Many evenings I witnessed conversations that, although they took place in the presence of other people, he was able to conduct as if he were alone, in private, with the only woman who at that moment appeared to interest him. He said nothing allusive, or compromising, he merely asked questions.

"And then what happened?"

"I left home. I left Lecce at eighteen and Naples wasn't an easy city."

"Where did you live?"

"In a run-down apartment in the Tribunali, with two other girls. There wasn't even a quiet corner where I could study."

"And men?"

"Certainly not."

"There must have been someone."

"There was one, and, just my luck, he's here, I'm married to him."

Although the woman had brought up her husband as if to include him in the conversation, Nino ignored him and continued to talk to her in his warm voice. He had a curiosity about the world of women that was genuine. But—this I knew very well by now—he didn't in the least resemble the men who in those years made a show of giving up at least a few of their privileges. I thought not only of professors, architects, artists who came to our house and displayed a sort of feminization of behaviors, feelings, opinions; but also of Carmen's husband, Roberto, who was really helpful, and Enzo, who with no hesitation would have sacrificed all his time to Lila's needs. Nino was sincerely interested in how women found themselves. There was no dinner at which he did not repeat that to think *along with* them was now the only way to a true thought. But he held tight to his spaces and his numerous activities, he put first of all, always and only, himself, he didn't give up an instant of his time.

On one occasion I tried, with affectionate irony, to show him up as a liar in front of everyone:

"Don't believe him. At first he helped me clear, he washed the dishes: today he doesn't even pick his socks up off the floor."

"That's not true," he protested.

"Yes, it is. He wants to liberate the women of others but not his."

"Well, your liberation shouldn't necessarily signify the loss of my freedom."

In remarks like this, too, uttered playfully, I soon recognized, uneasily, echoes of my conflicts with Pietro. Why had I gotten so angry at my ex-husband while with Nino I let it go? I thought: maybe every relationship with men can only reproduce the same contradictions and, in certain environments, even the same smug responses. But then I said to myself: I mustn't exaggerate, there's a difference, with Nino it's certainly going better.

But was it really? I was less and less sure. I remembered how, when he was our guest in Florence, he had supported me against Pietro, I thought again with pleasure of how he had encouraged me to write. But now? Now that it was crucial for me to seriously get to work, he seemed unable to instill in me the same confidence as before. Things had changed over the years. Nino always had his own urgent needs, and even if he wanted to he couldn't devote himself to me. To mollify me he had hurried to get, through his mother, a certain Silvana, a massive woman of around fifty, with three children, always cheerful, very lively, and good with the three girls. Generously he had glossed over what he paid her, and after a week had asked: Everything in order, it's working? But it was evident that he felt that the expense authorized him not to be concerned with me. Of course he was attentive, he regularly asked: Are you writing? But that was it. The central place that my effort to write had had at the start of our relationship had vanished. And it wasn't only that. I myself, with a certain embarrassment, no longer recognized him as the authority he had once been. I discovered, in other words, that the part of me that confessed I could not really depend on Nino also no longer saw around his every word the flaming halo I had seemed to perceive since childhood. I gave him a still shapeless paragraph to read and he exclaimed: Perfect. I summarized a plot and characters that I was sketching out and he said: Great, very intelligent. But he didn't convince me, I didn't believe him, he expressed enthusiastic opinions about the work of too many women. His recurring phrase after an evening with other couples was almost always: What a boring man, she is certainly better than he is. His women friends, inasmuch as they were his friends, were always judged extraordinary. And his judgment of women in general was, as a rule, tolerant. Nino could justify even the sadistic obtuseness of the employees of the post office, the ignorant narrow-mindedness of Dede and Elsa's teachers. In other words I no longer felt unique, I was a form that was valid for all women. But if for him I wasn't unique, what help could his opinion give me, how could I draw energy from it to do well?

Exasperated, one evening, by the praise he had heaped on a biologist friend in my presence, I asked him:

"Is it possible that a stupid woman doesn't exist?"

"I didn't say that: I said that as a rule you are better than us."

"I'm better than you?"

"Absolutely, yes, and I've known it for a very long time."

"All right, I believe you, but at least once in your life, have you met a bitch?"

"Yes."

"Tell me her name."

I knew what he would say, and yet I insisted, hoping he would say Eleonora. I waited, he became serious:

"I can't."

"Tell me."

"If I tell you you'll get mad."

"I won't get mad."

"Lina."

73.

If in the past I had believed somewhat in his recurring hostility toward Lila, now I found it less and less convincing, partly
because it was joined not infrequently to moments when, as had
happened a few nights earlier, he demonstrated a completely
different feeling. He was trying to finish an essay on work and
the automation of Fiat, but I saw that he was in trouble (*What
precisely is a microprocessor, what's a chip, how does this stuff
function in practice*). I had said to him: talk to Enzo Scanno, he's
smart. He had asked absentmindedly: Who is Enzo Scanno?
Lina's companion, I answered. He said with a half smile: Then
I prefer to talk to Lina, she certainly knows more. And, as if the
memory had returned, he added, with a trace of resentment:
Wasn't Scanno the idiot son of the fruit seller?

That tone struck me. Enzo was the founder of a small, innovative business—a miracle, considering that the office was in
the heart of the old neighborhood. Precisely because he was a
scholar, Nino should have displayed interest and admiration
toward him. Instead, he had returned him, thanks to that
imperfect—*was*—to the time of elementary school, when he
helped his mother in the shop or went around with his father
and the cart and didn't have time to study and didn't shine. He
had, with irritation, taken every virtue away from Enzo, and
given them all to Lila. That was how I realized that if I had
forced him to delve into himself, it would have emerged that
the highest example of female intelligence—maybe his own
worship of female intelligence, even certain lectures claiming
that the waste of women's intellectual resources was the greatest waste of all—had to do with Lila, and that if our season of

love was already darkening, the season of Ischia would always remain radiant for him. The man for whom I left Pietro, I thought, is what he is because his encounter with Lila reshaped him that way.

74.

This idea occurred to me one frigid fall morning when I was taking Dede and Elsa to school. I was driving distractedly, and the idea took root. I distinguished the love for the neighborhood boy, the high-school student—a feeling of *mine* that had as its object a fantasy of *mine*, conceived *before* Ischia—from the passion that had overwhelmed me for the young man in the bookstore in Milan, the person who had appeared in my house in Florence. I had always maintained a connection between those two emotional blocks, and that morning instead it seemed to me that there was no connection, that the continuity was a trick of logic. In the middle, I thought, there had been a rupture—his love for Lila—that should have cancelled Nino forever from my life, but which I had refused to reckon with. To whom, then, was I bound, and whom did I still love today?

Usually Silvana drove the children to school, and, while Nino was still asleep, I took care of Imma. That day, however, I had arranged things so that I could stay out all morning; I wanted to see if I could find in the Biblioteca Nazionale an old volume by Roberto Bracco, entitled *In the World of Women*. Meanwhile, I advanced slowly through the morning traffic with that thought in mind. I was driving, I was answering the children's questions, I was returning to a Nino made of two parts, one that belonged to me, the other alien. When, with countless warnings and bits of advice, I left Dede and Elsa at their respective schools, the thought had become an image and, as happened often in that period, had been transformed into the nucleus of a possible story. It could be, I said to myself as I descended toward the sea, a novel in which a woman marries the man she's been in love with since childhood, but on their wedding night she realizes that while a part of his body belongs to her, the other part is physically inhabited by a childhood friend of hers. Then in a flash everything was swept away by a sort of domestic alarm bell: I had forgotten to buy diapers for Imma.

Daily life frequently erupted, like a slap, making irrelevant if not ridiculous every meandering little fantasy. I pulled up, angry at myself. I was so burdened that, although I scrupulously wrote down on a notepad the things I needed to buy, I ended up forgetting the list itself. I fumed, I could never organize myself as I should. Nino had an important appointment for work, maybe he had already left, and anyway it was useless to count on him. I couldn't send Silvana to the pharmacy because she would have had to leave the baby alone in the house. As a result there were no diapers, Imma couldn't be changed and would have a rash for days. I went back to Via Tasso. I hurried to the pharmacy, I bought the diapers, I arrived home out of breath. I was sure I would hear Imma screaming from the landing but I opened the door with the key and entered a silent apartment.

I glimpsed the baby in the living room, sitting in her playpen, without a diaper, playing with a doll. I slipped past so that she wouldn't see me, or she would start howling to be picked up, and I wanted to hand over the package to Silvana and try again to get to the library. A faint noise came from the big bathroom (we had a small bathroom that Nino generally used, and a large one for the girls and me), I thought that Silvana must be straightening it. I went there, the door was half open, I pushed it. First I saw, in the luminous space of the long mirror, Silvana's head bent forward, and I was struck by the stripe of the center part, the two black bands of her hair

threaded with white. Then I became aware of Nino's closed
eyes, his open mouth. Suddenly, in a flash, the reflected image
and the real bodies came together. Nino was in his undershirt
and otherwise naked, his long thin legs parted, his feet bare.
Silvana, curved forward, with both hands resting on the sink,
had her big underpants at her knees and the dark smock
pulled up around her waist. He, while he stroked her sex holding her heavy stomach with his arm, was gripping an enormous
breast that stuck out of the smock and the bra, and meanwhile
was thrusting his flat stomach against her large white buttocks.

I pulled the door hard toward myself just as Nino opened
his eyes and Silvana suddenly raised her head, throwing me a
frightened gaze. I rushed to get Imma from the playpen and
while Nino shouted, Elena, wait, I was already out of the
house, I didn't even call the elevator, I ran down the stairs with
the baby in my arms.

75.

I took refuge in the car, I started the engine, and with Imma
on my knees I left. The baby seemed happy, she wanted to honk
the horn, as Elsa had taught her, she spoke her incomprehensible little words alternating with shrieks of joy at my presence. I
drove without a goal, I wanted only to get as far away from the
house as possible. Finally I found myself at Sant'Elmo. I
parked, turned off the engine, and discovered that I had no
tears, I wasn't suffering, I was only frozen with horror.

I couldn't believe it. Was it possible that that Nino whom I
had discovered as he was thrusting his taut sex inside the sex
of a mature woman—a woman who cleaned my house, did my
shopping, cooked, took care of my children; a woman marked
by the struggle to survive, large, worn-out, the absolute opposite of the cultivated, elegant women he brought to dinner—

was the boy of my adolescence? For the whole time I was driving blindly, perhaps scarcely feeling the weight of the half-naked Imma, who was pounding the horn in vain and happily calling me, I couldn't give him a stable identity. I felt as if, entering the house, I had suddenly found out in the open, in my bathroom, an alien creature who usually stayed hidden inside the skin of the father of my third daughter. The stranger had the features of Nino, but wasn't him. Was it the other, the one born after Ischia? But which one? The one who had impregnated Silvia? The lover of Mariarosa? The husband of Eleonora, unfaithful and yet closely bound to her? The married man who had said to me, a married woman, that he loved me, wanted me at all costs?

Along the entire route that led me to the Vomero, I had tried to cling to the Nino of the neighborhood and of high school, the Nino of tenderness and love, to get myself out of the revulsion. Only when I stopped at Sant'Elmo did the bathroom return to mind, and the moment when he had opened his eyes and seen me in the mirror, standing on the threshold. Then everything seemed clearer. There was no split between that man who came after Lila and the boy with whom—before Lila—I had been in love since childhood. Nino was only one, and the expression he had on his face while he was inside Silvana was the proof. It was the expression of his father, Donato, not when he deflowered me on the Maronti but when he touched me between the legs, under the sheet, in Nella's kitchen.

Nothing alien, then, but much that was ugly. Nino was what he wouldn't have wanted to be and yet always had been. When he rhythmically hammered against Silvana's buttocks and was also kindly taking care to give her pleasure, he wasn't lying, just as he wasn't lying when he wronged me and was sorry, apologized, begged me to forgive him, swore that he loved me. *He is like that*, I said to myself. But that didn't console me. I felt, rather, that the horror, instead of fading, found a more solid refuge in that statement. Then a warm liquid spread down to my knees. I shook myself: Imma was naked, she had peed on me.

76.

Going home seemed unthinkable, even though it was cold and Imma risked getting sick. I wrapped her in my coat as if we were playing, I bought a new package of diapers, I put one on after cleaning her with a baby wipe. Now I had to decide what to do. Dede and Elsa would get out of school soon, irritable and hungry; Imma was already hungry. I, my jeans wet, without a coat, nerves tense, was shivering with cold. I looked for a telephone, I called Lila, I asked:

"Can I come to lunch at your house with the children?"

"Of course."

"Enzo won't be annoyed?"

"You know he'll be pleased."

I heard Tina's happy little voice, Lila said to her: Quiet. Then she asked me with a wariness that she normally didn't have:

"Is something wrong?"

"Yes."

"What happened?"

"What you predicted."

"Did you fight with Nino?"

"I'll tell you later, I have to go now."

I arrived early at school. Imma had by now lost any interest in me, the steering wheel, the horn, and was howling. I forced her yet again to stay wrapped in the jacket and we went to find some cookies. I thought I was acting calmly—inside I felt tranquil: not fury but disgust still prevailed, a revulsion not different from what I would have felt if I had seen two lizards coupling—but I realized that the passersby were looking at me with curiosity, with alarm, as I hurried along the street in my wet pants, talking aloud to the baby, who, squeezed tight in the coat, was wriggling and wailing.

At the first cookie Imma quieted down, but her calm freed my anxiety. Nino must have put off his appointment, he was probably looking for me, I was in danger of finding him at school. Since Elsa came out before Dede, who was in her second year of middle school, I went and stood in a corner from which I could watch the entrance of the elementary school without being seen. My teeth were chattering with cold, Imma was smearing my coat with saliva-soaked cookie crumbs. I surveyed the area, nervously, but Nino didn't appear. And he didn't appear at the entrance of the middle school, from which Dede soon emerged in a flood of pushing and shoving, shouts, and insults in dialect.

The children paid little attention to me; they were very interested in the novelty of my coming to get them with Imma.

"Why are you holding her in the coat?" Dede asked.

"Because she's cold."

"Did you see she's ruining it?"

"It doesn't matter."

"Once when I got you dirty you slapped me," Elsa complained.

"It's not true."

"It's very true."

Dede investigated:

"Why is it that she has only a shirt and diaper on?"

"She's fine like that."

"Did something happen?"

"No. Now we're going to have lunch at Aunt Lina's."

They greeted the news with their usual enthusiasm, then they settled in the car, and while the baby talked to her sisters in her obscure language, happy to be the center of their attention, they began to fight over who got to hold her. I insisted that they hold her together, without pulling her this way and that: She's not made of rubber, I cried. Elsa wasn't pleased with that solution and swore at Dede in dialect. I tried to slap her, I said, staring at her in the rearview mirror: What did you say, repeat it, what did you say? She didn't cry, she abandoned Imma to Dede, muttering that taking care of her sister bored her. Then, when the baby reached out her hands to play, she pushed her away roughly. She shouted, assaulting my nerves: Imma, that's enough, you're bothering me, you're getting me dirty. And to me: Mamma, make her stop. I couldn't bear it anymore, I let out a scream that frightened all three of them. We crossed the city in a state of tension broken only by the whispering of Dede and Elsa, who were trying to understand if, again, something irreparable was about to happen in their lives.

I couldn't even tolerate that consultation. I couldn't bear anything anymore: their childhood, my role as mother, Imma's babbling. And then the presence of my daughters in the car clashed with the images of coitus that were constantly before me, with the odor of sex that was still in my nostrils, with the rage that was beginning to advance, along with the most vulgar dialect. Nino had fucked the servant and then gone to his appointment, not giving a shit about me or even about his daughter. Ah, what a piece of shit, all I did was make mistakes. Was he like his father? No, too simple. Nino was very intelligent, Nino was extraordinarily cultured. His propensity for fucking did not come from a crude, naïve display of virility based on half-fascistic, half-southern clichés. What he had done to me, what he was doing to me, was filtered by a very refined knowledge. He dealt in complex concepts, he knew that this way he would offend me to the point of destroying me. But he had done it just the same. He had thought: I can't give up my pleasure just because that shit can be a pain in the ass. Like that, just like that. And surely he judged as philistine—

that adjective was still very widespread in our world—my possible reaction. Philistine, philistine. I even knew the line he would resort to in sophisticated justification: What's the harm, the flesh is weak and I've read all the books. Exactly those words, nasty son of a bitch. Rage had opened up a pathway in the horror. I shouted at Imma—*even at Imma*—to be quiet. When I reached Lila's house I hated Nino as until that moment I had never hated anyone.

77.

Lila had made lunch. She knew that Dede and Elsa adored orecchiette with tomato sauce and she announced this, creating a rowdy scene of enthusiasm. That wasn't all. She took Imma from my arms and cared for her and Tina as if suddenly her daughter had doubled. She changed them both, washed them, dressed them identically, cuddled them with an extraordinary display of maternal care. Then, since the two little girls had recognized each other at once and were playing, she put them down on an old carpet, to crawl around, babble. How different they were. Bitterly I compared the daughter of Nino and me to the daughter of Lila and Enzo. Tina seemed prettier, healthier than Imma: she was the sweet fruit of a solid relationship.

Meanwhile Enzo came home from work, cordially laconic as usual. At the table neither he nor Lila asked me why I wasn't eating. Only Dede intervened, as if to take me away from her own bad thoughts and those of the others. She said: my Mamma always eats just a little because she doesn't want to get fat, and I'm doing that, too. I exclaimed, threatening: You have to clean your plate down to the last bite. And Enzo, perhaps to protect my daughters from me, started a comical contest to see who could eat the most and finish first. He patiently answered Dede's many questions about Rino—my daughter had hoped to see him at least for lunch—and explained that he had started a job in a workshop and was out all day. Then, at the end of the meal, in great secrecy, he took the two sisters into Gennaro's room to show them all the treasures there. After a few minutes there was a burst of furious music, and they didn't come back. I was alone with Lila, and I told her every detail, in a tone between sarcasm and suffering. She listened without interrupting. I realized, the more I put into words what had happened, the more ridiculous the scene of sex between that fat woman and skinny Nino seemed. He woke up—at a certain point the words emerged in dialect—he found Silvana in the bathroom, and even before peeing he pulled up her skirt and stuck it in. Then I burst out laughing in a vulgar fashion and Lila looked at me uneasily. She used such tones, she didn't expect them from me. You have to calm down, she said, and since Imma was crying we went into the other room.

My daughter, fair-haired, red in the face, was shedding large tears, her mouth open, and as soon as she saw me she raised her arms to be picked up. Tina, dark, pale, stared at her, disconcerted, and when her mother appeared she didn't move, she called to her as if she wanted her to help her understand, saying "Mamma" clearly. Lila picked up both babies, settled one on each arm, kissed mine, drying her tears with her lips, spoke to her, soothed her.

I was amazed. I thought: Tina says "Mamma" clearly, all the syllables, Imma doesn't do that yet and is almost a month older. I felt at a loss and sad. 1981 was about to end. I would get rid of Silvana. I didn't know what to write, the months would fly by, I wouldn't deliver my book, I would lose ground as well as my reputation as a writer. I would remain without a future, dependent on financial support from Pietro, alone with three daughters, without Nino. Nino lost, Nino over. The part of me that continued to love him appeared again, not as in Florence but, rather, as the child in elementary school had loved him, seeing him coming out of school. In confusion I searched for an excuse to forgive him in spite of the humiliation, I couldn't bear to drive him out of my life. Where was he? Was it possible that he hadn't even tried to look for me? I put together Enzo, who had immediately taken care of the two children, and Lila, who had freed me of every task and had listened, leaving me all the space I wanted. I finally understood that they had known everything before I arrived in the neighborhood. I asked:

"Did Nino call?"

"Yes."

"What did he say?"

"That it was foolish, that I should stay with you, that I should help you understand, that today people live like this. Talk."

"And you?"

"I slammed the telephone down on him."

"But he'll call again?"

"Of course he'll call again."

I felt discouraged.

"Lila, I don't know how to live without him. It all lasted such a short time. I broke up my marriage, I came to live here with the children, I had another child. Why?"

"Because you made a mistake."

I didn't like the remark, it sounded like the echo of an old offense. She was reminding me that I had made a mistake even though she had tried to get me out of the mistake. She was saying that I had *wanted* to make a mistake, and as a result *she* had been mistaken, I wasn't intelligent, I was a stupid woman. I said:

"I have to talk to him, I have to confront him."

"All right, but leave me the children."

"You can't do it, there are four."

"There are five, there's also Gennaro. And he's the most difficult of all."

"You see? I'll take them."

"Don't even mention it."

I admitted that I needed her help, I said:

"I'll leave them until tomorrow, I need time to resolve the situation."

"Resolve it how?"

"I don't know."

"You want to continue with Nino?"

I could hear her opposition and I almost shouted:

"What can I do?"

"The only thing possible: leave him."

For her it was the right solution, she had always wanted it to end like that, she had never concealed it from me. I said:

"I'll think about it."

"No, you won't think about it. You've already decided to pretend it was nothing and go on."

I avoided answering but she pressed me, she said that I shouldn't throw myself away, that I had another destiny, that if I went on like that I would lose myself. I noticed that she was becoming harsh, I felt that to restrain me she was on the point of telling me what for a long time I had wanted to know and what for a long time she had been silent about. I was afraid, but had I not myself, on various occasions, tried to urge her to be clear? And now, had I not come to her *also* so that finally she would tell me everything?

"If you have something to tell me," I said, "speak."

And she made up her mind, she looked at me, I looked down. She said that Nino had often sought her out. She said that he had asked her to come back to him, both before he had become involved with me and after. She said that when they took my mother to the hospital he had been particularly insistent. She said that while the doctors were examining my mother and they were waiting for the results in the waiting room he had sworn to her that he was with me only to feel closer to her.

"Look at me," she whispered. "I know I'm mean to tell you

these things, but he is much worse than I am. He has the worst kind of meanness, that of superficiality."

78.

I returned to Via Tasso determined to cut off every relation with Nino. I found the house empty and in perfect order, I sat beside the French door that led to the balcony. Life in that apartment was over, in a couple of years the reasons for my very presence in Naples had been consumed.

I waited with growing anxiety for him to appear. Several hours passed, I fell asleep, I woke with a start, when it was dark. The telephone was ringing.

I hurried to answer, sure that it was Nino, but it was Antonio. He was calling from a café nearby, he asked if I could meet him. I said: Come up. I heard his hesitation, then he agreed. I had no doubt that Lila had sent him, and he admitted it himself right away.

"She doesn't want you to do something foolish," he said, making an effort to speak in Italian.

"You can stop me?"

"Yes."

"How?"

He sat down in the living room, after refusing the coffee I wanted to make for him, and deliberately, in the tone of someone who is used to giving detailed reports, listed all Nino's lovers: names, surnames, professions, relatives. Some I didn't know, they were relationships from long ago. Others he had brought to dinner at my house and I remembered them, affectionate with me and the children. Mirella, who had taken care of Dede, Elsa, and also Imma, had been with him for three years. And his relationship with the gynecologist who had delivered my daughter, and Lila's too, was even longer. Antonio

enumerated a sizable number of females—he used that word—
with whom, at various times, Nino had applied the same
scheme: an intense period of meetings, then occasional encounters, in no case a definitive break. He's faithful, Antonio said,
sarcastically, he never really cuts off relations: now he goes to
that one, now he goes to that other.

"Does Lina know?"

"Yes."

"Since when?"

"Recently."

"Why didn't you tell me right away?"

"I wanted to tell you right away."

"And Lina?"

"She said to wait."

"And you obeyed her. You two let me cook and set the table
for people he had betrayed me with the day before or would
betray me with the day after. I ate with people whose foot or
knee or something else he touched under the table. I entrusted
my children to a girl he jumped on as soon as I looked away."

Antonio shrugged, he looked at his hands, clasped them,
and left them between his knees.

"If they tell me to do a thing I do it," he said in dialect.

But then he got confused. I almost always do it, he said, and
tried to explain: sometimes I obey money, sometimes respect,
in some cases myself. As for infidelities, he said, if you don't
find out about them at the right moment they're of no use:
when you're in love you forgive everything. For infidelities to
have their real impact some lovelessness has to develop first.
And he went on like that, piling up painful remarks about the
blindness of people in love. As if by way of example, he told
me again about how, years before, he had spied on Nino and
Lila for the Solaras. In that case, he said proudly, I didn't do
what they ordered. He hadn't felt like handing Lila over to
Michele and had called Enzo so that he could get her out of

trouble. He spoke again of the beating he had given Nino. I did it, he muttered, most of all because you loved him and not me, and then because if that piece of shit went back to Lina, she would have stayed faithful to him and would be ruined forever. You see, he concluded, in that case, too, there was little to be gained by talking, Lina wouldn't have listened to me, love not only doesn't have eyes, it doesn't have ears, either.

I asked him, stunned:

"In all these years you never told Lina that Nino was going back to her that night?"

"No."

"You should have."

"Why? When my head says, it's better to act in this way, I do it, and I don't think about it anymore. If you go back to it you only make trouble."

How wise he had become. That was when I learned that the story of Nino and Lila would have lasted a little longer if Antonio hadn't cut it off with a beating. But I immediately discarded the hypothesis that they would have loved each other all their lives, and perhaps both he and she would have become utterly different people: to me it seemed not only unlikely but unbearable. Instead I sighed with impatience. Antonio had decided for his own reasons to save Lila and now Lila had sent him to save me. I looked at him, I said with explicit sarcasm something about his role as a protector of women. He should have showed up in Florence, I thought, when I was hanging in the balance, when I didn't know what to do, and made the decision for me with his gnarled hands, as years before he had decided for Lila. I asked him teasingly:

"What orders do you have now?"

"Before sending me here, Lina forbade me to break the face of that shit. But I did it once and I'd like to do it again."

"You're unreliable."

"Yes and no."

"Meaning?"

"It's a complicated situation, Lenù, stay out of it. You just tell me that the son of Sarratore should repent the day he was born and I'll make him repent."

I couldn't contain myself, I burst out laughing at the mannered seriousness with which he expressed himself. It was the tone he had learned in the neighborhood as a boy, the formal tone of the upright male: he who in reality had been timid and fearful. What an effort it must have been, but now it was *his* tone, he wouldn't have known how to have any other. The only difference, in relation to the past, was that in that situation he was making an effort to speak in Italian and the difficult language was coming to him with a foreign accent.

He darkened because of my laughter, he looked at the black panes of the window, he said: Don't laugh. I saw that his forehead was shiny in spite of the cold, he was sweating from the shame of having seemed ridiculous to me. He said: I know I don't express myself well, I know German better than Italian. I became aware of his odor, the way it had smelled at the time of the ponds. I'm laughing, I apologized, at the situation, at you, who've wanted to kill Nino forever, and at me, who if he showed up now would say to you: Yes, kill him. I'm laughing out of despair, because I've never been so offended, because I feel humiliated in a way that I don't know if you can imagine, because at this moment I'm so ill that I think I'm fainting.

In fact I felt weak, and dead inside. So I was suddenly grateful to Lila for having had the sensitivity to send me Antonio, he was the only person whose affection at that moment I didn't doubt. Besides, his lean body, his big bones, his thick eyebrows, his coarse features had remained familiar to me, they didn't repel me, I wasn't afraid of them. At the ponds, I said, it was cold and we didn't feel it: I'm trembling, can I sit next to you?

He looked at me uncertainly, but I didn't wait for his assent. I got up, I sat on his knees. He didn't move, he extended only his arms, for fear of touching me, and let them fall to the sides of the chair. I leaned against him, resting my face between his neck and his shoulder, it seemed to me that for a few seconds I fell asleep.

"Lenù."

"Yes?"

"Do you not feel well?"

"Hold me, I have to warm up."

"No."

"Why?"

"I'm not sure you want me."

"I want you now, this time only: it's something you owe me and I you."

"I don't owe you anything. I love you and you, instead, have always loved only him."

"Yes, but I never desired anyone the way I desired you, not even him."

I talked for a long time, I told him the truth, the truth of that moment and the truth of the faraway time of the ponds. He was the discovery of excitement, he was the pit of the stomach that grew warm, that opened up, that turned liquid, releasing a burning indolence. Franco, Pietro, Nino had stumbled on that expectation but had never managed to satisfy it, because it was an expectation without a definite object, it was the hope of pleasure, the hardest to fulfill. The taste of Antonio's mouth, the perfume of his desire, his hands, the large sex taut between his thighs constituted a *before* that couldn't be matched. The *after* had never been truly equal to our afternoons hidden by the skeleton of the canning factory, although they consisted of love without penetration and often without orgasm.

I spoke in an Italian that was complex. I did it more to explain to myself what I was doing than to clarify to him, and this must have seemed to him an act of trust, he seemed content.

He held me, he kissed me on one shoulder, then on the neck, finally on the mouth. I don't think I've had any other sexual relation like that, which abruptly joined the ponds of more than twenty years earlier and the room on Via Tasso, the chair, the floor, the bed, suddenly sweeping away everything that was between us, that divided us, what was me, what was him. Antonio was delicate, he was brutal, and I was the same, no less than him. He demanded things and I demanded things with a fury, an anxiety, a need for violation that I didn't think I harbored. At the end he was annihilated by wonder and I was, too.

"What happened?" I asked, stunned, as if the memory of that absolute intimacy had already vanished.

"I don't know," he said, "but luckily it happened."

I smiled.

"You're like everybody else, you've betrayed your wife."

I wanted to joke, but he took me seriously, he said in dialect:

"I haven't betrayed anyone. My wife—*before now*—doesn't exist yet."

An obscure formulation but I understood. He was trying to tell me that he agreed with me, seeking to communicate, in turn, a sense of time outside the present chronology. He wanted to say that we had lived *now* a small fragment of a day that belonged to twenty years earlier. I kissed him, I whispered: Thank you, and I told him I was grateful because he had chosen to ignore the brutal reasons for all that sex—mine and his—and to see in it only the need to close our accounts.

Then the telephone rang, I went to answer, it might be Lila who needed me for the children. But it was Nino.

"Luckily you're home," he said breathlessly. "I'm coming right away."

"No."

"When?"

"Tomorrow."

"Let me explain, it's essential, it's urgent."

"No."

"Why?"

I told him and hung up.

79.

It was hard to separate from Nino; it took months. I don't think I've ever suffered so much for a man; it tortured me both to keep him away and to take him back. He wouldn't admit that he had made romantic and sexual offers to Lila. He insulted her, he mocked her, he accused her of wanting to destroy our relationship. But he was lying. At first he always lied, he even tried to convince me that what I had seen in the bathroom was a mistake due to weariness and jealousy. Then he began to give in. He confessed to some relationships but backdated them, as for others, indisputably recent, he said they had been meaningless, he swore that with those women it was friendship, not love. We quarreled all through Christmas, all winter. Sometimes I silenced him, worn out by his skill at accusing himself, defending himself, and *expecting* forgiveness, sometimes I yielded in the face of his despair, which seemed real—he often arrived drunk—sometimes I threw him out because, out of honesty, pride, maybe even dignity, he never promised that he would stop seeing those he called his friends, nor would he assure me that he would not lengthen the list.

On that theme he often undertook long, very cultured monologues in which he tried to convince me that it wasn't his fault but that of nature, of astral matter, of spongy bodies and their excessive liquids, of the immoderate heat of his loins—in short, of his exorbitant virility. No matter how much I add up all the books I've read, he murmured, in a tone that was sincere, pained, and yet vain to the point of ridiculousness, no matter how much I add up the languages I've learned, the mathematics, the sciences, the literature, and most of all my love for you—yes, the love and the need I have for you, the terror of not being able to have you anymore—believe me, I beg you, believe me, there's nothing to be done, I can't I can't I can't, the occasional desire, the most foolish, the most obtuse, prevails.

Sometimes he moved me, more often he irritated me, in general I responded with sarcasm. And he was silent, he nervously ruffled his hair, then he started again. But when I said to him coldly one morning that perhaps all that need for women was the symptom of a labile heterosexuality that in order to endure needed constant confirmation, he was offended, he harassed me for days, he wanted to know if I had been better with Antonio than with him. Since I was now tired of all that distraught talk, I shouted yes. And since in that phase of excruciating quarrels some of his friends had tried to get into my bed, and I, out of boredom, out of spite, had sometimes consented, I mentioned names of people he was fond of, and to wound him I said they had been better than him.

He disappeared. He had said that he couldn't do without Dede and Elsa, he had said that he loved Imma more than his other children, he had said that he would take care of the three children even if I hadn't wanted to go back to him. In reality not only did he forget about us immediately but he stopped paying the rent in Via Tasso, along with the bills for the electricity, the gas, the telephone.

I looked in vain for a cheaper apartment in the area: often, apartments that were uglier and smaller commanded even higher rents. Then Lila said to me that there were three rooms and a kitchen available just above her. The rent was almost nothing, from the windows you could see both the *stradone* and the courtyard. She said it in her way, in the tone of someone who signals: I'm only giving you the information, do as you like.

I was depressed, I was frightened. Elisa had recently yelled at me during a quarrel: Papa is alone, go live with him, I'm tired of having to take care of him myself. And naturally I had refused, in my situation I couldn't take care of my father, too. I was already the slave of my daughters. Imma was constantly sick, as soon as Dede got over the flu Elsa had it, she wouldn't do her homework unless I sat with her, Dede got mad and said: Then you have to help me, too. I was exhausted, a nervous wreck. And then, in the great chaos I had fallen into, I didn't have even that bit of active life that until then I had guaranteed myself. I turned down invitations and articles and trips, I didn't dare answer the telephone for fear it was the publisher asking for the book. I had ended up in a vortex that was pulling me down, and a hypothetical return to the neighborhood would be the proof that I had touched bottom. To immerse myself again, and my daughters, in that mentality, let myself be absorbed by Lila, by Carmen, by Alfonso, by everyone, just as in fact they wanted. No, no, I swore to myself that I would go and live in Tribunali, in Duchesca, in Lavinaio, in Forcella, amid the scaffolding that marked the earthquake damage, rather than return to the neighborhood. In that atmosphere the editor called.

"How far along are you?"

It was an instant, a flame kindled in my head illuminating it like day. I knew what I had to say and what I had to do.

"I finished just yesterday."

"Seriously? Send it today."

"Tomorrow morning I'll go to the post office."

"Thank you. As soon as the book arrives, I'll read it and let you know."

"Take your time."

I hung up. I went to a big box I kept in the bedroom closet, I pulled out the typescript that years before neither Adele nor Lila had liked, I didn't even attempt to reread it. The next morning I took the children to school and went with Imma to send the package. I knew that it was a risky move, but it seemed to me the only one possible to save my reputation. I had promised to deliver a novel and here it was. Was it an unsuccessful novel, irrefutably bad? Well, it wouldn't be published. But I had worked hard, I hadn't deceived anyone, I would soon do better.

The line at the post office was exhausting, I had to protest continually against people who didn't respect it. In that situation my disaster became obvious to me. *Why am I here, why am I wasting time like this. The girls and Naples have eaten me alive. I don't study, I don't write, I've lost all discipline.* I had gained a life very far from what might have been expected for me, and look how I had ended up. I felt exasperated, guilty toward myself and especially toward my mother. Furthermore, Imma had been making me anxious: when I compared her with Tina I was sure she was suffering from some developmental problem. Lila's daughter, although she was three weeks younger, was very lively, seemed more than a year old, whereas Imma seemed unresponsive and had a vacant look. I observed her obsessively, I harassed her with tests that I invented on the spot. I thought: it would be terrible if Nino not only had ruined my life but had given me a daughter with problems. And yet people stopped me on the street because she was so plump, so fair. Here, even at the post office, the women in line complimented her, how chubby she was. But she didn't even smile. A man offered her a candy and Imma stretched out her hand reluctantly, took it, dropped it. Ah, I was constantly anxious, every day a new worry was added to the others. When I came out of the post office and the package had been sent and there was no way to stop it, I jumped, I remembered my mother-in-law. Good Lord, what had I done. Was it possible that I hadn't considered that the publisher would give the manuscript to Adele? It was she, after all, who had wanted the publication of both my first book and the second, they owed it to her if only out of courtesy. And she would say: Greco is cheating you, this isn't a new text, I read it years ago and it's terrible. I broke out in a cold sweat, I felt weak. To plug one leak I had created another. I was no longer able to keep under control, even within the limits of the possible, the chain of my actions.

80.

Just then, to complicate things, Nino showed up again. He had never given me back the keys, even though I had insisted on having them, and so he reappeared without calling, without knocking. I told him to go, the house was mine, he wasn't paying the rent and wasn't giving me a cent for Imma. He swore that, annihilated by grief at our separation, he had forgotten. He seemed sincere; he had a feverish look, and was very thin. He promised with an involuntarily comical solemnity to start paying the next month, he spoke in a sorrowful voice of his love for Imma. Then, apparently in a good-humored way, he began to ask again about my encounter with Antonio, about how it had gone, first in general and then sexually. From Antonio he moved on to his friends. He tried to make me admit that I had yielded ("yield" seemed to him the right verb) to this one or that one not out of genuine attraction but only out of spite. I was alarmed when he began to caress my shoulder, my knee, my cheek. I soon saw—in his eyes and in his words—that what made him desperate was not that he had lost my love but that I had been with those other men, and that sooner or later I would be with others and would prefer them to him. He had showed up, that morning, only to reenter my bed. He demanded that I vilify those recent lovers by showing him that my only desire was to be penetrated again by him. He wanted, in other words, to reassert his primacy, then surely he would again disappear. I managed to get the keys back and I threw him out. I realized then, and to my surprise, that I no longer felt anything for him. The long time that I had loved him dissolved conclusively that morning.

The next day I began to ask about what I had to do to get a job, even as a substitute, in the middle schools. I quickly realized that it wouldn't be simple, and that in any case I would have to wait for the new school year. Since I took for granted the break with the publisher, which was followed in my imagination by the devastating collapse of my identity as a writer, I was frightened. From birth, the children had been used to a comfortable life, I myself—ever since my marriage to Pietro— couldn't imagine being without books, magazines, newspapers, records, movies, theater. I had to think immediately of some provisional job, and I put advertisements in the local shops offering private lessons.

Then one morning in June the editor called. He had received the manuscript, he had read it.

"Already?" I said with feigned indifference.

"Yes. And it's a book that I would never have expected from you, but that you, surprisingly, wrote."

"You're saying it's bad?"

"It is, from the first line to the last, pure pleasure of narration."

My heart was going crazy in my chest.

"Is it good or not?"

"It's extraordinary."

81.

I was proud. In a few seconds I not only regained faith in myself, I relaxed, I began to speak of my work with a childish enthusiasm, I laughed too much, I questioned the editor

closely to get a more articulated approval. I quickly understood that he had read my pages as a sort of autobiography, an
arrangement in novel form of my experience of the poorest
and most violent Naples. He said he had feared the negative
effects of a return to my city, but now he had to admit that that
return had helped me. I didn't say that the book had been written several years earlier in Florence. It's a harsh novel, he
emphasized, I would say masculine, but paradoxically also delicate, in other words a big step forward. Then he discussed
organizational questions. He wanted to move the publication
to the spring of 1983 to devote himself to careful editing and
to prepare the launch. He concluded, with some sarcasm:
"I talked about it with your ex-mother-in-law. She said that
she had read an old version and hadn't liked it; but evidently
either her taste has aged or your personal problems kept her
from giving a dispassionate evaluation."
I quickly admitted that long ago I had let Adele read a first
draft. He said: It's clear that the air of Naples has given free
rein to your talent. When he hung up I felt hugely relieved. I
changed, I became particularly affectionate toward my daughters. The publisher paid the rest of the advance and my economic situation improved. Suddenly I began to look at the city
and especially at the neighborhood as an important part of my
life; not only should I not dismiss it but it was essential to the
success of my work. It was a sudden leap, going from distrust
to a joyful sense of myself. What I had felt as a precipice not
only acquired literary nobility but seemed to me a determined
choice of a cultural and political arena. The editor himself had
sanctioned it authoritatively, saying: For you, returning to the
point of departure has been a step forward. Of course, I hadn't
said that the book was written in Florence, that the return to
Naples had had no influence on the text. But the narrative
material, the human depth of the characters came from the
neighborhood, and surely the turning point was there. Adele

hadn't had the sensitivity to understand, so she had lost. All the Airotas had lost. Nino had lost, too, as in essence he had considered me one of the women on his list, without distinguishing me from the others. And—what for me was even more significant—Lila had lost. She hadn't liked my book, she had been severe, it was one of the few times in her life she had cried, when she had had to wound me with her negative judgment. But I didn't want it from her, rather I was pleased that she was wrong. From childhood I had given her too much importance, and now I felt as if unburdened. Finally it was clear that what I was wasn't her, and vice versa. Her authority was no longer necessary to me, I had my own. I felt strong, no longer a victim of my origins but capable of dominating them, of giving them a shape, of taking revenge on them for myself, for Lila, for whomever. What before was dragging me down was now the material for climbing higher. One morning in July of 1982 I called her and said:

"All right, I'll take the apartment above you, I'm coming back to the neighborhood."

82.

I moved in midsummer, Antonio took care of the logistics. He assembled some brawny men who emptied the apartment on Via Tasso and arranged everything in the apartment in the neighborhood. The new house was dark and repainting the rooms didn't help brighten it. But, contrary to what I had thought since I returned to Naples, this didn't bother me; in fact the dusty light that had always struggled to penetrate the windows had the effect on me of an evocative childhood memory. Dede and Elsa, on the other hand, protested at length. They had grown up in Florence, Genoa, in the bright light of Via Tasso, and they immediately hated the floors of uneven tiles, the small dark bathroom, the din of the *stradone*. They resigned themselves only because now they could enjoy some not insignificant advantages: see Aunt Lina every day, get up later because the school was nearby, go there by themselves, spend time on the street and in the courtyard.

I was immediately seized by a yearning to regain possession of the neighborhood. I enrolled Elsa in the elementary school where I had gone and Dede in my middle school. I resumed contact with anyone, old or young, who remembered me. I celebrated my decision with Carmen and her family, with Alfonso, with Ada, with Pinuccia. Naturally I had misgivings, and Pietro, who was very unhappy with the decision, made them worse. He said on the telephone:

"On the basis of what criteria do you want to bring up our daughters in a place that you fled?"

"I won't bring them up here."

"But you've taken a house and enrolled them in school without considering that they deserve something else."

"I have a book to finish and I can only do it well here."

"I could have taken them."

"You would also take Imma? All three are my daughters and I don't want the third to be separated from the other two."

He calmed down. He was happy that I had left Nino and he soon forgave the move. Keep at your work, he said, I have confidence in you, you know what you're doing. I hoped it was true. I watched the trucks that passed noisily along the *stradone*, raising dust. I walked in the gardens that were full of syringes. I went into the neglected, empty church. I felt sad in front of the parish cinema, which had closed, in front of the party offices, which were like abandoned dens. I listened to the shouting of men, women, children in the apartments, especially at night. The feuds between families, the hostilities between neighbors, the ease with which things came to blows, the wars between gangs of boys. When I went to the pharmacy

I remembered Gino; I felt revulsion at the sight of the place where he had been killed, and went cautiously around it. I spoke compassionately to his parents, who were still behind the old dark-wood counter, more bent over, white-haired in their white smocks, and as kind as ever. As a child I endured all this, I thought, let's see if now I can control it.

"How is it that you decided to do it?" Lila asked some time after the move. Maybe she wanted an affectionate answer, or maybe a sort of recognition of the validity of her choices, words like: You were right to stay, going out into the world was of no use, now I understand. Instead I answered:

"It's an experiment."

"Experiment in what?"

We were in her office. Tina was near her, Imma was wandering on her own. I said:

"An experiment in recomposition. You've managed to have your whole life here, but not me: I feel I'm in pieces scattered all over."

She had an expression of disapproval.

"Forget these experiments, Lenù, otherwise you'll be disappointed and leave again. I'm also in pieces. Between my father's shoe repair shop and this office it's only a few meters, but it's as if they were at the North Pole and the South Pole."

I said, pretending to be amused:

"Don't discourage me. In my job I have to paste one fact to another with words, and in the end everything has to seem coherent even if it's not."

"But if the coherence isn't there, why pretend?"

"To create order. Remember the novel I gave you to read and you didn't like? There I tried to set what I know about Naples within what I later learned in Pisa, Florence, Milan. Now I've given it to the publisher and he thought it was good. It's being published."

She narrowed her eyes. She said softly:

"I told you that I don't understand anything."

I felt I had wounded her. It was as if I had thrown it in her face: if you can't connect your story of the shoes with the story of the computers, that doesn't mean that it can't be done, it means only that you don't have the tools to do it. I said hastily: You'll see, no one will buy the book and you'll be right. Then I listed somewhat randomly all the defects that I myself attributed to my text, and what I wanted to keep or change before it was published. But she escaped, it was as if she wanted to regain altitude, she started talking about computers and she did it as if to point out: You have your things, I mine. She said to the children: Do you want to see a new machine that Enzo bought?

She led us into a small room. She explained to Dede and Elsa: This machine is called a personal computer, it costs a lot of money but it can do wonderful things, look how it works. She sat on a stool and first she settled Tina on her knees, then she began patiently to explain every element, speaking to Dede, to Elsa, to the baby, never to me.

I looked at Tina the whole time. She talked to her mother, asked, pointing: What's this, and if her mother didn't pay attention she tugged on the edge of her shirt, grabbed her chin, insisted: Mamma, what's this. Lila explained it to her as if she were an adult. Imma wandered around the room, pulling a little wagon, and sometimes she sat down on the floor, disoriented. Come, Imma, I said, over and over, listen to what Aunt Lina is saying. But she continued to play with the wagon.

My daughter did not have the qualities of Lila's daughter. A few days earlier the anxiety that she was in some way retarded had dissipated. I had taken her to a very good pediatrician, the child showed no retardation of any sort. I was reassured. And yet comparing Imma to Tina continued to make me uneasy. How lively Tina was: to see her, to hear her talk put you in a good mood. And to see mother and daughter together was touching. As long as Lila talked about the computer—we were starting then to use that word—I observed them both with admiration. At that moment I felt happy, satisfied with myself, and so I also felt, very clearly, that I loved my friend for how she was, for her virtues and her flaws, for everything, even for that being she had brought into the world. The child was full of curiosity, she learned everything in an instant, she had a large vocabulary and a surprising manual dexterity. I said to myself: She has little of Enzo, she's like Lila, look how she widens her eyes, narrows them, look at the ears that have no lobe. I still didn't dare to admit that Tina attracted me more than my daughter, but when that demonstration of skill ended, I was very excited about the computer, and full of praise for the little girl, even though I knew that Imma might suffer from it (*How clever you are, how pretty, how well you speak, how many things you learn*), I complimented Lila, mainly to diminish the unease I had caused her by announcing the publication of my book, and, finally, I drew an optimistic portrait of the future that awaited my three daughters and hers. They'll study, I said, they'll travel all over the world, goodness knows what they'll be. But Lila, after smothering Tina with kisses—*yes, she's sooo clever*—replied bitterly: Gennaro was clever, too, he spoke well, he read, he was very good in school, and look at him now.

83.

One night when Lila was speaking disparagingly of Gennaro, Dede gathered her courage and defended him. She became red-faced, she said: He's extremely intelligent. Lila looked at her with interest, smiled, replied: You're very nice, I'm his mamma and what you say gives me great pleasure.

From then on Dede felt authorized to defend Gennaro on every occasion, even when Lila was very angry at him. Gennaro

was now a large boy of eighteen, with a handsome face, like his
father's as a youth, but he was stockier and had a surly nature.
He didn't even notice Dede, who was twelve, he had other
things on his mind. But she never stopped thinking of him as
the most astonishing human creature who had ever appeared
on the face of the earth and whenever she could she sang his
praises. Sometimes Lila was in a bad mood and didn't respond.
But on other occasions she laughed, she exclaimed: Certainly
not, he's a delinquent. You three sisters, on the other hand,
you're clever, you'll be better than your mother. And Dede,
although pleased with the compliment (when she could consider herself better than me she was happy), immediately began
to belittle herself in order to elevate Gennaro.

She adored him. She would often sit at the window to
watch for his return from the shop, shouting at him as soon as
he appeared: Hi, Rino. If he answered hi (usually he didn't) she
hurried to the landing to wait for him to come up the stairs and
then tried to start a serious conversation, like: You're tired,
what did you do to your hand, aren't you hot in those overalls,
things of that sort. Even a few words from him excited her. If
she happened to get more attention than usual, in order to pro-
long it she grabbed Imma and said: I'm taking her down to
Aunt Lina, so she can play with Tina. I didn't have time to give
her permission before she was out of the house.

Never had so little space separated Lila and me, not even
when we were children. My floor was her ceiling. Two flights
of stairs down brought me to her house, two up brought her to
mine. In the morning, in the evening, I heard their voices: the
indistinct sounds of conversations, Tina's trills that Lila
responded to as if she, too, were trilling, the thick tonality of
Enzo, who, silent as he was, spoke a lot to his daughter, and
often sang to her. I supposed that the signs of my presence also
reached Lila. When she was at work, when my older daughters
were at school, when only Imma and Tina—who often stayed

with me, sometimes even to sleep—were at home, I noticed the emptiness below, I listened for the footsteps of Lila and Enzo returning.

Things soon took a turn for the better. Dede and Elsa frequently looked after Imma; they carried her down to the courtyard with them or to Lila's. If I had to go out Lila took care of all three. It was years since I had had so much time available. I read, I revised my book, I was at ease without Nino and free of the anxiety of losing him. Also my relationship with Pietro improved. He came to Naples more often to see the girls, he got used to the small, dreary apartment and to their Neapolitan accents, Elsa's especially, and he often stayed overnight. At those times, he was polite to Enzo, and talked a lot to Lila. Even though in the past Pietro had had definitely negative opinions of her, it seemed clear that he was happy to spend time in her company. As for Lila, as soon as he left she began to talk about him with an enthusiasm she rarely showed for anyone. How many books must he have studied, she said seriously, fifty thousand, a hundred thousand? I think she saw in my ex-husband the incarnation of her childhood fantasies about people who read and write for knowledge, not as a profession.

"You're very smart," she said to me one evening, "but he has a way of speaking that I truly like: he puts the writing into his voice, but he doesn't speak like a printed book."

"I do?" I asked, as a joke.

"A little."

"Even now?"

"Yes."

"If I hadn't learned to speak like that I would never have had any respect, outside of here."

"He's like you, but more natural. When Gennaro was little, I thought—even though I didn't know Pietro yet—I thought I'd want him to become just like that."

She often talked about her son. She said she should have given him more, but she hadn't had time, or consistency, or ability. She accused herself of having taught him the little she could and of having then lost confidence and stopped. One night she went from her first child to the second without interruption. She was afraid that Tina, too, as she grew up would be a waste. I praised Tina, sincerely, and she said in a serious tone: "Now that you're here you have to help her become like your daughters. It's important to Enzo, too, he told me to ask you."

"All right."

"You help me, I'll help you. School isn't enough, you remember Maestra Oliviero, with me it wasn't enough."

"They were different times."

"I don't know. I gave Gennaro what was possible, but it went badly."

"It's the fault of the neighborhood."

She looked at me gravely, she said:

"I don't have much faith in it, but since you've decided to stay here with us, let's change the neighborhood."

84.

In a few months we became very close. We got in the habit of going out together to do the shopping, and on Sundays, rather than strolling amid the stalls on the *stradone*, we insisted on going to the center of town with Enzo so that our daughters could have the sun and the sea air. We walked along Via Caracciolo or in the Villa Comunale. He carried Tina on his shoulders, he pampered her, maybe too much. But he never forgot my daughters, he bought balloons, sweets, he played with them. Lila and I stayed behind them on purpose. We talked about everything, but not the way we had as adolescents: those times would never return. She asked questions about things she had heard on television and I answered volubly. I talked about the postmodern, the problems of publishing, the latest news of feminism, whatever came into my mind, and Lila listened attentively, her expression just slightly ironic, interrupting only to ask for further explanations, never to say what she thought. I liked talking to her. I liked her look of admiration, I liked it when she said: How many things you know, how many things you think, even when I felt she was teasing. If I pressed for her opinion she retreated, saying: No, don't make me say something stupid, you talk. Often she asked me about famous people, to find out if I knew them, and when I said no she was disappointed. She was also disappointed—I should say—when I reduced to ordinary dimensions well-known people I'd had dealings with.

"So," she concluded one morning, "those people aren't what they seem."

"Not at all. Often they're good at their work. But otherwise they're greedy, they like hurting you, they're allied with the strong and they persecute the weak, they form gangs to fight other gangs, they treat women like dogs on a leash, they'll utter obscenities and put their hands on you exactly the way they do on the buses here."

"You're exaggerating?"

"No, to produce ideas you don't have to be a saint. And anyway there are very few true intellectuals. The mass of the educated spend their lives commenting lazily on the ideas of others. They engage their best energies in sadistic practices against every possible rival."

"Then why are you with them?"

I answered: I'm not with them, I'm here. I wanted her to feel that I was part of an upper-class world and yet different. She herself pushed me in that direction. She was amused if I was sarcastic about my colleagues. Sometimes I had the impression that she insisted so that I would confirm that I really was one of those who told people how things stood and what they should think. The decision to live in the neighborhood made sense to her only if I continued to count myself among those who wrote books, contributed to magazines and newspapers, appeared sometimes on television. She wanted me as her friend, her neighbor, provided I had that aura. And I supported her. Her approval gave me confidence. I was beside her in the Villa Comunale, with our daughters, and yet I was definitively different, I had a wide-ranging life. It flattered me to feel that, compared to her, I was a woman of great experience and I felt that she, too, was pleased with what I was. I told her about France, Germany, and Austria, about the United States, the debates I had taken part in, here and there, the men there had been recently, after Nino. She was attentive to every word with a half smile, never saying what she thought. Not even the story of my occasional relationships set off in her a need to confide.

"Are you happy with Enzo?" I asked one morning.

"Enough."

"And you've never been interested in someone else?"

"No."

"Do you really love him?"

"Enough."

There was no way of getting anything else out of her, it was I who talked about sex and often in an explicit way. My ramblings, her silences. Yet, whatever the subject, during those walks, something was released from her very body that enthralled me, stimulating my brain as it always had, helping me reflect.

Maybe that was why I sought her out. She continued to emit an energy that gave comfort, that reinforced a purpose, that spontaneously suggested solutions. It was a force that struck not only me. Sometimes she invited me to dinner with the children, more often I invited her, with Enzo and, naturally, Tina. Gennaro, no, there was nothing to be done, he often stayed out and came home late at night. Enzo—I soon realized—was worried about him, whereas Lila said: He's grown-up, let him do as he likes. But I felt she spoke that way to reduce her partner's anxiety. And the tone was identical to that of our conversations. Enzo nodded, something passed from her to him like an invigorating tonic.

It was no different on the streets of the neighborhood. Going shopping with her never ceased to amaze me: she had become an authority. She was constantly stopped, people drew her aside with a respectful familiarity, they whispered something to her, and she listened, without reacting. Did they treat her like that because of the success she had had with her new business? Because she gave off the sense of someone who could do anything? Or because, now that she was nearly forty, the energy she had always had imbued her with the aura of a magician who cast spells and instilled fear? I don't know. Of course it struck me that people paid more attention to her than to me. I was a well-known writer and the publishing house was making sure that, in view of my new book, I was often mentioned in the newspapers: the *Repubblica* had come out with a fairly large photograph of me to illustrate a short article on forthcoming books, which at a certain point said: *Highly anticipated is the new novel by Elena Greco, a story set in an unknown Naples, with bloodred colors*, et cetera. And yet next to her, in the place where we were born, I was only a decoration, that is, I bore witness to Lila's merits. Those who had known us from birth attributed to her, to the force of her attraction, the fact that the neighborhood could have on its streets an esteemed person like me.

85.

I think there were many who wondered why I, who in the newspapers seemed rich and famous, had come to live in a wretched apartment, situated in an increasingly run-down area. Maybe the first not to understand were my daughters. Dede came home from school one day disgusted: "An old man peed in our doorway." Another day Elsa arrived terrified: "Today someone was knifed in the gardens." At such times I was afraid. The part of me that had long ago left the neighborhood was indignant, was worried about the children, and said, Enough. At home, Dede and Elsa spoke a good Italian, but occasionally I heard them from the window or coming up the stairs, and I realized that Elsa especially used a very aggressive, sometimes obscene dialect. I reprimanded her, she pretended to be sorry. But I knew that it took a lot of self-discipline to resist the lure of bad behavior and so many other temptations. Was it possible that while I was devoting myself to making literature they were getting lost? I calmed myself by repeating the temporal limit of this stay: after the publication of my book I would definitely leave Naples. I said it to myself and said it again: I needed only to reach a final draft of the novel.

The book was undoubtedly benefiting from everything that came from the neighborhood. But the work proceeded so well mainly because I was attentive to Lila, who had remained completely within that environment. Her voice, her gaze, her gestures, her meanness and her generosity, her dialect were all intimately connected to our place of birth. Even Basic Sight, in spite of the exotic name (people called her office *basissìt*), didn't seem some sort of meteorite that had fallen from outer space but rather the unexpected product of poverty, violence, and blight. Thus, drawing on her to give truth to my story seemed indispensable. Afterward I would leave for good, I intended to move to Milan.

I had only to sit in her office for a while to understand the background against which she moved. I looked at her brother, who was now openly consumed by drugs. I looked at Ada, who was crueler every day, the sworn enemy of Marisa, who had taken Stefano away from her. I looked at Alfonso—in whose face, in whose habits, the feminine and the masculine continually broke boundaries with effects that one day repelled me, the next moved me, and always alarmed me—who often had a black eye or a split lip because of the beatings he got, who knows where, who knows when. I looked at Carmen, who, in the blue jacket of a gas-pump attendant, drew Lila aside and interrogated her like an oracle. I looked at Antonio, who hovered around her with unfinished sentences or stood in a serene silence when he brought to the office, as if on a courtesy visit, his beautiful German wife, the children. Meanwhile I picked up endless rumors. Stefano Carracci is about to close the grocery, he doesn't have a lira, he needs money. It was Pasquale Peluso who kidnapped so-and-so, and if it wasn't him he certainly has something to do with it. That other so-and-so set fire to the shirt factory in Afragola by himself to fuck the insurance company. Watch out for Dede, they're giving children drugged candy. There's a faggot hanging around the elementary school who lures children away. The Solaras are opening a night club in the new neighborhood, women and drugs, the music will be so loud that no one will sleep again. Big trucks pass by on the *stradone* at night, transporting stuff that can destroy us faster than the atomic bomb. Gennaro has started hanging out with a bad crowd, and, if he continues like that, I won't even let him go to work. The person they found murdered in the tunnel looked like a woman but was a man: there was so much blood in the body that it flowed all the way down to the gas pump.

I observed, I listened, from the vantage point of what Lila and I as children had imagined becoming and what I had actually become: the author of a big book that I was polishing—or at times rewriting—and that would soon be published. In the first draft—I said to myself—I put too much dialect. And I erased it, rewrote. Then it seemed that I had put in too little and I added some. I was in the neighborhood and yet safe in that role, within that setting. The ambitious work justified my presence there and, as long as I was occupied with it, gave meaning to the poor light in the rooms, the rough voices of the street, the risks that the children ran, the traffic on the *stradone* that raised dust when the weather was good and water and mud when it rained, Lila and Enzo's swarm of clients, small provincial entrepreneurs, big luxury cars, clothes of a vulgar wealth, heavy bodies that moved sometimes aggressively, sometimes with servile manners.

Once when I was waiting for Lila at Basic Sight with Imma and Tina, everything seemed to become clearer: Lila was doing new work but totally immersed in our old world. I heard her shouting at a client in an extremely crude way about a question of money. I was shaken, where had the woman who graciously emanated authority suddenly gone? Enzo hurried in, and the man—a small man around sixty, with an enormous belly—went away cursing. Afterward I said to Lila:

"Who are you really?"

"In what sense?"

"If you don't want to talk about it, forget it."

"No, let's talk, but explain what you mean."

"I mean: in an environment like this, with the people you have to deal with, how do you behave?"

"I'm careful, like everyone."

"That's all?"

"Well, I'm careful and I move things around in order to make them go the way I say. Haven't we always behaved that way?"

"Yes, but now we have responsibilities, toward ourselves and our children. Didn't you say we have to change the neighborhood?"

"And to change it what do you think needs to be done?"

"Resort to the law."

I was startled myself by what I was saying. I made a speech in which I was, to my surprise, even more legalistic than my ex-husband and, in many ways, more than Nino. Lila said teasingly:

"The law is fine when you're dealing with people who pay attention if you merely say the word 'law'. But you know how it is here."

"And so?"

"So if people have no fear of the law, you have to instill the fear yourself. We did a lot of work for that shit you saw before, in fact a huge amount, but he won't pay, he says he has no money. I threatened him, I told him: I'll sue you. And he answered: Sue me, who gives a damn."

"But you'll sue him."

She laughed: "I'll never see my money that way. Some time ago, an accountant stole millions from us. We fired him and filed charges. But the law didn't lift a finger."

"So?"

"I was fed up with waiting and I asked Antonio. The money was returned immediately. And this money, too, will return, without a trial, without lawyers, and without judges."

86.

So Antonio did that sort of work for Lila. Not for money but out of friendship, or personal respect. Or, I don't know, maybe she asked Michele if she could borrow him, since Antonio worked for Michele, and Michele, who agreed to everything Lila asked, let her.

But did Michele really satisfy her every request? If it had certainly been true before I moved to the neighborhood, now it wasn't clear if things really were like that. First I noticed some odd signs: Lila no longer uttered Michele's name with condescension but, rather, with irritation or obvious concern; mainly, though, he hardly ever appeared at Basic Sight.

It was at the wedding celebration of Marcello and Elisa, which was ostentatious and lavish, that I became aware something had changed. During the entire reception Marcello stayed close to his brother; he often whispered to him, they laughed together, he put an arm around his shoulders. As for Michele, he seemed revived. He had returned to making long, pompous speeches, as he used to, while the children and Gigliola, now extraordinarily fat, sat obediently beside him, as if they had decided to forget the way he had treated them. It struck me how the vulgarity, which was still very provincial at the time of Lila's wedding, had been as if modernized. It had become a metropolitan vulgarity, and Lila herself was appropriate to it, in her habits, in her language, in her clothes. Nothing clashed, in other words, except for me and my daughters, who with our sobriety were completely out of place in that triumph of excessive colors, excessive laughter, excessive luxuries.

Perhaps that was why Michele's burst of rage was especially alarming. He was making a speech in honor of the newlyweds, but meanwhile little Tina was claiming something that Imma had taken away from her, and was screaming in the middle of the room. He was talking, Tina was crying. Suddenly Michele broke off and, with the eyes of a madman, shouted: Fuck, Lina, will you shut that piece of shit kid up? Like that, exactly in those words. Lila stared at him for a long second. She didn't speak, she didn't move. Very slowly, she placed one hand on the hand of Enzo, who was sitting next to her. I quickly got up from my table and took the two little girls outside.

The episode roused the bride, that is to say, my sister Elisa. At the end of the speech, when the sound of applause reached me, she came out, in her extravagant white dress. She said cheerfully: My brother-in-law has returned to himself. Then she added: But he shouldn't treat babies like that. She picked up Imma and Tina, and, laughing and joking returned to the hall with the two children. I followed her, confused.

For a while I thought that she, too, had returned to herself. Elisa in fact did change greatly, after her marriage, as if what had ruined her had been the absence, until that moment, of the marriage bond. She became a calm mother, a tranquil yet firm wife, her hostility toward me ended. Now when I went to her house with my daughters and, often, Tina, she welcomed me politely and was affectionate with the children. Even Marcello—when I ran into him—was courteous. He called me the sister-in-law who writes novels (*How is the sister-in-law who writes novels?*), said a cordial word or two, and disappeared. The house was always tidy, and Elisa and Silvio welcomed us dressed as if for a party. But my sister as a little girl—I soon realized—had vanished forever. The marriage had inaugurated a completely fake Signora Solara, never an intimate word, only a good-humored tone and a smile, all copied from her husband. I made an effort to be loving, with her and especially with my nephew. But I didn't find Silvio appealing, he was too much like Marcello, and Elisa must have realized it. One afternoon she turned bitter again for a few minutes. She said: You love Lina's child more than mine. I swore it wasn't true, I hugged the child, kissed him. But she shook her head, whispered: Besides, you went to live near Lina and not near me or Papa. She continued, in other words, to be angry with me and now also with our brothers. I think she accused them of behaving like ingrates. They lived and worked in Baiano and they weren't even in touch with Marcello, who had been so generous with them. Family ties, said Elisa, you think they're strong, but no. She talked as if she were stating a universal principle, then she added: To keep from breaking those ties, you need, as my husband has shown, goodwill. Michele had turned into an idiot, but Marcello restored his mind to him: Did you notice what a great speech he made at my wedding?

87.

Michele's return to his senses was marked not only by a return to his flowery speech but also by the absence among the guests of a person who during that period of crisis had been very close to him: Alfonso. Not to be invited was for my former schoolmate a source of great suffering. For days he did nothing but complain, asking aloud how he had wronged the Solaras. I worked for them for so many years, he said, and they didn't invite me. Then something happened that caused a sensation. One evening he came to dinner at my house with Lila and Enzo, very depressed. But Alfonso, who had never dressed as a woman in my presence except the day he tried on the maternity dress in the shop on Via Chiaia, arrived in women's clothes, leaving Dede and Elsa speechless. He was troublesome all evening; he drank a lot. He asked Lila obsessively: Am I getting fat, am I getting ugly, do I not look like you anymore? And Enzo: Who's prettier, her or me? At a certain point he complained that he had a blocked intestine, that he had a terrible pain in what—addressing the girls—he called his ass. And he began to insist that I look and see what was wrong. Look at my ass, he said, laughing in an obscene way, and Dede stared at him in bewilderment, Elsa tried to stifle a laugh. Enzo and Lila had to take him away in a hurry.

But Alfonso didn't calm down. The next day, without makeup, in male clothes, eyes red with crying, he left Basic Sight saying that he was going to have a coffee at the Bar Solara. At the entrance he met Michele, and they said something to each other. Michele, after a few minutes, began to punch and kick him, then he grabbed the pole that was used to lower the shutter and beat him methodically, for a long time. Alfonso returned to the office badly battered, but he couldn't stop repeating: It's my fault, I don't how to control myself. Control in what way we couldn't understand. Certainly, he got even worse, and Lila seemed worried. For days she tried in vain to soothe Enzo, who couldn't bear the violence of the strong against the weak, and wanted to go to Michele to see if he could beat him, Enzo, the way he had beaten Alfonso. From my apartment I heard Lila saying: Stop it, you're frightening Tina.

88.

January arrived, and my book was now enriched by echoes of many small details of the neighborhood. A great anguish came over me. When I was at the last stage of proofs I timidly asked Lila if she had the patience to reread it (*It's very changed*) but she answered decisively no. I didn't read the last one you published, she said, those are things in which I have no expertise. I felt alone, at the mercy of my own pages, and I was even tempted to call Nino to ask if he would do me a favor and read it. Then I realized that, although he knew my address and phone number, he had never appeared, in all those months he had ignored both me and his daughter. So I gave up. The text moved beyond the final provisional stage and disappeared. Separating from it frightened me, I would see it again only in its definitive guise, and every word would be irremediable.

The publicity office telephoned. Gina said: at *Panorama* they've read the proofs and are very interested, they'll send a photographer. Suddenly I missed the elegant apartment on Via Tasso. I thought: I don't want to be photographed again at the entrance of the tunnel, or in this dreary apartment, or even in the gardens, amid the syringes of the addicts; I'm not the girl of fifteen years ago, this is my third book, I want to be treated properly. But Gina insisted, the book had to be promoted. I told her: Give the photographer my phone number—I wanted at least to be notified ahead of time, attend to my appearance, put off the meeting if I didn't feel in good shape.

In those days I tried to keep the house in order, but no one called. I concluded that there were already enough photographs of me around and that *Panorama* had decided not to do the article. But one morning, when Dede and Elsa were at school and I was sitting on the floor, in jeans and a worn-out sweater, my hair uncombed, playing with Imma and Tina, the doorbell rang. The two little girls were building a castle with blocks that were scattered around, and I was helping them. In the past few months it had seemed to me that the distance between my daughter and Lila's had been bridged: they collaborated on the construction with precise gestures, and if Tina appeared more imaginative and often asked me surprising questions in a pure Italian, always clearly pronounced, Imma was more decisive, maybe more disciplined, and her only disadvantage was a constricted language that we often needed her friend to decipher. Since I delayed going to the door as I finished answering some question or other of Tina's, there was a commanding ring. I opened the door and found myself facing a beautiful woman of around thirty, with blond curls, a long blue raincoat. She was the photographer.

She turned out to be a very gregarious Milanese, expensively dressed. I lost your number, she said, but just as well—the less you expect to be photographed the better the photos. She looked around. What a job to get here, what a wretched place, but it's exactly what's needed: are these your babies? Tina smiled at her, Imma didn't, but it was obvious that they both considered her a kind of fairy. I introduced them: Imma is my daughter and Tina the daughter of a friend. But even as I was speaking, the photographer began to wander around, snapping photos constantly with different cameras and all her equipment. I have to pull myself together, I tried to say. Not at all, you're fine like that.

She pushed me into every part of the house: the kitchen, the children's room, my bedroom, even in front of the bathroom mirror.

"Do you have your book?"

"No, it's not out yet."

"A copy of the last one you wrote?"

"Yes."

"Take it and sit here, pretend to be reading."

I obeyed in a daze. Tina grabbed a book, too, and assumed the same pose, saying to Imma: Take a picture of me. This excited the photographer, she said: Sit on the floor with the children. She took a lot of pictures, Tina and Imma were happy. She exclaimed: Now let's do one alone with your daughter. I tried to pull Imma to me, but she said: No, the other one, she has a fantastic face. She pushed Tina toward me, she took an infinite number of pictures, Imma became upset. Me, too, she said. I opened my arms, I called to her: Yes, come to Mamma.

The morning flew by. The woman in the blue raincoat dragged us out of the house, but was somewhat tense. She asked a couple of times: They won't steal my equipment? Then she got carried away, she wanted to photograph every squalid corner of the neighborhood. She placed me on a broken-down bench, against a flaking wall, next to the old urinal. I said to Imma and Tina: Stay here, don't move, because the cars are going by, I'm warning you. They held each other by the hand, one fair and one dark, the same height, and waited.

Lila returned from work at dinnertime, and came up to get her daughter. Tina didn't wait for her to come in before she told her all about it.

"A beautiful lady came."

"More beautiful than me?"

"Yes."

"Even more beautiful than Aunt Lenuccia?"

"No."

"So Aunt Lenuccia is the prettiest of all?"

"No, me."

"You? What nonsense you talk."

"It's true, Mamma."

"And what did this lady do?"

"Took photos."

"Of whom?"

"Of me."

"Only you?"

"Yes."

"Liar. Imma, come here, tell me what you did."

89.

I waited for *Panorama* to come out. I was pleased now, the publicity office was doing a good job, I felt proud of being the subject of an entire photographic feature. But a week passed, and the feature didn't appear. Two weeks passed, nothing. It was the end of March, the book was in the bookstores, and still nothing. I was absorbed in other things, an interview on the radio, one in *Il Mattino*. At a certain point I had to go to Milan for the launch of the book. I did it in the same bookstore as fifteen years earlier, introduced by the same professor. Adele didn't come, nor did Mariarosa, but the audience was bigger than in the past. The professor talked about the book without much warmth but positively, and some members of the audience—it was mostly women—spoke up enthusiastically about the complex humanity of the protagonist. A rite that I knew well by now. I left the next morning and returned to Naples, exhausted.

I remember that I was heading home, dragging my suitcase, when a car pulled up along the *stradone*. At the wheel was Michele, next to him sat Marcello. I remembered when the two Solaras had tried to pull me into their car—they had done it with Ada, too—and Lila had defended me. I had on my wrist, as I had then, my mother's bracelet, and, though objects are impassive by nature, I drew back with a start to protect it. But Marcello stared straight ahead without greeting me, he didn't even say in his usual good-humored tone: Here's the sister-in-law who writes novels. Michele spoke, he was furious:

"Lenù, what the fuck did you write in that book? Despicable things about the place you were born? Despicable things about my family? Despicable things about the people who watched you grow up and who admire you and love you? Despicable things about this beautiful city of ours?"

He turned around and took from the backseat a copy of *Panorama*, fresh from the printer, and held it out through the window.

"You like talking shit?"

I looked. The weekly was open to the page about me. There was a big color photo that showed Tina and me sitting on the floor at my apartment. The caption struck me immediately: *Elena Greco with her daughter Tina*. At first I thought that the problem was the caption and I didn't understand why Michele was so angry. I said bewildered:

"They made a mistake."

But he shouted out a sentence, even more incomprehensible:

"They aren't the ones who made a mistake, it was *you two*."

At that point Marcello interrupted, he said with irritation:

"Forget it, Michè, Lina manipulates her and she doesn't even realize it."

He took off, tires screeching, and left me on the sidewalk with the magazine in my hand.

90.

I stood stock-still, my suitcase beside me. I read the article, four pages with pictures of the ugliest places in the neighborhood: the only one with me was the one with Tina, a beautiful picture in which the bleak background of the apartment gave our two figures a particular refinement. The writer wasn't reviewing my book and didn't speak of it as a novel, but used it to give an account of what he called "the dominion of the Solara brothers," a borderland territory, perhaps tied to the new organized Camorra, perhaps not. Of Marcello it said little, alluding mainly to Michele, to whom it attributed initiative, unscrupulousness, a tendency to jump from one political cart to the next, according to the logic of business. What business? *Panorama* made a list, mixing the legal and the illegal: the bar-pastry shop, hides, shoe factories, mini-markets, night clubs, loan sharking, cigarette smuggling, receiving stolen goods, drugs, infiltration of the post-earthquake construction sites.

I broke into a cold sweat.

What had I done, how could I have been so imprudent.

In Florence I had invented a plot, drawing on facts of my childhood and adolescence with the boldness that came from distance. Naples, seen from there, was almost a place of imagination, a city like the ones in films, which although the streets and buildings are real serve only as a background for crime stories or romances. Then, since I had moved and saw Lila every day, a mania for reality had gripped me, and although I hadn't named it I had told the story of the neighborhood. But I must have overdone it, and the relationship between truth and fiction must have gone awry: now every street, every building had become recognizable, and maybe even the people, even the violent acts. The photographs were proof of what my pages really contained, they identified the area conclusively, and the neighborhood ceased to be, as it had always been for me while I was writing, an invention. The author of the article told the history of the neighborhood, even mentioning the murders of Don Achille Carracci and Manuela Solara. He went on at length about the latter, hypothesizing that it had been either the visible point of a conflict between

Camorra families or an execution at the hands of the "dangerous terrorist Pasquale Peluso, born and raised in the area, former bricklayer, former secretary of the local section of the Communist Party." But I hadn't written anything about Pasquale, I hadn't written anything about Don Achille or Manuela. The Carraccis, the Solaras had been for me only outlines, voices that had been able to enrich, with the cadence of dialect, gestures, at times violent tonalities, a completely imagined scheme. I didn't want to stick my nose in their real business, what did "the dominion of the Solara brothers" have to do with it.

I had written a novel.

91.

I went to Lila's house in a state of great agitation, the children were with her. You're back already, said Elsa, who felt freer when I wasn't there. And Dede greeted me distractedly, murmuring with feigned restraint: Just a minute, Mamma, I'll finish my homework and then hug you. The only enthusiastic one was Imma, who pressed her lips to my cheek and kissed me for a long time, refusing to let go. Tina wanted to do the same. But I had other things on my mind, and paid them almost no attention. I immediately showed Lila *Panorama*. I told her about the Solaras, suppressing my anxiety. I said: They're angry. Lina read the article calmly and made a single comment: Nice photos. I exclaimed:

"I'll send a letter, I'll protest. Let them do a report on Naples, let them do it on, I don't know, the kidnapping of Cirillo, on Camorra deaths, on what they want, but they shouldn't use my book gratuitously."

"And why?"

"Because it's literature, I didn't narrate real events."

"I recall that you did."

I looked at her uncertainly.

"What do you mean?"

"You didn't use the names, but a lot of things were recognizable."

"Why didn't you tell me?"

"I told you I didn't like the book. Things are told or not told: you remained in the middle."

"It was a novel."

"Partly a novel, partly not."

I didn't answer, my anxiety increased. Now I didn't know if I was more unhappy about the Solaras' reaction or because she, serenely, had just repeated her negative judgment of years earlier. I looked at Dede and Elsa, who had taken possession of the magazine, but almost without seeing them. Elsa exclaimed:

"Tina, come see, you're in the newspaper."

Tina approached and looked at herself, eyes wide with wonder and a pleased smile on her face. Imma asked Elsa:

"Where am I?"

"You're not there because Tina is pretty and you're ugly," her sister answered.

Imma then turned to Dede to find out if it was true. And Dede, after reading the *Panorama* caption aloud twice, tried to convince her that since her name was Sarratore and not Airota, she wasn't truly my daughter. I couldn't take it anymore, I was tired, upset, I cried: That's enough, let's go home. They all three objected, supported by Tina and by Lila, who insisted that we stay for dinner.

I stayed. Lila tried to soothe me, she even tried to make me forget that she had again been critical of my book. She started off in dialect and then began to speak in the Italian she brought out on important occasions, which never failed to surprise me. She cited the experience of the earthquake, for more than two years she had done nothing except complain of how the city had deteriorated. She said that since then she had been careful never to forget that we are very crowded beings, full of physics, astrophysics, biology, religion, soul, bourgeoisie, proletariat, capital, work, profit, politics, many harmonious phrases, many unharmonious, the chaos inside and the chaos outside. So calm down, she said laughing, what do you expect the Solaras to be. Your novel is done: you wrote it, you rewrote it, being here was evidently useful to you, to make it truer, but now it's out and you can't take it back. The Solaras are angry? So what. Michele threatens you? Who gives a damn. There could be another earthquake at any moment, even stronger. Or the whole universe could collapse. And then what is Michele Solara? Nothing. And Marcello is nothing. The two of them are merely flesh that spouts out threats and demands for money. She sighed. She said in a low voice: The Solaras will always be dangerous beasts, Lenù, there's nothing to be done; I thought I had tamed one but his brother made him ferocious again. Did you see how many blows Michele gave Alfonso? They're blows he wanted to give me but he hasn't got the courage. And that rage at your book, at the article in *Panorama*, at the photos, is all rage against me. So don't give a shit, the way I don't give a shit. You put them in the newspaper and the Solaras can't tolerate it, it's bad for business and for scams. To us, on the other hand, it's a pleasure, no? What do we have to worry about?

I listened. When she talked like that, with those high-flown pronouncements, the suspicion returned that she had continued to consume books, the way she had as a girl, but that for incomprehensible reasons she kept it hidden from me. In her house not a single volume was to be seen, apart from the hyper-technical pamphlets that had to do with the work. She wanted to present herself as an uneducated person, and yet suddenly here she was talking about biology, psychology, about how complicated human beings are. Why did she act like that with me? I didn't know, but I needed support and I trusted her just the same. In other words, Lila managed to soothe me. I reread the article and I liked it. I examined the photographs: the neighborhood was ugly but Tina and I were pretty. We began to cook, and the preparations helped me reflect. I decided that the article, the photos, would be useful for the book and that the text of Florence, filled out in Naples, in the apartment above hers, really was improved. Yes, I said, let's screw the Solaras. And I relaxed, I was nice to the children again.

Before dinner, after who knows what councils, Imma came over to me, Tina trailing behind. In her language made up of words that were pronounced clearly and words that were barely comprehensible she said:

"Mamma, Tina wants to know if your daughter is me or her."

"And do you want to know?" I asked her.

Her eyes were shining: "Yes."

Lila said:

"We are mammas of you both and we love you both."

When Enzo returned from work he was excited about the photograph of his daughter. The next day he bought two copies of *Panorama* and stuck up in his office both the whole image and the image of his daughter alone. Naturally he cut off the mistaken caption.

92.

Today, as I write, I'm embarrassed at the way fortune continued to favor me. The book immediately aroused interest. Some were thrilled by the pleasure of reading it. Some praised the skill with which the protagonist was developed. Some talked about a brutal realism, some extolled my baroque imagination, some admired a female narrative that was gentle and embracing. In other words there were many positive judgments, but often in sharp contrast to one another, as if the reviewers hadn't read the book that was in the bookstores but, rather, each had evoked a fantasy book fabricated from his own biases. On one thing, after the article in *Panorama*, they all agreed: the novel was absolutely different from the usual kind of writing about Naples.

When my copies arrived from the publisher, I was so happy that I decided to give one to Lila. I hadn't given her my previous books, and I took it for granted that, at least for the moment, she wouldn't even look at it. But I felt close to her, she was the only person I could truly rely on, and I wanted to show her my gratitude. She didn't react well. Obviously that day she had a lot to do, and was involved in her usual aggressive way in the neighborhood conflicts over the forthcoming elections on June 26th. Or maybe something had annoyed her, I don't know. The fact is that I gave her the book and she didn't even look at it, she said I shouldn't waste my copies.

I was disappointed. Enzo saved me from embarrassment. Give it to me, he said, I've never had a passion for reading, but I'll save it for Tina, so when she grows up she'll read it. And he wanted me to write a dedication to the child. I remember that I wrote with some uneasiness: For Tina, who will do better than all of us. Then I read the dedication aloud and Lila exclaimed: It doesn't take much to do better than me, I hope she'll do much more. Pointless words, with no motivation: I had written *better than all of us* and she had reduced it to *better than me*. Both Enzo and I dropped it. He put the book on a shelf among the computer manuals and we talked about the invitations I was receiving, the trips I would have to make.

93.

In general those moments of hostility were open, but some-times they also persisted behind an appearance of availability and affection. Lila, for example, still seemed happy to take care of my daughters, and yet, with a mere inflection of her voice, she could make me feel indebted, as if she were saying: What you are, what you become, depends on what I, sacrificing, allow you to be, to become. If I perceived that tone I darkened and suggested getting a babysitter. But both she and Enzo were almost offended, it shouldn't even be mentioned. One morning when I needed her help she alluded in irritation to problems that were putting her under pressure and I said coldly that I could find other solutions. She became aggressive: Did I tell you I can't? If you need me, I'll arrange it: have your daughters ever complained, have I neglected them? So I convinced myself that she wanted only a sort of declaration of indispensability and I admitted with sincere gratitude that my public life would have been impossible if she had been less supportive. Then I gave in to my commitments without any more qualms.

Thanks to the competence of the publicity office, I appeared in a different newspaper every day, and a couple of times even on television. I was excited and extremely tense, I liked the increasing attention but I was afraid of saying the wrong thing. At the moments of greatest anxiety I didn't know whom to ask and I resorted to Lila for advice:

"If they ask me about the Solaras?"

"Say what you think."

"And if the Solaras get angry?"

"At the moment you're more dangerous for them than they are for you."

"I'm worried, Michele seems crazier and crazier."

"Books are written so their authors can be heard, not so that they remain silent."

In reality I always tried to be cautious. It was the middle of a heated electoral campaign, and I was careful, in interviews, not to get mixed up in politics, not to mention the Solaras, who—it was known—were involved in funneling votes for the five governing parties. Instead I talked a lot about the conditions of life in the neighborhood, of the further deterioration after the earthquake, of poverty and illegal trafficking, of institutional complicity. And then—depending on the questions and the whim of the moment—I talked about myself, about my education, about the effort I had had to make in order to study, about misogyny at the Normale, about my mother, about my daughters, about feminist thought. It was a complicated moment in the literary market; writers of my age, hesitating between the avant-garde and traditional storytelling, struggled to define and establish themselves. But I had an advantage. My first book had come out at the end of the sixties, with my second I had demonstrated a solid education and a broad range of interests, and I was one of the few who had a small publication history and even a following. So the telephone began to ring more and more often. But rarely, it should be said, did the journalists want opinions or comments on literary questions; they asked me mainly for sociological reflections and statements about the current state of Naples. I engaged in this willingly. And soon I began to contribute to *Il Mattino* on an array of subjects, and I accepted a column in *We Women*, I presented the book wherever I was invited, adapting it to the requirements of the audience I found. I couldn't believe what was happening to me. The preceding books had done well but not with the same momentum. A couple of well-known writers whom I had never had a chance to meet telephoned me. A famous director wanted to meet me, he wanted to make my novel into a film. Every day I learned that the book had been requested for reading by this or that foreign publisher. I was more and more content.

But I got particular satisfaction from two unexpected phone calls. The first was from Adele. She spoke to me very cordially, she asked about her grandchildren, she said that she knew all about them from Pietro, that she had seen pictures of them and they were beautiful. I listened to her, I confined myself to a few polite remarks. About the book she said: I read it again, well done, you improved it a lot. And as she said goodbye she made me promise that if I came to present the book in Genoa I should let her know, I should bring the children, leave them with her for a while. I promised, but I ruled out that I would keep my promise.

A few days later Nino called. He said that my novel was fantastic (*a quality of writing unimaginable in Italy*), he asked to see the three children. I invited him to lunch. He devoted himself to Dede, Elsa, and Imma, and then naturally he spoke a great deal about himself. He spent very little time in Naples now, he was always in Rome, he worked a lot with my former father-in-law, he had important responsibilities. He repeated: Things are going well, Italy is finally setting out on the road to modernity. Then suddenly he exclaimed, fixing his eyes on mine: Let's get back together. I burst out laughing: When you want to see Imma, call; but the two of us have nothing more to say to each other. It seems to me that I conceived the child with a ghost, certainly you weren't in the bed. He went away sulkily and didn't show up again. He forgot about us—Dede, Elsa, Imma, and me—for a long period. He probably forgot about us as soon as I closed the door behind him.

94.

At that point, what more did I want? My name, the name of a nobody, was definitely becoming the name of a somebody. That was why Adele Airota had telephoned me as if to

apologize, that was why Nino Sarratore had tried to be forgiven and to return to my bed, that was why I was invited
everywhere. Of course, it was difficult to separate from the
children and stop, if just for a few days, being their mother. But
even that tug became habitual. The need to make a good
impression in public soon replaced the sense of guilt. My head
became crowded with countless things, Naples and the neighborhood lost substance. Other landscapes imposed themselves, I went to beautiful cities I had never seen before, I
thought I would like to go and live in them. I met men who
attracted me, who made me feel important, who made me
happy. A range of alluring possibilities opened up before me in
the space of a few hours. And the chains of motherhood weakened, sometimes I forgot to call Lila, to say goodnight to the
girls. Only when I noticed that I would have been capable of
living without them did I return to myself, did I feel remorse.

Then there was an especially bad moment. I left for a long
promotional tour in the south. I was to stay away for a week,
but Imma didn't feel well, she looked depressed, she had a
bad cold. It was my fault, I couldn't be angry with Lila: she
was very attentive, but she had endless things to do and
couldn't keep an eye on the children if they got sweaty when
they ran around, and the drafts. Before I left I asked the publicity office to get me the telephone numbers of the hotels
where I was to stay and I left them with Lila for any eventuality. If there are problems, I insisted, telephone me and I'll be
right home.

I departed. At first I thought only of Imma and her illness,
I called whenever I could. Then I forgot about it. I arrived in
a place, I was welcomed with great courtesy, an intense program had been prepared for me, I tried to show that I was up
to it, I was celebrated at interminable dinners. Once I tried to
call, but the telephone rang unanswered, and I let it go; once
Enzo answered and said in his laconic way: Do what you have

to do, don't worry; once I talked to Dede, who said, in an adult voice, We're fine, Mamma, bye, have fun. But when I returned I discovered that Imma had been in hospital for three days. She had pneumonia, and had been admitted. Lila was with her, she had abandoned every commitment, had abandoned even Tina, had stayed in the hospital with my daughter. I was desperate, I protested that I had been kept in the dark. But she wouldn't give in, even when I returned, she continued to feel responsible for the child. Go, she said, you're always traveling, rest.

I was truly tired, but above all I was dazed. I regretted not having been with the child, of having deprived her of my presence just when she needed me. Because now I didn't know anything about how much and in what way she had suffered. Whereas Lila had in her head all the phases of my daughter's illness, her difficulty breathing, the suffering, the rush to the hospital. I looked at her, there in the corridor of the hospital, and she seemed more worn-out than I was. She had offered Imma the permanent and loving contact of her body. She hadn't been home for days, she had hardly slept, she had the blunted gaze of exhaustion. I, however, in spite of myself, felt inside—and maybe appeared outside—luminous. Even now that I knew about my daughter's illness, I couldn't get rid of the satisfaction for what I had become, the pleasure of feeling free, moving all over Italy, the pleasure of disposing of myself as if I had no past and everything were starting now.

As soon as the child was discharged, I confessed my state of mind to Lila. I wanted to find an order in the confusion of guilt and pride that I felt inside, I wanted to tell her how grateful I was but also hear from her in detail what Imma—since I hadn't been there to give it to her—had gotten from her. But Lila replied almost with irritation: Lenù, forget it, it's over, your daughter's fine, there are bigger problems now. I thought for a few seconds that she meant her problems at work but it wasn't that, the problems had to do with me. She had found out, just before Imma's illness, that a lawsuit was about to be brought against me. The person who was bringing it was Carmen.

95.

I was frightened, and I felt distressed. Carmen? Carmen had done a thing like that to me?

The thrilling phase of success ended at that moment. In a few seconds the guilt at having neglected Imma was added to the fear that by legal means everything would be taken away from me, joy, prestige, money. I was ashamed of myself, of my aspirations. I said to Lila that I wanted to talk to Carmen right away, she advised me against it. But I had the impression that she knew more than what she had said and I went to look for Carmen anyway.

First I went to the gas pump, but she wasn't there. Roberto was embarrassed in my presence. He was silent about the lawsuit, he said that his wife had gone with the children to Giugliano, to some relatives, and would be there for a while. I left him standing there and went to their house to see if he had told me the truth. But Carmen either really had gone to Giugliano or wouldn't open the door to me. It was very hot. I walked for a while to calm myself, then I looked for Antonio, I was sure he would know something. I thought it would be hard to track him down, he was always out. But his wife told me that he had gone to the barber and I would find him there. I asked him if he had heard talk of legal actions against me, and instead of answering he began to complain about the school, he said that the teachers were annoyed with his children, they complained that they spoke in German or in dialect, but meanwhile they didn't teach them Italian. Then out of the blue he almost whispered:

"Let me take this moment to say goodbye."

"Where are you going."

"I'm going back to Germany."

"When?"

"I don't yet know."

"Why are you saying goodbye now?"

"You're never here, we hardly see each other."

"It's you who never come to see me."

"You don't come to see me, either."

"Why are you going?"

"My family isn't happy here."

"Is it Michele who's sending you away?"

"He commands and I obey."

"So it's he who doesn't want you in the neighborhood anymore."

He looked at his hands, he examined them carefully.

"Every so often my nervous breakdown returns," he said, and he began to talk to me about his mother, Melina, who wasn't right in the head.

"You'll leave her to Ada?"

"I'll take her with me," he muttered. "Ada already has too many troubles. And I have the same constitution, I want to keep her in sight to see what I'm going to become."

"She's always lived here, she'll suffer in Germany."

"One suffers everywhere. You want some advice?"

I understood from the way he looked at me that he had decided to get to the point.

"Let's hear it."

"You get out of here, too."

"Why?"

"Because Lina believes that the two of you are invincible but it's not true. And I can't help you any longer."

"Help us in what?"

He shook his head unhappily.

"The Solaras are furious. Did you see how people voted here in the neighborhood?"

"No."

"It turned out that they no longer control the votes they used to control."

"So?"

"Lina has managed to shift a lot of them to the Communists."

"And what do I have to do with it?"

"Marcello and Michele see Lina behind everything, especially behind you. There is a lawsuit, and Carmen's lawyers are their lawyers."

96.

I went home, I didn't look for Lila. I assumed that she knew all about the elections, about the votes, about the Solaras, enraged, who were waiting in ambush behind Carmen. She told me things a little at a time, for her own ends. Instead I called the publishing house, I told the editor in chief about the lawsuit and what Antonio had reported to me. For now it's only a rumor, I said, nothing certain, but I'm worried. He tried to reassure me, he promised that he would ask the legal department to investigate and as soon as he found out anything he would telephone me. He concluded: Why are you so agitated, this is good for the book. Not for me, I thought, I've been wrong about everything, I shouldn't have returned here to live.

Days passed, I didn't hear from the publisher, but the notification of the lawsuit arrived at my house like a stab. I read it and was speechless. Carmen demanded that the editor and I withdraw the book from circulation, plus enormous damages for having tarnished the memory of her mother, Giuseppina. I had never seen a document that summed up in itself, in the letterhead, in the quality of the writing, in the decorative stamps and notarized seals, the power of the law. I discovered that what had never made an impression on me as an adolescent, even as a young woman, now terrified me. This time I hurried to see Lila. When I told her what it was about she started teasing me:

"You wanted the law, the law has arrived."

"What should I do?"

"Make a scene."

"What do you mean?"

"Tell the newspapers what's happening to you."

"You're crazy. Antonio said that behind Carmen are the Solaras' lawyers, and don't say you don't know."

"Of course I know."

"Then why didn't you tell me?"

"Because you see how nervous you are? But you don't have to worry. You're afraid of the law and the Solaras are afraid of your book."

"I'm afraid that with all the money they have they can ruin me."

"But it's precisely their money you have to go for. Write. The more you write about their disgusting affairs the more you ruin their business."

I was depressed. Lila thought this? This was her project? Only then did I understand clearly that she ascribed to me the power that as children we had ascribed to the author of *Little Women*. That was why she had wanted me to return to the neighborhood at all costs? I left without saying anything. I went home, I called the publisher again. I hoped that he was exerting himself in some way, I wanted news that would calm me, but I didn't reach him. The next day he called me. He announced gaily that in the *Corriere della Sera* there was an article by him—yes, by his hand—in which he gave an account of the lawsuit. Go and buy it, he said, and let me know what you think.

97.

I went to the newsstand more anxious than ever. There again was the photograph of me with Tina, this time in black-and-white. The lawsuit was announced in the headline; it was considered an attempt to muzzle one of the very few courageous writers et cetera, et cetera. The article didn't name the neighborhood, it didn't allude to the Solaras. Skillfully, it set the episode within a conflict that was taking place everywhere, "between the medieval remnants that are keeping this country from modernizing and the unstoppable advance, even in the South, of political and cultural renewal." It was a short piece, but it defended effectively, especially in the conclusion, the rights of literature, separating them from what were called "very sad local disputes."

I was relieved, I had the impression of being well protected. I telephoned, I praised the article, then I went to show the paper to Lila. I expected her to be be excited. That was what it seemed to me she wanted: a deployment of the power that she ascribed to me. Instead she said coolly:

"Why did you let this man write the article?"

"What's wrong? The publisher is standing behind me, they're attending to this mess, it seems a good thing."

"It's just talk, Lenù, this guy is only interested in selling the book."

"And isn't that good?"

"It's good, but you should have written the article."

I became nervous, I couldn't understand what she had in mind.

"Why?"

"Because you're smart and you know the situation well. You remember when you wrote the article against Bruno Soccavo?"

That reference, instead of pleasing me, upset me. Bruno was dead and I didn't like to remember what I had written. He wasn't very bright, ending up in the clutches of the Solaras and who knows how many others, given that they had killed him. I wasn't happy that I had been angry with him.

"Lila," I said, "the article wasn't against Bruno, it was an article about factory work."

"I know, and with this? You made them pay, and now that you're an even more important person you can do better. The Solaras shouldn't hide behind Carmen. You have to drag the Solaras out into the open, and they should no longer command."

I understood why she had disparaged the editor's article. She didn't care in the least about freedom of expression and the battle between backwardness and modernization. She was interested only in the sad local disputes. She wanted me, here, now, to contribute to the clash with real people, people we had known since childhood, and what they were made of. I said:

"Lila, the *Corriere* doesn't give a damn about Carmen, who sold herself, and the Solaras, who bought her. To be in a big newspaper, an article has to have a broad meaning, otherwise they won't publish it."

Her face fell.

"Carmen didn't sell herself," she said. "She's still your friend and she has brought the suit against you for one reason alone: they forced her."

"I don't understand, explain it."

She smiled at me, sneering, she was really angry.

"I'm not explaining anything to you: you write the books, you're the one who has to explain. I know only that here we don't have any publisher in Milan to protect us, no one who puts big articles in the newspaper for us. *We* are only a local matter and we fix things however we can: if *you* want to help us, good, and if not we'll do it alone."

98.

I went back to Roberto and harassed him until he gave me the address of the relatives in Giugliano, then I got in the car with Imma and left to look for Carmen.

The heat was suffocating. I had trouble locating the place, the relatives lived on the outskirts. At the door, a large woman answered who told me brusquely that Carmen had returned to Naples. Hardly persuaded, I went off with Imma, who, even though we had walked only a hundred meters, protested that she was tired. But as soon as I turned the corner to go back to the car I ran into Carmen, loaded with shopping bags. It was an instant, she saw me and burst into tears. I hugged her, Imma wanted to hug her, too. Then we found a café with a table in the shade and after ordering the child to play silently with her dolls I got Carmen to explain the situation. She confirmed what Lila had told me: she had been forced to bring a suit against me. And she also told me the reason: Marcello had made her believe that he knew where Pasquale was hiding.

"Is it possible?"

"It's possible."

"And do you know where he's hiding?"

She hesitated, she nodded.

"They said that they'll kill him whenever they want to."

I tried to soothe her. I told her that if the Solaras really knew where the person they believed had killed their mother was they would have seized him long ago.

"So you think they don't know?"

"Not that they don't know. But at this point for the good of your brother there's only one thing you can do."

"What?"

I told her that if she wanted to save Pasquale she should turn him in to the carabinieri.

The effect this produced on Carmen was not good. She

stiffened, I struggled to explain that it was the only way to protect him from the Solaras. But it was useless, I realized that my solution sounded to her like the worst of betrayals, something much more serious than her betrayal of me.

"This way you remain in their hands," I said. "They asked you to bring a suit against me, they can ask you any other thing."

"I'm his sister," she exclaimed.

"It's not a question of a sister's love," I said. "A sister's love in this case has harmed me, certainly won't save him, and risks ruining you, too."

But there was no way to convince her, in fact the more we talked, the more confused I got. Soon she began crying again: one moment she felt sorry for what she had done to me and asked my pardon, the next she felt sorry for what they could do to her brother and she despaired. I remembered how she had been as a girl, at the time I would never have imagined that she was capable of such stubborn loyalty. I left her because I wasn't able to console her, because Imma was all sweaty and I was afraid that she would get sick again, because it became increasingly less clear what I expected from Carmen. Did I want her to break off her long complicity with Pasquale? Why did I believe it was the right thing? Did I want her to choose the state over her brother? Why? To take her away from the Solaras and make her withdraw the suit? Did that count more than her anguish? I said to her:

"Do what you think is best, and remember that anyway I'm not mad at you."

But Carmen at that point had an unpredictable flash of anger in her eyes:

"And why should you be mad at me? What do you have to lose? You're in the newspapers, you're getting publicity, you'll sell more books. No, Lenù, you shouldn't say that, you advised me to give Pasquale up to the carabinieri, you were wrong."

I went away feeling bitter and already on the drive home I doubted that it had been a good idea to want to see her. I imagined that she would now go to the Solaras and that they would force her, after the editor's article in the *Corriere*, to take other actions against me.

99.

For days I expected new disasters, but nothing happened. The article created a certain sensation, the Neapolitan papers took it up and amplified it, I got phone calls and letters of support. The weeks passed, and I became used to the idea of being sued; I discovered that it had happened to many who did the same work I did and had been much more at risk than I was. Daily life asserted itself. For a while I avoided Lila, and I was especially careful not to let myself be drawn into making wrong moves.

The book never stopped selling. In August I went on vacation to Santa Maria di Castellabate; Lila and Enzo were also supposed to take a house at the sea, but work prevailed and it seemed natural for them to give Tina to me. The only pleasure, among the endless difficulties and tasks of that time (call this one, shout at that one, settle a quarrel, do the shopping, the cooking), was seeing a couple of readers sitting under their umbrella each with my book in their hands.

In the fall things started off better. I won a fairly important prize that came with a substantial sum, and I felt smart, skilled in public relations, with increasingly satisfying financial prospects. But the joy, the astonishment of the first weeks of success never returned. I felt the days as if the light had become opaque, and I perceived around me a widespread malaise. For a while there hadn't been a night when Enzo didn't raise his voice with Gennaro, something that had been very rare before.

When I stopped in at Basic Sight I found Lila plotting with Alfonso, and if I tried to approach she signaled me to wait a moment with a distracted gesture. She behaved the same way if she was talking to Carmen, who had returned to the neighborhood, or to Antonio, who for obscure reasons had put off his departure to some indeterminate time.

It was clear that things around Lila were getting worse, but she kept me out of it and I preferred to stay out of it. Then there were two terrible moments, one after the other. Lila happened to discover that Gennaro's arms were covered in needle marks. I heard her screaming as I had never heard her scream before. She incited Enzo, she drove him to give her son a beating: they were two strong men and they thrashed each other. The next day she threw her brother Rino out of Basic Sight, even though Gennaro begged her not to fire his uncle, he swore it wasn't Rino who had started him on heroin. That tragedy struck the girls deeply, especially Dede.

"Why does Aunt Lina treat her son like that?"

"Because he did something that he shouldn't do."

"He's grown-up, he can do what he wants."

"Not what can kill him."

"Why? It's his life, he has the right to do what he wants with it. You don't know what freedom is, and neither does Aunt Lina."

She, Elsa, and even Imma were as if stunned by that outburst of cries and curses that came from their beloved Aunt Lina. Gennaro was a prisoner in the house and he shouted all day. His Uncle Rino disappeared from Basic Sight after breaking a very expensive machine, and his curses could be heard throughout the neighborhood. Pinuccia came one evening with her children to beg Lila to rehire her husband and brought her mother-in-law, too. Lila treated both her mother and her sister-in-law rudely; the shouts and insults reached my house clearly. You are delivering us hand and foot to the

Solaras, Pinuccia cried desperately. And Lila replied: you deserve it, I'm fucking sick and tired of slaving for you without a drop of gratitude.

But that was petty compared to what happened a few weeks later. Things had scarcely calmed down when Lila began to quarrel with Alfonso, who was now indispensable to the operations of Basic Sight and yet had become increasingly unreliable. He missed important appointments, when he did make them his attitude was an embarrassment, he was heavily made up, he spoke of himself using the feminine. By now Lila had disappeared completely from his face and, in spite of his efforts, he was regaining his masculinity. In his nose, in his forehead, in his eyes something of his father, Don Achille, was appearing, and he himself was disgusted by it. As a result he seemed continuously in flight from his own body, which was putting on weight, and sometimes nothing was heard of him for days. When he reappeared he almost always showed signs of beatings. He went back to work but listlessly.

Then one day he disappeared for good. Lila and Enzo looked for him everywhere, without success. His body was found days later on the beach at Coroglio. He had been beaten to death somewhere else and then thrown into the sea. At the time I couldn't believe it. When I realized that it was all brutally true I was seized by a grief that wouldn't go away. I saw him again as he had been in our school days, gentle, attentive to others, beloved by Marisa, tormented by Gino, the pharmacist's son. Sometimes I even recalled him behind the counter at the grocery during his summer vacations, when he was obliged to do a job he detested. But I cut away the rest of his life, I knew little about it, I felt it as confused. I couldn't think of him as what he had become, every recent encounter faded, I even forgot the period when he worked in the shoe store in Piazza dei Martiri. Lila's fault, I thought in the heat of the moment: with her mania for forcing others by mixing everything up, she overwhelmed him. She had obscurely used him and then let him go.

But I changed my mind almost right away. Lila had learned the news several hours earlier. She knew that Alfonso was dead, but she couldn't get rid of the rage she had felt for days and kept insisting, rudely, on his unreliability. Then, right in the middle of a tirade like this, she collapsed on the floor of my house, evidently because her grief was unbearable. From that moment it seemed to me that she had loved him more than I did, even more than Marisa, and—as, besides, Alfonso had often told me—had helped him as no one else had. In the following hours she became listless, she stopped working, she lost interest in Gennaro, she left Tina with me. Between her and Alfonso there must have been a more complex relationship than I had imagined. She must have looked at him as at a mirror and seen herself in him and had wanted to draw out of his body a part of herself. The complete opposite, I thought uneasily, of what I had narrated in my second book. That work of Lila's must have pleased Alfonso very much, he had offered himself to her like a living material and she had molded him. Or at least so it seemed to me in the brief time in which I tried to put what had happened in order and calm myself. But, in the end, it was nothing but a vague impression of mine. In reality she never told me anything about their bond, not then or later. She was numbed by her suffering, harboring who knows what feelings, until the day of the funeral.

100.

There were very few of us at the funeral. None of Alfonso's friends from Piazza dei Martiri came, and his relatives didn't come, either. I was struck above all by the absence of Maria, his mother, even though none of his siblings came, neither Pinuccia nor Stefano, nor was Marisa there with the children, maybe his children, maybe not. Instead, surprisingly, the Solaras appeared. Michele was grim, very thin, he was constantly looking around with the eyes of a madman. Marcello, on the other hand, seemed contrite, an attitude that contrasted with the luxuriousness of every item of his clothing. They didn't limit themselves to the funeral service; they drove to the cemetery, and were present at the burial. The whole time I wondered why they had showed up at the service and I tried to catch Lila's eye. She never looked at me, she focused on them, she kept staring at them in a provocative manner. At the end, when she saw that they were leaving, she grabbed my arm, she was furious.

"Come with me."

"Where?"

"To talk to the two of them."

"I have the children."

"Enzo will take care of them."

I hesitated, I tried to resist, I said:

"Forget it."

"Then I'll go by myself."

I grumbled, it had always been like that: if I didn't agree to go with her she abandoned me. I nodded to Enzo to watch the girls—he seemed not to have noticed the Solaras—and in the same spirit with which I had followed her up the stairs to Don Achille's house or in the stone-throwing battles with the boys, I followed her through the geometry of whitish buildings, packed with burial niches.

Lila ignored Marcello, she stood in front of Michele:

"Why did you come? Do you feel some remorse?"

"Don't bother me, Lina."

"You two are finished, you'll have to leave the neighborhood."

"It's better if you go, while you still have time."

"Are you threatening me?"

"Yes."

"Don't you dare touch Gennaro, and don't touch Enzo.
Michè, do you understand me? Remember that I know enough
to ruin you, you and that other beast."

"You don't know anything, you have nothing in hand, and
above all you've understood nothing. Is it possible that you can
be so intelligent and you still don't know that by now I don't
give a fuck about you?"

Marcello pulled him by the arm, he said in dialect:
"Let's go, Michè, we're wasting time here."

Michele freed his arm forcefully, he turned to Lila:
"You think you scare me because Lenuccia is always in the
newspapers? Is that what you think? That I'm afraid of someone who writes novels? But this here is no one. You, however,
you are someone, even your shadow is better than any flesh-
and-blood person. But you would never understand, so much
the worse for you. I'll take away everything you have."

He said that last sentence as if he were suddenly sick to his
stomach, and then, as if reacting to the physical pain, before
his brother could stop him he punched Lila violently in the
face, knocking her to the ground.

101.

I was paralyzed by that utterly unpredictable gesture. Not
even Lila could have imagined it, we were now so used to the
idea that Michele not only would never touch her but would
kill anyone who did. I was unable to scream, not even a choked
sound came out of me.

Marcello dragged his brother away, but as he pulled and
pushed him, as Lila vomited in words dialect and blood (*I'll
kill you, by God, you are both dead already*), he said to me with
affectionate sarcasm: Put this in your next novel, Lenù, and tell

Lina, if she doesn't understand yet, that my brother and I have *truly* stopped loving her.

It was hard to convince Enzo that Lila's swollen face was due to the disastrous fall that, as we told him, had followed a sudden fainting fit. In fact I'm almost certain that he wasn't convinced at all, first because my version—agitated as I was—must have seemed anything but plausible, second because Lila didn't even make an effort to be persuasive. But when Enzo tried to object she said sharply that it was true, and he stopped discussing it. Their relationship was based on the idea that even an open lie from Lila was the only truth that could be uttered.

I went home with my daughters. Dede was frightened, Elsa incredulous, Imma asked questions like: Is there blood in a nose? I was disoriented, I was furious. Every so often I went down to see how Lila felt and to try and take Tina with me, but the child was alarmed by her mother's state and eager to help her. For both reasons she wouldn't leave her, even for a moment: she delicately spread an ointment, placed metal objects on her mother's forehead to cool it and make the headache go away. When I brought my daughters down as a lure to draw Tina up to my place, I merely made things more complicated. Imma tried every way she could to intervene in the treatment game, but Tina wouldn't yield at all and shrieked desperately even when Dede and Elsa attempted to take away her authority. The sick mamma was hers and she didn't want to give her up to anyone. Finally Lila sent everyone away, including me, and with such energy that it seemed to me she was already better.

She recovered quickly, in fact. Not me. My fury first became rage, then changed into contempt for myself. I couldn't forgive myself for remaining paralyzed in the face of violence. I said to myself: What have you become; why did you come back here to live, if you weren't capable of reacting against those two shits;

you're too well-meaning, you want to play the democratic lady who mixes with the working class, you like to say to the newspapers: I live where I was born, I don't want to lose touch with my reality; but you're ridiculous, you lost touch long ago, you faint at the stink of filth, of vomit, of blood. I had thoughts like that and meanwhile images came to my mind in which I let loose mercilessly against Michele. I hit him, scratched him, bit him, my heart pounding. Then the desire for violence died down and I said to myself: Lila is right, one writes not so much to write, one writes to inflict pain on those who wish to inflict pain. The pain of words against the pain of kicks and punches and the instruments of death. Not much, but enough. Of course, she still had in mind our dreams of childhood. She thought that if you gained fame, money, and power through writing, you became a person whose sentences were thunderbolts. Whereas I had long known that everything was more mediocre. A book, an article, could make noise, but ancient warriors before the battle also made noise, and if it wasn't accompanied by real force and immeasurable violence it was only theater. Yet I wished to redeem myself, the noise could do some damage. One morning I went downstairs, I asked her: What do you know that frightens the Solaras.

She looked at me with curiosity, she circled around reluctantly for a while, she answered: When I worked for Michele I saw a lot of documents, I studied them, some stuff he gave me himself. Her face was livid, she made a pained grimace, she added, in the crudest dialect: If a man wants pussy and he wants it so much that he can't even say I want it, even if you order him to stick his prick in boiling oil he does it. Then she held her head in her hands, she shook it hard as if it were a tin cup with dice in it, and I realized that she, too, at that moment despised herself. She didn't like the way she was forced to treat Gennaro, the way she had insulted Alfonso, the way she had thrown out her brother. She didn't like a single one of the very vulgar words that were coming out of her now. She couldn't bear herself, she couldn't bear anything. But at a certain point she must have felt that we were in the same mood and she asked me:

"If I give you things to write you'll write them?"

"Yes."

"And then what you write you'll get printed?"

"Maybe, I don't know."

"What does it depend on?"

"I have to be sure that it will do damage to the Solaras and not to me and my daughters."

She looked at me, unable to make up her mind. Then she said: Take Tina for ten minutes, and she left. She returned half an hour later with a floral-print bag full of documents.

We sat down at the kitchen table, while Tina and Imma chattered softly, moving dolls, horses, and carriages around the floor. Lila took out a lot of papers, her notes, also two notebooks with stained red covers. I immediately leafed through these with interest: graph-paper pages written in the calligraphy of the old elementary schools—account books, minutely annotated in a language full of grammatical mistakes and initialed on every page "M.S." I understood that they were part of what the neighborhood had always called Manuela Solara's red book. How the expression "red book" had echoed during our childhood and adolescence: evocative yet threatening—or perhaps evocative precisely because threatening. But whatever other word one might use in speaking of it—"register," for example—and no matter if the color was altered, Manuela Solara's book excited us like a secret document at the center of bloody adventures. Here it was, instead. It was a collection of school notebooks like the two I had before me: very ordinary dirty notebooks with the lower right edge raised like a wave. I realized in a flash that the memory was already literature and that perhaps Lila was right: my book—even though it was having

so much success—really was bad, and this was because it was
well organized, because it was written with obsessive care,
because I hadn't been able to imitate the disjointed, unaes-
thetic, illogical, shapeless banality of things.

While the children played—if they merely hinted at a quarrel we let out nervous cries to quiet them—Lila placed before
my eyes all the material in her possession, and explained the
meaning of it. We organized and summarized. It was a long
time since we had undertaken something together. She seemed
pleased, I understood that this was what she wanted and
expected from me. At the end of the day she disappeared again
with her bag and I returned to my apartment to study the
notes. Then, in the following days, she wanted us to meet at
Basic Sight. We locked ourselves in her office and sat at the
computer, a kind of television with a keyboard, very different
from what she had showed me and the children some time
before. She pressed the power button, she slid dark rectangles
into gray blocks. I waited, bewildered. On the screen luminous
tremors appeared. Lila began to type on the keyboard, I was
speechless. It was in no way comparable to a typewriter, even
an electric one. With her fingertips she caressed gray keys, and
the writing appeared silently on the screen, green like newly
sprouted grass. What was in her head, attached to who knows
what cortex of the brain, seemed to pour out miraculously and
fix itself on the void of the screen. It was power that, although
passing for act, remained power, an electrochemical stimulus
that was instantly transformed into light. It seemed to me like
the writing of God as it must have been on Sinai at the time of
the Commandments, impalpable and tremendous, but with a
concrete effect of purity. Magnificent, I said. I'll teach you, she
said. And she taught me, and dazzling, hypnotic segments
began to lengthen, sentences that I said, sentences that she
said, our volatile discussions were imprinted on the dark well
of the screen like wakes without foam. Lila wrote, I would

reconsider. Then with one key she erased, with others she made an entire block of light disappear, and made it reappear higher up or lower down in a second. But right afterward it was Lila who changed her mind, and everything was altered again, in a flash: ghostly moves, what's here now is no longer here or is there. And no need for pen, pencil, no need to change the paper, put another sheet in the roller. The page is the screen, unique, no trace of a second thought, it always seems the same. And the writing is incorruptible, the lines are all perfectly straight, they emit a sense of cleanliness even now that we are adding the filthy acts of the Solaras to the filthy acts of half of Campania.

We worked for days. The text descended from Heaven to earth through the noise of the printer, materialized in black dots laid on paper. Lila found it inadequate, we returned to pens, we labored to correct it. She was irritable: from me she expected more, she thought I could respond to all her questions, she got angry because she was convinced that I was a well of knowledge, while at every line she discovered that I didn't know the local geography, the tiny details of bureaucracies, how the communal councils functioned, the hierarchies of a bank, the crimes and the punishments. And yet, contradictorily, I hadn't felt her to be so proud of me and of our friendship in a long time. *We have to destroy them, Lenù, and if this isn't enough I'll murder them.* Our heads collided—for the last time, now that I think of it—one against the other, and merged until they were one. Finally we had to resign ourselves and admit that it was finished, and the dull period of what's done is done began. She printed it yet again, I put our pages in an envelope, and sent it to the publishing house and asked the editor to show it to the lawyers. I need to know—I explained on the telephone—if this stuff was sufficient to send the Solaras to jail.

102.

A week passed, two weeks. The editor telephoned one morning and was lavish in his praise.

"You're in a splendid period," he said.

"I worked with a friend of mine."

"It shows your hand at its best, it's an extraordinary text. Do me a favor: show these pages to Professor Sarratore, so he sees how anything can be transformed into passionate reading."

"I don't see Nino anymore."

"Maybe that's why you're in such good shape."

I didn't laugh, I needed to know urgently what the lawyers had said. The answer disappointed me. There's not enough material, the editor said, for even a day in jail. You can take some satisfaction, but these Solaras of yours aren't going to prison, especially if, as you recount, they're rooted in local politics and have money to buy whoever they want. I felt weak, my legs went limp, I lost conviction, I thought: Lila will be furious. I said, depressed: They're much worse than I've described. The editor perceived my disappointment, he tried to encourage me, he went back to praising the passion I had put into the pages. But the conclusion remained the same: with this you won't ruin them. Then, to my surprise, he insisted that I not put aside the text but publish it. I'll call *L'Espresso*, he suggested, if you come out with a piece like this right now, it'll be an important move for yourself, for your audience, for everyone, you'll show that the Italy we live in is much worse than the one we talk about. And he asked permission to submit the pages to the lawyers again to find out what legal risks I would run, what I would have to take out and what I could keep. I thought of how easy everything had been when it was a matter of scaring Bruno Soccavo, and I refused firmly. I said, I'll end up being sued again, I'd find myself in trouble for no reason, and I would be forced—

something I don't want to do, for the sake of my children—to think that the laws work for those who fear them, not for those who violate them.

I waited a while, then I gathered my strength and told Lila everything, word for word. She stayed calm, she turned on the computer, she scanned the text, but I don't think she reread it, she stared at the screen and meanwhile reflected. Then she asked me in a hostile tone:

"Do you trust this editor?"

"Yes, he's a smart person."

"Then why don't you want to publish the article?"

"What would be the point?"

"To clarify."

"It's already clear."

"To whom? To you, to me, to the editor?"

She shook her head, displeased, and said coldly that she had to work.

I said: "Wait."

"I'm in a hurry. Without Alfonso work's gotten complicated. Go on, please, go."

"Why are you angry at me?"

"Go."

We didn't see each other for a while. In the morning she sent Tina up to me, in the evening either Enzo came to get her or she shouted from the landing: Tina, come to Mamma. A couple of weeks passed, I think, then the editor telephoned me in a very cheerful mood.

"Good for you, I'm glad you made up your mind."

I didn't understand and he explained to me that his friend at *L'Espresso* had called, he urgently needed my address. From him he had learned that the text on the Solaras would come out in that week's issue, with some cuts. You could have told me, he said, that you changed your mind.

I was in a cold sweat, I didn't know what to say, I pretended nothing was wrong. But it took me a moment to realize that Lila had sent our pages to the weekly. I hurried to her to protest, I was indignant, but I found her especially affectionate and above all happy.

"Since you couldn't make up your mind, I did."

"I had decided not to publish it."

"Not me."

"You sign it alone, then."

"What do you mean? You're the writer."

It was impossible to communicate to her my disapproval and my anguish, every critical sentence of mine was blunted against her good humor. The article, six dense pages, was given great prominence, and naturally it had a single byline, mine. When I saw that, we quarreled. I said to her angrily:

"I don't understand why you behave like that."

"I understand," she said.

Her face still bore the marks of Michele's fist, but certainly it hadn't been fear that kept her from putting her name to it. She was terrified by something else and I knew it, she didn't give a damn about the Solaras. But I felt so resentful that I threw it in her face just the same—*You removed your name because you like to stay hidden, because it's convenient to throw stones and hide your hand, I'm tired of your plots*—and she began to laugh, it seemed to her a senseless accusation. I don't like that you think that, she said. She became sullen, she muttered that she had sent the article to *L'Espresso* with only my name on it because hers didn't count, because I was the one who had studied, because I was famous, because now I could give anyone a beating without fear. In those words I found the confirmation that she ingenuously overestimated my role, and I told her so. But she was annoyed, she answered that it was I who underrated myself, so she wanted me to take on more and better, to have even greater success, all she wanted was for my merits to be recognized. You'll see, she exclaimed, what will happen to the Solaras.

I went home depressed. I couldn't drive out the suspicion that she was using me, just as Marcello had said. She had sent me out to risk everything and counted on that bit of fame I had to win her war, to complete her revenge, to silence all her feelings of guilt.

103.

In reality, having my name on that article was a further step up for me. As a result of its wide circulation, many of my fragments were connected. I proved that not only did I have a vocation as a fiction writer but, as in the past I had been involved in the union struggles, as I had engaged in criticizing the condition of women, so I fought against the degradation of my city. The small audience I had won in the late sixties merged with the one that, amid ups and downs, I had cultivated in the seventies and the new, larger one of now. That helped the first two books, which were reprinted, and the third, which continued to sell well, while the idea of making a film from it became more concrete.

Naturally the article caused a lot of bother. I was summoned by the carabinieri. I was bugged by the financial police. I was vilified by local papers on the right with labels like *divorcée, feminist, Communist, supporter of terrorists*. I received anonymous phone calls that threatened me and my daughters in a dialect full of obscenities. But, although I lived in anxiety—a state of anxiety now seemed to me inherent to writing—I was in the end not as agitated as at the time of the article in *Panorama* and Carmen's lawsuit. It was my job, I was learning to do it better and better. And then I felt protected by the legal support of the publisher, by the success I had in newspapers on the left, by the increasingly well attended public appearances, and by the idea that I was right.

But, if I have to be honest, it wasn't only that. I calmed down mainly when it became evident that the Solaras would do absolutely nothing to me. My visibility drove them to be as invisible as possible. Marcello and Michele not only didn't bring a second lawsuit but were completely silent, the whole time, and even when I encountered them before law-enforcement officers, both confined themselves to cold but respectful greetings. Thus the waters subsided. The only concrete thing that happened was that various investigations were opened, along with an equal number of files. But, as the lawyers of the publishing house had predicted, the first soon came to a halt, the second ended—I imagine—under thousands of other files, and the Solaras remained free. The only harm the article caused was of an emotional nature: my sister, my nephew Silvio, even my father—not in words but in deeds—cut me out of their lives. Only Marcello continued to be polite. One afternoon I met him along the *stradone*, and I looked away. But he stopped in front of me, he said: Lenù, I know that if you could you wouldn't have done it, I'm not angry with you, it's not your fault. So remember that my house is always open. I replied: Elisa hung up on me just yesterday. He smiled: Your sister is the boss, what can I do?

104.

But the outcome, which was in essence conciliatory, depressed Lila. She didn't hide her disappointment and yet she didn't put it into words. She carried on, pretending that nothing was wrong: she dropped off Tina at my house and shut herself in the office. But sometimes she stayed in bed all day; she said her head was bursting, and she dozed.

I was careful not to remind her that the decision to publish our pages had been hers. I didn't say: I warned you that the

Solaras would come out of it unharmed, the publisher told me, now it's pointless for you to suffer over it. But stamped on her face was also regret that she had been wrong in her assessment. In those weeks she felt humiliated at having always ascribed a power to things that in the current hierarchies were insignificant: the alphabet, writing, books. Only then—I think today— did she, who seemed so disillusioned, so adult, come to the end of her childhood.

She stopped helping me. More and more often she gave me charge of her daughter and sometimes, though rarely, even of Gennaro, who was forced to hang around my house. Yet my life had become increasingly busy and I didn't know how to manage. One morning when I asked her about the children she answered in annoyance: Call my mother, get her to help you. It was a novelty, I withdrew in embarrassment, I obeyed. So it was that Nunzia arrived at my house, much aged, submissive, uneasy, but efficient as in the days when she took care of the house in Ischia.

My older daughters immediately treated her with disdain, especially Dede, who was going through puberty and had lost any sense of tact. Her face was inflamed, her body was swelling, becoming shapeless, driving out, day by day, the image she was used to, and she felt ugly, she became mean. We began to bicker:

"Why do we have to stay with that old lady? It's disgusting what she cooks, you should cook."

"Stop it."

"She spits when she talks, did you see she doesn't have any teeth?"

"I don't want to hear another word, that's enough."

"We already have to live in this toilet, now we have to have that person in the house? I don't want her to sleep here when you're not here."

"Dede, I said that's enough."

Elsa was no better, but in her own way: she remained serious,

assuming a tone that seemed to support me and yet was duplic-
itous.

"I like her, Mamma, you were right to have her come. She
smells nice, just like a corpse."

"Now I'll slap you. You know she can hear you?"

The only one who was immediately fond of Lila's mother
was Imma: she was Tina's slave and so she imitated her in
everything, even in her attachments. The two of them followed
Nunzia around as she worked in the apartment; they called her
grandma. But Grandma was brusque, especially with Imma.
She caressed her real grandchild, occasionally softening at her
chatter and her affection, while she worked in silence when her
pretend grandchild looked for attention. Meanwhile—I discovered—something was bothering her. At the end of the first
week she said, looking down: Lenù, we haven't talked about
how much you'll give me. I felt hurt: I had stupidly thought
that she came because her daughter had asked her to; if I had
known I had to pay I would have chosen a young person,
whom my daughters would like and from whom I could have
demanded what I needed. But I contained myself, we talked
about money and fixed on an amount. Only then Nunzia
cheered up a little. At the end of the negotiation she felt the
need to justify herself: My husband is sick, she said, he no
longer works, and Lina is crazy, she fired Rino, we don't have
a cent. I muttered that I understood, I told her to be nicer to
Imma. She obeyed. From then on, although she always favored
Tina, she made an effort to be kind to my daughter.

Toward Lila, however, her attitude didn't change. Neither
when she arrived nor when she left did Nunzia ever feel the
need to stop by at her daughter's, although Lila had gotten the
job for her. If they met on the stairs they didn't even greet each
other. She was an old woman who had lost her former wary
friendliness. But Lila, too, it must be said, was intractable, and
visibly worsening.

105.

With me she was always spiteful, for no reason. It especially irritated me that she acted as if everything that happened to my daughters escaped me.

"Dede got the curse."

"Did she tell you?"

"Yes, you weren't here."

"Did you use that expression with her?"

"What word should I have used?"

"Something less vulgar."

"You know how your daughters speak to each other? And have you ever heard the things they say about my mother?"

I didn't like that tone. She, who in the past had appeared so fond of Dede, Elsa, and Imma, seemed determined to disparage them to me, and she took every opportunity to show me that, because I was always traveling around Italy, I neglected them, with serious consequences for their upbringing. I was especially upset when she began accusing me of not seeing Imma's problems.

"What's wrong," I asked her.

"She has a tic in her eye."

"Not very often."

"I've seen it a lot."

"What do you think it means?"

"I don't know. I only know that she feels fatherless and isn't even sure she has a mother."

I tried to ignore her but it was difficult. Imma, as I've said, had always worried me a little, and even when she stood up well to Tina's vivacity she still seemed to lack something. Also, some time earlier I had recognized in her features of mine that I didn't like. She was submissive, she gave in immediately out of fear of not being liked, it depressed her that she had given in. I would have preferred her to inherit Nino's bold capacity for seduction, his thoughtless vitality, but she wasn't like that. Imma was unhappily compliant, she wanted everything and pretended to want nothing. Children, I said, are the product of chance, she's got nothing of her father. Lila didn't agree; she was always finding ways of alluding to the child's resemblance to Nino, but she didn't see it as positive, she spoke as if it were a congenital defect. And then she kept repeating: I'm telling you these things because I love them and I'm worried.

I tried to explain to myself her sudden persecution of my daughters. I thought that, since I had disappointed her, she was withdrawing from me by separating first of all from them. I thought that since my book was increasingly successful, which sanctioned my autonomy from her and from her judgment, she was trying to belittle me by belittling my children and my capacity to be a good mother. But neither of those hypotheses soothed me and a third advanced: Lila saw what I, as a mother, didn't know how or didn't want to see, and since she appeared critical of Imma in particular, I had better find out if her comments had any foundation.

So I began to observe the child and was soon convinced that she really suffered. She was the slave of Tina's joyful expansiveness, of her elevated capacity for verbalization, of the way she aroused tenderness, admiration, affection in everyone, especially me. Although my daughter was pretty, and intelligent, beside Tina she turned dull, her virtues vanished, and she felt this deeply. One day I witnessed an exchange between them, in a good Italian, Tina's pronunciation very precise, Imma's still missing some syllables. They were coloring in the outlines of animals and Tina had decided to use green for a rhinoceros, while Imma added colors randomly for a cat. Tina said:

"Make it gray or black."

"You mustn't give me orders about the color."

"It's not an order, it's a suggestion."

Imma looked at her in alarm. She didn't know the difference between an order and a suggestion. She said:
"I don't want to follow the suggestion, either."
"Then don't."
Imma's lower lip trembled.
"All right," she said, "I'll do it but I don't like it."
I tried to be more attentive to her. To begin with, I stopped
getting excited about everything Tina did, I reinforced Imma's
skills, I praised her for every little thing. But I soon realized it
wasn't enough. The two little girls loved each other. Dealing
with each other helped them grow, some extra artificial praise
was of no help in keeping Imma, looking at her reflection in
Tina, from seeing something that wounded her and that her
friend was certainly not the cause of.

At that point I began to turn over Lila's words: *she's fatherless and isn't even sure she has a mother.* I remembered the mistake in the *Panorama* caption. That caption, buttressed by
Dede and Elsa's mean jokes (*You don't belong to this family:
your name is Sarratore, not Airota*), must have done its damage.
But was that really the core of the problem? I ruled it out. Her
father's absence seemed to me something more serious and I
was sure that her suffering came from that.

Once I had started down this road I began to notice how
Imma sought Pietro's attention. When he called his daughters,
she sat in a corner and listened to the conversation. If the sisters had a good time she pretended to be having fun, too, and
when the conversation ended and they said goodbye to their
father in turn, Imma shouted: Bye. Often Pietro heard her and
said to Dede: Give me Imma so I can say hello. But in those
cases either she became shy and ran away or took the receiver
and remained mute. She behaved the same way when he came
to Naples. Pietro never forgot to bring her a little present, and
Imma hovered near him, played at being his daughter, was
happy if he said something nice or picked her up. Once when

my ex-husband came to get Dede and Elsa, the child's sadness must have seemed especially obvious, and as he left he said: Cuddle her, she's sorry that her sisters are leaving and she has to stay behind.

That observation increased my anxieties, I said to myself that I had to do something, I thought of talking to Enzo and asking him to be more present in Imma's life. But he was already very attentive. If he carried his daughter on his shoulders, after a while he put her down, picked up my daughter, and put her up there; if he got Tina a toy, he got an identical one for her; if he was pleased almost to the point of being moved at the intelligent questions his child asked, he managed to remember to show enthusiasm for the somewhat more prosaic questions of my child. But I spoke to him anyway, and sometimes Enzo admonished Tina, if she occupied the stage and didn't leave room for Imma. I didn't like that, it wasn't the child's fault. In those cases Tina was as if stunned, the lid that was suddenly lowered on her vivacity seemed an undeserved punishment. She didn't understand why the spell was broken, she struggled to regain her father's favor. At that point I would pull her to me, play with her.

In other words things were not going well. One morning I was in the office with Lila, I wanted her to teach me to write on the computer. Imma was playing with Tina under the desk and Tina was sketching in words imaginary places and characters with her usual brilliance. Monstrous creatures were pursuing their dolls, courageous princes were about to rescue them. But I heard my daughter exclaim with sudden rage:

"Not me."

"Not you?"

"I won't rescue myself."

"You don't have to rescue yourself, the prince rescues you."

"I don't have one."

"Then mine will rescue you."

"I said no."

The sudden leap with which Imma had gone from her doll to herself wounded me, even though Tina tried to keep her in the game. Because I was distracted, Lila became irritated, she said:

"Girls, either talk quietly or go outside and play."

106.

That day I wrote a long letter to Nino. I enumerated the problems that I thought were complicating our daughter's life: her sisters had a father who was attentive to them, she didn't; her playmate, Lila's daughter, had a very devoted father and she didn't; because of my work I was always traveling and often had to leave her. In other words, Imma was in danger of growing up feeling that she was continually at a disadvantage. I sent the letter and waited for him to respond. He didn't and so I decided to call his house. Eleonora answered.

"He's not here," she said listlessly. "He's in Rome."

"Would you please tell him that my daughter needs him?"

Her voice caught in her throat. Then she composed herself:

"Mine haven't seen their father, either, for at least six months."

"Has he left you?"

"No, he never leaves anyone. Either you have the strength to leave him yourself—and in this you were smart, I admire you—or he goes, comes, disappears, reappears, as it suits him."

"Will you tell him I called, and if he won't see the child I'll track him down, and take her to him wherever he is?"

I hung up.

It was a while before Nino made up his mind to call, but in the end he did. As usual he acted as if we had seen each other

a few hours earlier. He was energetic, cheerful, full of compliments. I cut him off, I asked:

"Did you get my letter?"

"Yes."

"Then why didn't you answer?"

"I've got no time."

"Find the time, as soon as possible, Imma's not well."

He said reluctantly that he would return to Naples for the
weekend, I insisted that he come to lunch on Sunday. I insisted
that he was not to talk to me, not joke with Dede or Elsa, but
focus the whole day on Imma. That visit, I said, has to become
a habit: it would be wonderful if you would come once a week,
but I won't ask that, I don't expect that from you; once a
month, however, is essential. He said in a serious tone that he
would come every week, he promised, and at that moment he
was surely sincere.

I don't remember the day of the phone call, but the day
when, at ten in the morning, Nino appeared in the neighborhood, elegantly dressed and driving a brand-new luxury car, I
will never forget. It was September 16, 1984. Lila and I had
just turned forty, Tina and Imma were almost four.

107.

I told Lila that Nino was coming to lunch at my house. I
said to her: I forced him, I want him to spend the whole day
with Imma. I hoped she would understand that for at least
that one day she shouldn't send Tina to my house, but she
didn't understand or didn't want to. Instead she acted helpful, she said: I'll tell my mother to cook for everyone and
maybe we'll eat here at my house where there's more room. I
was surprised, and annoyed. She hated Nino; what was that
intrusion all about? I refused, I said: I'll cook, and I repeated

that the day was dedicated to Imma, there would be no way and no time for anything else. But exactly at nine the next day Tina climbed the stairs with her toys and knocked at my door. She was tidy and neat, her black braids shiny, her eyes sparkling with affection.

I told her to come in, but I immediately had to fight with Imma, who was still in her pajamas, sleepy, she hadn't had breakfast, and yet she wanted to start playing immediately. Since she refused to obey me and kept making faces and laughing with her friend, I got mad and closed Tina—frightened by my tone—in a room to play by herself, then I made Imma wash. I don't want to, she screamed. I told her: You have to get dressed, Papa is coming. I had been announcing it for days, but she, hearing that word, became even more rebellious. I myself, in using it to signal to her the imminence of his arrival, became more anxious. The child writhed, screamed: I don't want Papa, as if Papa were a repellent medicine. I ruled out that she remembered Nino, she wasn't expressing a rejection of a definite person. I thought: Maybe I was wrong to make him come; when Imma says she doesn't want Papa, she means that she doesn't want just anyone, she wants Enzo, she wants Pietro, she wants what Tina and her sisters have.

At that point I remembered the other child. She hadn't protested, she hadn't poked her head out. I was ashamed of my behavior. Tina was not responsible for the day's tensions. I called her affectionately, she reappeared and sat happily on a stool in a corner of the bathroom giving me advice on how to braid Imma's hair. My daughter brightened, she let me dress her up without protesting. Finally they ran away to play and I went to get Dede and Elsa out of bed. Elsa jumped up very happily, she was glad to see Nino again and was ready in a short time. But Dede spent an infinite amount of time washing and came out of the bathroom only because I started yelling. She couldn't accept her transformation. I'm disgusting, she said, with tears in her eyes. She shut herself in the bedroom crying that she didn't want to see anyone.

I got myself ready in a hurry. I didn't care about Nino, but I didn't want him to find me neglected and aged. And I was afraid that Lila would show up and I was well aware that, if she wanted, she could focus a man's gaze totally on her. I was agitated and at the same time lethargic.

108.

Nino was exceedingly punctual, and he came up the stairs loaded with presents. Elsa ran to wait for him on the landing, immediately followed by Tina and then, cautiously, Imma. I saw the tic appear in her right eye. Here's Papa, I told her, and she feebly shook her head no.

But Nino behaved well. Already on the stairs he began to sing: Where's my little Imma, I have to give her three kisses and a little bite. When he reached the landing he said hi to Elsa, pulled one of Tina's braids absentmindedly, and grabbed his daughter, covered her with kisses, told her he had never seen such pretty hair, complimented her dress, her shoes, everything. He came in without even a greeting for me. Instead he sat down on the floor, lifted Imma onto his crossed legs, and only then gave some encouragement to Elsa, and warmly greeted Dede (*Good Lord, how you've grown, you're magnificent*), who had approached with a timid smile.

I saw that Tina was puzzled. Strangers, without exception, were dazzled by her and cuddled her as soon as they saw her, whereas Nino had begun to distribute the gifts and was ignoring her. She turned to him with her caressing little voice and tried to take a place on his knees next to Imma, but she couldn't and leaned against his arm, put her head with a languid expression on one shoulder. No, Nino gave Dede and Elsa each a book, then he focused on his daughter. He had bought her all kinds of things. He waited for her to unwrap one gift and immediately gave her another. Imma seemed charmed, moved. She looked at that man as if he were a wizard who had come to cast spells for her alone and when Tina tried to take a gift she cried: It's mine. Tina quickly drew back with her lower lip trembling, I picked her up, I said: Come with aunt. Only then did Nino seem to realize that he was overdoing it and he dug in his pocket, took out an expensive-looking pen, said: This is for you. I put the child down on the floor, she took the pen whispering thank you and he seemed to really see her for the first time. I heard him mutter in amazement:

"You look exactly like your mother."

"Shall I write my name for you?" Tina asked, serious.

"You already know how to write?"

"Yes."

Nino pulled a folded piece of paper out of his pocket, she put it on the floor and wrote: "Tina." Very good! he praised her. But a moment afterward he sought my gaze, afraid of being reprimanded, and to remedy the situation he turned to his daughter: I bet you're very good, too. Imma wanted to show him, and, snatching the pen away from her friend, scribbled on the page with intense concentration. He complimented her profusely, even as Elsa tormented her little sister (*No one can understand that, you don't know how to write*) and Tina tried in vain to get her pen back, saying: I know how to write other words, too. Finally, Nino, to cut it off, stood up with his daughter and said: Now let's go see the most beautiful car in the world, and he carried them all off, Imma in his arms, Tina trying to get him to take her hand, Dede pulling her away and keeping her close, Elsa taking possession of the expensive pen with a greedy gesture.

109.

The door closed behind them. I heard Nino's thick voice on the stairs—he was promising to buy sweets, to take them for a ride in the car—and Dede, Elsa, and the two little girls shouting their excitement. I imagined Lila on the floor below, shut in her apartment, in silence, while the same voices that reached me reached her, too. Separating us was only a layer of floor, and yet she could shorten the distance further or expand it according to her mood and convenience and the movements of her mind, which shifted like the sea when the moon seizes it whole and pulls it upward. I tidied, cooked, I thought Lila— below—was doing the same. We were both waiting to hear again the voices of our daughters, the steps of the man we had loved. It occurred to me that she must have recognized Nino's features in Imma countless times, as he had just now recognized hers in Tina. Had she always felt an aversion, all these years, or was her loving concern for the child a result of that resemblance? Did she still, in secret, like Nino? Was she observing him from the window? Had Tina managed to get him to take her hand and was she looking at her daughter beside that tall thin man, thinking: If things had gone differently she could be his. What was she planning? Would she come up to my house, in a moment, to wound me with a malicious comment? Or would she open the door of her house just as he was passing by, returning with the four girls, and would she invite him to come in and then call up from below, so that I would be compelled to invite her and Enzo to lunch, too?

The apartment was very silent, but outside there was a mixture of Sunday sounds: the pealing bells of midday, the cries of vendors in the stalls, the trains passing on the siding, the traffic of the trucks heading to work sites busy every day of the week. Nino would no doubt let the girls fill up on sweets, without thinking that they would not eat their lunch later. I knew him well: he granted every request, he bought everything without batting an eye, he overdid it. As soon as lunch was ready and the table set, I looked out the window onto the *stradone*. I wanted to call them to say it was time to come home. But the stalls impeded my view, all I could see was Marcello walking with my sister on one side and Silvio on the other. The image of the *stradone* from above gave me a sense of anguish. Sundays had always seemed to me a paint concealing the decay, but that day the impression was stronger. What was I doing in that place, why did I continue to live there, when I had enough money and could go anywhere. I had given Lila too much rope, I had let her retie too many knots, I myself had believed that, reassigning myself publicly to my origins, I would be able to write better. Everything struck me as ugly, I felt a strong repulsion for the food I had prepared. Then I pulled myself together, brushed my hair, made sure that I looked all right, and went out. I passed Lila's door almost on tiptoe; I didn't want her to hear me and decide to come with me.

Outside there was a strong odor of toasted almonds, I looked around. First I saw Dede and Elsa, eating cotton candy and examining a stall selling junk: bracelets, earrings, necklaces, hairpins. Not far away I could make out Nino, standing at the corner. Only after a fraction of a second did I discover that he was talking to Lila, beautiful the way she was when she wanted to be, and Enzo, serious, frowning.

She was holding Imma, who was tormenting one of her ears, as she usually did with mine when she felt neglected. Lila let the child twist it roughly, without stopping her, she was apparently so absorbed by Nino, who was talking in his pleasing way, smiling, gesturing with his long arms, his long hands. I was enraged. That's why Nino had gone out and hadn't been seen again. Here was how he cared for his daughter. I called him, he didn't hear me. Dede turned, she laughed with Elsa at my faint voice, they always did when I shouted. I called again. I wanted Nino to come back right away, return home, *alone*, alone with my daughters. But there was the deafening whistle of the peanut seller and the din of a truck passing, every one of its parts rattling, raising clouds of dust. I grumbled, I joined them. Why was Lila holding my daughter in her arms, what need was there? And why was Imma not playing with Tina? I didn't say hello, I said to Imma: What are you doing being held, you're a big girl, come down, and I pulled her away from Lila. Then I turned to Nino: The children have to eat, it's ready. Meanwhile I realized that my daughter was attached to my skirt, she hadn't left me to run to her friend. I looked around, I asked Lila: Where is Tina?

She still had on her face the expression of cordial assent with which until a minute earlier she had been listening to Nino's conversation. She must be with Dede and Elsa, she said. I answered: She's not. And I wanted her to see about her daughter, together with Enzo, instead of inserting herself between mine and her father on the only day he had made himself available. But while Enzo looked around for Tina, Lila continued talking to Nino. She told him about the times Gennaro had disappeared. She laughed, saying: One morning he couldn't be found, everyone had gone to school and he wasn't there. I was terrified, I imagined the worst things, and instead he was sitting quietly in the gardens. But it was precisely as she remembered that episode that she lost color. Her eyes emptied, in a changed voice she asked Enzo:

"Did you find her, where is she?"

110.

We looked for Tina along the *stradone*, then throughout the whole neighborhood, then again along the *stradone*. Many people joined us. Antonio came, Carmen came, Roberto, Carmen's husband, came, and even Marcello Solara mobilized some of his people, walking the streets himself, until late into the night. Lila now seemed like Melina, she ran here and there with no reason. But Enzo seemed even crazier than she was. He screamed, he got angry at the peddlers, he threatened terrible things, he wanted to look in their cars and vans and carts. The carabinieri had to intervene to calm him.

At every moment it seemed that Tina had been found and there was a sigh of relief. Everyone knew the child, there was no one who wouldn't swear to have seen her a moment before standing at this stall or that corner or in the courtyard or in the gardens over by the tunnel with a tall man, a short one. But every sighting turned out to be illusory, people lost faith and goodwill.

In the evening a rumor took hold that later prevailed. The child had left the sidewalk to chase a blue ball. But just at that moment a truck was passing. The truck was a mud-colored hulk, traveling at high speed, clattering and bouncing because of the holes in the *stradone*. No one had seen anything else, but the collision was heard, the collision that passed directly from the story into the memory of whoever was listening. The truck hadn't braked, or even tried to, and had disappeared at the end of the *stradone* along with Tina's body, her braids. On the asphalt not a drop of blood remained, nothing, nothing at all. In that nothing the vehicle was lost, the child was lost forever.

OLD AGE
THE STORY OF BAD BLOOD

1.

I left Naples definitively in 1995, when everyone said that the city was reviving. But I no longer believed in its resurrections. Over the years I had seen the advent of the new railway station, the dull tower of the skyscraper on Via Novara, the soaring structures of Scampia, the proliferation of tall, shining buildings above the gray stone of Arenaccia, of Via Taddeo da Sessa, of Piazza Nazionale. Those buildings, conceived in France or Japan and rising between Ponticelli and Poggioreale with the usual breakdowns and delays, had immediately, at high speed, lost all their luster and become dens for the desperate. So what resurrection? It was only cosmetic, a powder of modernity applied randomly, and boastfully, to the corrupt face of the city.

It happened like that every time. The scam of rebirth raised hopes and then shattered them, became crust upon ancient crusts. Thus, just as the obligation arose to stay in the city and support the revival under the leadership of the former Communist party, I decided to leave for Turin, drawn by the possibility of running a publishing house that at the time was full of ambition. Once I turned forty, time had begun to race, I couldn't keep up. The real calendar had been replaced by one of contract deadlines, the years leaped from one publication to the next; giving dates to the events that concerned me, and my daughters, cost me a lot, and I forced them into the writing, which took me more and more time. When had this or that happened? In an almost heedless way I oriented myself by the publication dates of my books.

I now had quite a few books behind me, and they had won me some authority, a good reputation, a comfortable life. Over time the weight of my daughters had greatly diminished. Dede and Elsa—first one, then the other—had gone to study in Boston, encouraged by Pietro, who for seven or eight years had had a professorship at Harvard. They were at ease with their father. Apart from the letters in which they complained about the cruel climate and the pedantry of the Bostonians, they were satisfied, with themselves and with escaping the choices that, in the past, I had compelled them to confront. At that point, since Imma was desperate to do what her sisters had, what was I doing in the neighborhood? If at first the image of the writer who, although able to live elsewhere, had stayed in a dangerous outlying neighborhood to continue to nourish herself on reality, had been useful to me, now there were many intellectuals who prided themselves on the same cliché. And my books had taken other paths, the material of the neighborhood had been set aside. Wasn't it therefore hypocritical to have a certain fame, and many advantages, and yet to limit myself, to live in a place where I could only record uneasily the deterioration of the lives of my siblings, my friends, their children and grandchildren, maybe even of my last daughter?

Imma was then fourteen; I didn't deprive her of anything, and she studied hard. But if necessary she spoke in a harsh dialect, she had schoolmates I didn't like, I was so worried if she went out after dinner that often she decided to stay home. I, too, when I was in the city, had a limited life. I saw my friends from cultured Naples, I let myself be courted and embarked on relationships, but they never lasted. Even the most brilliant men sooner or later turned out to be disillusioned, raging at a cruel fate, witty and yet subtly malicious. At times I had the impression that they wanted me mainly so that they could give me their manuscripts to read, ask me about television or the movies, in some cases borrow money that they never paid back. I made the best of it, exerting myself to have a social and emotional life. But going out at night, dressed up, wasn't a pleasure, it was a cause of anxiety. On one occasion I didn't have time to close the street door behind me before I was beaten and robbed by two kids who were no more than thirteen. The taxi driver, who was waiting right out front, didn't even look out the window. So in the summer of 1995 I left Naples with Imma.

I rented an apartment on the Po, near the Isabella Bridge, and my life and that of my third daughter immediately improved. From there it became simpler to reflect on Naples, to write about it and let myself write about it with lucidity. I loved my city, but I uprooted from myself any dutiful defense of it. I was convinced, rather, that the anguish in which that love sooner or later ended was a lens through which to look at the entire West. Naples was the great European metropolis where faith in technology, in science, in economic development, in the kindness of nature, in history that leads of necessity to improvement, in democracy, was revealed, most clearly and far in advance, to be completely without foundation. To be born in that city—I went so far as to write once, thinking not of myself but of Lila's pessimism—is useful for only one thing: to have always known, almost instinctively, what today, with endless fine distinctions, everyone is beginning to claim: that the dream of unlimited progress is in reality a nightmare of savagery and death.

In 2000 I was left alone; Imma went to study in Paris. I tried to convince her that there was no need, but since many of her friends had decided to go, she didn't want to be left out. At first it didn't bother me, I had a busy life. But within a few years I began to feel old age, it was as if I were fading along with the world in which I had established myself. Although I had won, at various times and with various works, some prestigious prizes, my books were now hardly selling at all: in 2003, for example, the thirteen novels and two volumes of essays I had published earned altogether twenty-three hundred and twenty-three euros before taxes. I had to acknowledge, at that point, that my audience expected nothing more from me and that younger readers—it would be more accurate to say younger women readers; from the start it was mainly women who read my books—had other tastes, other interests. The newspapers were no longer a source of income, either. They weren't interested in me; they rarely asked for articles, and paid nothing or next to nothing. As for television, after some successful experiences in the nineties, I had tried to do an afternoon show devoted to classics of Greek and Latin literature, an idea that was accepted only thanks to the regard of some friends, including Armando Galiani, who had a show on Channel 5 but good relations with public television. It was an unquestionable fiasco and I had not had other opportunities. Things also deteriorated at the publishing house I had run for many years. In the fall of 2004 I was pushed out by a clever young man, scarcely over thirty, and reduced to an external consultant. I was sixty, I felt my journey was ending. In Turin the winters were too cold, the summers too hot, the cultured classes unwelcoming. I was anxious, I didn't sleep much. Men no longer noticed me. I looked out at the Po from my balcony, at the rowers, the hill, and I was bored.

I began to go more frequently to Naples, but I had no wish to see friends and relatives, and friends and relatives had no wish to see me. I saw only Lila, but often, by my choice, not even her. She made me uneasy. In recent years she had become passionate about the city with a chauvinism that seemed crude, so I preferred to walk alone on Via Caracciolo, or go up to the Vomero, or walk through the Tribunali. So it happened that in the spring of 2006, shut up in an old hotel on Corso Vittorio Emanuele during an incessant rain, I wrote, in a few days, to pass the time, a narrative of scarcely eighty pages that was set in the neighborhood and told the story of Tina. I wrote it rapidly in order not to give myself time to invent. The pages were terse, direct. The story took off imaginatively only at the end.

I published the book in the fall of 2007 with the title *A Friendship*. It was very well received, and it still sells well today; teachers recommend it to students as summer reading.

But I hate it.

Just two years earlier, when Gigliola's body was found in the gardens—she had died of a heart attack, in solitude, a death terrible in its bleakness—Lila had made me promise that I would never write about her. Instead, here, I had done it, and I had done it in the most direct way. For a few months I believed that I had written my best book, and my fame as a writer took off again; it was a long time since I'd had such success. But already by the end of 2007—during the Christmas season—when I went to Feltrinelli in Piazza dei Martiri to present *A Friendship*, I suddenly felt ashamed and was afraid of seeing Lila in the audience, maybe the front row, ready to interrupt and make trouble for me. But the evening went very well, I was much celebrated. When I returned to the hotel, a bit more confident, I tried to telephone her, first on the regular phone, then on the cell, then again on the other. She didn't answer, she hasn't answered me since.

2.

I don't know how to recount Lila's grief. What befell her, what had perhaps been lying in wait in her life forever, was not the death of a daughter through illness, an accident, an act of violence, but her daughter's sudden disappearance. The grief couldn't coagulate around anything. She had no lifeless body to cling to in despair, there was no one for whom to hold a funeral, she couldn't linger before a corpse that had walked, run, talked, hugged her, and had ended up a broken thing. Lila felt, I think, as if a limb, which until a moment before had been part of her body, had lost form and substance without undergoing any trauma. But I don't know the suffering that derived from it well enough, nor can I imagine it.

In the ten years that followed the loss of Tina, although I continued to live in the same building, although I met Lila every day, I never saw her cry, I never witnessed a crisis of despair. After at first rushing through the neighborhood, day and night, in that vain search for her daughter, she gave in as if she were too weary. She sat beside the kitchen window and didn't move for a long period, even though from there you could see only a slice of the railroad and a little sky. Then she pulled herself together and began normal life again, but without resignation. The years washed over her, her nasty character got even worse, she sowed uneasiness and fear, she grew old screeching, quarreling. At first she talked about Tina on every occasion and with anyone, she clung to the name of the child as if uttering it would serve to bring her back. But later it was impossible even to mention that loss in her presence, and even if it was I who did so she got rid of me rudely after a few seconds. She seemed to appreciate only a letter from Pietro, mainly—I think—because he managed to write to her lovingly without ever mentioning Tina. Even in 1995, before I left, except on very rare occasions she acted as if nothing had happened. Once Pinuccia spoke of the child as a little angel watching over us all. Lila said: Get out.

3.

No one in the neighborhood put faith in the forces of order or in the journalists. Men, women, even gangs of kids spent days and weeks looking for Tina, ignoring the police and television. All the relatives, all the friends were mobilized. The

only one who turned up just a couple of times—and by telephone, with generic phrases that existed only to be repeated: I
have no responsibility, I had just handed the child over to Lina
and Enzo—was Nino. But I wasn't surprised, he was one of
those adults who when they play with a child and the child falls
and skins his knee behave like children themselves, afraid that
someone will say: It was you who let him fall. Besides, no one
gave him any importance, we forgot about him in a few hours.
Enzo and Lila trusted Antonio above all, and he put off his
departure for Germany yet again, to track down Tina. He did
it out of friendship but also, as he himself explained, surprising us, because Michele Solara had ordered him to.

The Solaras undertook more than anyone else in that business of the child's disappearance and—I have to say—they
made their involvement highly visible. Although they knew
they would be treated with hostility they appeared one evening
at Lila's house with the attitude of those who are speaking for
an entire community, and they vowed they would do everything
possible to return Tina safe and sound to her parents. Lila
stared at them the whole time as if she saw them but didn't hear
them. Enzo, extremely pale, listened for a few minutes and
then cried that it was they who had taken his daughter. He said
it then and on many other occasions, he shouted it everywhere:
the Solaras had taken Tina away from them because he and
Lila had refused to give them a percentage of the profits of
Basic Sight. He wanted someone to object so that he could
murder him. But no one ever objected in his presence. That
evening not even the two brothers objected.

"We understand your grief," Marcello said. "If they had
taken Silvio I would have gone mad, just like you."

They waited for someone to calm Enzo and they left. The
next day they sent on a courtesy call their wives, Gigliola and
Elisa, who were welcomed without warmth but more politely.
And later they multiplied their initiatives. Probably it was the

Solaras who organized a sort of roundup of all the street peddlers who were usually present in the neighborhood on Sundays and holidays and of all the Gypsies in the area. And certainly they were at the head of a real surge of anger against the police when they arrived, sirens blasting, to arrest Stefano, who had his first heart attack at that time and ended up in the hospital, and then Rino, who was released in a few days, and finally Gennaro, who wept for hours, swearing that he loved his little sister more than any other person in the world and would never harm her. Nor can it be ruled out that they were the ones responsible for surveillance of the elementary school—thanks to which the "faggot seducer of children," who until then had been only a popular fantasy, materialized. A slender man of around thirty who, although he didn't have children to deliver to the entrance and pick up at the exit, appeared just the same at the school, was beaten, managed to escape, was pursued by a furious mob to the gardens. There he would surely have been murdered if he hadn't managed to explain that he wasn't what they thought but a trainee at *Il Mattino* looking for news.

After that episode the neighborhood began to settle down, people slowly slipped back into the life of every day. Since no trace of Tina was found, the rumor of the truck hitting her became increasingly plausible. Those who were tired of searching took it seriously, both police and journalists. Attention shifted to the construction sites in the area and remained there for a long time. It was at that point that I saw Armando Galiani, the son of my high-school teacher. He had stopped practicing medicine, had lost in the parliamentary elections of 1983, and now, thanks to a scruffy local television station, he was attempting an aggressive type of journalism. I knew that his father had died a little over a year earlier and that his mother lived in France but wasn't in good health, either. He asked me to take him to Lila's, I said Lila wasn't at all well. He insisted, I telephoned. Lila struggled to remember Armando, but when she did

she—who until that moment hadn't spoken to journalists—
agreed to see him. Armando explained that he had been inves-
tigating the aftermath of the earthquake and that traveling
around to the construction sites he had heard of a truck that
was scrapped in a hurry because of a terrible thing it had been
involved in. Lila let him speak, then said:

"You're making it all up."

"I'm saying what I know."

"You don't care a thing about the truck, the construction
sites, or my daughter."

"You're insulting me."

"No, I'll insult you now. You were disgusting as a doctor,
disgusting as a revolutionary, and now you're disgusting as a
journalist. Get out of my house."

Armando scowled, nodded goodbye to Enzo, and left. Out
on the street he looked annoyed. He said: Not even that great
sorrow has changed her, tell her I wanted to help. Then he did
a long interview with me and we said goodbye. I was struck by
his kind manners, by his attentiveness to words. He must have
been through some bad times both when Nadia made her decisions and when he separated from his wife. Now, though, he
seemed in good shape. His old attitude, of a know-it-all who
follows a strict anticapitalist line, had turned into a painful
cynicism.

"Italy has become a cesspool," he said in an aggrieved tone,
"and we've all ended up in it. If you travel around, you see that
the respectable people have understood. What a pity, Elena,
what a pity. The workers' parties are full of honest people who
have been left without hope."

"Why did you start doing this job?"

"For the same reason you do yours."

"What's that?"

"Once I was unable to hide behind anything, I discovered I
was vain."

"Who says I'm vain?"

"The comparison: your friend isn't. But I'm sorry for her, vanity is a resource. If you're vain you pay attention to yourself and your affairs. Lina is without vanity, so she lost her daughter."

I followed his work for a while, he seemed good at it. He tracked down the burned-out wreck of an old vehicle in the neighborhood of the Ponti Rossi, and connected it to Tina's disappearance. The news caused a certain sensation, it reverberated in the national dailies, and remained in the news for several days. Then it was ascertained that there was no possible connection between the burned vehicle and the child's disappearance. Lila said to me:

"Tina is alive, I never want to see that piece of shit again."

4.

I don't know how long she believed that her daughter was still alive. The more Enzo despaired, worn out by tears and rage, the more Lila said: You'll see, they'll give her back. Certainly she never believed in the hit-and-run truck, she said that she would have noticed right away, that before anyone else she would have heard the collision, or at least a cry. And it didn't seem to me that she gave credence to Enzo's thesis, either, she never alluded to involvement on the part of the Solaras. Instead for a long period she thought that one of her clients had taken Tina, someone who knew what Basic Sight earned and wanted money in exchange for the child. That was also Antonio's thesis, but it's hard to say what concrete facts inspired it. Of course the police were interested in that possibility, but since there were never any telephone calls asking for ransom they finally let it go.

The neighborhood was soon divided into a majority that believed Tina was dead and a minority that thought she was

alive and a prisoner somewhere. We who loved Lila dearly
were part of that minority. Carmen was so sure of it that she
repeated it insistently to everyone, and if, as time passed, someone was persuaded that Tina was dead she became that person's enemy. I once heard her whisper to Enzo: Tell Lina that
Pasquale is with you, he thinks the child will be found. But the
majority prevailed, and those who kept on looking for Tina
seemed to the majority either stupid or hypocritical. People
also began to think that Lila's intelligence wasn't helping her.

Carmen was the first to intuit that the respect our friend
had inspired before Tina's disappearance and the solidarity
that arose afterward were both superficial, an old aversion
toward her lurked underneath. Look, she said to me, once they
treated her as if she were the Madonna and now they pass by
her without even a glance. I began to pay attention and saw
that it was true. Deep inside, people thought: we're sorry you
lost Tina, but it means that if you had truly been what you
wanted us to believe, nothing and no one would have touched
you. On the street, when we were together, they began to greet
me but not her. They were put off by her troubled expression
and the cloud of misfortune they saw around her. In other
words, the part of the neighborhood that had become used to
thinking of Lila as an alternative to the Solaras withdrew in disappointment.

Not only that. An initiative was undertaken that at first
seemed kind but then became malicious. In the early weeks,
flowers, emotional notes addressed to Lila or directly to Tina,
even poems copied from schoolbooks appeared at the entrance
to the house, at the door of Basic Sight. Then there were old
toys brought by mothers, grandmothers, and children. Then
barrettes, colorful hair ribbons, old shoes. Then puppets sewed
by hand, with ugly sneers, stained with red, and animal carcasses wrapped in dirty rags. Since Lila calmly picked everything up and threw it into the trash, but suddenly began

screaming horrible curses at anyone who passed by, especially
the children, who observed her from a distance, she went from
being a mother who inspired pity to a madwoman who spread
terror. When a girl she had been angry with because she had
seen her writing with chalk on the doorway, *the dead are eating
Tina*, became seriously ill, old rumors joined the new and people avoided Lila, as if just to look at her could bring misfortune.

Yet she seemed not to realize it. The certainty that Tina was
still alive absorbed her completely and it was what, I think,
pushed her toward Imma. In the first months I had tried to
reduce the contact between her and my youngest daughter, I
was afraid that seeing her would cause more suffering. But Lila
soon seemed to want her around constantly, and I let her keep
her even to sleep. One morning when I went to get her the
door of the house was half open, I went in. My child was asking about Tina. After that Sunday I had tried to soothe her by
telling her that Tina had gone to stay for a while with Enzo's
relatives in Avellino, but she kept asking when she would
return. Now she was asking Lila directly, but Lila seemed not
to hear Imma's voice, and instead of answering was telling her
in detail about Tina's birth, her first toy, how she attached herself to her breast and never let go, things like that. I stopped in
the doorway for a few seconds, I heard Imma interrupt her
impatiently:

"But when is she coming back?"

"Do you feel lonely?"

"I don't know who to play with."

"I don't, either."

"Then when is she coming back?"

Lila said nothing for a long moment, then scolded her:

"It's none of your business, shut up."

Those words, uttered in dialect, were so brusque, so harsh,
so unsuitable that I was alarmed. I said something, brought my
child home.

I had always forgiven Lila her excesses and in those circumstances I was inclined to do so even more than in the past.
She often went too far, and as much as possible I tried to get
her to be reasonable. When the police interrogated Stefano
and she was immediately convinced that he had taken Tina—
so that at first she refused even to visit him in the hospital after
the heart attack—I mollified her, and we went together to visit
him. And it was thanks to me that she hadn't attacked her
brother when the police questioned him. I had also done all I
could on the awful day when Gennaro was summoned to the
police station and, once at home, felt himself accused; there
was a quarrel, and he went to live at his father's house, shouting at Lila that she had lost forever not only Tina but also him.
The situation, in other words, was terrible and I could understand why she fought with everyone, even me. But with Imma,
no, I couldn't allow it. From then on, when Lila took the child
I became anxious, I pondered, I looked for ways out.

But there was little to do; the threads of her grief were tangled and Imma was for a time part of that tangle. In the general
chaos where we had all ended up, Lila, despite her weariness,
continued to tell me about my daughter's every little difficulty,
as she had done until I decided to insist that Nino visit. I felt
angry, I was irritated, and yet I tried *also* to see a positive aspect:
she's slowly shifting onto Imma—I thought—her maternal love,
she's saying to me: Since you've been lucky, and you still have
your daughter, you ought to take advantage of it, pay attention
to her, give her all the care you haven't given her.

But that was only the appearance of things. Soon I had a
different theory: that, more deeply, Imma—her body—must
be a symbol of guilt. I thought often of the situation in which
the little girl had been lost. Nino had handed her over to Lila
but *Lila hadn't attended to her.* She had said to her daughter,
You wait here, and to my daughter, *Come with your aunt.* She
had done it, perhaps, to show off Imma to her father, to praise

her to him, to stir his affection, who knows. But Tina was lively, or more simply she had felt neglected, offended, and had wandered off. As a result Lila's suffering had made a nest in the weight of Imma's body in her arms, in the contact, in the living warmth it still gave off. But my daughter was fragile, slow, different in every way from Tina, who was shining, vivacious. Imma could in no way become a substitute, she was only holding back time. I imagined, in other words, that Lila kept her nearby in order to stay within that terrible Sunday, and meanwhile thought: Tina is here, soon she'll pull on my skirt, she'll call me, and then I'll pick her up in my arms, and everything will return to its place. That was why she didn't want the child to upset everything. When the little girl kept asking for her friend, when she merely reminded Lila that in fact Tina wasn't there, Lila treated her with the same harshness with which she treated us adults. But I couldn't accept that. As soon as she came to get Imma, I found some excuse or other to send Dede or Elsa to watch her. If she had used that tone when I was present, what might happen when she took her away for hours?

5.

Every so often I escaped from the apartment, from the flight of stairs between my rooms and hers, from the gardens, the *stradone*, and left for work. These were moments when I sighed with relief: I put on makeup, stylish clothes, even the slight limp that remained from the pregnancy was a sort of pleasingly distinctive trait. Although I frequently made sarcastic remarks about the ill-humored behavior of literary people and artists, at the time everything having to do with publishing, cinema, television—every type of aesthetic display—seemed to me a fantastic landscape in which it was marvelous to appear. I liked being present in the extravagant, festive chaos of big conventions, big conferences, big theater productions, big exhibitions, big films, big operas, and I was flattered on the few occasions when I had a place in the front rows, the reserved seats, from which, sitting among famous people, I could observe the spectacle of powers large and small. Lila, on the other hand, remained at the center of *her* horror, without any distraction. Once I had an invitation to an opera at the San Carlo—a magnificent place where not even I had been—and I insisted on taking her; she didn't want to go, and persuaded Carmen to go instead. The only distraction, if that is the right word for it, she would allow was another reason for suffering. A new affliction acted on her as a sort of antidote. She became combative, determined, she was like someone who knows she has to drown but in spite of herself agitates her arms and legs to stay afloat.

One night she discovered that her son had started shooting up again. Without saying a word, without even telling Enzo, she went to get him from Stefano, in the house in the new neighborhood where decades earlier she had lived as a bride. But he wasn't there: Gennaro had quarreled with his father, too, and a few days earlier had moved to his uncle Rino's. She was greeted with open hostility by Stefano and Marisa, who now lived together. That once handsome man was now skin and bones, and very pale; his clothes seemed several sizes too big. The heart attack had crushed him, he was frightened, he scarcely ate, he didn't drink, he no longer smoked, he wasn't supposed to get upset, because of his bad heart. But on that occasion he became extremely upset and had reason to be. He had closed the grocery because of his illness. Ada demanded money for herself and their daughter. His sister Pinuccia and his mother, Maria, also demanded money. Marisa demanded it for herself and her children. Lila understood immediately that Stefano wanted that money from her and that the excuse for getting it was Gennaro. In fact, although he had thrown his son out of the house, he took his side; he said, and Marisa supported him, that it would take a lot of money to get treatment for Gennaro. And since Lila replied that she would never give a cent to anyone, she didn't give a damn about relatives, friends, or the whole neighborhood, the quarrel became furious. With tears in his eyes, Stefano listed all he had lost over the years—from the grocery stores to the house itself—and for those losses he in some obscure way blamed Lila. But the worst came from Marisa, who yelled at her: Alfonso was ruined because of you, you've ruined us all, you're worse than the Solaras, whoever stole your child did a good thing.

Only at that point did Lila become silent, she looked around for a chair to sit on. She couldn't find one and leaned against the living room wall, which, decades earlier, had been her living room, a white room at the time, the furniture brand-new, nothing yet damaged by the havoc of the children who had grown up there, by the carelessness of the adults. Let's go, Stefano said to her, perhaps realizing that Marisa had gone too far, let's go get Gennaro. And they left together; he took her by the arm, and they went to Rino's house.

Once they were outside, Lila recovered, and freed herself. They walked, she a few steps ahead. Her brother lived in the Carraccis' old house, with his mother-in-law, Pinuccia, their children. Gennaro was there and as soon as he saw his parents he began shouting. So another fight broke out, first between father and son, then between mother and son. For a while Rino was silent, then, his eyes dull, he began whining about the harm his sister had done since they were children. When Stefano intervened Rino got angry at him, insulted him, insisted that all the trouble had started when he wanted to make people think he was someone and instead he had been cheated first by Lila and then by the Solaras. They were about to come to blows and Pinuccia had to restrain her husband, muttering, You're right, but calm down, this isn't the moment, while the old lady, Maria, had to restrain Stefano, wheezing: That's enough, son, pretend you didn't hear him, Rino is sicker than you. At that point Lila grabbed her son forcefully by the arm and took him away.

But Rino followed them to the street, they heard him limping after them. He wanted money, he wanted it at all costs, right away. He said: You'll kill me if you leave me like this. Lila kept walking while he pushed her, laughed, moaned, held her back by the arm. Gennaro began to cry, he yelled at her: You have money, Ma, give it to him. But Lila drove her brother away and brought her son home, hissing: You want to become like that, you want to end up like your uncle?

6.

With the return of Gennaro the apartment below became an even worse inferno; at times I was compelled to go down because I was afraid they'd kill each other. Lila opened the door, said coldly: What do you want. I answered just as coldly: You're overdoing it, Dede's crying, she wants to call the police, and Elsa is scared. She answered: Stay in your own home and plug up your children's ears if they don't want to hear.

In that period she showed less and less interest in the two girls; with explicit sarcasm she called them the young ladies. But my daughters' attitude toward her changed as well. Dede especially stopped feeling her fascination, as if in her eyes, too, Tina's disappearance had taken away Lila's authority. One evening she asked me:

"If Aunt Lina didn't want another child why did she have one?"

"How do you know she didn't want one?"

"She told Imma."

"Imma?"

"Yes, I heard it with my own ears. She talks to her as if she weren't a child, I think she's insane."

352 · ELENA FERRANTE

"It's not insanity, Dede, it's grief."

"She's never shed a tear."

"Tears aren't grief."

"Yes, but without tears how can you be sure that the grief is there?"

"It's there and often it's an even greater suffering."

"That's not her case. You want to know what I think?"

"All right."

"She lost Tina on purpose. And now she also wants to lose Gennaro. Not to mention Enzo, don't you see how she treats him? Aunt Lina is just like Elsa, she doesn't love anyone."

Dede was like that, she wanted to be someone who is more perceptive than everyone else, and loved to formulate judgments without appeal. I forbade her to repeat those terrible words in Lila's presence and tried to explain to her that not all human beings react in the same way, Lila and Elsa had emotional strategies different from hers.

"Your sister, for example," I said, "doesn't confront emotional issues the way you do; she finds feelings that are too intense ridiculous, and she always stands back a step."

"By standing back a step she's lost any sensitivity."

"Why are you so annoyed with Elsa?"

"Because she's just like Aunt Lina."

A vicious circle: Lila was wrong because she was like Elsa, Elsa was wrong because she was like Lila. In reality at the center of this negative judgment was Gennaro. According to Dede, precisely in this crucial situation Elsa and Lila were making the same mistaken assessment and showed the same emotional disorder. Just as for Lila, for Elsa, too, Gennaro was worse than a beast. Her sister—Dede reported to me—often told her, to offend her, that Lila and Enzo were right to beat him as soon as he tried to stick his nose out of the house. Only someone as stupid as you—she taunted her—who doesn't know anything about men, could be dazzled by a mass of unwashed flesh without a crumb of intelligence. And Dede replied: Only a bitch like you could describe a human being that way.

Since they both read a lot, they quarreled in the language of books, so that, if they didn't slip suddenly into the most brutal dialect to insult each other, I would have listened to their squabbling almost with admiration. The positive side of the conflict was that Dede's rancor toward me diminished, but the negative side burdened me greatly: her sister and Lila became the object of all her malice. Dede was constantly reporting to me Elsa's disgraceful actions: she was hated by her schoolmates because she considered herself the best at everything and was always humiliating them; she boasted of having had relations with adult men; she skipped school and forged my signature on the absence slips. Of Lila she said: She's a fascist, how can you be her friend? And she took Gennaro's side with no equivocation. In her view drugs were a rebellion of sensitive people against the forces of repression. She swore that sooner or later she would find a way of getting Rino out—she always called him that, and only that, habituating us to call him that, too—from the prison in which his mother kept him.

I tried whenever I could to throw water on the flames, I reprimanded Elsa, I defended Lila. But sometimes it was hard to take Lila's part. The peaks of her bitter grief frightened me. On the other hand I was afraid that, as had happened in the past, her body wouldn't hold up, and so, even though I liked Dede's lucid and yet passionate aggression, even though I found Elsa's quirky impudence amusing, I was careful not to let my daughters set off crises with reckless words. (I knew that Dede would have been more than capable of saying: *Aunt Lina, tell things as they are, you wanted to lose Tina, it didn't happen by chance.*) But every day I feared the worst. The young ladies, as Lila called them, although they were immersed in the reality of the neighborhood, had a strong sense that they were different. Especially when they returned from Florence they felt they were of superior quality and did all they could to demonstrate it. Dede was doing very well in high school and when her professor—a very cultivated man no more than forty, awestruck by the surname Airota—interrogated her he seemed more worried that he would make a mistake in the questions than that she would make a mistake in the answers. Elsa was less brilliant scholastically, and her midyear report cards were generally poor, but what made her intolerable was the ease with which at the end she shuffled the cards and came in among the top. I knew their insecurities and terrors, I felt them to be fearful girls, and so I didn't put much credence in their domineering attitudes. But others did, and seen from the outside they must surely have seemed odious. Elsa, for example, gleefully bestowed offensive nicknames in class and outside, she had no respect for anyone. She called Enzo the mute bumpkin; she called Lila the poisonous moth; she called Gennaro the laughing crocodile. But she was especially irked by Antonio, who went to Lila's almost every day, either to the office or to her house, and as soon as he arrived drew her and Enzo into a room to conspire. Antonio, after the episode of Tina, had become cantankerous. If I was present he more or less explicitly took his leave; if it was my daughters, he cut them off by closing the door. Elsa, who knew Poe well, called him the mask of yellow death, because Antonio had a naturally jaundiced complexion. It was obvious, therefore, that I should fear some blunder on their part. Which duly happened.

I was in Milan. Lila rushed into the courtyard, where Dede was reading, Elsa was talking to some friends, Imma was playing. They weren't children. Dede was sixteen, Elsa almost thirteen; only Imma was little, she was five. But Lila treated all three as if they had no autonomy. She dragged them into the house without explanation (they were used to hearing explanations), crying only that staying outside was dangerous. My oldest daughter found that behavior unbearable, she said:

"Mamma entrusted my sisters to me, it's up to me to decide whether to go inside or not."

"When your mother isn't here I'm your mother."

"A shit mother," Dede answered, moving to dialect. "You lost Tina and you haven't even cried."

Lila slapped her, crushing her. Elsa defended her sister and was slapped in turn, Imma burst into tears. You don't go out of the house, my friend repeated, gasping, outside it's dangerous, outside you'll die. She kept them inside for days, until I returned.

When I returned, Dede recounted the whole episode, and, honest as she was, on principle, she also reported her own ugly response. I wanted her to understand that what she had said was terrible, and I scolded her harshly: I warned you not to. Elsa sided with her sister, she explained to me that Aunt Lina was out of her mind, she was possessed by the idea that to escape danger you had to live barricaded in the house. It was hard to convince my daughters that it wasn't Lila's fault but the Soviet empire's. In a place called Chernobyl a nuclear power plant had exploded and emitted dangerous radiation that, since the planet was small, could be absorbed by anyone. Aunt Lina was protecting you, I said. But Elsa shouted: It's not true, she beat us, the only good thing is that she fed us only frozen food. Imma: I cried a lot, I don't like frozen food. And Dede: She treated us worse than she treats Rino. I said: Aunt Lina would have behaved the same way with Tina, think of what torture it must have been for her to protect you, imagining that her daughter is somewhere and no one's taking care of her. But it was a mistake to express myself like that in front of Imma. While Dede and Elsa looked skeptical, she was upset, and ran away to play.

A few days later Lila confronted me in her direct way:

"Is it you who tell your daughters that I lost Tina and never cried?"

"Stop it, do you think I would say a thing like that?"

"Dede called me a shit mother."

"She's a child."

"She's a very rude child."

At that point I committed errors no less serious than those of my daughters. I said:

"Calm down. I know how much you loved Tina. Try not to keep it all inside, you should let it out, you should say whatever comes into your mind. I know the birth was difficult, but you shouldn't elaborate on it."

I got everything wrong: the past tense of "you loved," the allusion to the birth, the fatuous tone. She answered curtly: Mind your own business. And then she cried, as if Imma were an adult: Teach your daughter that if someone tells her something, she shouldn't go around repeating it.

7.

Things got even worse when, one morning—I think it was in June of 1986—there was another disappearance. Nunzia arrived, grimmer than usual, and said that Rino hadn't returned home the previous night, that Pinuccia was looking for him all over the neighborhood. She gave me the news without looking at me, as she did when what she was telling me was really meant for Lila.

I went downstairs to report it. Lila immediately summoned Gennaro—she took it for granted that he would know where his uncle was. The boy resisted, he didn't want to reveal anything that might lead his mother to become even harsher. But when the entire day passed and Rino still couldn't be found, he decided to cooperate. The next morning he refused to let Enzo and Lila come with him on the search, but resigned himself to the company of his father. Stefano arrived out of breath, nervous because of yet another difficulty that his brother-in-law was causing, apprehensive because of his own ill health, and, continually touching his throat, said, ashen-faced: I can't breathe. Finally father and son—the boy large, the man looking like a stick in his oversized clothes—set off for the railroad.

They crossed the switching yard and walked along the old tracks where disused cars had been abandoned. In one of them they found Rino. He was seated, his eyes were open. His nose seemed enormous, his unshaved beard, still black, covered his face, up to the cheekbones, like an overgrown plant. Stefano, seeing his brother-in-law, forgot his health and had a real fit of rage. He shouted insults at the corpse, he wanted to kick it. You were a shit as a boy—he screamed—and a shit you've remained. You deserve this death, you died like a shit. He was angry because he had ruined his sister Pinuccia, because he had ruined his nephews, and because he had ruined his son. Look, he said to Gennaro, look what's waiting for you. Gennaro grabbed him from behind and gripped him hard to restrain him while, kicking and thrashing, Stefano tried to get free.

It was early morning but already starting to get hot. The car stank of shit and pee, the seats were broken, the windows so dirty you couldn't see out. Since Stefano continued to struggle and howl, the boy lost his temper and said ugly things to his father. He said that it disgusted him to be his son, that the only people in the whole neighborhood he respected were his mother and Enzo. At that point Stefano began to cry. They sat together for a while beside Rino's body, not to watch over him, only to calm down. They went home to deliver the news.

8.

Nunzia and Fernando were the only ones who felt the loss of Rino. Pinuccia mourned her husband only as much as was indispensable and then seemed to be reborn. Two weeks afterward she showed up at my house to ask if she could replace her mother-in-law, who was crushed by grief and didn't feel like working anymore: she would clean the house, cook, and take care of my daughters in my absence for exactly the same sum. She was less efficient than Nunzia but more talkative and above all more appealing to Dede, Elsa, and Imma. She was full of compliments for all three of them and for me as well. How well you look, she said, you're a lady: I see you've got beautiful dresses and a lot of shoes in the closet, it's obvious that you're important and you go out with important people: is it true that they're making a film out of your book?

At first she acted like a widow, but then she asked if there were dresses I didn't wear anymore, even if she was large and they didn't fit her. I'll let them out, she said, and I chose some for her. She altered them carefully and skillfully, and then she appeared at work as if she were going to a party, parading back and forth along the hall so that the girls and I could give her our opinion. She was very grateful to me; at times she was so content that she wanted to talk rather than work, and she recalled the days of Ischia. She often alluded to Bruno Soccavo, becoming emotional, and saying in a low voice: What a terrible end he had. A few times she made a remark that must have pleased her greatly: I was widowed twice. One morning she confided to me that Rino had been a real husband only for a few years, otherwise he had behaved like a boy: even in bed, one minute and off he got, sometimes not even the minute. Ah, yes, he was immature, he was a braggart, a liar, but also arrogant, arrogant like Lina. It's a characteristic of the race of the Cerullos—she grew angry—they're bigmouths and they've got no feelings. Then she began to speak ill of Lila, she said she had appropriated everything that was a product of her brother's intelligence and hard work. I replied: It's not true, Lina loved Rino, it was he who exploited her in every way. Pinuccia looked at me bitterly, out of the blue she began to praise her husband. Cerullo shoes, she pronounced, he invented, but then Lina took advantage, she cheated Stefano, she made him marry her, she stole a lot of money—Papa had left us millionaires—and then she made a deal with Michele Solara, she ruined us all. She added: Don't defend her, you know it perfectly well.

It wasn't true, naturally, I knew something quite different, Pinuccia spoke like that because of old resentments. And yet Lila's only real reaction to the death of her brother was that she confirmed many of those lies. I had long since realized that each of us organizes memory as it suits him, I'm still surprised when I do it myself. But it surprised me that one could go so far as to give the facts an arrangement that went against one's own interests. Lila began almost immediately to attribute to Rino all the merits of the business with the shoes. She said that her brother had had extraordinary imagination and skill since he was a boy, that if the Solaras hadn't interfered he might have surpassed Ferragamo. She strove to stop the flow of Rino's life at the exact moment when her father's workshop was transformed into a small factory, and from all the rest—everything that he had done and had done to her—she removed shape and form. She kept alive and solid only the figure of the boy who had defended her against a violent father, who had indulged the yearnings of a girl who sought outlets for her own intelligence.

This must have seemed to her a good remedy for grief, because in that same period she revived, and she began to do the same thing with Tina. She no longer spent her days as if the child might return at any moment, but tried to fill the void in the house and in herself with a luminous little figure, as if it were the product of a computer program. Tina became a sort of hologram, she was there and not there. Lila called her up rather than recalling her. She showed me the photos in which she looked best or made me listen to her voice that Enzo had recorded on a tape recorder at one year, at two, at three, or quoted her funny little questions, her extraordinary answers, taking care to speak of her always in the present: Tina has, Tina does, Tina says.

This didn't soothe her, naturally, in fact she yelled more than before. She yelled at her son, at her clients, at me, at Pinuccia, at Dede and Elsa, sometimes at Imma. She yelled at Enzo, in particular, if, while he was working, he burst into tears. But sometimes she sat down, as she had done in the first days, and talked to Imma about Rino and about the child, as if for some reason they had left together. If the little girl asked, when are they coming back, she answered without getting angry: They'll come back when they feel like it. But this, too, became less frequent. After our fight about my daughters she didn't seem to need Imma anymore. In fact, she gradually reduced Imma's visits, and, though with more affection, began to treat her like her sisters. One evening when we had just come into the shabby entranceway of our building—and Elsa complained because she had seen a cockroach, and Dede at the mere idea was disgusted, and Imma wanted me to pick her up—Lila said to all three, as if I weren't present: You're the daughters of a lady, what are you doing here, persuade your mother to take you away.

9.

Apparently, then, after Rino's death she seemed to improve. She stopped narrowing her eyes in alarm. The skin of her face, which seemed a pure white canvas sail flattened by a strong wind, softened. But it was a momentary improvement. Soon there was a jumble of wrinkles, on her forehead, at the edges of her eyes, even on her cheeks, where they looked like fake pleats. And her whole body began to age, her back was bent, her stomach swelled.

Carmen one day used an expression of her own, she said anxiously: Tina is encysted in her, we have to get her out. And she was right, we had to find a way to flush out the story of the child. But Lila refused, everything about her daughter was fixed. I think that something shifted, very painfully, only with Antonio and with Enzo but, out of necessity, in secret. And when suddenly Antonio left—without saying goodbye to anyone, taking his blond family and crazy Melina, now old—she no longer had even the mysterious reports he gave her. She was left alone to rage at Enzo and Gennaro, often setting one against the other. Or distracted, with her own thoughts, as if she were waiting.

I stopped by every day, even when I was pressed by deadlines, and did all I could to revive our intimacy. Since she was always idle, I asked her once:

"Do you still like your work?"

"I never liked it."

"You're lying, I remember you liked it."

"No, you don't remember anything: Enzo liked it and so I made myself like it."

"Then find something else to do."

"I'm fine like this. Enzo's head is in the clouds and if I don't help we'll go out of business."

"You both need to emerge from your suffering."

"What suffering, Lenù, we have to emerge from our rage."

"Then emerge from rage."

"We're trying."

"Try with more conviction. Tina doesn't deserve it."

"Forget Tina, think about your own daughters."

"I am thinking about them."

"Not enough."

She always found, in those years, cracks through which to turn a situation upside down and force me to look at the flaws of Dede, of Elsa, of Imma. You neglect them, she said. I accepted the criticisms, some were well-founded, I too often pursued my own life, neglecting theirs. But meanwhile I waited for an opportunity to shift the conversation back to her and Tina. At a certain point, I began to harass her about her pasty complexion.

"You're very pale."

"You're too red: look, you're purple."

"I'm talking about you: what's wrong?"

"Anemia."

"What anemia."

"My period comes when it likes, but then it doesn't go away."

"Since when?"

"Forever."

"Tell the truth, Lila."

"The truth."

I pressed her, often I provoked her, and she reacted but never to the point of losing control and letting go.

It occurred to me that it was now a linguistic question. She resorted to Italian as if to a barrier; I tried to push her toward dialect, our language of candor. But while her Italian was translated from dialect, my dialect was increasingly translated from Italian, and we both spoke a false language. She needed to explode, lose control of the words. I wanted her to say in the authentic Neapolitan of our childhood: What the fuck do you want, Lenù, I'm like this because I lost my daughter, and maybe she's alive, maybe she's dead, but I can't bear either of those possibilities, because if she's alive she's alive far away from me, she's in a place where horrible things are happening to her, which I see clearly, I see them all day and all night as if they were happening right before my eyes; but if she's dead I'm dead, too, dead here inside, a death more unbearable than real death, which is death without feeling, while this death forces you to feel everything, every day, to wake up, wash, dress, eat and drink, work, talk to you who don't understand or won't understand, to you who even if I just see you, all set, fresh from the hairdresser, with your daughters who do well in school, who always do everything perfectly, who aren't spoiled even by this place of shit, which, rather, seems to do them good— makes them even more confident, even more arrogant, even more sure they have the right to take everything—all this makes me more furious than I already was: so go, go, leave me in peace, Tina would have been better than all of you, and instead they took her, and I can't bear it anymore.

I would have liked to lead her into a conversation like that, jumbled, intoxicated. I felt that if she made up her mind she would extract from the tangled mass of her brain words of that sort. But it didn't happen. In fact, as I think back, in that phase she was less aggressive than in other periods of our story. Maybe the outburst I hoped for was made up of my own feelings, which therefore hindered me from seeing the situation clearly and made Lila even more elusive. Sometimes I wondered if she had in her mind something unutterable that I wasn't even capable of imagining.

10.

Sundays were the worst. Lila stayed home, she didn't work, and from outside came the holiday voices. I went down, I said: Let's go out, let's take a walk to the center, let's go to the sea. She refused, and got angry if I was too insistent. So, to make up for her rudeness, Enzo said: I'll go, come on. She shouted immediately: Yes, go, leave me in peace, I'll take a bath and wash my hair, let me breathe.

We would go out, my daughters came with us and sometimes also Gennaro—who, after the death of his uncle, we all called Rino. During those hours of our walks Enzo confided in me, in his laconic, sometimes obscure way. He said that without

Tina he didn't know what the point of making money was. He said that stealing children to make their parents suffer was a sign of the wretched times that were coming. He said that after the birth of his daughter it was as if a light had switched on in his head, and now the light had gone out. He said: You remember when right here, on this street, I carried her on my shoulders? He said: Thank you, Lenù, for the help you give us, don't be angry with Lina, this is a time of tribulation, but you know her better than I do, sooner or later she'll recover.

I listened, I asked him: She's very pale, physically how is she? I meant: I know she is tortured by grief, but tell me, is she healthy, have you noticed worrying symptoms? But in the face of "physically" Enzo was embarrassed. He knew almost nothing about Lila's body, he adored it as one adores an idol, warily and with respect. And he answered without conviction: fine. Then he grew nervous, he was in a hurry to get home, he said: Let's try to persuade her at least to take a short walk in the neighborhood.

Useless. Only very rarely could I get Lila outside on a Sunday. But it wasn't a good idea. She walked quickly, carelessly dressed, her hair loose and disheveled, flashing angry glances. My daughters and I followed haltingly behind her, supportive, like handmaidens more beautiful, more richly adorned than our mistress. Everyone knew her, even the peddlers, who remembered the troubles they had had because of Tina's disappearance and, afraid there could be others, avoided her. To everyone she was the terrifying woman who, stricken by a great misfortune, carried its potency with her, spreading it wherever she went. Lila walked along the *stradone* with her fierce gaze, toward the gardens, and people lowered their eyes, looked in another direction. But even if someone greeted her she paid no attention, and didn't respond. From the way she walked she seemed to have an urgent goal. The truth is, she was running from the memory of that Sunday two years earlier.

When we went out together we inevitably met the Solaras. Lately, they hadn't been straying from the neighborhood much; there had been a lengthy list of people murdered in Naples, and, at least on Sundays, they preferred to remain peacefully on the streets of their childhood that for them were as safe as a fortress. The two families always did the same things. They went to Mass, they walked amid the stalls, they brought their children to the neighborhood library, which by long tradition, since the days when Lila and I were young, was open on Sundays. I thought it must be Elisa or Gigliola who imposed that educated ritual, but once when I stopped to exchange a few words I discovered that it was Michele. He said, pointing to his children, who although they were grown obeyed him, evidently out of fear, while they had no respect for their mother:

"They know that if they don't read at least one book a month from the first page to the last I won't give them a lira. I'm doing the right thing, no, Lenù?"

I don't know if they really took out books, they had enough money to buy the entire Biblioteca Nazionale. But whether they did it out of real need or as a performance, they now had this habit: they went up the stairs, pushed open the glass door, a relic of the forties, went in, stayed for no more than ten minutes, and came out.

When I was alone with my daughters, Marcello, Michele, Gigliola, and the boys, too, were cordial; only my sister was cool. With Lila, on the other hand, things were complicated, and I was afraid that the tension would rise dangerously. But on those very rare Sunday walks she always pretended that they didn't exist. And the Solaras behaved the same way, and since I was with Lila they preferred to ignore me as well. Elsa, however, one Sunday morning, decided not to follow that unwritten rule and with her queen-of-hearts manners greeted the children of Michele and Gigliola, who responded uneasily.

As a result, although it was very cold, we were forced to stop for a few minutes. The two Solaras pretended to have urgent things to talk about with each other, I spoke to Gigliola, the girls to the boys, Imma studied her cousin Silvio attentively, since we saw him so infrequently. No one addressed a word to Lila, and Lila, for her part, was silent. Only Michele, when he broke off his conversation with his brother and spoke to me in his teasing way, referred to her without looking at her:

"Now, Lenù, we're going to look in at the library and then we're going to eat. Would you like to come with us?"

"No, thank you," I said, "we have to go. Another time, though, certainly."

"Good, then tell the boys what they should read and what they shouldn't. You are an example for us, you and your daughters. When we see you pass by on the street we always say: once Lenuccia was like us, and look how she is now. She doesn't know what pride is, she is democratic, she lives here with us, just like us, even though she's an important person. Ah, yes, those who study become good. Today everyone goes to school, everyone keeps his eyes on the books, and so in the future we'll have so much of that goodness it'll be coming out of our ears. But if you don't read and you don't study, which is what happened to Lina, it happened to all of us, you stay malicious, and malice is ugly. Isn't it true, Lenù?"

He grabbed me by the wrist, his eyes were shining. He repeated sarcastically: Isn't it true? and I nodded yes, but I freed my wrist too forcefully, my mother's bracelet remained in his hand.

"Oh," he exclaimed, and this time he sought Lila's gaze, but didn't find it. He said with feigned regret: "I'm sorry, I'll have it fixed for you."

"It's nothing."

"Absolutely not, it's my duty: you'll have it back like new. Marcè, you'll go by the jeweler's?"

Marcello nodded yes.

People were passing, eyes lowered; it was almost time for lunch. When we managed to get rid of the brothers Lila said to me:

"You're even more defenseless than you used to be: you'll never see that bracelet again."

11.

I was convinced that she was about to have one of her crises. I saw that she was debilitated and anguished, as if she expected something uncontrollable to break the building in two, the apartment, herself. For several days, knocked out by the flu, I didn't hear anything about her. Dede, too, had a cough and a fever, and I assumed that the virus would soon be transmitted to Elsa and to Imma. Also, I had an article to hand in urgently (I was supposed to do something for a magazine that was devoting an entire issue to the female body) and I didn't have the desire or the strength to write.

Outside a cold wind had arisen; it shook the windowpanes, blades of cold penetrated the loose frames. On Friday Enzo came to tell me that he had to go to Avellino because an old aunt of his was ill. As for Rino, he would be spending Saturday and Sunday with Stefano, who had asked him to help dismantle the fixtures in the grocery and take them to a man who was willing to buy them. Lila therefore would be alone, and Enzo said that she was a little depressed, he wanted me to keep her company. But I was tired, I barely had time to focus on a thought when Dede called me, Imma wanted me, Elsa protested, and the thought vanished. When Pinuccia came to clean the house I asked her to cook enough for Saturday and Sunday, then I shut myself in my bedroom, where I had a table to work at.

The next day, since I hadn't heard from Lila, I went down to invite her to lunch. She came to the door in sandals, an old green bathrobe over her pajamas, her hair disheveled. But to my amazement her eyes and mouth were heavily made up. The house was a mess, and there was an unpleasant smell. She said: If the wind blows any harder the neighborhood will fly away. Nothing but an overused hyperbole and yet I was alarmed: she had said it as if she were convinced that the neighborhood really could be torn from its foundations and carried off to shatter near Ponti Rossi. Once she realized that I had perceived how odd her tone was, she smiled in a forced way, whispered: I was joking. I nodded, I listed the good things there were for lunch. She became excited in an exaggerated way, but a moment later her mood abruptly changed, she said: Bring me lunch here, I don't want to come to your house, your daughters get on my nerves.

I brought her lunch and also dinner. The stairs were cold, I didn't feel well, and I didn't want to go up and down just to have unpleasant things said to me. But this time I found her surprisingly cordial, she said Wait, sit with me for a moment. She drew me into the bathroom, she brushed her hair carefully, and meanwhile spoke about my daughters with tenderness, with admiration, as if to convince me that she didn't seriously believe what she had said to me earlier.

"At first," she said, dividing the hair into two, and beginning to braid it without losing sight of her image in the mirror, "Dede resembled you, now instead she's becoming like her father. The opposite is happening with Elsa: she seemed identical to her father and now instead she's starting to look like you. Everything moves. A wish, a fantasy travels more swiftly than blood."

"I don't understand."

"You remember when I thought Gennaro was Nino's?"

"Yes."

"To me he really seemed so, he was identical to Nino, his exact image."

"You mean that a desire can be so strong as to seem ful-filled?"

"No, I mean that for a few years Gennaro was *truly* Nino's child."

"Don't exaggerate."

She stared at me spitefully for a moment, she took a few steps in the bathroom, limping, she burst out laughing in a slightly artificial way.

"So it seems to you that I'm exaggerating?"

I realized with some annoyance that she was imitating my walk.

"Don't make fun of me, my hip hurts."

"Nothing hurts, Lenù. You invented that limp in order not to let your mother die completely, and now you really do limp, and I've studied you, it's good for you. The Solaras took your bracelet and you said nothing, you weren't sorry, you weren't worried. At the time I thought it was because you don't know how to rebel, but now I understand it's not that. You're getting old properly. You feel strong, you stopped being a daughter, you truly became a mother."

I felt uneasy, I repeated:

"It's just a little pain."

"Even pain does you good. You just needed a slight limp and now your mother stays quietly inside you. Her leg is glad that you limp and so you, too, are glad. Isn't that true?"

"No."

She gave me an ironic look to reassert that she didn't believe me, and with her made-up eyes narrowed to cracks said:

"Do you think that when Tina is forty-two, she'll be like this?"

I stared at her. She had a provocative expression, her hands tight around the braids. I said:

"It's likely, yes, maybe so."

12.

My daughters had to fend for themselves, I stayed to eat with Lila, even though I felt cold in my bones. We talked the whole time about physical resemblances; I tried to understand what was happening in her mind. But I also mentioned to her the work I was doing. Talking to you helps, I said to give her confidence, you make me think.

The idea seemed to cheer her, she said: Knowing I'm useful to you I feel better. Right afterward, thanks to the effort involved in being useful to me, she moved on to contorted or illogical arguments. She had put on a lot of powder to hide her pallor, and she didn't seem herself but a Carnival mask with very red cheeks. At times I followed her with interest, at times I recognized only the signs of the illness that I was well acquainted with by now, and was alarmed. For example, she said, laughing: For a while I brought up Nino's child, just as you've done with Imma, a flesh and blood child; but when that child became Stefano's where did Nino's child go, does Gennaro still have him inside, do I have him? Remarks like that: she got lost. Then she started abruptly to praise my cooking, she said she had eaten with pleasure, something she hadn't done for a long time. When I said it wasn't mine but Pinuccia's, she darkened, she grumbled that she didn't want anything from Pinuccia. At that point Elsa called me from the landing, she shouted that I had to come home right away, Dede with a fever was even worse than Dede healthy. I urged Lila to call me whenever she needed me, I told her to rest, I hurried up to my apartment.

For the rest of the day I tried to forget about her; I worked late into the night. The children had grown up with the idea that when I really had my back to the wall they had to look after themselves and not disturb me. In fact they left me in peace, and I worked well. As usual a half sentence of Lila's was enough and my brain recognized her aura, became active, liberated my intelligence. By now I knew that I could do well especially when she, even just with a few disjointed words, assured the more insecure part of me that I was right. I gave to her digressive complaints a concise, elegant organization. I wrote about my hip, about my mother. Now that I was surrounded by admiration, I could admit without uneasiness that talking to her incited ideas, pushed me to make connections between distant things. In those years of being neighbors, I on the floor above, she below, it often happened. A slight push was enough and the seemingly empty mind discovered that it was full and lively. I attributed to her a sort of farsightedness, as I had all our lives, and I found nothing wrong with it. I said to myself that to be adult was to recognize that I needed her impulses. If once I had hidden, even from myself, that spark she induced in me, now I was proud of it, I had even written about it somewhere. *I was I* and for that very reason I could make space for her in me and give her an enduring form. *She instead didn't want to be her*, so she couldn't do the same. The tragedy of Tina, her weakened physical state, her drifting brain surely contributed to her crises. But *that* was the underlying cause of the illness that she called "dissolving boundaries." I went to bed around three, I woke at nine.

Dede's fever was gone, but in compensation Imma had a cough. I straightened the apartment, I went to see how Lila was. I knocked for a long time, she didn't open the door. I pressed the bell until I heard her dragging footsteps and her voice grumbling insults in dialect. Her braids were half undone, her makeup was smeared, even more than the day before it was a mask with a pained expression.

"Pinuccia poisoned me," she said with conviction. "I couldn't sleep, my stomach is splitting."

I went in, I had an impression of carelessness, of filth. On the floor, next to the sink, I saw toilet paper soaked with blood. I said:

"I ate the same things you ate and I'm fine."

"Then explain to me what's wrong with me."

"Menstruation?"

She got mad:

"I'm always menstruating."

"Then you should be examined."

"I'm not going to have my stomach examined by anyone."

"What do you think is wrong?"

"I know what it is."

"I'll go get you a painkiller at the pharmacy."

"You must have something in the house?"

"I don't need them."

"And Dede and Elsa?"

"They don't, either."

"Ah, you're perfect, you never need anything."

I was irked, it was starting up again.

"You want to quarrel?"

"You want to quarrel, since you say I have menstrual cramps. I'm not a child like your daughters, I know if I have that pain or something else."

It wasn't true, she knew nothing about herself. When it came to the workings of her body she was worse than Dede and Elsa. I realized that she was suffering, she pressed her stomach with her hands. Maybe I was wrong: certainly she was overwhelmed with anguish, but not because of her old fears— she really was ill. I made her some chamomile tea, forced her to drink it. I put on a coat and went to see if the pharmacy was open. Gino's father was a skilled pharmacist, he would surely give me good advice. But I had barely emerged onto the *stradone*, among the Sunday stalls, when I heard explosions— *pah, pah, pah, pah*—similar to the sound of the firecrackers that children set off at Christmastime. There were four close together, then came a fifth: *pah*.

I turned onto the street where the pharmacy was. People

seemed disoriented, Christmas was still weeks away, some walked quickly, some ran.

Suddenly the litany of sirens began: the police, an ambulance. I asked someone what had happened, he shook his head, he admonished his wife because she was slow and hurried off. Then I saw Carmen with her husband and two children. They were on the other side of the street, I crossed. Before I could ask a question Carmen said in dialect: They've killed both Solaras.

13.

There are moments when what exists on the edges of our lives, and which, it seems, will be in the background forever—an empire, a political party, a faith, a monument, but also simply the people who are part of our daily existence—collapses in an utterly unexpected way, and right when countless other things are pressing upon us. This period was like that. Day after day, month after month, task was added to task, tremor to tremor. For a long time it seemed to me that I was like certain figures in novels and paintings who stand firm on a cliff or on the prow of a ship in the face of a storm, which doesn't overwhelm them and in fact doesn't even touch them. My telephone rang continuously. The fact that I lived in the dominion of the Solaras compelled me to an infinite chain of words, written and spoken. After the death of her husband, my sister Elisa became a terrified child, she wanted me with her day and night, she was sure that the murderers would return to kill her and her son. And above all I had to tend to Lila, who that same Sunday was suddenly torn from the neighborhood, from her son, from Enzo, from her job, and ended up in the hands of the doctors, because she was weak, she saw things that seemed real but weren't, she was losing blood. They discovered a fibromatous uterus, they operated and took it out. Once—she was still in the hospital—she woke suddenly, exclaimed that Tina had come out of her belly again and now was taking revenge on everyone, even on her. For a fraction of a second she was sure that the killer of the Solaras was her daughter.

14.

Marcello and Michele died on a Sunday in December of 1986, in front of the church where they had been baptized. Just a few minutes after their murder the whole neighborhood knew the details. Michele had been shot twice, Marcello three times. Gigliola had run away, her sons had instinctively followed her. Elisa had grabbed Silvio and held him tight, turning her back on the murderers. Michele had died immediately, Marcello, no, he had sat down on a step and tried to button his jacket, but couldn't.

When it came to saying who had actually killed the Solara brothers, those who appeared to know everything about the murders realized they had seen almost nothing. It was a single man who fired the shots, then had got calmly into a red Ford Fiesta and left. No, there had been two, two men, and at the wheel of the yellow Fiat 147 in which they escaped there was a woman. Not at all, the murderers were three, men, faces covered by ski masks, and they had fled on foot. In some cases it seemed that no one had fired the shots. In the story Carmen told me, for example, the Solaras, my sister, my nephew, Gigliola, her children became agitated in front of the church as if they had been hit by effects without cause: Michele fell to the ground backward and hit his head hard on the lava stone; Marcello sat down cautiously on a step and since he couldn't close his jacket over the blue turtleneck sweater he cursed and lay down on one side; the wives, the children hadn't got even a scratch and in a few seconds had gone into the church to hide. It seemed that those present had looked only in the direction of the killed and not that of the killers.

Armando, in this situation, returned to interview me for his television station. He wasn't the only one. At that moment I said, and recounted in writing, in various places, what I knew. But in the two or three days that followed I realized that in particular the reporters for the Neapolitan papers knew much more than I did. Information that until not long before could be found nowhere was suddenly flooding in. An impressive list of criminal enterprises I had never heard of were attributed to the Solara brothers. Equally impressive was the list of their assets. What I had written with Lila, what I had published when they were still alive was nothing, almost nothing in comparison with what appeared in the papers after their death. On the other hand I realized that I knew other things, things that no one knew and no one wrote, not even me. I knew that the Solaras had always seemed very handsome to us as girls, that they went around the neighborhood in their Fiat 1100 like ancient warriors in their chariots, that one night they had defended us in Piazza dei Martiri from the wealthy youths of Chiaia, that Marcello would have liked to marry Lila but then had married my sister Elisa, that Michele had understood the extraordinary qualities of my friend long before that and had loved her for years in a way so absolute that he had ended up losing himself. Just as I realized that I knew these things I discovered that they were important. They indicated how I and countless other respectable people all over Naples had been within the world of the Solaras, we had taken part in the opening of their businesses, had bought pastries at their bar, had celebrated their marriages, had bought their shoes, had been guests in their houses, had eaten at the same table, had directly or indirectly taken their money, had suffered their violence and pretended it was nothing. Marcello and Michele were, like it or not, part of us, just as Pasquale was. But while in relation to Pasquale, even with innumerable distinctions, a clear line of separation could immediately be drawn, the line of separation in relation to people like the Solaras had been and was, in Naples, in Italy, vague. The farther we jumped back in horror, the more certain it was that we were behind the line.

The concreteness that being behind the line assumed in the reduced and overfamiliar space of the neighborhood depressed me. Someone, to sling mud on me, wrote that I was related to the Solaras and for a while I avoided going to see my sister and my nephew. I even avoided Lila. Of course, she had been the brothers' bitterest enemy, but hadn't she gotten the money to start her little business working for Michele, maybe stealing it from him? I wandered around that theme for a while. Then time passed, the Solaras, too, joined the many who every day ended up on the list of the murdered, and slowly what began to worry us was only that people less familiar and more violent would take their place. I forgot them to the point that when a teenage boy delivered a package from a jeweler in Montesanto, I didn't immediately guess what it contained. The red case inside amazed me, the envelope addressed to Dottoressa Elena Greco. I had to read the note to realize what it was. Marcello had, in a laborious handwriting, written only "Sorry," and had signed it with a swirling "M," of the type that used to be taught in elementary school. In the case was my bracelet, so highly polished that it seemed new.

15.

When I told Lila about that package and showed her the polished bracelet she said: Don't wear it and don't even let your daughters wear it. She had returned home very weak;

when she went up a flight of stairs you could hear the breath straining in her chest. She took pills and gave herself injections, but she was so pale that she seemed to have been in the kingdom of the dead and spoke of the bracelet as if she were sure that it had come from there.

The death of the Solaras overlapped with her emergency admission to the hospital, the blood she had shed was mixed— in my feeling of that chaotic Sunday—with theirs. But whenever I tried to talk to her about that execution, so to speak, in front of the church, she became irritated, she reacted with remarks like: They were shits, Lenù, who gives a damn about them, I'm sorry for your sister but if she had been a little smarter she wouldn't have married Marcello, everyone knows that people like him end up getting killed.

Sometimes I tried to draw her into the sense of contiguity that at that time embarrassed me, I thought she should feel it more than I did. I said something like:

"We'd known them since they were boys."

"All men were once boys."

"They gave you work."

"It was convenient for them and it was convenient for me."

"Michele was certainly a bastard but so were you sometimes."

"I should have done worse."

She made an effort to limit herself to contempt, but she had a malicious look, she entwined her fingers and gripped them, making her knuckles turn white. I saw that behind those words, fierce in themselves, there were even fiercer ones that she avoided saying, but that she had ready in her mind. I read them in her face, I heard them shouted: If it was the Solaras who took Tina away from me, then too little was done to them, they should have been drawn and quartered, their hearts ripped out, and their guts dumped on the street; if it wasn't them, whoever murdered them did a good thing just the same, they deserved that and more; if the assassins had whistled I would have hurried to give them a hand.

But she never expressed herself in that way. To all appearances the abrupt exit from the scene of the two brothers seemed to have little effect on her. Only it encouraged her to walk in the neighborhood more frequently, since there was no longer any chance of meeting them. She never mentioned returning to the activities of the time before Tina's disappearance, she never resumed the life of home and office. She made her convalescence last for weeks and weeks, as she wandered around the tunnel, the *stradone*, the gardens. She walked with her head down, she spoke to no one, and since, partly because of her neglected appearance, she continued to seem dangerous to herself and others, no one spoke to her.

Sometimes she insisted that I go with her, and it was hard to say no. We often passed the bar-pastry shop, which bore a sign saying "Closed for mourning." The mourning never ended, the shop never reopened, the time of the Solaras was over. But Lila glanced every time at the lowered shutters, the faded sign, and said with satisfaction: It's still closed. The fact seemed to her so positive that, as we passed by, she might even give a small laugh, just a small laugh, as if in that closure there was something ridiculous.

Only once did we stop at the corner as if to take in its ugliness, now that it was without the old embellishments of the bar. Once, there had been tables and colored chairs, the fragrance of pastries and coffee, the coming and going of people, secret trafficking, honest deals and corrupt deals. Now there was the chipped gray wall. When the grandfather died, Lila said, after their mother's murder, Marcello and Michele carpeted the neighborhood with crosses and Madonnas, they made endless lamentations; now that they're dead, zero. Then she remembered when she was still in the clinic and I had told her that, according to the reticent words of the people, the bullets that killed the Solaras hadn't been fired by anyone. No one killed them—she smiled—no one weeps for them. And she stopped, and was silent for a few seconds. Then, without any obvious connection, she told me that she didn't want to work anymore.

16.

It didn't seem like a random manifestation of a bad mood, surely she had thought about it for a long time, maybe since she had left the clinic. She said:

"If Enzo can do it by himself, good, and if not we'll sell it."

"You want to give up Basic Sight? And what will you do?"

"Does a person necessarily have to do something?"

"You have to use your life."

"The way you do?"

"Why not?"

She laughed, she sighed:

"I want to waste time."

"You have Gennaro, you have Enzo, you have to think of them."

"Gennaro is twenty-three years old, I've been too taken up with him. And I have to separate Enzo from me."

"Why?"

"I want to go back to sleeping alone."

"It's terrible to sleep alone."

"You do, don't you?"

"I don't have a man."

"Why should I have one?"

"Aren't you fond of Enzo anymore?"

"Yes, but I have no desire for him or anyone. I'm old and no one should disturb me when I sleep."

"Go to a doctor."

"Enough with doctors."

"I'll go with you, those are problems that can be solved."

She became serious.

"No, I'm fine like this."

"No one is fine like this."

"I am. Fucking is very overrated."

"I'm talking about love."

"I have other things on my mind. You've already forgotten Tina, not me."

I heard Enzo and her arguing more frequently. Rather, in the case of Enzo, only his heavy voice reached me, slightly more emphatic than usual, while Lila did nothing but scream. Only a few phrases of his reached me upstairs, filtered through the floor. He wasn't angry—he was never angry with Lila—he was desperate. In essence he said that everything had gotten worse—Tina, the work, their relationship—but she wasn't doing anything to redefine the situation; rather she wanted everything to continue getting worse. You talk to us, he said to me once. I answered that it was no use, she just needed more time to find an equilibrium. Enzo, for the first time, replied roughly: Lina has never had any equilibrium.

It wasn't true. Lila, when she wanted, could be calm, thoughtful, even in that phase of great tension. She had good days, when she was serene and very affectionate. She took care of me and my daughters, she asked about my trips, about what I was writing, about the people I met. She followed—often with amusement, sometimes with indignation—the stories Dede, Elsa, even Imma told about school failures, crazy teachers, quarrels, loves. And she was generous. One afternoon, with Gennaro's help, she brought me up an old computer. She taught me how it worked and said: I'm giving it to you.

The next day I began writing on it. I got used to it quickly, even though I was obsessed by the fear that a power outage would sweep away hours of work. Otherwise I was excited about the machine. I told my daughters, in Lila's presence: Imagine, I learned to write with a fountain pen, then moved on to a ballpoint pen, then the typewriter—and also an electric typewriter—and finally here I am, I tap on the keys and this miraculous writing appears. It's absolutely beautiful, I'll never go back, I'm finished with the pen, I'll always write on the computer, come, touch the callus I have here on my index finger, feel how hard it is: I've always had it but now it will disappear.

Lila enjoyed my satisfaction, she had the expression of someone who is happy to have made a welcome gift. Your mother, however, she said, has the enthusiasm of someone who understands nothing, and she drew them away to let me work. Although she knew she had lost their confidence, when she was in a good mood she often took them to the office to teach them what the newest machines could do, and how and why. She said, to win them back: Signora Elena Greco, I don't know if you know her, has the attention of a hippopotamus sleeping in a swamp, whereas you girls are very quick. But she couldn't regain their affection, in particular Dede and Elsa's. The girls said to me: It's impossible to understand what she has in mind, Mamma, first she urges us to learn and then she says that these machines are useful for making a lot of money by destroying all the old ways of making money. Yet, while I knew how to use the computer only for writing, my daughters, and even Imma to a small extent, soon acquired knowledge and skills that made me proud. Whenever I had a problem I began to depend especially on Elsa, who always knew what to do and then boasted to Aunt Lina: I fixed it like this and like that, what do you say, was I clever?

Things went even better when Dede began to involve Rino. He, who had never even wanted to touch one of those objects of Enzo and Lila's, began to show some interest, if only not to be admonished by the girls. One morning Lila said to me, laughing:

"Dede is changing Gennaro."
I answered:
"Rino just needs some confidence."
She replied with ostentatious vulgarity:
"I know what kind of confidence he needs."

17.

Those were the good days. But soon the bad ones arrived: she was hot, she was cold, she turned yellow, then she flared up, she yelled, she demanded, she broke out in a sweat, then she quarreled with Carmen, whom she called stupid and whiny. After the operation her body seemed even more confused. Suddenly she put an end to the kindnesses; she found Elsa unbearable, reprimanded Dede, treated Imma harshly; while I was speaking to her she abruptly turned her back and went off. In those dark periods she couldn't stand to be in the house and had even less tolerance for the office. She took a bus or the subway and off she went.

"What are you doing?" I asked.
"I'm traveling around Naples."
"Yes, but where?"
"Do I have to account for myself to you?"

Any occasion could provide a pretext for a fight; it took nothing. She quarreled mainly with her son but ascribed the cause of their disagreements to Dede and Elsa. In fact she was right. My oldest daughter happily spent time with Rino, and now her sister, in order not to feel excluded, made an effort to accept him, and was often with them. The result was that both were inoculating him with a sort of permanent insubordination, an attitude that, while in their case was only a passionate verbal exercise, for Rino became confused and self-indulgent chatter that Lila couldn't bear. Those two girls, she scolded her son, put intelligence into it, you repeat nonsense like a parrot. In those days she was intolerant, she wouldn't accept clichéd phrases, maudlin expressions, any form of sentimentality, or, especially, the spirit of rebellion fed by old slogans. And yet at the opportune moment she herself displayed an affected anarchism that to me seemed out of place now. We confronted each other harshly when, at the approach of the electoral campaign of '87, we read that Nadia Galiani had been arrested in Chiasso.

Carmen hurried to my house in the grip of a panic attack, she couldn't think, she said: Now they'll seize Pasquale, you'll see, he escaped the Solaras but the carabinieri will murder him. Lila answered: The carabinieri didn't arrest Nadia, she turned herself in to bargain for a lighter sentence. That hypothesis seemed sensible to me. There were a few lines in the papers, but no talk of pursuits, shooting, capture. To soothe Carmen I again advised her: Pasquale would do well to turn himself in, you know what I think. All hell broke loose, Lila became furious, she began to shout:

"Turn himself over to whom."

"To the state."

"To the state?"

She made a concise list of thefts and criminal collaborations old and new by ministers, simple parliamentarians, policemen, judges, secret services from 1945 until then, showing herself as usual more informed than I could have imagined. And she yelled:

"*That* is the state, why the fuck do you want to give it Pasquale?" Then she pushed me: "Let's bet that Nadia does a few months in jail and comes out, while, if they get Pasquale, they'll lock him in a cell and throw away the key?" She was almost on top of me, repeating aggressively: "Do you want to bet?"

I didn't answer. I was worried, this sort of conversation

wasn't good for Carmen. After the death of the Solaras she had immediately withdrawn the lawsuit against me, she had done endless nice things for me, she was always available to my daughters, even if she was burdened by obligations and worries. I was sorry that instead of soothing her we were tormenting her. She was trembling, she said, addressing me but invoking Lila's authority: If Nadia turned herself in, Lenù, it means that she's repented, that now she's throwing all the blame on Pasquale and will get herself off. Isn't it true, Lina? But then she spoke bitterly to Lila, invoking my authority: It's no longer a matter of principle, Lina, we have to think of what's right for Pasquale, we have to let him know that it's better to live in prison than to be killed: isn't it true, Lenù?

At that point Lila insulted us grossly and, although we were in her house, went out, slamming the door.

18.

For Lila, going out, wandering around, was now the solution to all the tensions and problems she struggled with. Often she left in the morning and returned in the evening, paying no attention to Enzo, who didn't know how to deal with the clients, or to Rino, or to the commitments she made to me, when I had to travel and left her my daughters. She was now unreliable, all it took was some small setback and she dropped everything, without a thought of the consequences.

Carmen maintained that Lila took refuge in the old cemetery on the Doganella, where she chose the grave of a child to think about Tina, who had no grave, and then she walked along the shaded paths, amid plants, old niches, stopping in front of the most faded photographs. The dead—Carmen said to me—are a certainty, they have stones, the dates of birth and death, while her daughter doesn't, her daughter will remain forever with only the date of birth, and that is terrible, that poor child will never have a conclusion, a fixed point where her mother can sit and be tranquil. But Carmen had a propensity for fantasies about death and so I took no notice. I imagined that Lila walked through the city paying no attention to anything, only to numb the grief that after years continued to poison her. Or I hypothesized that she really had decided, in her way, extreme as always, not to devote herself anymore to anything or anyone. And since I knew that her mind needed exactly the opposite, I feared that she would have a nervous breakdown, that at the first opportunity she would let loose against Enzo, against Rino, against me, against my daughters, against a passerby who annoyed her, against anyone who gave her an extra glance. At home I could quarrel, calm her down, control her. But on the street? Every time she went out I was afraid she'd get in trouble. But frequently, when I had something to do and heard the door below close and her steps on the stairs, then out in the street, I drew a sigh of relief. She wouldn't come up to me, she wouldn't drop in with provocative words, she wouldn't taunt the girls, she wouldn't disparage Imma, she wouldn't try in every possible way to hurt me.

I went back to thinking insistently that it was time to leave. Now it was senseless for me, for Dede, for Elsa, for Imma to remain in the neighborhood. Lila herself, besides, after her stay in the hospital, after the operation, after the imbalances of her body, had begun to say more often what she first said sporadically: Go away, Lenù, what are you doing here, look at you, it's as if you're staying only because you made a vow to the Madonna. She wanted to remind me that I hadn't met her expectations, that my living in the neighborhood was only an intellectual pretense, that in fact for her, for the place where we were born—with all my studies, with all my books—I had been useless, I was useless. I was irritated and I thought: she treats me as if she wanted to fire me for poor performance.

19.

A period began in which I racked my brains constantly over what to do. My daughters needed stability and I had to work hard to get their fathers to attend to them. Nino remained the bigger problem. Occasionally he telephoned, said some sweet thing to Imma on the telephone, she responded in monosyllables, that was it. Recently he had made a move that was, all in all, predictable, considering his ambitions: during the elections he had appeared on the socialist party lists. For the occasion he had sent me a letter in which he asked me to vote for him and get people to vote. In the letter, which ended with *Tell Lina, too!* he had enclosed a flyer that included an attractive photograph of him and a biographical note. Underlined in pen was a line in which he declared to the electors that he had three children: Albertino, Lidia, and Imma. Next to it he had written: *Please read this to the child.*

I hadn't voted and I had done nothing to get people to vote for him, but I had shown the flyer to Imma and she had asked if she could keep it. When her father was elected I explained briefly the meaning of people, elections, representation, parliament. Now he lived permanently in Rome. After his electoral success he had been in touch only once, with a letter as hasty as it was self-satisfied, which he asked me to read to his daughter, Dede, and Elsa. No telephone number, no address, only words whose meaning was an offer of protection at a distance *(Be sure that I will watch over you)*. But Imma also wanted to keep that testimony to her father's existence. And when Elsa said to her things like, You're boring, that's why you're called Sarratore and we're Airota, she seemed less disoriented—perhaps less worried—by having a surname that was different from that of her sisters. One day the teacher had asked her: Are you the daughter of the Honorable Sarratore, and the next day she had brought in as proof the flyer, which she kept for any eventuality. I was pleased with that pride and planned to try to consolidate it. Nino's life was, as usual, crowded and turbulent? All right. But his daughter wasn't a rosette to use and then put back in the drawer until the next occasion.

With Pietro in recent years I had never had any problems. He contributed money for his daughters' maintenance punctually (from Nino I had never received a lira) and was as far as possible a conscientious father. But not long ago he had broken up with Doriana, he was tired of Florence, he wanted to go to the United States. And, stubborn as he was, he would manage it. That alarmed me. I said to him: You'll abandon your daughters, and he replied: it seems a desertion now but you'll see, soon it will be an advantage for them especially. He was probably right, in that his words had something in common with Nino's *(Be sure that I will watch over you)*. In fact, however, Dede and Elsa, too, would remain without a father. And if Imma had always done without, Dede and Elsa clung to Pietro, they were used to having recourse to him when they wanted. His departure would sadden and limit them, that I was sure of. Of course they were old enough, Dede was eighteen, Elsa almost fifteen. They were in good schools, they both had good teachers. But was it enough? They had never become assimilated, neither of them had close schoolmates or friends, they seemed comfortable only with Rino. And what did they really have in common with that large boy who was much older and yet more childish than they?

No, I had to leave Naples. I could try to live in Rome, for example, and for Imma's sake resume relations with Nino, only on the level of friendship, of course. Or return to Florence, so that Pietro could be closer to his daughters, and thus would not move across the ocean. The decision seemed particularly urgent when one night Lila came upstairs with a quarrelsome look, evidently in a bad mood, and asked me:

"Is it true that you told Dede to stop seeing Gennaro?"

I was embarrassed. I had only explained to my daughter that she shouldn't be stuck to him all the time.

"See him—she can see him when she wants: I'm only afraid that Gennaro might be annoyed, he's grown-up, she's a girl."

"Lenù, be clear. You think my son isn't good for your daughter?"

I stared at her in bewilderment.

"Good how?"

"You know perfectly well she's in love."

I burst out laughing.

"Dede? Rino?"

"Why, don't you think it's possible that your child has lost her head over mine?"

20.

Until that moment I had paid little attention to the fact that Dede, unlike her sister, who happily changed suitors every month, had never had a declared and ostentatious passion. I had attributed that withdrawn attitude partly to the fact that she didn't feel pretty, partly to her rigor, and from time to time I had teased her (*Are all the boys in your school unappealing?*). She was a girl who didn't forgive frivolity in anyone, above all in herself, but especially in me. The times she had seen me, I wouldn't say flirt but even just laugh with a man—or, I don't know, give a warm welcome to some boy who had brought her home—she made her disapproval clear and on one unpleasant occasion some months earlier had even gone so far as to use a vulgarity in dialect to me, which had made me furious.

But maybe it wasn't a question of a war on frivolity. After Lila's words I began to observe Dede and I realized that her protective attitude toward Lila's son could not be reduced, as I had thought until then, to a long childhood affection or a heated adolescent defense of the humiliated and offended. I realized, rather, that her asceticism was the effect of an intense and exclusive bond with Rino that had endured since early childhood. That frightened me. I thought of the long duration of my love for Nino and I said to myself in alarm: Dede is setting off on the same path, but with the aggravating factor that if Nino was an extraordinary boy and had become a handsome, intelligent, successful man, Rino is an insecure, uneducated youth, without attractions, without any future, and, if I thought about it, more than Stefano he physically recalled his grandfather, Don Achille.

I decided to speak to her. It was a few months until her final exams, she was very busy, it would be easy for her to say to me: I've got a lot to do, let's put it off. But Dede wasn't Elsa, who was able to reject me, who could pretend. With my oldest daughter it was enough to ask and I was sure that she, at any moment, whatever she was doing, would answer with the greatest frankness. I asked:

"Are you in love with Rino?"

"Yes."

"And he?"

"I don't know."

"Since when have you had that feeling?"

"Forever."

"But if he doesn't reciprocate?"

"My life would no longer have meaning."

"What are you thinking of doing?"

"I'll tell you after the exams."

"Tell me now."

"If he wants me we'll go away."

"Where?"

"I don't know, but certainly away from here."

"He also hates Naples?"

"Yes, he wants to go to Bologna."

"Why?"

"It's a place where there's freedom."

I looked at her with affection.

"Dede, you know that neither your father nor I will let you go."

"There's no need for you to let me go. I'm going and that's it."

"What about money?"

"I'll work."

"And your sisters? And me?"

"Some day or other, Mamma, we'll have to separate anyway."

I emerged from that conversation drained of strength. Although she had presented unreasonable things in an orderly fashion, I tried to behave as if she were saying very reasonable things.

Later, anxiously, I tried to think what to do. Dede was only an adolescent in love, one way or another I would make her obey. The problem was Lila, I was afraid of her, I knew immediately that the fight with her would be bitter. She had lost Tina, Rino was her only child. She and Enzo had gotten him away from drugs in time, using very harsh methods; she wouldn't accept that I, too, would cause him suffering. All the more since the company of my two daughters was doing him good; he was even working a little with Enzo, and it was possible that separating him from them would send him off the rails again. Besides, any possible regression of Rino worried me, too. I was fond of him, he had been an unhappy child and was an unhappy youth. Certainly he had always loved Dede, certainly giving her up would be unbearable for him. But what to do. I became more affectionate, I didn't want any misunderstandings: I valued him, I would always try to help him in everything, he had only to ask; but anyone could see that he and Dede were very different and that any solution they came up with would in a short time be disastrous. Thus I proceeded, and Rino became in turn kinder, he fixed broken blinds, dripping faucets, with the three sisters acting as helpers. But Lila didn't appreciate her son's availability. If he spent too much time at our house she summoned him with an imperious cry.

21.

I didn't confine myself to that strategy, I telephoned Pietro. He was about to move to Boston; now he seemed determined. He was mad at Doriana, who—he said with disgust—had turned out to be an untrustworthy person, completely without ethics. Then he listened to me attentively. He knew Rino, he remembered him as a child and knew what he had become as an adult. He asked a couple of times, to be sure of not making a mistake: He has no drug problems? And once only: Does he work? Finally he said: It's preposterous. We agreed that between the two of them, taking account of our daughter's sensitivity, even a flirtation had to be ruled out.

I was glad that we saw things the same way, I asked him to come to Naples and talk to Dede. He promised he would, but he had endless commitments and appeared only near Dede's exams, in essence to say goodbye to his daughters before leaving for America. We hadn't seen each other for a long time. He had his usual distracted expression. His hair was by now grizzled, his body had become heavier. He hadn't seen Lila and Enzo since Tina's disappearance—when he came to see the girls he would stay only a few hours or take them off on a trip—and he devoted himself to them. Pietro was a kind man, careful not to cause embarrassment with his role as a prestigious professor. He talked to them at length, assuming that serious and sympathetic expression that I knew well and that in the past had irritated me, but that today I appreciated because it wasn't feigned, and was natural also to Dede. I don't know what he said about Tina, but while Enzo remained impassive Lila cheered up, she thanked him for his wonderful letter of years earlier, said it had helped her a lot. Only then did I learn that Pietro had written to her about the loss of her daughter, and Lila's genuine gratitude surprised me. He was modest; she excluded Enzo from the conversation completely and began to speak to my ex-husband about Neapolitan things. She dwelt at length on the Palazzo Cellamare, about which I knew nothing except that it was above Chiaia, while she—I discovered then—knew in minute detail the structure, the history, the treasures. Pietro listened with interest. I fumed, I wanted him to stay with his daughters and, especially, deal with Dede.

When Lila finally left him free and Pietro, after spending some time with Elsa and Imma, found a way of going off with Dede, father and daughter talked a lot, peacefully. I observed them from the window as they walked back and forth along the *stradone*. It struck me, I think for the first time, how similar they were physically. Dede didn't have her father's bushy hair but she had his large frame and also something of his clumsy walk. She was a girl of eighteen, she had a feminine softness, but at every gesture, every step, she seemed to enter and exit Pietro's body as if it were her ideal dwelling. I stayed at the window hypnotized by the sight. The time extended, they talked so long that Elsa and Imma began to get restless. I also have things to tell Papa, said Elsa, and if he leaves when will I tell him? Imma murmured: He said he'd talk to me, too.

Finally Pietro and Dede returned, they seemed in a good mood. In the evening all three girls gathered around to listen to him. He said he was going to work in a very big, very beautiful redbrick building that had a statue at the entrance. The statue represented a man whose face and clothes were dark, except for one shoe, which the students touched every day for good luck and so it had become highly polished, and sparkled in the sun like gold. They had a good time together, leaving me out. I thought, as always on those occasions: now that he doesn't have to be a father every day he's a very good father, even Imma adores him; maybe with men things can't go otherwise: live with them for a while, have children, and then they're gone. The superficial ones, like Nino, would go without feeling any type of obligation; the serious ones, like Pietro, wouldn't fail in any of their duties and would if necessary give the best of themselves. Anyway, the time of faithfulness and permanent relationships was over for men and for women. But then why did we look at poor Gennaro, called Rino, as a threat? Dede would live her passion, would use it up, would go on her way. Every so often she would see him again, they would exchange some affectionate words. The process was that: why did I want something different for my daughter?

The question embarrassed me, I announced in my best authoritarian tone that it was time to go to bed. Elsa had just finished vowing that in a few years, once she got her high school diploma, she would go and live in the United States with her father, and Imma was tugging on Pietro's arm, she wanted attention, she was no doubt about to ask if she could join him, too. Dede sat in uncertain silence. Maybe, I thought, things are already resolved, Rino has been put aside, now she'll say to Elsa: You have to wait four years, I'm finishing high school now and in a month at most I'm going to Papa's.

22.

But as soon as Pietro and I were alone I had only to look at his face to understand that he was very worried. He said:

"There's nothing to do."

"What do you mean?"

"Dede functions by theorems."

"What did she tell you?"

"It's not important what she said but what she will certainly do."

"She'll go to bed with him?"

"Yes. She has a very firm plan, with the stages precisely marked out. Right after her exams she'll make a declaration to Rino, lose her virginity, they'll leave together and live by begging, putting the work ethic in crisis."

"Don't joke."

"I'm not joking, I'm reporting her plan to you word for word."

"Easy for you to be sarcastic, since you can avoid it, leaving the role of the bad mother to me."

"She's counting on me. She said that as soon as that boy wants, she'll come to Boston, with him."

"I'll break her legs."

"Or maybe he and she will break yours."

We talked into the night, at first about Dede, then also about Elsa and Imma, finally everything: politics, literature, the books I was writing, the newspaper articles, a new essay he was working on. We hadn't talked so much for a long time. He teased me good-humoredly for always taking, in his view, a middle position. He made fun of my halfway feminism, my halfway Marxism, my halfway Freudianism, my halfway Foucault-ism, my halfway subversiveness. Only with me, he said in a slightly harsher tone, you never used half measures. He sighed: Nothing was right for you, I was inadequate in everything. That other man was perfect. But now? He acted like the rigorous person and he ended up in the socialist gang. Elena, Elena, how you have tormented me. You were angry with me even when those kids pointed a gun at me. And you brought to our house your childhood friends who were murderers. You remember? But so what, you're Elena, I loved you so much, we have two children, and of course I still love you.

I let him talk. Then I admitted that I had often held sense-less positions. I even admitted that he was right about Nino, he

had been a great disappointment. And I tried to return to
Dede and Rino. I was worried, I didn't know how to manage
the issue. I said that to keep the boy away from our daughter
would cause, among other things, trouble with Lila and that I
felt guilty, I knew she would consider it an insult. He nodded.

"You have to help her."

"I don't know how to."

"She's trying everything possible to engage her mind and
emerge from her grief, but she's unable to."

"It's not true, she did before, now she's not even working,
she's not doing anything."

"You're wrong."

Lila had told him that she spent entire days in the Biblioteca
Nazionale: she wanted to learn all she could about Naples. I
looked at him dubiously. Lila again in a library, not the neighborhood library of the fifties but the prestigious, inefficient
Biblioteca Nazionale? That's what she was doing when she disappeared from the neighborhood? That was her new mania?
And why had she not told me about it? Or had she told Pietro
just so that he would tell me?

"She hid it from you?"

"She'll talk to me about it when she needs to."

"Urge her to continue. It's unacceptable that a person so
gifted stopped school in fifth grade."

"Lila does only what she feels like."

"That's how you want to see her."

"I've known her since she was six."

"Maybe she hates you for that."

"She doesn't hate me."

"It's hard to observe every day that you are free and she has
remained a prisoner. If there's an inferno it's inside her unsatisfied mind, I wouldn't want to enter it even for a few seconds."

Pietro used precisely the phrase "enter it," and his tone was
of horror, of fascination, of pity. I repeated:

"Lina doesn't hate me at all."

He laughed.

"All right, as you like."

"Let's go to bed."

He looked at me uncertainly. I hadn't made up the cot as I usually did.

"Together?"

It was a dozen years since we had even touched each other. All night I was afraid that the girls would wake up and find us in the same bed. I lay looking in the shadowy light at that large, disheveled man, snoring faintly. Rarely, when we were married, had he slept with me for long. Usually he tormented me for a long time with his sex and his arduous orgasm, he fell asleep, then he got up and went to study. This time lovemaking was pleasant, a farewell embrace, we both knew it wouldn't happen again and so we felt good. From Doriana Pietro had learned what I had been unable or unwilling to teach him, and he did all he could so that I would notice.

Around six I woke him, I said: It's time for you to go. I went out to the car with him, he urged me yet again to look after the girls, especially Dede. We shook hands, we kissed each other on the cheeks, he left.

I walked idly to the newsstand, the news dealer was unpacking the papers. I went home with, as usual, three dailies, whose headlines I would look at but no more. I was making breakfast, I was thinking about Pietro, and our conversation. I could have lingered on any subject—his bland resentment, Dede, his somewhat facile psychologizing about Lila—and yet sometimes a mysterious connection is established between our mental circuits and the events whose echo is about to reach us. His description of Pasquale and Nadia—the childhood friends he had polemically alluded to—as murderers had stayed with me. To Nadia—I realized—I by now applied the word "murderer" naturally, to Pasquale, no, I continued to reject it. Yet again, I was asking myself why when the telephone rang. It was Lila calling from downstairs. She had heard me when I went out with Pietro and when I returned. She wanted to know if I had bought the papers. She had just heard on the radio that Pasquale had been arrested.

23.

That news absorbed us entirely for weeks, and I was more involved—I admit—in the story of our friend than in Dede's exams. Lila and I hurried to Carmen's house, but she already knew everything, or at least the essentials, and she appeared serene. Pasquale had been arrested in the mountains of Serino, in the Avellinese. The carabinieri had surrounded the farmhouse where he was hiding and he had behaved in a reasonable way, he hadn't reacted violently, he hadn't tried to escape. Now—Carmen said—I only have to hope that they don't let him die in prison the way Papa did. She continued to consider her brother a good person, in fact on the wave of her emotion she went so far as to say that the three of us—she, Lila, and I— carried within us a quantity of wickedness much greater than his. We have been capable of attending only to our own affairs—she murmured, bursting into tears—not Pasquale, Pasquale grew up as our father taught him.

Owing to the genuine suffering in those words, Carmen managed, perhaps for the first time since we had known one another, to have the better of Lila and me. For example, Lila didn't make objections, and, as for me, I felt uneasy at her speech. The Peluso siblings, by their mere existence in the background of my life, confused me. I absolutely ruled out that their father the carpenter had taught them, as Franco had done with Dede, to challenge the silly moral fable of Menenius Agrippa, but both—Carmen less, Pasquale more—had always known instinctively that the limbs of a man are not nourished when he fills the belly of another, and that those who would make you believe it should sooner or later get what they deserve. Although they were different in every way, with their history they formed a block that I couldn't relate to me or to Lila, but that I couldn't distance us from, either. So maybe one day I said to Carmen: You should be happy, now that Pasquale is in the hands of the law we can understand better how to help him; and the next day I said to Lila, in complete agreement with her: Laws and guarantees count for nothing, whereas they should protect those who have no power—in prison they'll kill him. At times, I even admitted, with the two of them, that, although the violence we had experienced from birth now disgusted me, a modest amount was needed to confront the fierce world we lived in. Along those confusing lines I undertook to do everything possible for Pasquale. I didn't want him to feel—unlike his companion Nadia, who was treated with great consideration—like a nobody whom nobody cared about.

24.

I looked for reliable lawyers, I even decided, through telephone calls, to track down Nino, the only member of parliament I knew personally. I never managed to speak to him but a secretary, after lengthy negotiations, made an appointment for me. Tell him—I said coldly—that I'll bring our daughter. At the other end of the line there was a long moment of hesitation. I'll let him know, the woman said finally.

A few minutes later the telephone rang. It was the secretary again: the Honorable Sarratore would be very happy to meet us in his office in Piazza Risorgimento. But in the following days the place and hour of the appointment changed continuously: the Honorable had left, the Honorable had returned but was busy, the Honorable had an interminable sitting in parliament. I marveled at how difficult it was to have direct contact—in spite of my modest fame, in spite of my journalist's credentials, in spite of the fact that I was the mother of his child—with a representative of the people. When everything was finally set— the location was nothing less than Montecitorio, the parliament itself—Imma and I got dressed up and left for Rome. She asked if she could take her precious electoral flyer, I said yes. In the train she kept looking at it, as if to prepare for a comparison between the photograph and the reality. In the capital, we took a taxi, we presented ourselves at Montecitorio. At every obstacle I showed our papers and said, mainly so that Imma could hear: We're expected by the Honorable Sarratore, this is his daughter Imma, Imma Sarratore.

We waited a long time, the child at one point said, in the grip of anxiety: What if the people hold him up? I reassured her: They won't hold him up. Nino finally arrived, preceded by the secretary, a very attractive young woman. Well dressed, radiant, he hugged and kissed his daughter rapturously, picked her up and held her the whole time, as if she were still little. But what surprised me was the immediate assurance with which Imma clung to his neck and said to him happily, unfolding the leaflet: You're handsomer than in this photo, you know my teacher voted for you?

Nino was very attentive to her; he had her tell him about school, about her friends, about the subjects she liked best. He paid only the slightest attention to me, by now I belonged to another life—an inferior life—and it seemed pointless to waste his energies. I talked about Pasquale, he listened, but without neglecting his daughter, and nodded at the secretary to take notes. At the end of my account he asked seriously:

"What do you expect from me?"

"To find out if he's in good health and is getting the full protection of the law."

"Is he cooperating with the law?"

"No, and I doubt that he ever will."

"He'd be better off."

"Like Nadia?"

He gave a small, embarrassed laugh.

"Nadia is behaving in the only way possible, if she doesn't intend to spend the rest of her life in jail."

"Nadia is a spoiled girl, Pasquale isn't."

He didn't answer right away, he pressed Imma's nose as if it were a button and imitated the sound of a bell. They laughed together and then he said:

"I'll see what your friend's situation is, I'm here to be sure that the rights of everyone are protected. But I'll tell him that the relatives of the people he killed also have rights. You don't play at being a rebel, shed real blood, and then cry: we have rights. Do you understand, Imma?"

"Yes."

"Yes, Papa."

"Yes, Papa."

"And if the teacher mistreats you, call me."

I said:

"If the teacher mistreats her, she'll manage by herself."

"The way Pasquale Peluso managed?"

"Pasquale never asked anyone to protect him."

"And that vindicates him?"

"No, but it's significant that if Imma has to assert her right you tell her: call me."

"For your friend Pasquale aren't you calling me?"

I left very nervous and unhappy, but for Imma it was the most important day of her first seven years of life.

The days passed. I thought it had been a waste of time, but in fact Nino kept his word, he looked into Pasquale's situation. It was from him I learned, later, things that the lawyers either didn't know or didn't tell us about. The involvement of our friend in some notorious political crimes that had afflicted Campania was at the center of Nadia's detailed confession, but this had also been common knowledge for some time. The new information, instead, was that she now tended to ascribe everything to him, even acts of minor interest. Thus the long list of Pasquale's crimes included mentions of the murder of Gino, of Bruno Soccavo, the death of Manuela Solara, and, finally, that of her sons, Marcello and Michele.

"What agreement did your old girlfriend make with the carabinieri?" I asked Nino the last time I saw him.

"I don't know."

"Nadia is telling a pile of lies."

"I don't rule it out. But one thing I know for sure: she is ruining a lot of people who thought they were safe. So tell Lina to be careful, Nadia has always hated her."

25.

So many years had passed, and yet Nino didn't miss a chance to mention Lila, to show that he was solicitous of her even at a distance. I was there with him, I had loved him, I had beside me his daughter who was licking a chocolate ice-cream cone. But he considered me only a friend of his youth to whom he could show off the extraordinary path he had traveled, from his high school desk to a seat in parliament. In that last encounter of ours his greatest compliment was to put me on the same rung of the ladder. I don't remember in relation to what subject he said: The two of us climbed very high. But even as he uttered that sentence I read in his gaze that the declaration of equality was a sham. He considered himself much better than me and the proof was that, in spite of my successful books, I stood before him as a petitioner. His eyes smiled at me cordially, suggesting: Look what you lost by losing me.

I left in a hurry with the child. I was sure that he would have had quite a different attitude if Lila had been present. He would have mumbled, he would have felt mysteriously crushed, maybe even a little ridiculous with that preening. When we reached the garage where I had left the car—that time I had come to Rome by car—something occurred to me for the first time: only with Lila had Nino put at risk his own ambitions. On Ischia, and for the following year, he had given in to a romance that could have caused him nothing but trouble. An anomaly, in the journey of his life. At the time he was already a well-known and very promising university student. He had taken up with Nadia—that was clear to me now—because she was the daughter of Professor Galiani, because he had considered her the key to gaining access to what then appeared to us a superior class. His choices had always been consistent with his ambitions. Hadn't he married Eleonora out of self-interest? And I myself, when I had left Pietro for him, wasn't I in fact a well-connected woman, a writer of some success, with ties to an important publishing house—useful, in short, to his career? And all the other women who had helped him: didn't they come under the same logic? Nino loved women, certainly, but he was above all a cultivator of useful relations. What his intelligence produced would never, alone, have had sufficient energy to assert itself, without the web of power that he had been weaving since he was a boy. What about Lila? She had gone to school up to fifth grade, she was the very young wife of a shopkeeper, if Stefano had known of their relationship he could have killed them both. Why had Nino in that case gambled his entire future?

I put Imma in the car, I scolded her for letting the ice cream drip on the dress bought for the occasion. I started the car, I left Rome. Maybe what had attracted Nino was the impression of having found in Lila what he, too, presumed he had and that now, just by comparison, he discovered that he didn't have.

She possessed intelligence and didn't put it to use but, rather, wasted it, like a great lady for whom all the riches of the world are merely a sign of vulgarity. That was the fact that must have beguiled Nino: the gratuitousness of Lila's intelligence. *She stood out among so many because she, naturally, did not submit to any training, to any use, or to any purpose.* All of us had submitted and that submission had—through trials, failures, successes—reduced us. Only Lila, nothing and no one seemed to reduce her. Rather, even if over the years she became as stupid and intractable as anyone, the qualities that we had attributed to her would remain intact, maybe they would be magnified. Even when we hated her we ended by respecting her and fearing her. It didn't surprise me, when I thought about it, that Nadia, although she had met Lila only a few times, detested her and wanted to hurt her. Lila had taken Nino from her. Lila had humiliated her in her revolutionary beliefs. Lila was mean and could hit before being hit. Lila was from the proletariat but rejected any deliverance. In other words Lila was an honorable enemy and hurting her could be pure satisfaction, without the store of guilt that a designated victim like Pasquale would certainly arouse. Nadia could truly think of her in that way. How tawdry everything had become over the years: Professor Galiani, her house with a view of the bay, her thousands of books, her paintings, her cultured conversations, Armando, Nadia herself. She was so pretty, so well brought up, when I saw her beside Nino, outside the school, when she welcomed me to the party at her parents' beautiful house. And there was still something incomparable about her when she stripped herself of every privilege with the idea that, in a radically new world, she would have a more dazzling garment. But now? The noble reasons for that denuding had all dissolved. There remained the horror of so much blood stupidly shed and the villainy of unloading the blame on the former bricklayer, who had once seemed to her the avant-garde of a new humanity, and who now, along with so many others, served to reduce her own responsibilities almost to nothing.

I was upset. As I drove toward Naples I thought of Dede. I felt she was close to making a mistake similar to Nadia's, similar to all mistakes that take you away from yourself. It was the end of July. The day before Dede had got the highest grades on her graduation exam. She was an Airota, she was my daughter, her brilliant intelligence could only produce the best results. Soon she would be able to do much better than I had and even than her father. What I had gained by hard work and much luck, she had taken, and would continue to take, with ease, as if by birthright. Instead, what was her plan? To declare her love for Rino. To sink with him, to rid herself of every advantage, lose herself out of a spirit of solidarity and justice, out of fascination with what doesn't resemble us, because in the muttering of that boy she saw some sort of extraordinary mind. I asked Imma suddenly, looking at her in the rearview mirror:

"Do you like Rino?"

"No, but Dede likes him."

"How do you know?"

"Elsa told me."

"And who told Elsa?"

"Dede."

"Why don't you like Rino?"

"Because he's very ugly."

"And who do you like?"

"Papa."

I saw in her eyes the flame that in that moment she saw blazing around her father. A light—I thought—that Nino would never have had if he had sunk with Lila; the same light that Nadia had lost forever, sinking with Pasquale; and that would abandon Dede if she were lost following Rino. Suddenly I felt with shame that I could understand, and excuse, the irritation of Professor Galiani when she saw her daughter on

Pasquale's knees, I understood and excused Nino when, one way or another, he withdrew from Lila, and, why not, I understood and excused Adele when she had had to make the best of things and accept that I would marry her son.

26.

As soon as I was back in the neighborhood I rang Lila's bell. I found her listless, absent, but now it was typical of her and I wasn't worried. I told her in detail what Nino had said and only at the end did I report that threatening phrase that concerned her. I asked:

"Seriously, can Nadia hurt you?"

She assumed a look of nonchalance.

"You can be hurt only if you love someone. But I don't love anyone."

"And Rino?"

"Rino's gone."

I immediately thought of Dede and her intentions. I was frightened.

"Where?"

She took a piece of paper from the table, she handed it to me, muttering:

"He wrote so well as a child and now look, he's illiterate."

I read the note. Rino, very laboriously, said he was tired of everything, insulted Enzo heavily, announced that he had gone to Bologna to a friend he had met during his military service. Six lines in all. No mention of Dede. My heart was pounding in my chest. That writing, that spelling, that syntax, what did they have to do with my daughter? Even his mother considered him a failed promise, a defeat, perhaps even a prophecy: look what would have happened to Tina if they hadn't taken her.

"He left by himself?" I asked.

"Who would he have left with?"

I shook my head uncertainly. She read in my eyes the reason for my concern, she smiled:

"You're afraid he left with Dede?"

27.

I hurried home, trailed by Imma. I went in, I called Dede, I called Elsa. No answer. I rushed into the room where my older daughters slept and studied. I found Dede lying on the bed, her eyes burning with tears. I felt relieved. I thought that she had told Rino of her love and that he had rejected her.

I didn't have time to speak: Imma, maybe because she hadn't realized her sister's state, began talking enthusiastically about her father, but Dede rebuffed her with an insult in dialect, then sat up and burst into tears. I nodded to Imma not to get mad, I said to my oldest daughter gently: I know it's terrible, I know very well, but it will pass. The reaction was violent. As I was caressing her hair she pulled away with an abrupt movement of her head, crying: What are you talking about, you don't know anything, you don't understand anything, all you think about is yourself and the crap you write. Then she handed me a piece of graph paper—rather—she threw it in my face and ran away.

Once Imma realized that her sister was desperate, her eyes began to tear up in turn. I whispered, to keep her occupied: Call Elsa, see where she is, and I picked up the piece of paper. It was a day of notes. I immediately recognized the fine handwriting of my second daughter. Elsa had written at length to Dede. She explained to her that one can't control feelings, that Rino had loved her for a long time and that little by little she, too, had fallen in love. She knew, of course, that she was causing her pain and she was sorry, but she also knew that a possible renunciation of the loved person would not fix things. Then she addressed me in an almost amused tone. She wrote that she had decided to give up school, that my cult of study had always seemed to her foolish, that it wasn't books that made people good but good people who made some good books. She emphasized that Rino was good, and yet he had never read a book; she emphasized that her father was good and had made very good books. The connection between books, people, and goodness ended there: I wasn't cited. She said goodbye with affection and told me not to be too angry: Dede and Imma would give me the satisfactions that she no longer felt able to give me. To her younger sister she dedicated a little heart with wings.

I turned into a fury. I was angry with Dede, who hadn't realized how her sister, as usual, intended to steal what she valued. You should have known, I scolded her, you should have stopped her, you're so intelligent and you let yourself be tricked by a vain sly girl. Then I ran downstairs, I said to Lila:

"Your son didn't go alone, your son took Elsa with him."

She looked at me, disoriented:

"Elsa?"

"Yes. And Elsa is a minor. Rino is nine years older, I swear to God I'll go to the police and report him."

She burst out laughing. It wasn't a mean laugh but incredulous. She laughed and said, alluding to her son:

"But look how much damage he was able to do, I underrated him. He made both young ladies lose their heads, I can't believe it. Lenù, come here, calm down, sit down. If you think about it, there's more to laugh at than cry about."

I said in dialect that I found nothing to laugh at, that what Rino had done was very serious, that I really was about to go to the police. Then she changed her tone, she pointed to the door, she said:

"Go to the cops, go on, what are you waiting for?"

I left, but for the moment I gave up the idea of the police. I went home, taking the steps two at a time. I shouted at Dede: I want to know where the fuck they went, tell me immediately. She was frightened, Imma put her hands over her ears, but I wouldn't calm down until Dede admitted that Elsa had met Rino's Bolognese friend once when he came to the neighborhood.

"Do you know his name?"

"Yes."

"Do you have the address, the phone number?"

She trembled, she was on the point of giving me the information I wanted. Then, although by now she hated her sister even more than Rino, she must have thought it would be shameful to collaborate and was silent. I'll find it myself, I cried, and began to turn her things upside down. I rummaged through the whole house. Then I stopped. While I was looking for yet another piece of paper, a note in a school diary, I realized that a lot else was missing. All the money was gone from the drawer where I normally kept it, and all my jewelry was gone, even my mother's bracelet. Elsa had always been very fond of that bracelet. She said, partly joking and partly serious, that her grandmother, if she had made a will, would have left it to her and not to me.

28.

That discovery made me even more determined, and Dede finally gave me the address and telephone number I was looking for. When she made up her mind, despising herself for giving in, she shouted at me that I was just like Elsa, we didn't respect anything or anyone. I silenced her and went to the telephone. Rino's friend was called Moreno, I threatened him. I told him that I knew he sold heroin, that I would get him in such deep trouble that he would never get out of jail. I got nothing. He swore that he didn't know anything about Rino, that he remembered Dede, but that this daughter I was talking about, Elsa, he had never met.

I went back to Lila. She opened the door, but now Enzo was there, who made me sit down, and treated me kindly. I said I wanted to go to Bologna right away, I ordered Lila to go with me.

"There's no need," she said, "you'll see that when they run out of money they'll be back."

"How much money did Rino take?"

"Nothing. He knows that if he touches even ten lire I'll break his bones."

I felt humiliated. I muttered:

"Elsa took my money and my jewelry."

"Because you didn't know how to bring her up."

Enzo said to her:

"Stop it."

She turned against him sharply:

"I say what I like. My son is a drug addict, my son didn't study, my son speaks and writes poorly, my son is a good-for-nothing, my son has all the sins. But the one who steals is her daughter, the one who betrays her sister is Elsa."

Enzo said to me:

"Let's go, I'll go with you to Bologna."

We left in the car, we traveled at night. I had scarcely returned from Rome, the trip in the car had tired me. The sorrow and the fury that had arisen had absorbed all my remaining forces and now that the tension was easing I felt exhausted. Sitting next to Enzo, as we left Naples and got on the highway, what took hold was anxiety for the state in which I had left Dede, fear for what could happen to Elsa, some shame for the way I had frightened Imma, the way I had spoken to Lila, forgetting that Rino was her only child. I didn't know whether to telephone Pietro in America and tell him to come back right away, I didn't know if I really should go to the police. "We'll solve it ourselves," Enzo said, feigning confidence. "Don't worry, it's pointless to hurt the boy."

"I don't want to report Rino," I said. "I just want them to find Elsa."

It was true. I muttered that I wanted to recover my daughter, go home, pack my bags, not remain a minute longer in that house, in the neighborhood, in Naples. It makes no sense, I said, that now Lila and I start fighting about who brought up her children better, and if what happened is her fault or mine—I can't bear it.

Enzo listened to me at length, in silence, then, although I felt he had been angry at Lila for a long time, he began to make excuses for her. He didn't speak about Rino, about the problems he caused his mother, but about Tina. He said: If a being a few years old dies, she's dead, it's over, sooner or later you resign yourself. But if she disappears, if you no longer know anything about her, there's not a thing that remains in her place, in your life. Will Tina never return or will she return? And when she returns, will she be alive or dead? Every moment—he murmured—you're asking where she is. Is she a Gypsy on the street? Is she at home with rich people who have no children? Are people making her do horrible things and selling the photographs and films? Did they cut her up and sell her heart for a high price so it could be transplanted to another child's chest? Are the other pieces underground, or were they burned? Or is she under the ground intact, because she died accidentally after she was abducted? And if earth and fire didn't take her, and she is growing up who knows where, what does she look like now, what will she become later, if we meet her on the street will we recognize her? And if we recognize her who will give us back everything we lost of her, everything that happened when we weren't there and little Tina felt abandoned?

At a certain point, while Enzo spoke in his laborious but dense sentences, I saw his tears in the glow of the headlights, I knew he wasn't talking only about Lila but was trying to express his own suffering as well. That trip with him was important; I still find it hard to imagine a man with a finer sensibility than his. At first he told me what, every day, every night in those four years Lila had whispered or shouted. Then he urged me to talk about my work and my dissatisfactions. I told him about the girls, about books, about men, about resentments, about the need for approval. And I mentioned all my writing, which now had become obligatory, I struggled day and night to feel myself present, to not let myself be marginalized, to fight against those who considered me an upstart little woman without talent: persecutors—I muttered—whose only purpose is to make me lose my audience, and not because they're inspired by any elevated motives but, rather, for the enjoyment of keeping me from improvement, or to carve out for themselves or for their protégés some wretched power harmful to me. He let me vent, he praised the energy I put into things. You see—he said—how excited you get. The effort has anchored you to the world you've chosen, it's given you broad and detailed expertise in it, above all it has engaged your feelings. So life has dragged you along, and Tina, for you, is certainly an atrocious episode, thinking about it makes you sad, but it's also, by now, a distant fact. For Lila, on the other hand, in all these years, the world collapsed as if it were hearsay, and slid into the void left by her daughter, like the rain that rushes down a drainpipe. She remains frozen at Tina, and feels bitter toward everything that continues to be alive, that grows and prospers. Of course, he said, she is strong, she treats me terribly, she gets angry with you, she says ugly things. But you don't know how many times she has fainted just when she seemed tranquil, washing the dishes or staring out the window at the *stradone*.

29.

In Bologna we found no trace of Rino and my daughter, even though Moreno, frightened by Enzo's fierce calm, dragged us through streets and hangouts where, according to him, if they were in the city, the two would certainly have been welcomed. Enzo telephoned Lila often, I Dede. We hoped that there would be good news, but there wasn't. At that point I was seized by a new crisis, I no longer knew what to do. I said again:

"I'm going to the police."

Enzo shook his head.

"Wait a little."

"Rino has ruined Elsa."

"You can't say that. You have to try to look at your daughters as they really are."

"It's what I do continuously."

"Yes, but you don't do it well. Elsa would do anything to make Dede suffer and they are in agreement on a single point: tormenting Imma."

"Don't make me say mean things: it's Lila who sees them like that and you're repeating what she says."

"Lila loves you, admires you, is fond of your daughters. It's me who thinks these things, and I'm saying them to help you be reasonable. Calm down, you'll see, we'll find them."

We didn't find them, we decided to return to Naples. But as we were nearing Florence Enzo wanted to call Lila again to find out if there was any news. When he hung up he said, bewildered:

"Dede needs to talk to you but Lina doesn't know why."

"Is she at your house?"

"No, she's at yours."

I called immediately, I was afraid that Imma was sick. Dede didn't even give me a chance to speak, she said:

"I'm leaving tomorrow for the United States, I'm going to study there."

I tried not to shout:

"Now is not the moment for that conversation, as soon as possible we'll talk about it with Papa."

"One thing has to be clear, Mamma: Elsa will return to this house only when I am gone."

"For now the most urgent thing is to find out where she is."

She cried to me in dialect:

"That bitch telephoned a little while ago, she's at Grandma's."

30.

The grandma was, of course, Adele; I called my in-laws. Guido answered coldly and put his wife on. Adele was cordial, she told me that Elsa was there and added, Not only her.

"The boy's there, too?"

"Yes."

"Would you mind if I came to you?"

"We're expecting you."

I had Enzo leave me at the station in Florence. The journey was complicated, with delays, waits, annoyances of every type. I thought about how Elsa, with her sly capriciousness, had ended up involving Adele. If Dede was incapable of deception, Elsa was at her best when it came to inventing strategies that could protect her and perhaps let her win. She had planned, it was clear, to impose Rino on me in the presence of her grandmother, a person who—she and her sister knew well—had been very unwilling to accept me as a daughter-in-law. For the entire journey I felt relieved because I knew she was safe and hated her for the situation she was putting me in.

I arrived in Genoa ready for a hard battle. But I found Adele very welcoming and Guido polite. As for Elsa—dressed for a party, heavily made up, on her wrist my mother's bracelet, and on full display the ring that years earlier her father had given me—she was affectionate and relaxed, as if she found it inconceivable that I could be mad at her. The only silent one, eyes perpetually downcast, was Rino, so that I felt sorry for him and ended up more hostile toward my daughter than toward him. Maybe Enzo was right, the boy had had scant importance in that story. Of his mother's hardness, her insolence, he had no trace, it was Elsa who had dragged him along, beguiling him, and only to hurt Dede. The rare times he had the courage to look at me his glances were those of a faithful dog.

I quickly understood that Adele had received Elsa and Rino as a couple: they had their own room, their own towels, they slept together. Elsa had no trouble flaunting that intimacy authorized by her grandmother, maybe she even accentuated it for me. When the two withdrew after dinner, holding hands, my mother-in-law tried to push me to confess my aversion for Rino. She's a child, she said at a certain point, I really don't know what she sees in that young man, she has to be helped to get out of it. I tried, I said: He's a good kid, but even if he weren't, she's in love and there's little to be done. I thanked her for welcoming them with affection and broad-mindedness, and went to bed.

But I spent the whole night thinking about the situation. If I said the wrong thing, even just a wrong word, I would probably ruin both my daughters. I couldn't make a clean break between Elsa and Rino. I couldn't oblige the two sisters to live together at that impossible moment: what had happened was serious and for a while the two girls couldn't be under the same roof. To think of moving to another city would only complicate things, Elsa would make it her duty to stay with Rino. I quickly realized that if I wanted to take Elsa home and get her to graduate from high school I would have to lose Dede—actually send her to live with her father. So the next day, instructed by Adele about the best time to call (she and her son—I discovered—talked to each other constantly), I talked to Pietro. His mother had informed him in detail about what had happened

and from his bad mood I deduced that Adele's true feelings
were certainly not what she showed me. Pietro said gravely:

"We have to try to understand what sort of parents we've
been and how we've failed our daughters."

"Are you saying that I haven't been and am not a good
mother?"

"I'm saying that there's a need for continuity of affection
and that neither you nor I have been able to insure that Dede
and Elsa have that."

I interrupted him, announcing that he would have a chance
to be a full-time father to at least one of the girls: Dede wanted
to go and live with him immediately, she would leave as soon
as possible.

He didn't take the news well, he was silent, he prevaricated,
he said he was still adapting and needed time. I answered: You
know Dede, you're identical, even if you tell her no you'll find
her there.

The same day, as soon as I had a chance to talk to Elsa alone,
I confronted her, ignoring her blandishments. I had her give back
the money, the jewelry, my mother's bracelet, which I immediately put on, stating: You must never touch my things again.

She was conciliatory, I wasn't, I hissed that I wouldn't hes-
itate for a moment to report first of all Rino, and then her. As
soon as she tried to answer I pushed her against a wall, I raised
my hand to hit her. I must have had a terrible expression, she
burst into terrified tears.

"I hate you," she sobbed. "I don't ever want to see you again,
I will never go back to that shitty place where you made us live."

"All right, I'll leave you here for the summer, if your grandparents don't kick you out first."

"And then?"

"Then in September you'll come home, you'll go to school,
you'll study, you'll live with Rino in our apartment until you've
had enough of him."

She stared at me, stunned; there was a long instant of incredulity. I had uttered those words as if they contained the most terrible punishment, she took them as a surprising gesture of generosity.

"Really?"

"Yes."

"I'll never have enough of him."

"We'll see."

"And Aunt Lina?"

"Aunt Lina will agree."

"I didn't want to hurt Dede, Mamma, I love Rino, it happened."

"It will happen countless more times."

"It's not true."

"Worse for you. It means you'll love Rino your whole life."

"You're making fun of me."

I said no, I felt only all the absurdity of that verb in the mouth of a child.

31.

I returned to the neighborhood, I told Lila what I had proposed to the children. It was a cold exchange, almost a negotiation.

"You'll have them in your house?"

"Yes."

"If it's all right with you, it's all right with me, too."

"We'll split the expenses."

"I can pay it all."

"For now I have money."

"For now I do, too."

"We're agreed, then."

"How did Dede take it?"

"Fine. She's leaving in a couple of weeks, she's going to visit her father."

"Tell her to come and say goodbye."

"I don't think she will."

"Then tell her to say hello to Pietro for me."

"I'll do that."

Suddenly I felt a great sorrow, I said:

"In just a few days I've lost two daughters."

"Don't use that expression: you haven't lost anything, rather you've gained a son."

"It's you who pushed him in that direction."

She wrinkled her forehead, she seemed confused.

"I don't know what you're talking about."

"You always have to incite, shove, poke."

"Now you want to get mad at me, too, for what your children get up to?"

I muttered, I'm tired, and left.

For days, for weeks, in fact, I couldn't stop thinking that Lila couldn't bear the equilibrium in my life and so aimed at disrupting it. It had always been so, but after Tina's disappearance it had worsened: she made a move, observed the consequences, made another move. The objective? Maybe not even she knew. Of course the relationship of the two sisters was ruined, Elsa was in terrible trouble, Dede was leaving, I would remain in the neighborhood for an indeterminate amount of time.

32.

I was preoccupied with Dede's departure. Occasionally I said to her: Stay, you're making me very unhappy. She answered: You have so many things to do, you won't even notice I'm gone. I insisted: Imma adores you and so does Elsa, you'll clear things up, it will pass. But Dede didn't want to hear her sister's name, as soon as I mentioned it she assumed an expression of disgust and went out, slamming the door.

A few nights before her departure she suddenly grew very pale—we were having dinner—and began to tremble. She muttered: I can't breathe. Imma quickly poured her a glass of water. Dede took a sip, then left her place and came to sit on my lap. It was something she had never done. She was big, taller than me, she had long since cut off even the slightest contact between our bodies; if by chance we touched she sprang back as if by a force of repulsion. Her weight surprised me, her warmth, her full hips. I held her around the waist, she put her arms around my neck, she wept with deep sobs. Imma left her place at the table, came over and tried to be included in the embrace. She must have thought that her sister wouldn't leave, and for the next days she was happy, she behaved as if everything had been put right. But Dede did leave; rather, after that breakdown she seemed tougher and more determined. With Imma she was affectionate, she kissed her hundreds of times, she said: I want at least one letter a week. She let me hug and kiss her, but without returning it. I hovered around her, I struggled to predict her every desire, it was useless. When I complained of her coldness she said: It's impossible to have a real relationship with you, the only things that count are work and Aunt Lina; there's nothing that's not swallowed up inside them, the real punishment, for Elsa, is to stay here. Bye, Mamma.

On the positive side there was only the fact that she had gone back to calling her sister by name.

33.

When, in early September of 1988, Elsa returned home, I hoped that her liveliness would drive out the impression that

Lila really had managed to pull me down into her void. But it wasn't so. Rino's presence in the house, instead of giving new life to the rooms, made them bleak. He was an affectionate youth, completely submissive to Elsa and Imma, who treated him like their servant. I myself, I have to say, got into the habit of entrusting to him endless boring tasks—mainly the long lines at the post office—which left me more time to work. But it depressed me to see that big slow body around, available at the slightest nod and yet moping, always obedient except when it came to basic rules like remembering to raise the toilet seat when he peed, leaving the bathtub clean, not leaving his dirty socks and underwear on the floor.

Elsa didn't lift a finger to improve the situation, rather she purposely complicated it. I didn't like her coy ways with Rino in front of Imma, I hated her performance as an uninhibited woman when in fact she was a girl of fifteen. Above all I couldn't bear the state in which she left the room where once she had slept with Dede and which now she occupied with Rino. She got out of bed, sleepily, to go to school, had breakfast quickly, slipped away. After a while Rino appeared, ate for an hour, shut himself in the bathroom for at least another half hour, got dressed, hung around, went out, picked up Elsa at school. When they got back they ate cheerfully and immediately shut themselves in the room.

That room was like a crime scene, Elsa didn't want me to touch anything. But neither of them bothered to open the windows or tidy up a little. I did it before Pinuccia arrived; it annoyed me that she would smell the odor of sex, that she would find traces of their relations.

Pinuccia didn't like the situation. When it came to dresses, shoes, makeup, hairstyles, she admired what she called my modernity, but in this case she let me understand quickly and in every possible way that I had made a decision that was too modern, an opinion that must have been widespread in the neighborhood. It was very unpleasant, one morning, to find her there, as I was trying to work, with a newspaper on which lay a condom, knotted so that the semen wouldn't spill. I found it at the foot of the bed, she said disgusted. I pretended it was nothing. There's no need to show it to me, I remarked, continuing to type on the computer, there's the wastebasket for that.

In reality I didn't know how to behave. At first I thought that over time everything would improve. Every day there were clashes with Elsa, but I tried not to overdo it; I still felt wounded by Dede's departure and didn't want to lose her as well. So I went more and more often to Lila to say to her: Tell Rino, he's a good boy, try to explain that he has to be a little neater. But she seemed just to be waiting for my complaints to pick a quarrel.

"Send him back here," she raged one morning, "enough of that nonsense of staying at your house. Rather, let's do this: there's room, when your daughter wants to see him she comes down, knocks, and sleeps here if she wants."

I was annoyed. My child had to knock and ask if she could sleep with hers? I muttered:

"No, it's fine like this."

"If it's fine like this, what are we talking about?"

I fumed.

"Lila, I'm just asking you to talk to Rino: he's twenty-four years old, tell him to behave like an adult. I don't want to be quarreling with Elsa continuously, I'm in danger of losing my temper and driving her out of the house."

"Then the problem is your child, not mine."

On those occasions the tension rose rapidly but had no outlet; she was sarcastic, I went home frustrated. One evening we were having dinner when, from the stairs, her intransigent cry reached us, she wanted Rino to come to her immediately. He got agitated, Elsa offered to go with him. But as soon as Lila saw her she said: This is our business, go home. My daughter returned sullenly and meanwhile downstairs a violent quarrel erupted. Lila shouted, Enzo shouted, Rino shouted. I suffered for Elsa, who was anxiously wringing her hands, she said: Mamma, do something, what's happening, why do they treat him like that?

I said nothing, I did nothing. The quarrel stopped, some time passed, Rino didn't return. Elsa then insisted that I go see what had happened. I went down and Enzo, not Lila, opened the door. He was tired, depressed, he didn't invite me to come in. He said:

"Lila told me that the boy doesn't behave well, so from now on he's staying here."

"Let me talk to her."

I discussed it with Lila until late into the night; Enzo, gloomy, shut himself in another room. I understood almost immediately that she wanted to be thanked. She had intervened, she had taken back her son, had humiliated him. Now she wanted me to say to her: Your son is like a son of mine, it's fine with me that he's at my house, that he sleeps with Elsa, I won't come and complain anymore. I resisted for a long time, then I gave in and brought Rino back to my house. As soon as we left the apartment I heard her and Enzo start fighting again.

34.

Rino was grateful.

"I owe you everything, Aunt Lenù, you're the best person I know and I'll always love you."

"Rino, I'm not good at all. All you owe me is the favor of remembering that we have a single bathroom and, besides Elsa, Imma and I also use that bathroom."

"You're right, I'm sorry, sometimes I get distracted, I won't do it anymore."

He constantly apologized, he was constantly distracted. He was, in his way, in good faith. He declared endlessly that he wanted to find a job, that he wanted to contribute to the household expenses, that he would be very careful not to cause me trouble in any way, that he had an unbounded respect for me. But he didn't find a job, and life, in all the most dispiriting aspects of dailiness, continued as before, and perhaps worse. At any rate, I stopped going to Lila. I told her: Everything's fine.

It was becoming very clear to me that the tension between her and Enzo was increasing, and I didn't want to be the fuse for their rages. What had been upsetting me, for a while, was that the nature of their arguments had changed. In the past Lila yelled and Enzo for the most part was silent. But now it wasn't like that. She yelled, I often heard Tina's name, and her voice, filtered through the floor, seemed a kind of sick whine. Then suddenly Enzo exploded. He shouted and his shouting extended into a tumultuous torrent of exasperated words, all in violent dialect. Lila was silent then; while Enzo shouted she couldn't be heard. But as soon as he was silent you could hear the door slam. I strained my ears for the shuffling of Lila on the stairs, in the entrance. Then her steps vanished in the sounds of the traffic on the *stradone*.

Enzo used to run after her, but now he didn't. I thought: maybe I should go down, talk to him, tell him: You yourself told me how Lina continues to suffer, be understanding. But I gave up and hoped that she would return soon. But she stayed away the whole day and sometimes even the night. What was she doing? I imagined that she took refuge in some library, as Pietro had told me, or that she was wandering through Naples, noting every building, every church, every monument, every plaque. Or that she was combining the two things: first she explored the city, then she dug around in books to find information. Overwhelmed by events, I had never had the wish or the time to mention that new mania, nor had she ever talked to me about it. But I knew how she could become obsessively focused when something interested her, and it didn't surprise me that she could dedicate so much time and energy to it. I thought about it with some concern only when her disappearances followed the shouting, and the shadow of Tina joined the one vanishing into the city, even at night. Then the tunnels of tufa under the city came to mind, the catacombs with rows of death's-heads, the skulls of blackened bronze that led to the unhappy souls of the church of Purgatorio ad Arco. And sometimes I stayed awake until I heard the street door slam and her footsteps on the stairs.

On one of those dark days the police appeared. There had been a quarrel, she had left. I looked out at the window in alarm, I saw the police heading toward our building. I was frightened, I thought something had happened to Lila. I hurried onto the landing. The police were looking for Enzo, they had come to arrest him. I tried to intervene, to understand. I was rudely silenced, they took him away in handcuffs. As he went down the stairs Enzo shouted to me in dialect: When Lina gets back tell her not to worry, it's a lot of nonsense.

35.

For a long time it was hard to know what he was accused of. Lila stopped being hostile toward him, gathered her strength, and concerned herself only with him. In that new ordeal she was silent and determined. She became enraged only when she discovered that the state—since she had no official bond with Enzo and, furthermore, had never been separated from Stefano—wouldn't grant her a status equivalent to a wife or, as a result, the possibility of seeing him. She began to spend a lot of money so that, through unofficial channels, he would feel her closeness and her support.

Meanwhile I went back to Nino. I knew from Marisa that it was useless to expect help from him, he wouldn't lift a finger even for his own father, his mother, his siblings. But with me he again readily made an effort, maybe to make a good impression on Imma, maybe because it meant showing Lila, if indirectly, his power. Not even he, however, could understand precisely what Enzo's situation was and at different times he gave me different versions that he himself admitted were not reliable. What had happened? It was certain that Nadia, in the course of her sobbing confessions, had mentioned Enzo's name. It was certain that she had dug up the period when Enzo, with Pasquale, had frequented the worker-student collective in Via dei Tribunali. It was certain that she had implicated them both in small demonstrations, carried out, many years earlier, against the property of NATO officials who lived in Via Manzoni. It was certain that the investigators were trying to involve Enzo, too, in many of the crimes that they had attributed to Pasquale. But at this point certainties ended and suppositions began. Maybe Nadia had claimed that Enzo had had recourse to Pasquale for crimes of a nonpolitical nature. Maybe Nadia had claimed that some of those bloody acts—in particular the murder of Bruno Soccavo—had been carried out by Pasquale and planned by Enzo. Maybe Nadia had said she had learned from Pasquale himself that it was three men who killed the Solara brothers: him, Antonio Cappuccio, Enzo Scanno, childhood friends who, incited by a longtime solidarity and by an equally longstanding resentment, had committed that crime.

They were complicated years. The order of the world in which we had grown up was dissolving. The old skills resulting from long study and knowledge of the correct political line suddenly seemed senseless. Anarchist, Marxist, Gramscian, Communist, Leninist, Trotskyite, Maoist, worker were quickly becoming obsolete labels or, worse, a mark of brutality. The exploitation of man by man and the logic of maximum profit, which before had been considered an abomination, had returned to become the linchpins of freedom and democracy everywhere. Meanwhile, by means legal and illegal, all the accounts that remained open in the state and in the revolutionary organizations were being closed with a heavy hand. One might easily end up murdered or in jail, and among the common people a stampede had begun. People like Nino, who had a seat in parliament, and like Armando Galiani—who was now famous, thanks to television—had intuited for a while that the climate was changing and had quickly adapted to the new season. As for those like Nadia, evidently they had been well advised and were cleansing their consciences by informing. But not people like Pasquale and Enzo. I imagine that they continued to think, to express themselves, to attack, to defend, resorting to watchwords they had learned in the sixties and seventies. In truth, Pasquale carried on his war even in prison, and to the servants of the state said not a word, either to implicate or to exonerate himself. Enzo, on the other hand, certainly talked. In his usual laborious way, weighing every word with care, he displayed his feelings as a Communist but at the same time denied all the charges that had been brought against him.

Lila, for her part, focused her acute intelligence, her bad character, and very expensive lawyers on the battle to get him out of trouble. Enzo a strategist? A combatant? And when, if he had been working for years, from morning to night, at Basic Sight? How would it have been possible to kill the Solaras with Antonio and Pasquale if he was in Avellino at the time and Antonio was in Germany? Above all, even admitting that it was possible, the three friends were well known in the neighborhood and, masked or not, would have been recognized.

But there was little to do, the wheels of justice, as they say, advanced, and at a certain point I was afraid that Lila, too, would be arrested. Nadia named names upon names. They arrested some of those who had been part of the collective of Via dei Tribunali—one worked at the U.N., one at the F.A.O., one was a bank employee—and even Armando's former wife, Isabella, a peaceful housewife married to a technician at Enel, got her turn. Nadia spared only two people: her brother and, in spite of widespread fears, Lila. Maybe the daughter of Professor Galiani thought that by involving Enzo she had already struck her deeply. Or maybe she hated her and yet respected her, so that after much hesitation she decided to keep her out of it. Or maybe she was afraid of her, and feared a direct confrontation. But I prefer the hypothesis that she knew the story of Tina and took pity on her, or, better still, she had thought that if a mother has an experience like that, there is nothing that can truly hurt her.

Meanwhile, eventually, the charges against Enzo proved to be without substance, justice lost its grip, got tired. After many months, very little remained standing: his old friendship with Pasquale, militancy in the worker-student committee in the days of San Giovanni a Teduccio, the fact that the run-down farmhouse in the mountains of Serino, the one where Pasquale had been hiding, was rented to one of his Avellinese relations. Step by judicial step, he who had been considered a dangerous leader, the planner and executor of savage crimes, was demoted to sympathizer with the armed struggle. When finally even those sympathies proved to be generic opinions that had never been transmuted into criminal actions, Enzo returned home.

But by then almost two years had passed since his arrest, and in the neighborhood a reputation as a terrorist who was much more dangerous than Pasquale Peluso had solidified around him. Pasquale—said people on the streets and in the shops— we've all known him since he was a child, he always worked, his only crime was that he was always an upright man who, even after the fall of the Berlin Wall, didn't shed the uniform of a Communist his father sewed on him, who took on himself the sins of others and will never surrender. Enzo, on the other hand—they said—is very intelligent, he is well camouflaged by his silences and by the Basic Sight millions, above all he has behind him, directing him, Lina Cerullo, his black soul, more intelligent and more dangerous than he is: the two of them, yes, they must have done horrible things. Thus, as spiteful rumors accumulated, they were both marked out as people who not only had shed blood but had been clever enough to get away with it.

In that climate their business, already in trouble because of Lila's indifference and the money she had spent on lawyers and other things, couldn't get going again. By mutual consent they sold it, and although Enzo had often imagined that it was worth a billion lire, they barely got a couple of hundred million. In the spring of 1992, when they had stopped fighting, they separated both as business partners and as a couple. Enzo left a good part of the money to Lila and went to look for work in Milan. To me he said one afternoon: Stay near her, she's a woman who isn't comfortable with herself, she'll have a hard old age. For a while he wrote regularly, I did the same. A couple of times he called me. Then that was all.

36.

More or less around the same time another couple broke up, Elsa and Rino. Their love and complicity lasted for five or six months, at which point my daughter took me aside and confided that she felt attracted to a young mathematics teacher, a teacher in another section who didn't even know of her existence. I asked:

"And Rino?"

She answered:

"He is my great love."

I understood, as she added jokes to sighs, that she was making a distinction between love and attraction, and that her love for Rino wasn't affected in the least by her attraction to the teacher.

Since I was as usual stressed—I was writing a lot, publishing a lot, traveling a lot—it was Imma who became the confidante of both Elsa and Rino. My youngest daughter, who respected the feelings of both, gained the trust of both and became a reliable source of information for me. I learned from her that Elsa had succeeded in her intention of seducing the professor. I learned from her that Rino had eventually begun to suspect that things with Elsa weren't going well. I learned from her that Elsa had abandoned the professor so that Rino wouldn't suffer. I learned from her that, after a break of a month, she had started up again. I learned from her that Rino, suffering for almost a year, finally confronted her, weeping, and begged her to tell him if she still loved him. I learned from her that Elsa had shouted at him: I don't love you anymore, I love someone else. I learned from her that Rino had slapped her, but *only* with his fingertips, just to show he was a man. I learned from her that Elsa had run to the kitchen, grabbed the broom, and beaten him furiously, with no reaction from him.

From Lila, however, I learned that Rino—when I was absent and Elsa didn't come home from school and stayed out all night—had gone to her in despair. Pay some attention to your daughter, she said one evening, try to understand what she wants. But she said it indifferently, without concern for Elsa's future or for Rino's. In fact she added: Besides, look, if you have your commitments and you don't want to do anything it's all right just the same. Then she muttered: We weren't made for children. I wanted to respond that I felt I was a good mother and wore myself out trying to do my work without taking anything away from Dede, Elsa, and Imma. But I didn't, I perceived that at that moment she wasn't angry with me or my daughter, she was only trying to make her own indifference toward Rino seem normal.

Things were different when Elsa left the professor, and began going out with a classmate with whom she was studying for her final exams. She told Rino right away, so that he would understand that it was over. Lila then came up to my house, and, taking advantage of the fact that I was in Turin, made an ugly scene. What did your mother put in your head, she said in dialect, you have no sensitivity, you hurt people and don't realize it. Then she yelled at her: My dear, you think you're so important, but you're a whore. Or at least Elsa reported that, entirely confirmed by Imma, who said to me: It's true, Mamma, she called her a whore.

Whatever Lila had said, my second daughter was marked by it. She lost her lightness. She also gave up the schoolmate she was studying with, and became nice to Rino, but she left him alone in the bed and moved to Imma's room. When the exams were over she decided to visit her father and Dede, even though Dede had never given any sign of wanting to reconcile with her. She left for Boston, and there the two sisters, helped by Pietro, agreed on the fact that being in love with Rino had been a mistake. Once they made peace they had a good time, traveling around the United States, and when Elsa returned to Naples she seemed more serene. But she didn't stay with me for long. She enrolled in Physics, she became frivolous and sharp again, she changed boyfriends frequently. Since she was pursued by her schoolmate, by the young mathematics teacher, and naturally by Rino, she didn't take her exams, returned to her old loves, mixed them with new ones, accomplished nothing. Finally she flew off again to the United States, having decided to study there. She, like Dede, left without saying goodbye to Lila, but completely unexpectedly she spoke of her positively. She said that she understood why I had been her friend for so many years, and, without irony, called her the best person she had ever known.

37.

That was not Rino's opinion, however. Elsa's departure did not stop him, surprising as it may seem, from continuing to live with me. He was in despair for a long time, afraid of falling again into the physical and moral wretchedness from which *I* had rescued him. Full of devotion he attributed that and many other virtues to me. And he continued to occupy the room that had been Dede and Elsa's. He naturally did many jobs for me. When I left he drove me to the station and carried my suitcase, when I returned he did the same. He became my driver, my errand boy, my factotum. If he needed money he asked me for it politely, affectionately, and without the least scruple.

At times, when he made me nervous, I reminded him that he had some obligations toward his mother. He understood and disappeared for a while. But sooner or later he returned discouraged, muttering that Lila was never home, that the empty apartment made him sad, or he grumbled: She didn't even say hello, she sits at her computer and writes.

Lila was writing? What was she writing?

My curiosity at first was faint, the equivalent of an absent-minded observation. I was nearly fifty at the time, I was in the period of my greatest success, I was publishing two books a year, and selling well. Reading and writing had become a career, and, like all careers, it began to burden me. I remember thinking: in her place I'd sit on a beach in the sun. Then I said to myself: if writing helps her, good. And I went on to something else, I forgot about it.

38.

Dede's departure and then Elsa's grieved me. It depressed me that both, in the end, preferred their father to me. Of course they loved me, of course they missed me. I sent letters constantly, at moments of melancholy I telephoned without caring about the expense. And I liked Dede's voice when she said, I dream of you often; how moved I was if Elsa wrote, I'm looking everywhere for your perfume, I want to use it, too. But the fact was that they were gone, I had lost them. Every letter of theirs, every telephone call attested to the fact that, even if they suffered because of our separation, with their father they didn't have the conflicts they had had with me, he was the point of entry to their true world.

One morning Lila said to me in a tone that was hard to decipher: It makes no sense for you to keep Imma here in the neighborhood, send her to Rome to Nino, it's very clear that she wants to be able to say to her sisters, I've done what you did. Those words had an unpleasant effect on me. As if she were giving dispassionate advice, she was suggesting that I separate also from my third child. She seemed to be saying: Imma would be better off and so would you. I replied: If Imma leaves me, too, my life will no longer have meaning. But she smiled: Where is it written that lives should have a meaning? So she began to disparage all that struggle of mine to write. She said mockingly: Is the meaning that line of black markings that look like insect shit? She invited me to take a rest, she exclaimed: What need is there to work so hard. Enough.

I had a long period of uneasiness. On the one hand I thought: she wants to deprive me of Imma, too. On the other I said to myself: she's right, I should bring Imma and her father together. I didn't know whether to cling to the affection of the only child who remained or, for her sake, to try to reinforce her bond with Nino.

This last was not easy, and the recent elections had been proof of it. Imma was eleven—but she was inflamed by political passion. She wrote, I remember, to her father, she called him, she offered in every possible way to campaign for him and wanted me to help him, too. I hated the socialists even more than in the past. When I saw Nino I'd made remarks like: What's become of you, I no longer recognize you. I went so far as to say, with some rhetorical exaggeration: We were born in poverty and violence, the Solaras were criminals who stole everything, but you are worse, you are gangs of looters who make laws against the looting of others. He had answered lightheartedly: You've never understood anything about politics and you never will understand anything, play with literature and don't talk about things you don't know about.

But then the situation came to a head. Long-standing corruption—commonly practiced and commonly submitted to at every level as an unwritten rule but always in force among the most widely respected—came to the surface thanks to a sudden determination of the judiciary. The high-level crooks, who at first seemed few and so inexperienced that they were caught with their hands in the till, multiplied, became the true face of the management of the republic. As the elections approached I saw that Nino was less carefree. Since I had my fame and a certain reputation, he used Imma to ask me to stand behind him publicly. I said yes to the child in order not to upset her, but then in fact I withdrew. Imma was angry, she repeated her support for her father and when he asked her to stand next to him in a campaign ad she was enthusiastic. I rebelled and found myself in a terrible situation. On the one hand I didn't refuse Imma permission—it would have been impossible without a rift—on the other I scolded Nino on the telephone: Put Albertino, put Lidia in your ad, and don't dare use my daughter in this way. He insisted, he hesitated, finally he gave in. I forced him to tell Imma that he had inquired and that children weren't allowed in the ads. But she understood that I was the reason she had been deprived of the pleasure of standing publicly next to her father, and she said: You don't love me, Mamma, you send Dede and Elsa to Pietro, but I can't even spend five minutes with Papa. When Nino wasn't reelected Imma began to cry, she muttered between her sobs that it was my fault.

In other words, it was all complicated. Nino was bitter, he became intractable. For a while he seemed to be the only victim of those elections, but it wasn't so, soon the entire system of the parties was swept away and we lost track of him. The voters were angry with the old, the new, and the very new. If people had been horrified at those who wanted to overthrow the state, now they were disgusted by those who, pretending to serve it, had consumed it, like a fat worm in the apple. A black wave, which had lain hidden under gaudy trappings of power and a flow of words as impudent as it was arrogant, became increasingly visible and spread to every corner of Italy. The neighborhood of my childhood wasn't the only place untouched by any grace, Naples wasn't the only irredeemable city. I met Lila on the stairs one morning, she seemed cheerful. She showed me the copy of the *Repubblica* she had just bought. There was a photograph of Professor Guido Airota. The photographer had caught on his face, I don't know when, a frightened expression that made him almost unrecognizable. The article, full of they-says and perhapses, advanced the hypothesis that even the prestigious scholar, not to mention old political operator, might soon be summoned by the judges as one who was well informed about the corruption of Italy.

39.

Guido Airota never appeared before the judges, but for days dailies and weeklies drew maps of corruption in which even he played a part. I was glad, in that situation, that Pietro was in America, that Dede and Elsa, too, now had a life on the other side of the ocean. But I was worried about Adele, I thought I should at least telephone her. But I hesitated, I said to myself: she'll think that I'm enjoying it and it will be hard to convince her it's not true.

Instead I called Mariarosa, it seemed to me an easier path to take. I was wrong. It was years since I'd seen or spoken to her, she answered coldly. She said with a note of sarcasm: What a career you've had, my dear, now you're read everywhere, one can't open a newspaper or a journal without finding your name. Then she spoke in detail about herself, something she had never done in the past. She cited books, she cited articles, she cited travels. It struck me mainly that she had left the university.

"Why?" I asked.

"It disgusted me."

"And now?"

"Now what?"

"How do you live?"

"I have a rich family."

But she regretted that phrase as soon as she uttered it, she laughed uneasily, and it was she, right afterward, who spoke of her father. She said: It was bound to happen. And she quoted Franco, she said that he had been among the first to understand that either everything would change, and in a hurry, or even harder times would come and there would be no more hope. She was angry: My father thought you could change one thing here and one there, deliberately. But when you change almost nothing like that you're forced to enter into the system of lies and either you tell them, like the others, or they get rid of you. I asked her:

"Guido is guilty, he took money?"

She laughed nervously:

"Yes. But he is entirely innocent, in his whole life he never put a single lira that wasn't more than legal in his pocket."

Then she turned again to me, but in an almost offensive tone. She repeated: You write too much, you no longer surprise me. And although I had been the one to call, it was she who said goodbye and hung up.

The incongruous double judgment that Mariarosa had pronounced on her father was true. The media storm around Guido slowly faded and he returned to his study, but as an innocent who surely was guilty and, if you like, as a guilty man who surely was innocent. It seemed to me that at that point I could telephone Adele. She thanked me ironically for my concern, showed that she was better informed than I was regarding the life and studies of Dede and Elsa, uttered remarks like: This is a country where one is exposed to every insult, respectable people should be in a hurry to emigrate. When I asked if I could say hello to Guido she said: I'll say it for you, he's resting now. Then she exclaimed bitterly: His only crime was to be surrounded by newly literate types with no ethics, young arrivistes ready for anything, scum.

That very evening the television showed a particularly cheerful image of the former socialist deputy Giovanni Sarratore—who was not exactly a youth, at the time: he was fifty—and inserted him in the increasingly crowded list of corrupters and corrupt.

40.

That news especially upset Imma. In those first years of her conscious life she had seen her father very little, and yet had made him her idol. She boasted of him to her schoolmates, she boasted to her teachers, she showed everyone a photograph from the newspapers in which they were hand in hand right at the entrance to Montecitorio. If she had to imagine the man she would marry, she said: He will surely be very tall, dark, and handsome. When she learned that her father had ended up in jail like an ordinary inhabitant of the neighborhood—a place that she considered horrible: now that she was growing up she said in no uncertain terms that she was afraid of it, and, increasingly, she had reason to be—she lost the bit of serenity I had been able to guarantee her. She sobbed in her sleep, she woke in the middle of the night and wanted to get in bed with me.

Once we met Marisa, worn-out, shabby, angrier than usual. She said, paying no attention to Imma: Nino deserves it, he's always thought only of himself, and, as you well know, he never wanted to give us any help, he acted like an honest man only with his relatives, that piece of shit. My daughter couldn't bear even a word of it, she left us on the *stradone* and ran away. I quickly said goodbye to Marisa, I chased after Imma, I tried to console her: You mustn't pay any attention, your father and his sister never got along. But I stopped speaking critically of Nino in front of her. In fact I stopped speaking critically of him in front of anyone. I remembered when I went to him to find out about Pasquale and Enzo. You always needed some patron saint in Paradise to navigate the calculated opacity of the underworld, and Nino, although far from any sanctity, had helped me. Now that the saints were falling into the inferno, I had no one to ask to find out about him. Unreliable news came to me only from the infernal circle of his many lawyers.

41.

Lila, I have to say, never showed any interest in Nino's fate; she reacted to the news of his legal troubles as if it were something to laugh about. She said, with the expression of someone who has remembered a detail that explained everything: Whenever he needed money he got Bruno Soccavo to give it to him, and he certainly never paid it back. Then she muttered that she could imagine what had happened to him. He had smiled, he had shaken hands, he had felt he was the best of all, he had continuously wanted to demonstrate that he was equal to any possible situation. If he had done something wrong he had done it out of a desire to be more likable, to seem the most intelligent, to climb higher and higher. That's it. And later she acted as if Nino no longer existed. As much as she had exerted herself for Pasquale and Enzo, so she appeared completely indifferent to the problems of the former Honorable Sarratore. It's likely that she followed the proceedings in the papers and on television, where Nino appeared often, pale, suddenly grizzled, with the expression of a child who says: I swear it wasn't me. Certainly she never asked me what I knew about him, if I had managed to see him, what he expected, how his father, his mother, his siblings had reacted. Instead, for no clear reason, her interest in Imma was rekindled, she got involved with her again.

While she had abandoned her son Rino to me like a puppy who, having grown fond of another mistress, no longer greets the old one, she became very attached to my daughter again, and Imma, always greedy for affection, went back to loving her. I saw them talking, and they often went out together. Lila said to me: I showed her the botanic garden, the museum, Capodimonte.

In the last phase of our life in Naples, she guided Imma all over the city, transmitting an interest in it that remained with her. Aunt Lina knows so many things, Imma said in admiration. And I was pleased, because Lila, taking her around on her wanderings, managed to diminish her anguish about her father, the anger at the fierce insults of her classmates, prompted by their parents, and the loss of the attention she had received from her teachers thanks to her surname. But it wasn't only that. I learned from Imma's reports, and with greater and greater precision, that the object in which Lila's mind was engaged, and on which she was writing for perhaps hours and hours, bent over her computer, was not this or that monument but Naples in its entirety. An enormous project that she had never talked to me about. The time had passed in which she tended to involve me in her passions, she had chosen my daughter as her confidante. To her she repeated the things she learned, or dragged her to see what had excited or fascinated her.

42.

Imma was very receptive, and memorized everything rapidly. It was she who taught me about Piazza dei Martiri, so important for Lila and me in the past. I knew nothing about it, whereas Lila had studied its history and told her about it. She repeated it to me right in the piazza, one morning when we went shopping, mixing up, I think, facts, her fantasies, fantasies of Lila's. Here, Mamma, in the eighteenth century it was all countryside. There were trees, there were the peasants' houses, inns, and a road that went straight down to the sea called Calata Santa Caterina a Chiaia, from the name of the church there at the corner, which is old but quite ugly. After May 15, 1848, when, right in this spot, many patriots who wanted a constitution and a parliament were killed, the Bourbon King Ferdinando II, to show that peace had returned, decided to construct a Road of Peace and put up in the piazza a column with a Madonna at the top. But when the annexation of Naples by the Kingdom of Italy was proclaimed and the Bourbon was driven out, the mayor Giuseppe Colonna di Stigliano asked the sculptor Enrico Alvino to transform the column with the Madonna of Peace at the top into a column in memory of the Neapolitans who had died for freedom. So Enrico Alvino put at the base of the column these four lions, which symbolized the great moments of revolution in Naples: the lion of 1799, mortally wounded; the lion of the movements of 1820, pierced by the sword but still biting the air; the lion of

1848, which represents the force of the patriots subdued but
not conquered; finally, the lion of 1859, threatening and avenging. Then, Mamma, up there, instead of the Madonna of Peace
he put the bronze statue of a beautiful young woman, that is,
Victory, who is balanced on the world: that Victory holds the
sword in her left hand and in the right a garland for the
Neapolitan citizens, martyrs for Freedom, who, fallen in battle
and on the gallows, avenged the people with their blood, et
cetera et cetera.

I often had the impression that Lila used the past to make
Imma's tempestuous present normal. In the Neapolitan facts as
she recounted them there was always something terrible, disorderly, at the origin, which later took the form of a beautiful
building, a street, a monument, only to be forgotten, to lose
meaning, to decline, improve, decline, according to an ebb and
flow that was by its nature unpredictable, made of waves, flat
calm, downpours, cascades. The essential, in Lila's scheme,
was to ask questions. Who were the martyrs, what did the lions
mean, and when had the battles and the gallows occured, and
the Road of Peace, and the Madonna, and the Victory. The stories were a lineup of the befores, the afters, the thens. Before
elegant Chiaia, the neighborhood for the wealthy, there was the
playa cited in the letters of Gregory, the swamps that went
down to the beach and the sea, the wild forest that crept up to
the Vomero. Before the Risanamento, or cleanup, of the end of
the nineteenth century, before the railroad cooperatives, there
was an unhealthy area, polluted in every stone, but also with
quite a few splendid monuments, swept away by the mania for
tearing down under the pretense of cleaning up. And one of
the areas to be cleaned up had, for a very long time, been
called Vasto. Vasto was a place name that indicated the terrain
between Porta Capuana and Porta Nolana, and the neighborhood, once cleaned up, had kept the name. Lila repeated that
name—Vasto—she liked it, and Imma, too, liked it: Vasto and

Risanamento, waste and good health, a yearning to lay waste, sack, ruin, gut, and a yearning to build, order, design new streets or rename the old, for the purpose of consolidating new worlds and hiding old evils, which, however, were always ready to exact their revenge.

In fact, before the Vasto was called Vasto and was in essence wasteland—Aunt Lina recounted—there had been villas, gardens, fountains. In that very place the Marchese di Vico had built a palace, with a garden, called Paradise. The garden of Paradise was full of hidden water games, Mamma. The most famous was a big white mulberry tree, which had a system of almost invisible channels: water flowed through them, falling like rain from the branches or coursing like a waterfall down the trunk. Understand? From the Paradise of the Marchese di Vico to the Vasto of the Marchese del Vasto, to the Cleanup of Mayor Nicola Amore, to the Vasto again, to further renaissances and so on at that rate.

Ah, what a city, said Aunt Lina to my daughter, what a splendid and important city: here all languages are spoken, Imma, here everything was built and everything was torn down, here the people don't trust talk and are very talkative, here is Vesuvius which reminds you every day that the greatest undertaking of powerful men, the most splendid work, can be reduced to nothing in a few seconds by the fire, and the earthquake, and the ash, and the sea.

I listened, but at times I was baffled. Yes, Imma was consoled but only because Lila was introducing her to a permanent stream of splendors and miseries, a cyclical Naples where everything was marvelous and everything became gray and irrational and everything sparkled again, as when a cloud passes over the sun and the sun appears to flee, a timid, pale disk, near extinction, but now look, once the cloud dissolves it's suddenly dazzling again, so bright you have to shield your eyes with your hand. In Lila's stories the palaces with

paradisiacal gardens fell into ruin, grew wild, and sometimes
nymphs, dryads, satyrs, and fauns inhabited them, sometimes
the souls of the dead, sometimes demons whom God sent to
the castles and also the houses of common people to make
them atone for their sins or to put to the test good-hearted
inhabitants, to reward them after death. What was beautiful
and solid and radiant was populated with nighttime imagin-
ings, and they both liked stories of shades. Imma informed me
that at the cape of Posillipo, a few steps from the sea, opposite
Gajóla, just above the Grotta delle Fate, there was a famous
building inhabited by spirits. The spirits, she told me, were also
in the buildings of Vico San Mandato and Vico Mondragone.
Lila had promised her that they would go together to look in
the streets of Santa Lucia for a spirit called Faccione, called that
because of his broad face, who was dangerous and threw big
stones at anyone who disturbed him. Also—she had told her—
many spirits of dead children lived in Pizzofalcone and other
places. A child could often be seen at night in the neighborhood of Porta Nolana. Did they really exist, or did they not
exist? Aunt Lina said that the spirits existed, but not in the
palaces, or in the alleys, or near the ancient gates of the Vasto.
They existed in people's ears, in the eyes when the eyes looked
inside and not out, in the voice as soon as it begins to speak, in
the head when it thinks, because words are full of ghosts but
so are images. Is it true, Mamma?

Yes, I answered, maybe yes: if Aunt Lina says so, it could
be. This city is full of events, both large and small—Lila had
told her—you can even see spirits if you go to the museum, the
painting gallery, and, especially, the Biblioteca Nazionale, there
are a lot of them in the books. You open one and, for example,
Masaniello jumps out. Masaniello is a funny and terrible spirit,
he makes the poor laugh and the rich tremble. Imma liked it in
particular when, with his sword, he killed not the duke of
Maddaloni, not the father of the duke of Maddaloni, but their

portraits, *zac, zac, zac.* In fact, in her opinion, the most enter-taining moment was when Masaniello cut off the heads of the duke and his father in the portraits, or hanged the portraits of other ferocious noblemen. *He cut off the heads in the portraits,* Imma laughed, in disbelief, *he hanged the portraits.* And after those decapitations and hangings Masaniello put on an outfit of blue silk embroidered with silver, placed a gold chain around his neck, stuck a diamond pin in his hat, and went to the market. He went like that, Mamma, all decked out like a marquis, a duke, a prince, he who was a workingman, a fisher-man, and didn't know how to read or write. Aunt Lina had said that in Naples that could happen and other things, openly, without the pretense of making laws and decrees and entire conditions better than the previous ones. In Naples one could get carried away without subterfuges, with clarity and com-plete satisfaction.

The story of a minister had made a great impression on her. It involved the museum of our city, and Pompeii. Imma told me in a serious tone: You know, Mamma, that a Minister of Education, Nasi, a representative of the people almost a hun-dred years ago, accepted as a gift from workers at the excava-tions of Pompeii a small, valuable statue they had just dug up? You know that he had models made of the best artworks found at Pompeii to adorn his villa in Trapani? This Nasi, Mamma, even though he was a Minister of the Kingdom of Italy, acted instinctively: the workers brought him a beautiful little statue as a gift and he took it, he thought it would make a very fine impression at his house. Sometimes you make a mistake, but when as a child you haven't been taught what the public good is, you don't understand what a crime is.

I don't know if she said the last part because she was report-ing the words of Aunt Lina, or because she had made her own arguments. Anyway I didn't like those words and I decided to intervene. I made a cautious speech, but explicit: Aunt Lina tells you so many wonderful things, I'm pleased, when she gets excited no one can stop her. But you mustn't think that people carry out terrible acts lightly. You mustn't believe it, Imma, especially if it concerns members of parliament and ministers and senators and bankers and Camorrists. You mustn't believe that the world is chasing its tail—now it's going well, now badly, now it's going well again. We have to work with consistency, with discipline, step by step, no matter how things are going around us, and be careful not to make a mistake, because we pay for our mistakes.

Imma's lower lip trembled, she asked me:

"Papa won't go to parliament anymore?"

I didn't know what to say and she realized it. As if to encourage me to give a positive response, she said:

"Aunt Lina thinks so, that he'll return."

I hesitated, then made up my mind.

"No, Imma, I don't think so. But there's no need for Papa to be an important person for you to love him."

43.

It was the completely wrong answer. Nino, with his usual ability, slipped out of the trap he had ended up in. Imma found out and was very pleased. She asked to see him, but he disappeared for a while, it was difficult to track him down. When we made a date he took us to a pizzeria in Mergellina, but he didn't display his usual liveliness. He was nervous, distracted, to Imma he said one should never rely on political alignments, he described himself as the victim of a left that wasn't a left, in fact it was worse than the fascists. You'll see—he reassured her—Papa will fix everything up.

Later I read some very aggressive articles of his in which he returned to a thesis that he had espoused long ago: legal power had to be subject to executive power. He wrote indignantly: How can the judges one day be fighting against those who want to strike at the heart of the state and the next make the citizens believe that very same heart is sick and should be thrown out. He fought not to be thrown out. He passed through the old parties now out of commission, shifting further to the right, and in 1994, radiant, he regained a seat in parliament.

Imma was joyful when she learned that her father was again the Honorable Sarratore and that Naples had given him a very high number of preferences. As soon as she heard the news she came to tell me: You write books but you can't see the future the way Aunt Lina does.

44.

I didn't get angry with her, in essence my daughter wanted only to point out to me that I had been spiteful about her father, that I hadn't understood how great he was. But those words (*You write books but you can't see the future the way Aunt Lina does*) had an unexpected function: they pushed me to pay attention to the fact that Lila, the woman who in Imma's opinion could see the future, at fifty had returned officially to books, to studying, and was even writing. Pietro had imagined that with that decision she had self-prescribed a kind of therapy to fight the anguishing absence of Tina. But in my last year in the neighborhood I wasn't satisfied with Pietro's sensitivity or Imma's mediation: as soon as I could, I broached the subject, I asked questions.

"Why all this interest in Naples?"

"What's wrong with it?"

"Nothing, in fact I envy you. You're studying for your own pleasure, while I now read and write only for work."

"I'm not studying. I limit myself to seeing a building, a

street, a monument, and maybe I spend a little time looking for information, that's all."

"And that's studying."

"You think?"

She was evasive, she didn't want to confide in me. But sometimes she became excited, the way she could be, and began to speak of the city as if it were not made up of the usual streets, of the normality of everyday places, but had revealed only to her a secret sparkle. So in a few brief sentences she transformed it into the most memorable place in the world, into the place richest in meanings, and after a little conversation I returned to my things with my mind on fire. What a grave negligence it had been to be born and live in Naples without making an effort to know it. I was about to leave the city for the second time, I had been there altogether for thirty full years of my life, and yet of the place where I was born I knew almost nothing. Pietro, in the past, had admonished me for my ignorance, now I admonished myself. I listened to Lila and felt my insubstantiality.

Meanwhile, she, who learned with effortless speed, now seemed able to give to every monument, every stone, a density of meaning, a fantastic importance such that I would have happily stopped the nonsense that I was busy with to start studying in turn. But "the nonsense" absorbed all my energy, thanks to it I lived comfortably, I usually worked even at night. Sometimes in the silent apartment I stopped, I thought that perhaps at that moment Lila, too, was awake, maybe she was writing like me, maybe summarizing texts she'd read in the library, maybe putting down her reflections, maybe she moved on from there to recount episodes of her own, maybe the historic truth didn't interest her, she sought only starting points from which to let imagination wander.

Certainly she proceeded in her usual extemporaneous way, with unexpected interests that later weakened and vanished.

Now, as far as I could tell, she was concerned with the porcelain factory near the Palazzo Reale. Now she was gathering information on San Pietro a Majella. Now she sought testimonies of foreign travelers in which it seemed to her she could trace a mixture of attraction and repulsion. Everyone, she said, everyone, century after century, praised the great port, the sea, the ships, the castles, Vesuvius tall and black with its disdainful flames, the city like an amphitheater, the gardens, the orchards, the palaces. But then, century after century, they began to complain about the inefficiency, the corruption, the physical and moral poverty. No institution—behind the façade, behind the pompous name and the numerous employees—truly functioned. No decipherable order, only an unruly and uncontrollable crowd on streets cluttered with sellers of every possible type of merchandise, people speaking at the top of their lungs, urchins, beggars. Ah, there is no city that gives off so much noise and such a clamor as Naples.

Once she talked to me about violence. We believed, she said, that it was a feature of the neighborhood. We had it around us from birth, it brushed up against us, touched us all our lives, we thought: we were unlucky. You remember how we used words to cause suffering, and how many we invented to humiliate? You remember the beatings that Antonio, Enzo, Pasquale, my brother, the Solaras, and even I, and even you, gave and took? You remember when my father threw me out the window? Now I'm reading an old article on San Giovanni a Carbonara, where it explains what the Carbonara or Carboneto was. I thought that there was coal there once, and coal miners. But no, it was the place for the garbage, all cities have them. It was called Fosso Carbonario, dirty water ran in it, animal carcasses were tossed into it. And since ancient times the Fosso Carbonario of Naples was where the church of San Giovanni a Carbonara stands today. In the area called Piazza di Carbonara the poet Virgil in his time ordered that every year the *ioco de Carbonara* take place, gladiator games that didn't lead to the death of men, as they did later—*morte de homini come de po è facto* (she liked that old Italian, it amused her, she quoted it to me with visible pleasure)—but gave men practice in deeds of arms: *li homini ali facti de l'arme*. Soon, however, it wasn't a matter of *ioco* or practice. In that place where they threw out beasts and garbage a lot of human blood was shed. It seems that the game of throwing the *prete* was invented there, the stone throwing that we did as girls, you remember, when Enzo hit me in the forehead—I still have the scar—and he was desperate and gave me a garland of sorb apples. But then, in Piazza di Carbonara, from stones she moved on to weapons, and it became the place where men fought to the last drop of blood. Beggars and gentlemen and princes hurried to see people killing each other in revenge. When some handsome youth fell, pierced by a blade beaten on the anvil of death, immediately beggars, bourgeois citizens, kings and queens offered applause that rose to the stars. Ah, the violence: tearing, killing, ripping. Lila, between fascination and horror, spoke to me in a mixture of dialect, Italian, and very educated quotations that she had taken from who knows where and remembered by heart. The entire planet, she said, is a big Fosso Carbonario. And at times I thought that she could have held crowded rooms fascinated, but then I brought her down to size. She's a barely educated woman of fifty, she doesn't know how to do research, she doesn't know what the documentary truth is: she reads, she is excited, she mixes truth and falsehood, she imagines. No more. What seemed to interest and absorb her most was that all that filth, all that chaos of broken limbs and dug-out eyes and split heads was then covered—literally covered—by a church dedicated to San Giovanni Battista and by a monastery of Augustinian hermits who had a valuable library. Ah, ah—she laughed—underneath there's blood and above, God, peace, prayer, and books. Thus the coupling of San Giovanni and the Fosso Carbonario, that is to say the place name of San Giovanni a Carbonara: a street we've walked on thousands of times, Lenù, it's near the station, near Forcella and the Tribunali.

I knew where the street of San Giovanni a Carbonara was, I knew it very well, but I didn't know those stories. She talked about it at length. She talked so as to let me know—I suspected—that the things she was telling me orally she had in substance already written, and they belonged to a vast text whose structure, however, escaped me. I wondered: what does she have in mind, what are her intentions? Is she just organizing her wandering and readings or is she planning a book of Neapolitan curiosities, a book that, naturally, she'll never finish but that it's good for her to keep working on, day after day, now that not only Tina is gone but Enzo is gone, the Solaras are gone, I, too, am going, taking away Imma, who, one way and another, has helped her survive?

45.

Shortly before I left for Turin I spent a lot of time with her, we had an affectionate farewell. It was a summer day in 1995. We talked about everything, for hours, but finally she focused on Imma, who was now fourteen; she was pretty, and lively, and had just graduated from middle school. She praised her without sudden malice, and I listened to her praise, I thanked her for helping her at a difficult time. She looked at me in bafflement, she corrected me:

"I've always helped Imma, not just now."

"Yes, but after Nino's troubles you were really helpful to her."

She didn't like those words, either, it was a moment of confusion. She didn't want me to associate with Nino the attention she had devoted to Imma, she reminded me that she had taken care of the child from the start, she said she had done it because Tina loved her dearly, she added: Maybe Tina loved Imma even more than me. Then she shook her head in discontent.

"I don't understand you," she said.

"What don't you understand?"

She became nervous, she had something in mind that she wanted to tell me but restrained herself.

"I don't understand how it's possible that in all this time you never thought of it even once."

"Of what, Lila?"

She was silent for a few seconds, then spoke, eyes down.

"You remember the photograph in *Panorama*?"

"Which one?"

"The one where you were with Tina and the caption said that it was you and your daughter."

"Of course I remember."

"I've often thought that they might have taken Tina because of that photo."

"What?"

"They thought they were stealing your daughter, and instead they stole mine."

She said it, and that morning I had the proof that of all the infinite hypotheses, the fantasies, the obsessions that had tormented her, that still tormented her, I had perceived almost nothing. A decade hadn't served to calm her, her brain couldn't find a quiet corner for her daughter. She said:

"You were always in the newspapers and on television, beautiful, elegant, blond: maybe they wanted money from you and not from me, who knows, I don't know anything anymore, things go one way and then they change direction."

She said that Enzo had talked to the police, that she had talked about it with Antonio, but neither the police nor Antonio had taken the possibility seriously. Yet she spoke to me as if at that moment she were again sure that that was what had happened. Who knows what else she had brooded over and was still brooding over that I hadn't realized. Nunziatina had been taken in place of my Immacolata? My success was responsible for the kidnapping of her daughter? And that bond of hers with Imma was an anxiety, a protection, a safeguard? She imagined that the kidnappers, having thrown away the wrong child, would return to get the right one? Or what else? What had passed and was passing through her mind? Why was she talking to me about this only now? Did she want to inject in me a final poison to punish me for leaving her? Ah, I understood why Enzo had left. Living with her had become too harrowing.

She realized that I was looking at her with concern and, as if to reach safety, began to speak about what she was reading. But now in a jumbled way; her unease contorted her features. She muttered, laughing, that evil took unpredictable pathways. You cover it over with churches, convents, books—they seem so important, the books, she said sarcastically, you've devoted your whole life to them—and the evil breaks through the floor and emerges where you don't expect it. Then she calmed down and began to speak again of Tina, Imma, me, but in a conciliatory way, as if apologizing for what she had said to me. When there's too much silence, she said, so many ideas come to mind, I don't pay attention. Only in bad novels people always think the right thing, always say the right thing, every effect has its cause, there are the likable ones and the unlikable, the good and the bad, everything in the end consoles you. She whispered: It might be that Tina will return tonight and then who gives a damn how it happened, the essential thing will be that she's here again and forgives me for the distraction. You forgive me, too, she said, and, embracing me, concluded: Go, go, do better things than you've done so far. I've stayed near Imma *also* out of fear that someone might take her, and you loved my son truly *also* when your daughter left him. How many things you've endured for him, thank you. I'm so glad we've been friends for so long and that we are still.

46.

The idea that Tina had been taken in the belief that she was my daughter upset me, but not because I considered that it had some foundation. I thought rather of the tangle of obscure feelings that had generated it, and I tried to put them in order. I even remembered, after so long, that for completely coincidental reasons—under the most insignificant coincidences expanses of quicksand lie hidden—Lila had given her daughter the name of my beloved doll, the one that, as a child, she herself had thrown into a cellar. It was the first time, I recall, that I fantasized about it, but I couldn't stand it for long, I looked into a dark well with a few glimmers of light and drew back. Every intense relationship between human beings is full of traps, and if you want it to endure you have to learn to avoid them. I did so then, and finally it seemed that I had only come up against yet another proof of how splendid and shadowy our friendship was, how long and complicated Lila's suffering had been, how it still endured and would endure forever. But I went to Turin convinced that Enzo was right: Lila was very far from a quiet old age within the confines she had established for herself. The last image she gave me of herself was that of a woman of fifty-one who looked ten years older and who from time to time, as she spoke, was hit by waves of heat, and turned fiery red. There were patches on her neck, too, her gaze dimmed, she grabbed the edge of her dress with her hands and fanned herself, showing Imma and me her underwear.

47.

In Turin now everything was ready: I had found an apartment near the Isabella bridge and had worked hard to get most of my things and Imma's moved. We departed. The train, I remember, had just left Naples, my daughter was sitting across from me, and for the first time she seemed sad about what she was leaving behind. I was very tired from the traveling back and forth of the past months, from the thousands of things I had had to arrange, from what I had done, from what I had forgotten to do. I collapsed against the seat back, I looked out the window at the outskirts of the city and Vesuvius as they grew distant. Just at that moment the certainty sprang to mind that Lila, writing about Naples, would write about Tina, and the text—precisely because it was nourished by the effort of expressing an inexpressible grief—would be extraordinary.

That certainty took hold forcefully and never weakened. In the years of Turin—as long as I ran the small but promising publishing house that had hired me, as long as I felt much more respected, I would say in fact more powerful, than Adele had been in my eyes decades earlier—the certainty took the form of a wish, a hope. I would have liked Lila to call me one day and say: I have a manuscript, a notebook, a *zibaldone*, in other words a text of mine that I'd like you to read and help me arrange. I would have read it immediately. I would have worked to give it a proper form, probably, passage by passage, I would have ended up rewriting it. Lila, in spite of her intellectual liveliness, her extraordinary memory, the reading she must have done all her life, at times talking to me about it, more often hiding it from me, had an absolutely inadequate basic education and no skill as a narrator. I was afraid it would be a disorderly accumulation of good things badly formulated, splendid things put in the wrong place. But it never occurred to me—never—that she might write an inane little story, full of clichés, in fact I was absolutely sure that it would be a worthy text. In the periods when I was struggling to put together an editorial plan of a high standard, I even went so far as to urgently interrogate Rino, who, for one thing, showed up frequently at my house; he would arrive without calling, say I came to say hello, and stay at least a couple of weeks. I asked him: Is your mother still writing? Have you ever happened to take a look, to see what it is? But he said yes, no, I don't remember, it's her business, I don't know. I insisted. I fantasized about the series in which I would put that phantom text, about what I would do to give it the maximum visibility and get some prestige from it myself. Occasionally I called Lila, I asked how she was, I questioned her discreetly, sticking to generalities: Do you still have your passion for Naples, are you taking more notes? She automatically responded: What passion, what notes, I'm a crazy old woman like Melina, you remember Melina, who knows if she's still alive. Then I dropped the subject, we moved on to other things.

48.

In the course of those phone calls we spoke more and more frequently of the dead, which was an occasion to mention the living, too.

Her father, Fernando, had died, and a few months later Nunzia died. Lila then moved with Rino to the old apartment where she was born and that she had bought long ago with her own money. But now the other siblings claimed that it was the property of her parents and harassed her by claiming rights to a part of it.

Stefano had died after another heart attack—they hadn't had time even to call an ambulance, he had fallen facedown on the ground—and Marisa had left the neighborhood, with her children. Nino had finally done something for her. Not only had he found her a job as a secretary in a law firm on Via Crispi but he gave her money to support her children at the university.

A man I had never met but who was known to be the lover of my sister, Elisa, had died. She had left the neighborhood but neither she nor my father nor my brothers had told me. I found out from Lila that she had gone to Caserta, had met a lawyer who was also a city councilman, and had remarried, but hadn't invited me to the wedding.

We talked about things like this, she kept me updated on all the news. I told her about my daughters, about Pietro, who had married a colleague five years older than he, of what I was writing, of how my publishing experience was going. Only a couple of times did I go so far as to ask somewhat explicit questions on the subject important to me.

"If you, let's say, were to write something—it's a hypothesis—would you let me read it?"

"What sort of something?"

"Something. Rino says you're always at the computer."

"Rino talks nonsense. I'm going on the Internet. I'm finding out new information about electronics. That's what I'm doing when I'm at the computer."

"Really?"

"Of course. Do I never respond to your e-mails?"

"No, and you make me mad: I always write to you and you write nothing."

"You see? I write nothing to no one, not even to you."

"All right. but if you should write something, you'd let me read it, you'd let me publish it?"

"You're the writer."

"You didn't answer me."

"I did answer you, but you pretend not to understand. To write, you have to want something to survive you. I don't even have the desire to live, I've never had it strongly the way you have. If I could eliminate myself now, while we're speaking, I'd be more than happy. Imagine if I'm going to start writing."

She had often expressed that idea of eliminating herself, but, starting in the late nineties—and especially from 2000 on—it became a sort of teasing chorus. It was a metaphor, of course. She liked it, she had resorted to it in the most diverse circumstances, and it never occurred to me, in the many years of our friendship—not even in the most terrible moments following Tina's disappearance—that she would think of suicide. Eliminating herself was a sort of aesthetic project. One can't go on anymore, she said, electronics seems so clean and yet it dirties, dirties tremendously, and it obliges you to leave traces of yourself everywhere as if you were shitting and peeing on yourself continuously: I want to leave nothing, my favorite key is the one that deletes.

That yearning had been more true in some periods, in others less. I remember a malicious tirade that started with my fame. Eh, she said once, what a fuss for a name: famous or not, it's only a ribbon tied around a sack randomly filled with blood, flesh, words, shit, and petty thoughts. She mocked me at length on that point: I untie the ribbon—*Elena Greco*—and the sack stays there, it functions just the same, haphazardly, of course, without virtues or vices, until it breaks. On her darkest days she said with a bitter laugh: I want to untie my name, slip it off me, throw it away, forget it. But on other occasions she was more relaxed. It happened—let's say—that I called her hoping to persuade her to talk to me about her text and, although she forcefully denied its existence, continuing to be evasive, it sounded as if my phone call had surprised her in the middle of a creative moment. One evening I found her happily dazed. She made the usual speech about annihilating all hierarchies—*So much fuss about the greatness of this one and that one, but what virtue is there in being born with certain qualities, it's like admiring the bingo basket when you shake it and good numbers come out*—but she expressed herself with imagination and with precision, I perceived the pleasure of inventing images. Ah, how she could use words when she wanted to. She seemed to safeguard a secret meaning that took meaning away from everything else. Perhaps it was that which began to sadden me.

49.

The crisis arrived in the winter of 2002. At that time, in spite of the ups and downs, I again felt fulfilled. Every year Dede and Elsa returned from the United States, sometimes alone, sometimes with temporary boyfriends. The first was involved in the same things as her father, the second had precociously won a professorship in a very mysterious area of algebra. When her sisters returned Imma freed herself of every obligation and spent all her time with them. The family came together again, we were four women in the house in Turin, or out in the city, happy to be together at least for a short period, attentive to one another, affectionate. I looked at them and said to myself: How lucky I've been.

But at Christmas of 2002 something happened that depressed me. The three girls all returned for a long period. Dede had married a serious engineer of Iranian origin, she had a very energetic two-year-old named Hamid. Elsa came with one of her colleagues from Boston, also a mathematician, even more youthful, and rowdy. Imma returned from Paris, where she had been studying philosophy for two years, and brought a classmate, a tall, not very good-looking, and almost silent Frenchman. How pleasant that December was. I was fifty-eight, a grandmother, I cuddled Hamid. I remember that on Christmas evening I was in a corner with the baby and looking serenely at the young bodies of my daughters, charged with energy. They all resembled me and none of them did, their lives were very far from mine and yet I felt them as inseparable parts of me. I thought: how much work I've done and what a long road I've traveled. At every step I could have given in and yet I didn't. I left the neighborhood, I returned, I managed to leave again. Nothing, nothing pulled me down, along with these girls I produced. We're safe, I brought them all to safety. Oh, they now belong to other places and other languages.

They consider Italy a splendid corner of the planet and, at the same time, an insignificant and ineffectual province, habitable only for a short vacation. Dede often says to me: Leave, come and stay in my house, you can do your work from there. I say yes, sooner or later I will. They're proud of me and yet I know that none of them would tolerate me for long, not even Imma by now. The world has changed tremendously and belongs more and more to them, less and less to me. But that's all right—I said to myself, caressing Hamid—in the end what counts is these very smart girls who haven't encountered a single one of the difficulties I faced. They have habits, voices, requirements, entitlements, self-awareness that even today I wouldn't dare allow myself. Others haven't had the same luck. In the wealthier countries a mediocrity that hides the horrors of the rest of the world has prevailed. When those horrors release a violence that reaches into our cities and our habits we're startled, we're alarmed. Last year I was dying of fear and I made long phone calls to Dede, to Elsa, even to Pietro, when I saw on television the planes that set the towers in New York ablaze the way you light a match by gently striking the head. In the world below is the inferno. My daughters know it but only through words, and they become indignant, all the time enjoying the pleasures of existence, while it lasts. They attribute their well-being and their success to their father. But I—I who did not have privileges—am the foundation of their privileges.

While I was reasoning like this, something depressed me. I suppose it was when the three girls led the men playfully to the shelf that held my books. Probably none of them had ever read one, certainly I had never seen them do so, nor had they ever said anything to me about them. But now they were paging through them, they even read some sentences aloud. Those books originated in the climate in which I had lived, in what had influenced me, in the ideas that had impressed me. I had followed my time, step by step, inventing stories, reflecting. I had pointed out evils, I had staged them. Countless times I had anticipated redemptive changes that had never arrived. I had used the language of every day to indicate things of every day. I had stressed certain themes: work, class conflicts, feminism, the marginalized. Now I was hearing my sentences chosen at random and they seemed embarrassing. Elsa—Dede was more respectful, Imma more cautious—was reading in an ironic tone from my first novel, she read from the story about the invention of women by men, she read from books with many prizes. Her voice skillfully highlighted flaws, excesses, tones that were too exclamatory, the aged ideologies that I had supported as indisputable truths. Above all she paused with amusement on the vocabulary, she repeated two or three times words that had long since passed out of fashion and sounded foolish. What was I witnessing? An affectionate mockery in the Neapolitan manner—certainly my daughter had learned that tone there—which, however, line by line, was becoming a demonstration of the scant value of all those volumes, sitting there along with their translations?

Elsa's friend the young mathematician was the only one, I think, who realized that my daughter was hurting me and he interrupted her, took away the book, asked me questions about Naples as if it were a city of the imagination, similar to those which the most intrepid explorers brought news of. The holiday slipped away. But something inside me changed. Occasionally I took down one of my volumes, read a few pages, felt its fragility. My old uncertainties gained strength. I increasingly doubted the quality of my works. Lila's hypothetical text, in parallel, assumed an unforeseen value. If before I had thought of it as a raw material on which I could work with her, shaping it into a good book for my publishing house, now it was transformed into a completed work and so into a possible touchstone. I was surprised to ask myself: and if sooner or later a story much better than mine emerges from her files? If

I have never, in fact, written a memorable novel and she, she, on the other hand, has been writing and rewriting one for years? If the genius that Lila had expressed as a child in *The Blue Fairy*, disturbing Maestra Oliviero, is now, in old age, manifesting all its power? In that case her book would become—even only for me—the proof of my failure, and reading it I would understand how I should have written but had been unable to. At that point, the stubborn self-discipline, the laborious studies, every page or line that I had published successfully would vanish as when a storm arriving over the sea collides with the violet line of the horizon and blots out everything. My image as a writer who had emerged from a blighted place and gained success, esteem, would reveal its insubstantiality. My satisfactions would diminish: with my daughters who had turned out well, with my fame, even with my most recent lover, a professor at the Polytechnic, eight years younger than me, twice divorced, with a son, whom I saw once a week in his house in the hills. My entire life would be reduced merely to a petty battle to change my social class.

50.

I kept depression at bay, I called Lila less. Now I no longer hoped, but *feared*, feared she would say: Do you want to read these pages I've written, I've been working for years, I'll send them by e-mail. I had no doubts about how I would react if I discovered that she really had irrupted into my professional identity, emptying it. I would certainly remain admiring, as I had with *The Blue Fairy*. I would publish her text without hesitation. I would exert myself to make it successful in every way possible. But I was no longer that little being who had had to discover the extraordinary qualities of her classmate. Now I was a mature woman with an established profile. I was what

Lila herself, sometimes joking, sometimes serious, had often repeated: Elena Greco, the brilliant friend of Raffaella Cerullo. From that unexpected reversal of destinies I would emerge annihilated.

But in that phase things were still going well for me. A full life, a still youthful appearance, the obligations of work, a reassuring fame didn't leave much room for those thoughts, reduced them to a vague uneasiness. Then came the bad years. My books sold less. I no longer had my position in the publishing house. I gained weight, I lost my figure, I felt old and frightened by the possibility of an old age of poverty, without fame. I had to acknowledge that, while I was working according to the mental approach I had imposed decades earlier, everything was different now, including me.

In 2005 I went to Naples, I saw Lila. It was a difficult day. She was further changed, she tried to be sociable, she neurotically greeted everyone, she talked too much. Seeing Africans, Asians in every corner of the neighborhood, smelling the odors of unknown cuisines, she became excited, she said: I haven't traveled around the world like you, but, look, the world has come to me. In Turin by now it was the same, and I liked the invasion of the exotic, how it had been reduced to the everyday. Yet only in the neighborhood did I realize how the anthropological landscape had altered. The old dialect had immediately taken in, according to an established tradition, mysterious languages, and meanwhile it was dealing with different phonic abilities, with syntaxes and sentiments that had once been very distant. The gray stone of the buildings had unexpected signs, old trafficking, legal and illegal, was mixed with new, the practice of violence opened up to new cultures.

That was when the news spread of Gigliola's corpse in the gardens. At the time we still didn't know that she had died of a heart attack, I thought she had been murdered. Her body, supine on the ground, was enormous. How she must have suffered from that transformation, she who had been beautiful and had caught the handsome Michele Solara. I am still alive—I thought—and yet I can't feel any different from that big body lying lifeless in that sordid place, in that sordid way. It was so. Although I paid excessive attention to my appearance, I no longer recognized myself, either: I moved more hesitantly, my physical expression was not what I had been used to for decades. As a girl I had felt so different and now I realized that I was like Gigliola.

Lila, on the other hand, seemed not to notice old age. She moved with energy, she shouted, she greeted people with expansive gestures. I didn't ask her, yet again, about her possible text. Whatever she said I was certain that it wouldn't reassure me. I didn't know how to get out of this depression, what to hold on to. The problem was no longer Lila's work, or its quality, or at least I didn't need to be aware of that threat to feel that everything I had written, since the end of the sixties, had lost weight and force, no longer spoke to an audience as it seemed to me it had done for decades, had no readers. Rather, on that melancholy occasion of death, I realized that the very nature of my anguish had changed. Now I was distressed that nothing of me would endure through time. My books had come out quickly and with their minor success had for decades given me the illusion of being engaged in meaningful work. But suddenly the illusion faded, I could no longer believe in the importance of my work. On the other hand, for Lila, too, everything had passed by: she led an obscure life; shut up in her parents' small apartment, she filled the computer with impressions and thoughts. And yet, I imagined, there was the possibility that her name—whether it was just a ribbon or not—now that she was an old woman, or even after her death, would be bound to a single work of great significance: not the thousands of pages that I had written, but a book whose success she would never enjoy, as I instead had done with mine, yet that nevertheless would endure through time and would be read and reread for hundreds of years. Lila had that possibility, I had squandered it. My fate was no different from Gigliola's, hers might be.

51.

For a while I let myself go. I did very little work, but then again, neither the publisher nor anyone else asked me to work more. I saw no one, I only made long phone calls to my daughters, insisting that they put the children on, and I spoke to them in baby talk. Now Elsa, too, had a boy, named Conrad, and Dede had given Hamid a sister, whom she had called Elena.

Those childish voices which expressed themselves with such precision made me think of Tina again. In the moments of greatest darkness I was sure that Lila had written the detailed story of her daughter, sure that she had mixed it into the history of Naples with the arrogant naïveté of the uneducated person who, perhaps for that very reason, obtains tremendous results. Then I understood that it was a fantasy of mine. Without wanting to, I was adding apprehension to envy, bitterness, and affection. Lila didn't have that type of ambition, she had never had ambitions. To carry out any project to which you attach your own name you have to love yourself, and she had told me, she didn't love herself, she loved nothing about herself. On the evenings of greatest depression I went so far as to imagine that she had lost her daughter in order not to see herself reproduced, in all her antipathy, in all her malicious reactivity, in all her intelligence without purpose. She wanted to eliminate herself, cancel all the traces, because she couldn't tolerate herself. She had done it continuously, for her entire existence, ever since she had shut herself off within a suffocating perimeter, confining herself at a time when the planet wanted to eliminate borders. She had never gotten on a train,

not even to go to Rome. She had never taken a plane. Her
experience was extremely limited, and when I thought about it
I felt sorry for her, I laughed, I got up with a groan, I went to
the computer, I wrote yet another e-mail saying: Come and see
me, we'll be together for a while. At those moments I took it
for granted that there was not and never would be a manuscript of Lila's. I had always overestimated her, nothing memorable would emerge from her—something that reassured me
and yet truly upset me. I loved Lila. I wanted her to last. But I
wanted it to be I who made her last. I thought it was my task.
I was convinced that she herself, as a girl, had assigned it to me.

52.

The story that I later called *A Friendship* originated in that
mildly depressive state, in Naples, during a week of rain. Of
course I knew that I was violating an unwritten agreement
between Lila and me, I also knew that she wouldn't tolerate it.
But I thought that if the result was good, in the end she would
say: I'm grateful to you, these were things I didn't have the
courage to say even to myself, and you said them in my name.
There is this presumption, in those who feel destined for art
and above all literature: we act as if we had received an investi-
ture, but in fact no one has ever invested us with anything, it is
we who have authorized ourselves to be authors and yet we are
resentful if others say: This little thing you did doesn't interest
me, in fact it bores me, who gave you the right. Within a few
days I wrote a story that over the years, hoping and fearing that
Lila was writing it, I had imagined in every detail. I did it
because everything that came from her, or that I ascribed to
her, had seemed to me, since we were children, more meaningful, more promising, than what came from me.

When I finished the first draft I was in a hotel room with a balcony that had a beautiful view of Vesuvius and the gray semicircle of the city. I could have called Lila on the cell phone, said to her: I've written about me, about you, about Tina, about Imma, do you want to read it, it's only eighty pages, I'll come by your house, I'll read it aloud. I didn't do that out of fear. She had explicitly forbidden me not only to write about her but also to use persons and episodes of the neighborhood. When I had, she always found a way of telling me—even if painfully—that the book was bad, that either one is capable of telling things just as they happened, in teeming chaos, or one works from imagination, inventing a thread, and I had been able to do neither the first thing nor the second. So I let it go, I calmed myself, saying: it will happen as it always does, she won't like the story, she'll pretend it doesn't matter, in a few years she'll make it known to me, or tell me clearly, that I have to try to achieve more. In truth, I thought, if it were up to her I would never publish a line.

The book came out, I was swept up by a success I hadn't felt for a long time, and since I needed it I was happy. *A Friendship* kept me from joining the list of writers whom everyone considers dead even when they're still alive. The old books began to sell again, interest in me was rekindled, in spite of approaching old age life became full again. But that book, which at first I considered the best I had written, I later did not love. It's Lila who made me hate it, by refusing in every possible way to see me, to discuss it with me, even to insult me and hit me. I called her constantly, I wrote endless e-mails, I went to the neighborhood, I talked to Rino. She was never there. And on the other hand her son never said: My mother is acting like this because she doesn't want to see you. As usual he was vague, he stammered: You know how she is, she's always out, she either turns off the cell phone or forgets it at home, sometimes she doesn't even come home to sleep. So I had to acknowledge that our friendship was over.

53.

In fact I don't know what offended her, a detail, or the whole story. *A Friendship* had the quality, in my opinion, of being linear. It told concisely, with the necessary disguises, the story of our lives, from the loss of the dolls to the loss of Tina. Where had I gone wrong? I thought for a long time that she was angry because, in the final part, although resorting to imagination more than at other points of the story, I related what in fact had happened in reality: Lila had given Imma more importance in Nino's eyes, in doing so had been distracted, and as a result lost Tina. But evidently what in the fiction of the story serves in all innocence to reach the heart of the reader becomes an abomination for one who feels the echo of the facts she has really lived. In other words I thought for a long time that what had assured the book's success was also what had hurt Lila most.

Later, however, I changed my mind. I'm convinced that the reason for her repudiation lay elsewhere, in the way I recounted the episode of the dolls. I had deliberately exaggerated the moment when they disappeared into the darkness of the cellar, I had accentuated the trauma of the loss, and to intensify the emotional effects I had used the fact that one of the dolls and the lost child had the same name. The whole led the reader, step by step, to connect the childhood loss of the pretend daughters to the adult loss of the real daughter. Lila must have found it cynical, dishonest, that I had resorted to an important moment of our childhood, to her child, to her sorrow, to satisfy my audience.

But I am merely piecing together hypotheses, I would have to confront her, hear her protests, explain myself. Sometimes I feel guilty, and I understand her. Sometimes I hate her for this decision to cut me off so sharply right now, in old age, when we are in need of closeness and solidarity. She has always acted like that: when I don't submit, see how she excludes me, punishes me, ruins even my pleasure in having written a good book. I'm exasperated. Even this staging of her own disappearance, besides worrying me, irritates me. Maybe little Tina has nothing to do with it, maybe not even her ghost, which continues to obsess Lila both in the more enduring form of the child of nearly four, and in the labile form of the woman who today, like Imma, would be thirty. It's only and always the two of us who are involved: she who wants me to give what her nature and circumstances kept her from giving, I who can't give what she demands; she who gets angry at my inadequacy and out of spite wants to reduce me to nothing, as she has done with herself, I who have written for months and months and months to give her a form whose boundaries won't dissolve, and defeat her, and calm her, and so in turn calm myself.

EPILOGUE
RESTITUTION

1.

I can't believe it myself. I've finished this story that I thought would never end. I finished it and patiently reread it not so much to improve the quality of the writing as to find out if there are even a few lines where it's possible to trace the evidence that Lila entered my text and decided to contribute to writing it. But I have had to acknowledge that all these pages are mine alone. What Lila often threatened to do—enter my computer—she hasn't done, maybe she wasn't even capable of doing, it was long a fantasy I had as an old woman inexperienced in networks, cables, connections, electronic spirits. Lila is not in these words. There is only what I've been able to put down. Unless, by imagining what she would write and how, I am no longer able to distinguish what's mine and what's hers.

Often, during this work, I telephoned Rino, I asked about his mother. He doesn't know anything, the police limited themselves to summoning him three or four times to show him the bodies of nameless old women—so many of them disappear. A couple of times I had to go to Naples, and I met him in the old apartment in the neighborhood, a space darker, more run-down than it had been. There really wasn't anything of Lila anymore, everything that had been hers was gone. As for the son, he seemed more distracted than usual, as if his mother had definitively gone out of his head.

I returned to the city for two funerals, first my father's, then Lidia's, Nino's mother. I missed the funeral of Donato, not out of bitterness, only because I was abroad. When I came to the neighborhood for my father there was a great uproar because a young man had just been murdered at the entrance to the library. That made me think that this story would continue forever, recounting now the efforts of children without privileges to improve themselves by getting books from the old shelves, as Lila and I had done as girls, and now the thread of seductive chatter, promises, deceptions, of blood that prevents any true improvement in my city or in the world.

The day of Lidia's funeral was overcast, the city seemed tranquil, I felt tranquil, too. Then Nino arrived and all he did was talk loudly, joke, even laugh, as if we were not at his mother's funeral. I found him large, bloated, a big ruddy man with thinning hair who was constantly celebrating himself. Getting rid of him, after the funeral, was difficult. I didn't want to listen to him or even look at him. He gave me an impression of wasted time, of useless labor, that I feared would stay in my mind, extending into me, into everything.

On the occasion of both funerals I made plans ahead of time to visit Pasquale. In those years I did that whenever I could. In prison he had studied a lot, had received his high school diploma, and, recently, a degree in astronomical geography.

"If I'd known that to get a diploma and a degree all you needed to have was free time, to be shut up in a place without worrying about earning a living, and, with discipline, learning by heart pages and pages of some books, I would have done it before," he said once, in a teasing tone.

Today he's an old man, he speaks serenely, he is much better preserved than Nino. With me he rarely resorts to dialect. But he hasn't moved even a hairsbreadth out of the space of generous ideas in which his father enclosed him as a boy. When I saw him after Lidia's funeral and told him about Lila he burst out laughing. She must be doing her intelligent and imaginative things somewhere, he muttered. And it moved him to remember the time in the neighborhood library when the teacher assigned prizes to the most diligent readers, and the most diligent was Lila, who took out books illegally with her relatives' cards. Ah, Lila the shoemaker, Lila who imitated Kennedy's wife, Lila the artist and designer, Lila the worker, Lila the programmer, Lila always in the same place and always out of place.

"Who took Tina from her?" I asked.

"The Solaras."

"Sure?"

He smiled, showing his bad teeth. I understood that he wasn't telling the truth—maybe he didn't know it and it didn't even interest him—but was proclaiming the unshakable faith, based on the primary experience of injustice, the experience of the neighborhood, that—in spite of the reading he had done, the degree he had taken, the clandestine journeys, the crimes he had committed or been accused of—remained the currency of every certainty he had. He answered:

"Do you also want me to tell you who murdered those two pieces of shit?"

Suddenly I read in his gaze something that horrified me— an inextinguishable rancor—and I said no. He shook his head, and continued to smile. He said:

"You'll see that when Lila decides to, she'll show up."

But there was not a trace of her. On those two occasions for mourning I walked through the neighborhood, I asked around out of curiosity: no one remembered her, or maybe they were pretending. I couldn't even talk about her with Carmen. Roberto died, she left the gas pump, went to live with one of her sons, in Formia.

What is the point of all these pages, then? I intended to capture her, to have her beside me again, and I will die without knowing if I succeeded. Sometimes I wonder where she vanished. At the bottom of the sea. Through a fissure or down some subterranean tunnel whose existence she alone knows. In an old bathtub filled with a powerful acid. In an ancient garbage pit, one of those she devoted so many words to. In the crypt of an abandoned church in the mountains. In one of the many dimensions that we don't know yet but Lila does, and now she's there with her daughter.

Will she return?

Will they return together, Lila old, Tina a grown woman?

This morning, sitting on the balcony that looks out over the Po, I'm waiting.

2.

I have breakfast every day at seven, I go to the newsstand with the Labrador I got recently, I spend a good part of the morning in the Valentino playing with the dog, leafing through the papers. Yesterday, when I got back, I found on top of my mailbox a package roughly wrapped in newspaper. I took it, perplexed. Nothing indicated that it had been left for me or for any other tenant. There was no note with it and it didn't even have my last name written in pen somewhere.

I cautiously opened one edge of the wrapping, and that was enough. Tina and Nu leaped out of memory even before I got them completely out of the newspaper. I immediately recognized the dolls that one after the other, almost six decades earlier, had been thrown—mine by Lila, Lila's by me—into a cellar in the neighborhood. They were the dolls we had never found, although we had descended underground to look for them. They were the ones that Lila had pushed me to go and retrieve from the house of Don Achille, ogre and thief, and Don Achille had claimed that he hadn't taken them, and maybe he had imagined that it was his son Alfonso who stole them, and so had compensated us with money to buy new ones. But we hadn't bought dolls with that money—how could we have replaced Tina and Nu?—instead we bought *Little Women*, the novel that had led Lila to write *The Blue Fairy* and me to become what I was today, the author of many books and, most important, of a remarkably successful story entitled *A Friendship*.

The lobby of the building was silent, no voices or other sounds came from the apartments. I looked around anxiously. I wanted Lila to emerge from stairway A or B or from the deserted porter's room, thin, gray, her back bent. I wished it more than any other thing, I wished it more than an unexpected visit from my daughters with their children. I expected that she would say in her usual mocking way: Do you like this gift? But it didn't happen and I burst into tears. Here's what she had done: she had deceived me, she had dragged me wherever she wanted, from the beginning of our friendship. All our lives she had told a story of redemption that was *hers*, using *my* living body and *my* existence.

Or maybe not. Maybe those two dolls that had crossed more than half a century and had come all the way to Turin meant only that she was well and loved me, that she had broken her confines and finally intended to travel the world by now no less small than hers, living in old age, according to a new truth, the life that in youth had been forbidden to her and that she had forbidden herself.

I went up in the elevator, I shut myself in my apartment. I examined the two dolls carefully, I smelled the odor of mold, I arranged them against the spines of my books. Seeing how cheap and ugly they were I felt confused. Unlike stories, real life, when it has passed, inclines toward obscurity, not clarity. I thought: now that Lila has let herself be seen so plainly, I must resign myself to not seeing her anymore.

About the Author

Elena Ferrante was born in Naples. She is the author of *The Days of Abandonment*, *Troubling Love*, and *The Lost Daughter*. Her Neapolitan Novels include *My Brilliant Friend*, *The Story of a New Name*, *Those Who Leave and Those Who Stay*, and the fourth and final book in the series, *The Story of the Lost Child*.

THE NEAPOLITAN NOVELS
By Elena Ferrante

BOOK 1

"Ferrante's novels are intensely, violently personal, and because of this they seem to dangle bristling key chains of confession before the unsuspecting reader."
—James Wood, *The New Yorker*

978-1-60945-078-6 • September 2012

BOOK 2

"Stunning . . . cinematic in the density of its detail."
—The *Times Literary Supplement*

978-1-60945-134-9 • September 2013

BOOK 3

"Everyone should read anything with Ferrante's name on it."—Eugenia Williamson, *The Boston Globe*

978-1-60945-233-9 • September 2014

BOOK 4

"One of modern fiction's richest portraits of a friendship."—John Powers, *NPR's Fresh Air*

978-1-60945-286-5 • September 2015

"Imagine if Jane Austen got angry and you'll have some idea how explosive these works are."
—John Freeman, critic and author of *How to Read a Novelist*